# bitten

## A Romantic Comedy

by

Robert Smith

DESERE
BOOK

SALT LAKE CITY, UTAH

*For Krista, the most incredible person I've ever had the privilege of hanging out with*

The contents of *Bitten* were previously published as *All Is Swell: Trust in Thelma's Way* (1999) and *Falling for Grace: Trust at the End of the World* (1999) and have been abridged for this edition.



**Library of Congress Cataloging-in-Publication Data**

Smith, Robert F., 1970–
Bitten : a romantic comedy / Robert Smith.
p. cm.
Summary: When Trust Williams completes his two-year mission in Thelma's Way, Tennessee, he finds he cannot break his connection to the people there, especially Grace Heck, who comes back home with him to Southdale so they can see if they have a future together, despite his parents' objections.
ISBN 978-1-59038-904-1 (pbk.)
[1. Coming of age—Fiction. 2. Missionaries—Fiction. 3. Mormons—Fiction. 4. Dating (Social customs)—Fiction. 5. Family life—Fiction. 6. Tennessee—Fiction.] I. Title.
PZ7.S657616Bit 2008
[Fic]—dc22 2008000468

Printed in the United States of America
Worzalla Publishing Co., Stevens Point, WI

10 9 8 7 6 5 4 3 2 1

1

# Order Up

It was here. I stuck my hand in the mailbox and pulled out the letter—my mission call had arrived. With a patience nurtured by TV and the flash of everyday life, I tore it open. I couldn't wait to see where I'd be serving. My stomach exploded with butterflies.

I couldn't believe this!

I shook the paper, as if jostling it about might rearrange its contents.

The words remained the same. Forget the fact that I had prayed for it every night for the last year. Forget the fact that I had taken language courses in school. God had not seen fit to send me someplace prestigious and foreign in the world. My blue eyes simmered as I stared at the paper. This was not the mission call I had envisioned receiving. The population of Knoxville, Tennessee, was about to increase by one clean-cut, dark-suited, two-year missionary. I could feel the bug bites already.

God was keeping me stateside.

2

# Fared Well

The chapel was packed. People pushed up against each other like putty, making room for more. The place was filled to capacity. I couldn't believe it. Even some of my Catholic and Baptist friends from work and school had come to say good-bye.

Wendy, our non-Mormon neighbor, was sitting in the front row, obviously unaware that we Mormons discouraged eating in church. She had a bag of chips and a Coke balanced on the edge of the pew. I guess she thought Church was like a trip to the movies. She was probably hoping for a few good laughs. She'd probably get them.

Showtime.

The chapel organ began to bellow the first notes of the opening song as I reached up to feel my newly shorn brown hair. I stared at the odd-looking wing tips on my feet. I brushed the leg of my dark suit.

Heaven help itself, I was turning into a missionary.

I looked at my hands as I sat there on the stand listening to Bishop Leen say nice things about me. My fingers seemed . . . longer? Or shorter? Different.

For a moment, I wanted to jump out of who I was becoming and run home barefooted. I wanted to climb one of the big trees out in front of my house and spend the afternoon throwing seed pods down at passing cars. I wanted to work on math homework with my mom, torment my brother, Abel, and sit in wonder over Lucy, my first and only love.

I looked at my family sitting out in the crowd. None of them had wanted to speak today. Dad was a pillar in the community but no more than a flimsy support beam to the Church. He had more money than faith and sort of liked it that way. Mom was the believing one, but despite her Noah-like faith, she still couldn't be talked into taking the stand in front of all those people. My twelve-year-old sister, Margaret, was not about to give a talk, and my eight-year-old brother, Abel, had wanted to speak but had been banned from coming to the microphone ever since the "incident" in fast and testimony meeting last summer. Yes, I would be the only Williams on the program today.

Trust Andrew Williams. I had a name like a political sound bite.

My parents had named me Trust out of fear. I was their firstborn, and I had come out boy when they had specifically asked the heavens for something frilly and pink. It wasn't that they hated boys, it was just that they had heard so many bad things about tiny males from our neighbor Wendy. So they named me Trust, hoping it would help the budding hellion in me surface slowly if at all.

I had grown up all right.

Sure, if pressed, my parents could produce a list of trespasses and transgressions, but I had managed for the most part to keep my life on track. Now here I was, about to embark on a two-year mission for The Church of Jesus Christ of Latter-day Saints. Scared. Nervous. But embarking. Mom was thrilled, and Dad, despite his own inactivity, was happy too. He saw the whole mission thing as a big training camp for my future career in business—sort of a divine gospel salesman internship.

I gazed at the tip of my tie as I sat there on the stand, my childhood suddenly seeming too short. I felt my heart tighten. My nerves were buzzing just below my skin. I wasn't ready for this, was I? I didn't know how to feel.

The call to Tennessee had been a surprise, but I was determined to make the best of it. After all, if I believed anything about what I was going to be preaching, it was that the Lord was at the head. And while I had sort of imagined myself looking sharp in France or stunning in Greece, I guess He sort of saw me in Tennessee. I'm not saying that didn't concern me, but I would do this favor for God. There had to be *something* worth seeing in Tennessee. I was just hoping it wasn't the bugs.

The heavens were consoling me, sending down a calming silence to my troubled soul. I sat in relative peace and quiet—actually a little too quiet.

There was no one at the podium, and everyone was staring at me. I realized it was my turn to speak.

I had daydreamed my way through two talks and an intermediate hymn sung by our home teacher's sixteen-year-old daughter. I picked up my scriptures and rose to my feet.

I spotted Lucy Fall in the crowd three rows back and to the left. Her blonde hair was shining under the bright fluorescent lights. She acknowledged me with her blue eyes. I was going to miss Lucy. She nodded at me as if to say, *Go on.* Her lips parted a tad, giving the world a rare glimpse of her perfect white teeth. She sat there looking better than everyone else and knowing it. Some people thought Lucy was stuck-up. True or not, I was too stuck on her to care. All I knew then was that I was going to miss her.

I stood at the pulpit and cleared my throat. There were so many faces looking up at me. I tried to smile. I made a lame attempt at a joke. The crowd laughed mercifully.

I was going to miss the Clearview First Ward. I had always thought it odd that Mormons called their congregations wards. Typically the word "ward" went better with words like "psyche," or "mental," or "burn." But for some reason we Mormons felt it described us. Regardless, I liked the Clearview Ward, and I didn't want it to change while I was gone. I wanted to come back in two years and see each family sitting just where they were in front of me: the Johnsons three pews back and to the right; the Lewises strategically sitting on the back row next to the door—to make it easier for Sister Lewis to haul out the twins if necessary; the Falls in the middle section, boxed in by Sister Cravitz and Bishop Leen's wife and family; Brother Vastly in his designated spot, the last padded bench to the right, in front of the overflow chair sitters.

If there was any rift in our congregation, it was between the bench sitters and the chair sitters. The chair sitters were always complaining about the awful treatment they received sitting in the back: cold metal chairs, poor sound, an uneven ratio of noisy kids to listening parishioners, and there were never enough hymnbooks. Week after week the chair sitters were forced to hum.

The bench sitters had little compassion. They figured that if the chair sitters wanted to badly enough, they could show up on time and claim one of the soft benches for themselves. Most of the bench sitters also piously considered themselves worthy of sitting so close to the podium because of their clear consciences, claiming that the chair sitters parked their behinds on the fringes due to some sort of subconscious unworthiness.

There was a true division.

One time when Brother Treat stepped out of the chair section and tried to retrieve a hymnbook for his wife from the back of one of the benches, Sister Cravitz almost drew blood by jabbing him with a small easel she was planning to use later in her Relief Society lesson to prop up a picture of Christ. Three days later Brother Treat accidentally spilled two gallons of bleach across Sister Cravitz's prize-winning azaleas and front lawn. The bishop had to step in to smooth things out. He used part of the Young Women's budget to buy more hymnbooks for the chair sitters.

Of course, Sister Luke, the Young Women's leader, was not at all happy about the cut in her budget, and the Young Women were not compassionately giddy over their money providing hymnal text to the subconsciously guilty chair sitters. They were even less thrilled about it later that year at girls' camp when, due to their depleted budget, they went without warm meals and mattress pads.

But things had smoothed out for the time being. The chair sitters sang, and the bench sitters continued to sit, somewhat self-righteously, on their pampered behinds, always looking forward.

But none of that seemed to matter now. I was speaking at my mission farewell.

I talked a little about my desire to serve a mission. I was hoping the words I was using would help trick my soul into feeling comfortable with the whole idea. I mentioned my fear of being bitten by bugs. I told a story about myself as a child. I bore my testimony. I closed, clutched at my scriptures, and sat down.

At meeting's end, everyone came up to me and wished me well. Every handshake and hug made me more and more frightened to leave it all behind. Sister Johnson kissed me on the cheek. Brother Vastly shook my hand without lecturing me. Lucy was kind enough to hug me. Then she just stood there looking gorgeous. We had grown up together. We had dated a couple of times, but more than that, we had just always been. She liked me like a brother, and I liked her like a love-crazed, emotionally wavering, wishful-thinking third cousin.

"Good luck," Lucy said, her hands clasped together in front of her. She was impeccably dressed, as usual, her cutting-edge fashion sense clashing with the rest of the congregation's outdated wardrobe.

"Thanks," I replied.

Lucy wriggled her nose and bit her bottom lip, as if on cue.

"I'll write," I offered.

"I can't believe we're this old," she replied, showing a sliver of the soft under-self she usually kept locked up behind her perfect exterior.

"I'm going to—" I started to say, "really miss you," but Lucy sensed my borderline blubbering and interrupted.

"I'll be here when you return," she said almost coldly.

I wanted to fall on my knees, to beg her not to make me go. But I figured that wouldn't really leave a favorable last impression. I would do this. I would turn my fledgling testimony into a true conviction. I would take two years to better the kingdom. I would even try not to be bitter about the whole Tennessee thing. I would do anything if the heavens would only promise me that on my return I would be good enough for Lucy Fall.

Before I could say anything else, Sister Cravitz slipped between me and Lucy and hugged me tightly. She sort of stroked the back of my hair and whispered something about being so very proud. I watched Lucy slip off the stage and out of my life for two years.

Sister Cravitz squeezed me tighter. The big brooch she was wearing on her lapel dug into my chest.

"So, so, very, very proud," she said again.

3

# Big Things, Small Packages

## Week Three

I spent a couple weeks at the Missionary Training Center in Provo, Utah, and three nights in the mission home in Knoxville with President and Sister Clasp before my mission really began.

President Clasp was big, loud, and funny—three attributes I would never have envisioned my mission president having. He was also stern, a trait I had expected. He had very little hair, but he insisted he wasn't bald. It was just that he had an extra wide part. The enormous part topped off big eyes and crooked teeth. Before being called as mission president, he had been a safety inspector at a toy company in Wisconsin. Sister Clasp, who was also big, loud, and funny, dispensed hugs like an overzealous mother bear. She always wore a billowy blouse tucked into an elastic-banded skirt.

President Clasp taught us quite a bit in those first three days. At the conclusion he interviewed me and went on and on about how he used to have a dog named Trust. I felt like part of the family.

After those few days in the mission home, I was driven in a big gray van to a small town called Collin's Blight, Tennessee. I had tried to take in the scenery and figure out which direction we were going, but it sped by so fast that my eyes couldn't properly digest it. My poor sense of direction asserted itself.

From Collin's Blight I was transported in a tiny green car to the mid-sized town of Virgil's Find. At Virgil's Find—which, by the way, was no great find—I was met by the companion I would be serving with, Elder Boone, who then escorted me on foot to our destination: Thelma's Way, Tennessee.

To get there, we had to hike along a well-worn footpath that cut through the mountains like a poorly sewn seam. Next to the trail ran a line of weathered utility poles that were heavy with wire. On every other pole was posted an orange piece of paper that read:

**COME ONE, COME ALL**

Pre-planning meeting

this Saturday at 6:00 A.M. for the

Thelma's Way Sesquicentennial Pageant

Together the posted poles and tiny path provided a lifeline to my new home. After following the trail for about four miles, through thick trees and steep hills, we came to the meadow where Thelma's Way lay. With one glance I could take in everything the town had to offer. The mountains all around it sloped their soft shoulders down to a clearing where a few shacks and dwellings sat huddled together. There were maybe eight poorly built buildings in all, laid out as if they had been thrown down during a spoiled fit. Bushy trees surrounded the meadow, and a smoky gray sky gave the place a closed-in feeling and charged the air with uneasiness. A thick river ran swiftly along the far side of the clearing.

"This is it?" I asked as we stood up on a hill looking down.

"This is it," Elder Boone replied.

"There's nothing here!"

"There's more people hidden in the hills."

I couldn't tell if he was attempting to warn me or comfort me.

What was I doing here? Thelma's Way was a weed patch, a city so hidden that even upon discovery it was nothing. It was a few shacks and a large meadow. It was a bad neighborhood smack-dab in the middle of Mother Nature's lower back. It was remote, regressive, repulsive, and really making me homesick. The moist air gummed up my brain. I swallowed hard, willing myself to do my best regardless of where I was, and blinked a few times, hoping the rapid eye movement would make this green town in front of me appear more like home.

Elder Boone saw my expression and sensed the need to explain a few things. We sat down on a soft patch of grass. Big grasshopper-like bugs the size of Twinkies jumped about, chirping.

"I hate bugs," I said.

"Don't worry," he replied. "I've never been bitten."

Elder Boone swatted a black-winged thing away from his face and proceeded to give me an oral history.

Thelma's Way was the most remote spot in the entire mission—remote and difficult. According to Elder Boone, the missionaries in the town of Virgil's Find had it easy compared to us. They had running water and electricity.

"Luckily, the big Girth River runs right next to our place," he consoled.

*What luck,* I thought.

Thelma's Way had just been opened up in the mission. There had been no missionaries since the early days of the Church, when the apostle Parley P. Pratt stopped off and got sick from eating some bad ham. It was a small place with a small number of active members and inactives aplenty.

Two months previous President Clasp had felt impressed to open up Thelma's Way to the good word of the gospel. There had been some big problems with apostasy in the area, and the Church felt that full-time missionaries would be able to help reactivate and reconstruct what Elder Boone referred to as the crumbling Thelma's Way Ward.

Elder Boone had opened this area with Elder Frates, whom I was replacing. Elder Frates had not done very well here in Thelma's Way. He just didn't have the patience to put up with these laid-back country folks, having come directly from a rather affluent "Seven-Habits" family in Orem, Utah. Elder Frates couldn't handle everyone's casualer-than-thou attitude toward life.

During his second week in Thelma's Way, Elder Frates had had his parents FedEx fifty day planners for him to distribute among the locals. FedEx brought them in by motorcycle, and Elder Frates distributed them to the desperately disorganized inhabitants.

Well, the locals accepted the gift but didn't exactly understand the application of pen and paper planning. A couple of the women in town propped their floral day planner binders up in the front windows of their homes for decoration, and some of the men found that they came in handy when a body needed something soft to sit on. A boy by the name of Digby Heck had collected a few of the unused ones and incorporated them in the construction of his small rock fort down by the Girth River.

The infraction that got Frates's goat, however, was when far-from-feminine Sybil Porter used her day planner as a place to store her fishing worms. Sybil had emptied the planner's innards and had been storing worms and soil inside the zippered case.

"Dark and moist," she had reasoned.

Elder Frates lost it. He started yelling and called her a heathen gentile. Sybil in turn picked Elder Frates up and threw him into a muddy hole full of stagnant water. Furious, he pulled himself up, got his bearings, and stormed off to Virgil's Find, never to return. Elder Boone waited with the Virgil's Find missionaries until the mission president was able to send me as a replacement.

"The people here didn't exactly like Frates," Elder Boone said, exercising diplomatic restraint.

"Great," I said, pulling at the long grass we were sitting in.

"Life's a little slower in Thelma's Way, and the missionary work's a little different here than in the rest of the mission."

"Any good things?" I asked hopefully.

"Church is only two hours long," he offered. "There aren't enough active members right now to staff Sunday School."

This didn't seem like a perk. The last thing we needed was more free time. I couldn't see clearly how we would be able to fill our days here in Thelma's Way as it was.

"Anything else I should know?" I asked.

"Everyone here mistrusts each other. The local apostate, Paul, has torn the ward apart, leaving everyone bitter and hurt."

And to think I had wanted to go foreign.

"President Clasp didn't say anything about all this," I said, frustrated.

"Maybe he didn't want to ruin the surprise."

I was surprised all right.

"Listen," Elder Boone said, "if you're anything like me, after you got your mission call you probably rushed out to the local bookstore or library and read up on Tennessee."

I nodded.

"Well, forget everything you think you learned," he went on. "Thelma's Way is not your typical Tennessee town. It's a bunch of Mormons who got lost on their way to Utah over a hundred years ago. The rest of Tennessee likes to pretend Thelma's Way doesn't even exist. You see, Tennessee is the buckle of the Bible Belt, and this little community of inactive Mormons is an unsightly smudge. It's an embarrassment to the rest of the state."

I was embarrassed for them.

"But you'll learn to like these people," Elder Boone added. "On the surface they may seem like misfits, but they'll grow on you. This is actually an exciting time for the town. This Saturday they're holding their first pre-planning meeting for the big sesquicentennial celebration."

"I saw the signs," I said. "So when's the actual celebration?"

"Oh, it's not for over a year and a half. They just want to get a real jump on it. They've been waiting a hundred and fifty years for this."

The anticipation was already killing me.

We sat there for a moment shooing bugs in silence.

"Are you sure they won't bite?" I asked.

"Who knows for sure?" he replied.

I swatted more vigorously.

"Ready?" Elder Boone finally asked.

We stood up, dusted ourselves off, and shuffled slowly into the thriving metropolis of Thelma's Way.

# 4

# LUCY

Lucy was pretty. Pretty spoiled, pretty demanding, and pretty stubborn. She liked herself as much as she enjoyed the company of those who felt likewise. Lucy spent her days thinking about what she should wear the next day, and her nights dreaming of how she would look when she did. Rumor had it that someplace beneath her expensive clothes and hardened exterior, Lucy did possess a soft spot. As it stood, however, no witnesses had yet stepped up to corroborate such an opinion.

Lucy's life was tight, with no give. She had no patience for the unexpected. Surprises to Lucy were like an embarrassing blemish on the glossy lips of life. Today was planned, tomorrow was scheduled, and she already had a pretty good idea of what the next two years of her life would entail.

Piece by piece.

Lucy admired her perfect cheekbones as she walked past the hall mirror and into her bedroom. She closed her door and took a few minutes to write down the day in her diary. Journal keeping was more than a commandment to Lucy, it was an accurate way to chronicle her remarkable existence. She knew she couldn't possibly count on some future historian's doing justice to her story.

After one full page of writing, Lucy closed the diary and changed into her pajamas. She then sat on the edge of her bed and read the letter she had received from Trust. The letter was simple, with three spelling errors and tired penmanship. Trust would have to do better if he had any hopes of her waiting around for him.

Lucy sighed. The moment seemed to call for it, and she liked her moments to be traditional and normal. She folded the letter up and stuck it into her stationery drawer.

Lucy liked Trust. He had been gone for only three weeks, but already she was considering missing him. Trust was tall, blue-eyed, and handsome in a rustically un-oafish way. Trust was also the only Mormon her age that Lucy could even tolerate, and her life plans called for a Mormon. Her hometown of Southdale didn't offer too many great options. Lucy would settle for Trust. Sure, he was a little rough around the edges, but she could mold him into someone truly worthy of her love.

Lucy was confident that Trust liked her. For years he had existed with an eye single to her glory. She could make him blush like a modest Mormon in a nudist camp simply by calling his name slowly. Trust tripped over himself constantly in her presence, subtly announcing to the world that he was enamored of her. He had asked her out a thousand times, and she had replied *no* almost as many, issuing a *yes* on only a few occasions.

Despite all the *no's,* Lucy knew Trust would keep asking. In two years, when he returned home from his mission, she would size him up. If he had improved in the ways she thought he should, then maybe she would utter another *yes* and usher in the beginning of what could be a lasting relationship.

Piece by piece.

She brushed her blonde hair for ten minutes. Then she studied her blue eyes in the mirror next to her bed. She was beautiful.

"Maybe Trust isn't good enough," she said to herself as she kneeled down to recite the same prayer with which she had vainly petitioned God for the last couple of years.

After her prayer, she laid down and pulled her comforter up to her neck. It wasn't terribly late, but she closed her eyes and beckoned sleep. She had two of her more important college classes tomorrow, and she wanted to make sure she got enough rest.

Sleep smothered Lucy like a big warm cat.

# 5

# Thelma's Way, Tennessee

I tried to smile as Elder Boone and I shuffled into town along the small footpath. I squinted, as if doing so might mercifully pull hidden houses out from the surrounding hills and drag them into the clearing. We came to a stop at the center of town or, more appropriately, the pit.

We were standing in front of a small boardinghouse and store. There was a big poster tacked to the front of the store informing everyone about the distant sesquicentennial celebration. Two older men sat on the front porch staring at us. One was extremely heavy—heavy beard, heavy glance, and heavy stature. He sat upon that porch as if he had been destined to do so, his large, bushy face flushed simply from sitting. The other elderly man was as thin as the wooden chair he was pinched into. His puckered-up head bobbed and dipped with each rocking motion, and a smoking pipe hung from his sliver-like lips. His pitch-black pupils looked like magnets, each one attracted to the other and coming together at the top of his nose. The heavy gentleman fanned himself with a faded hat, seeking relief from the warm afternoon.

"Hello," I said like some great explorer presenting himself to the natives. *Disappointed, I presume.*

Elder Boone introduced us. "This is Roswell Ford," he said, pointing to the skinny man, "and this is Feeble, his brother," he went on, indicating the heavy one. "They're twins."

They both sniffed the air, as if my presence had presented a new scent.

"Bet he's the new elder," Roswell said to Feeble. They then turned back to whatever it was they were talking about before. It had something to do with possum fur.

"Nice to meet you," I said to no one, thinking how very un-twin-like they looked.

In front of the boardinghouse, the footpath widened to the size of a large dirt road, circling around the house and then running off in a couple of different directions. It made this place the center of town, the crossroads of the backwoods. To the east was our church building, a big, run-down wooden cabin with a new sign out front announcing the meeting times. It had a bell on top and a roof made of mismatched pieces of rough wood and sheet metal. Its wooden walls were dry and cracking, and weeds filled the flowerpots that were sitting out front. The entire thing had "community service project" written all over it.

To the west of the boardinghouse was a school. It was flat-roofed and leaned to one side. It had no front door, so I could easily see inside. Each desk was currently occupied by a wiggling child. A short woman with thick arms was standing in front of a chalkboard pronouncing the word "offspring."

I looked away from the school toward the sprawling meadow. It was full of wildflowers and weeds, and stitched with small paths where people had trampled down the growth to move across it. Two rusted and rotting pioneer-era wagons lay in the center of the meadow. Their metal bindings were bent and corroded, their wooden bodies splintered and dry.

Elder Boone saw me gazing at the wagons and spoke. "That's sort of the town park," he said. "During lunch and recess the school kids play on those."

"Fun," I commented dryly.

Elder Boone pointed to a small, outhouse-looking shack off in the distance. "That's Wad's shop," he informed me. "He's the town barber."

"Wad?"

"You'll understand once you meet him."

I wasn't sure I wanted to understand.

"He cuts the missionaries' hair for free," Elder Boone added.

Way past Wad's place was a bridge that spanned the mouth of the river, looking like an awkward set of braces. Though the bridge was far away from the boardinghouse, I could see that it was burnt and unusable. I didn't have the courage to ask what the story behind its condition was.

We picked up our feet and walked past the church and then past a small cemetery that lay between the church and what turned out to be our house. The cemetery ran back and over beyond our place, touching the river with its backside. Headstones and flowers dotted its layout like a poorly finished paint-by-number. In the middle of the cemetery was a big cement mausoleum with the name "Watson" carved into its top. The mausoleum was surrounded by trees and bushes, and in front of it stood a large statue of a woman. It looked to me like more people had died here in Thelma's Way than had lived.

Our place was wedged between the cemetery and the river. It was a small cabin with very little besides two beds and a hard dirt floor. There was a round table to eat on and a washbasin with a mirror above it. In the center of it all was a black iron stove for cooking and heating the place. A thick quilt was hanging on a wire, providing some privacy to whoever was standing behind it.

"Primitive," I observed.

"Home sweet home," Elder Boone clarified.

"Where do we keep our food?" I asked, noticing that there was no refrigerator.

"In the winter we can hang it out the windows, but for now we keep it over at the boardinghouse. Roswell and Feeble don't mind."

I thought maybe I did.

"We can shower at the boardinghouse and do our laundry over at Bishop Watson's place," Elder Boone continued. "It's not perfect, but hey, President Clasp just opened this area back up."

In my humble opinion, the area should have remained closed. This was nowhere, nothing, and no way all wrapped into one. This was the edge of the earth, the end of civilization, the dropping-off point for all things backward and isolated. Dirt floors, wood walls, and bugs the size of those in any foreign mission flashed before my eyes as I tried to find the silver lining in this very dark cloud. I pretended I was in some exotic country, living out in the uncharted forest. It helped a little.

"Toilet's out back," Elder Boone said. "And all mail gets delivered to the boardinghouse. President Clasp promised he would look into making improvements on this place, but I can't imagine either of us being here long enough to see any of them."

Elder Boone was skinny—too skinny. He had green eyes and a posture that the elitely prim would have been complimentary toward. He stood straight, walked straight, and talked straight. At the moment, however, I wished that he would make up a few crooked lies to help disguise the unpleasant truth. The truth being that I was stuck in Thelma's Way for at least a month.

I took a few steps into the cabin and set my backpack down on the bed. I was just about to sit down myself when a horrible noise exploded from outside. It sounded as if someone had just sucker-punched a hyena. The noise grew louder and louder until it eventually ended up on our doorstep, taking the shape of a little blonde girl with long braids and big feet. She was wearing a small, baggy dress and ankle-high boots, and her big head rotated in circles as she hollered.

"Elders, my dad is . . . ! He needs . . . !!"

Elder Boone grabbed the girl by the arm. "Calm down, Narlette," he ordered.

Narlette? This town needed a sensible baby-name book.

"But my . . . ," she wailed, "my . . . it's awful!"

She had that right.

"There's water in that pitcher, and a cup!" Elder Boone instructed me loudly, pointing over his shoulder.

I looked. Against the wall was a small shelf with a big bowl, a pitcher, and a glass on it. I grabbed the pitcher, quickly poured a glass of water, and ran back to my companion.

"Give it to her," he shouted.

Had I taken a second to think about it, I would have administered it differently. But, caught up in the movement of the moment, I threw the water into her face.

For a second she was silent. Then the calm was shattered as her young brain instructed her small vocal cords to stop holding back. She wailed, hollered, screamed, and yelped all in one incessant and steady shriek.

"To drink!" Elder Boone snapped. "Give it to her to drink!"

It was, of course, too late for that.

Elder Boone picked the girl up and set her on his bed. "Narlette," he said kindly, "I can't help you unless you calm down."

She looked at me with dislike and took in air. "My father is hurt bad," she finally managed to say.

"Should we get a doctor?" I asked, wanting to help.

"Not the bloody kind of hurt," she cried, shaking water off her like a dog. "Satan's got him again."

"Let's go," Elder Boone said authoritatively. He took Narlette's hand and pulled her out the door. I considered just waiting around and resting while he went out, but then I remembered I was a missionary. I will go; I will do. For the next two years I would be tied to my companion.

We stomped past the cemetery. We stomped past the church. We stomped past the un-identical twins Roswell and Feeble Ford. Feeble shifted his weight and yelled out, "Things okay, Narlette?"

"Daddy's in trouble again," she yelled back, having regained her composure.

"Tell him hello," he offered.

We crossed into the meadow and wove down one of the stamped-out trails. The long meadow stretched on for a few hundred feet along the river. Then came the trees, followed by the slope of the mountains. We hiked up through the forest, Narlette leading the way.

We soon came to a big home with a nice new roof and a freshly painted porch. There was a picture of Christ taped up in one of the front windows, and a dog with only two legs lay on the ground. The dog was chewing on something that I couldn't identify, although at first glance it sort of reminded me of my homesick stomach—mangled.

Narlette led us back around her house and up to a good-sized chicken coop. Loud fowl and colorful language came from within. We stopped a few steps away and just stood there listening.

"Brother Heck," Elder Boone finally hollered.

There was a brief pause, "Who's out there?"

"It's the missionaries. Your daughter brought us."

For another moment there was silence.

"Go on your way," a voice finally yelled back. "I ain't fit for you to waste your time on."

I would have been happy to obey. Apparently, Elder Boone felt differently.

"We're not leaving," he informed Brother Heck.

"Send Narlette away," he yelled out from the coop. "I don't want her to see me like this."

Narlette skipped off as if this were suddenly just a big game.

"She's gone," Elder Boone hollered.

I was born a member. I had grown up singing, "I hope they call me on a mission when I have grown a foot or two." Well, I had grown a foot or two—topping out at a couple of inches over the six-foot mark. I had also seen dozens of videos, taken classes, and read sacks full of books on the missionary experience. I had been prepped and readied. Or so I thought.

Brother Heck stepped out of the chicken coop and stood there. He looked to be about forty-five years old, and he wore no shirt or shoes, just a pair of ripped and ragged pants. He was covered in blue paint and feathers. His painted hair was sticking up in clumps and matted in strips. There were bits of straw and dirt and feathers all over him. His round belly contracted and expanded like a blue balloon with each breath. As he stepped out of the coop, he was followed by a flock of spotted blue chickens. He hung his head dejectedly.

"What have you done?" Elder Boone asked.

Brother Heck looked up at the two of us and then hung his head back down. With his voice and gaze directed toward the ground, he spoke. "I see you got yourself a new companion."

"This is Elder Williams," Elder Boone introduced. "We just got into town."

"Nice to meet you," Brother Heck mumbled, still looking at the ground.

"Good to meet you," I replied, trying hard not to smile.

"Have you been smoking again?" Elder Boone asked.

Brother Heck glumly nodded. "I'm helpless."

"And . . . ?" Elder Boone prodded.

"And I felt so awful about indulging that I tarred and feathered myself. 'Cepin I didn't have no tar, so I used paint."

We stood there silently for a moment.

"Patty's going to be awful sore," he said. "She was planning to use that paint on the house."

"There are other ways to repent," Elder Boone offered.

"I'm just so carnal," he moaned. "Weak as taffy."

The chickens grew bored and wandered off to find something more exciting to watch. Brother Heck took a seat on an overturned paint can. He put his head in his hands, smearing more paint on his face as he did so.

"Where is Sister Heck?" Elder Boone asked.

"Virgil's Find," he replied. "She went after some fabric. Narlette needs a new dress."

We sprayed Brother Heck off with a hose and then helped him clean up the paint in the chicken coop. During the cleanup we gave him a lesson on repentance and respecting ourselves enough not to paint our body-temples. He seemed forlorn and overly willing to change. It was obvious he had been through this sort of thing before. He showed us where he hid his cigarettes, and we burned them in one of the metal trash receptacles out back.

We left before his wife, Patty, came home. As we walked down through the forest and into the meadow, Elder Boone told me about the other times he had been summoned out here to help Brother Heck. Once they had to coax him out of a tree after Brother Heck had exiled himself to its tallest branches. On another occasion he had taped his legs to the spigot out back and then commenced to whip himself on his bare back with a fly swatter. As a form of punishment, that one was largely ineffective. Folks never knew what Brother Heck would submit himself to after a moment of nicotine-tinged weakness. Elder Boone also informed me that Brother Heck was one of the more dedicated members in the area.

We came down out of the forest and into the meadow. The place was now alive. School was out, and children ran around, climbing through the two aged and dilapidated wagons. Like small mounds of earth, they would rise and crumble above the long grass. Collectively they gave the meadow a soul. We walked past Roswell and Feeble again, past the cemetery, and home to our abode.

I lay down on my bed and stared at the ceiling.

"Really, it gets better," Elder Boone said.

"It gets better, or I get numb?"

"Some of both, I suppose."

One thing was for sure, I couldn't see it getting any worse. I was so homesick. I closed my eyes. Darkness helped. With my eyes closed I could almost imagine myself on a normal mission. I inventoried the few things I had going for me. My companion seemed like a decent person. If I had been put with anyone else, I would probably have been unable to suppress the urge to simply run away.

My gloomy thoughts were interrupted by a knock at the door.

Elder Boone opened the door to skinny old Roswell Ford, who was dancing with anticipation.

"What's up?" Elder Boone asked.

"Feeble's having a vision," he hollered. "Come quickly, I'm betting this one's a big'un." He ran off.

"Feeble's having a vision," Elder Boone repeated to me.

"What?" I asked.

Elder Boone ignored me and ran out the door. I followed.

Thelma's Way was moving. Waves of people washed across the meadow and lapped against the boardinghouse. Soon the place was surrounded by kids and adults of all makes and models. The feature attraction: Feeble Ford.

He was on the porch, standing with his arms outstretched. He was dancing a little jig. I was amazed. Feeble had looked so planted in that chair of his; now here he was wiggling about like an over-stimulated teenager. The crowd was humming with excitement.

"Look at Feeble."

"Feeble's on one."

"What's Feeble going to say?"

Feeble was stamping his feet and shimmying as if he heard music playing. He waved his hat around, and then kicked one of the porch chairs for effect. It was very dramatic.

I came to a standstill behind Elder Boone. The crowd stood quietly, watching Feeble's every twitch and slither. Finally he stopped, clapped his hands, and sang, "Praise God, from Whom All Blessings Flow." Then he pointed at me.

At me!

His arm shook, and his feet stamped. Then, as if they had been poured into the top of his head, words ran out of his mouth. "Things are going to change!" he yelled. "Things are going to change. Don't take life at face value. A nickel can appear to be a dime." He clapped his hands and fell back into a chair, closing his eyes. His red nose sizzled. His vision was completed.

Everyone turned to look at me. I looked behind me, hoping they were focusing on something else. My short brown hair felt as if it were contracting, and my face was painted red with the blush of prophecy.

The townsfolk gawked, eyeing me like fuzzy food that had been left in the back of the refrigerator. Seconds later, almost in unison, they turned their attention from me and began the work of critiquing Feeble's vision.

"Awful short."

"Not much substance."

"He sure got all fired up for just a few words."

"I liked his last one better."

Roswell spoke. "Has Feeble ever been wrong?"

The crowd collectively shook their heads no.

"I'd wager any one of yous that Feeble's words will come true," Roswell ranted. "Anyone?"

No takers.

"Chickens," Roswell spat. "Afraid of a little bet."

"What the heck did Feeble mean?" a woman shouted, ignoring Roswell and getting back to the vision. "Things are always changing here."

Folks went on speculating for a few minutes. I saw Brother Heck through the crowd. He had Narlette in hand and was wearing a big pair of overalls. I could see spots of blue in his ears and on one of his elbows where we had failed to wash him clean. His graying hair was wet, and his foggy eyes looked full of thoughts he wasn't properly thinking. He was tall, and his wide shoulders gave the impression of constant attentiveness. He was actually a rather distinguished-looking man, if you could mentally get past the first impression he had so vividly painted.

The crowd broke up. People wandered off pondering Feeble's prophetic words. Brother Heck sheepishly sidled up to us. "Elders," he acknowledged.

Narlette smiled.

"Feeble had at it," Brother Heck commented. "I hope this vision don't make everyone crazy again."

Again?

"He didn't say much," Elder Boone pointed out.

"Appears he's taken a shine to this'un," Brother Heck said, nodding toward me. "I guess big things are in store for you." He stuck out his hand and introduced himself, as if this were the first time we had ever met. I suppose he was hoping to start anew. I couldn't fault him for that.

"I'm Brother Ricky Heck," he said proudly.

"I'm Elder Trust Williams," I responded, shaking his hand.

Brother Heck took Narlette's hand and walked off.

"I think he likes you," Elder Boone said.

I couldn't do this. This was not right. I must have gotten the wrong mission assignment. That was it. My real call must have gotten mixed up in the mail. I had to tell someone. Right now there was some missionary in France who should be here, someone who had a command of backwoods etiquette. Someone who was fluent in *'ceptin's* and *ain'ts.*

Elder Boone patted me on the back as we walked back to our home. "I'm glad you're here," he said.

I missed Southdale.

I missed civilization.

# 6

# Green Eyes

Grace Heck was perceptive. She could sense and tell things about others that were unknown even to them. Grace's father figured this was a result of her having accidentally hit her head against a large piece of limestone down by the Girth when she was seven. Her mother saw the gift as coming directly from God at her birth. Either way, Grace was pretty perceptive. Unfortunately, she couldn't seem to see her own future too clearly these days.

When Grace had turned twenty, her whole world had changed. Her reflection in the river looked unfamiliar. She had grown up being liked by everyone, but at the moment she didn't even know if she cared for herself. For the first time, she saw her life as lacking. What place did she as a woman have here in Thelma's Way?

She had hoped that having missionaries would be good for the town. But so far they had proved to be little more than an irritant—a new set of outsiders to look down their noses at everyone. Elder Frates had treated Thelma's Way as if he were the master teacher, and they were all the same slow child who couldn't quite grasp what he was saying. His act of trying to pompously reorganize the town was too much for Grace. She had promised herself that she wouldn't return to church until the missionaries were a thing of the past.

She closed the cupboards and sat back in one of the wooden chairs. She looked around the quaint little home and sighed. A few months back, she had discovered this small cabin hidden deep among the thick mountain trees. She observed it for a while before bravely trying the door handle and finding it unlocked. Curiosity took her inside.

It was a nice place, though clearly abandoned. She had cleaned it out and fixed it up a bit. She spent many days and nights in it hidden away from everything besides her books. She was always checking out books from the Virgil's Find public library in hopes of broadening her universe. She dreamed about life outside of Thelma's Way, about any life different from the one she knew.

Grace was moving and simple in appearance. Her most recognizable features were her dark green eyes and her thick red hair, which was usually tied back behind her neck. The oldest of the three Heck children, she loved her family, although she found herself being more and more compelled to stay away these days.

What with the shelter of her newfound cabin, it was becoming increasingly rare for her to leave the sanctuary of the forest and wander into the open meadow, and now, after what she had just witnessed, she was determined never to come down. She had been secretly watching as her painted father had humiliated himself in front of the missionaries. She had looked on in horror as the elders had hosed her dad off and then lectured him on the dangers of smoking. *Embarrassed* was too mild a word.

She had considered storming out of the trees and insisting that the missionaries leave her father alone, but something in her seemed to snap. The emptiness that had been creeping up on her for months was suddenly upon her in full force.

All she could do was watch.

Later, from behind the boardinghouse, she watched Feeble prophesy and point at the new elder. Curiosity wiggled through her veins, her mind flipping back and forth like the adjusting blades of a mini-blind. The new elder intrigued her. He was good-looking. Grace feared the new feelings that were growing inside of her—feared and fanned.

After Feeble finished prophesying, she slipped through the back of the cemetery and down to the Girth River. She sat down on the edge of the ground and stuck her feet into the water like prongs into a socket. Her body jolted to the touch of the water. She washed her hands and took her hair out of its tie.

"Missionaries," she whispered.

Grace was lonely.

# 7

# It Starts

Saturday, our early morning companionship study was interrupted by reveille. I looked out our window to see Roswell blowing a bugle in the middle of the meadow as the sun rose. It was pre-planning meeting day. We went outside, hurrying over as if something important were actually happening. A small crowd had already gathered by the time we got there. Roswell put down the bugle and caught his breath.

"We will now hear from Sister Watson," he announced.

Sister Watson, the bishop's wife, stepped up beside Roswell.

"I expected more of a crowd," she said.

There weren't too many people in the meadow. Feeble's vision a few days back had been a much bigger draw. But then, Feeble had had the courtesy to prophesy at a reasonable hour of the day.

"I'm certain our ancestors are disappointed," Sister Watson scolded. "Here it is the pre-planning meeting for our sesquicentennial, and you're all that have shown up."

I couldn't tell if she was insulting us or not.

"Some may say, 'But Sister Watson, the celebration isn't for almost two years.' To that I respond, 'Remember the slow turtle.'"

Everyone nodded as if they knew exactly what she was talking about. Having nothing to lose, I nodded too.

"I feel inspired," Sister Watson continued, "to have the missionaries come up and give you all an impromptu lesson on participation. Elders."

I looked at Elder Boone. He was too busy pushing me forward to meet my eyes.

"You go do it, Elder," he said, smiling. "It will be good for you."

I wanted to protest, but Elder Boone *shhhed* me. The tiny crowd split. I reluctantly walked through and to the front. Sister Watson glanced at my tag to make sure she was remembering my name correctly.

"Some of you may remember Elder Williams from Feeble's last vision a couple days back. Well, Bishop Watson and I had the opportunity to meet with him the other day, and I can honestly say that he seems to have fewer flaws than the last missionary the church sent us—the one with the funny, puffy booklets. With that, I give you: Elder Williams."

I looked at the small group. Brother Heck was there, and Feeble, and a few other folks I was beginning to recognize. Elder Boone smiled at me. I really hated public speaking.

"Well," I began. "I know that participation is important. I think that people need to participate in things that are worthwhile.

"I came out on my mission a little later than most Mormon elders. I attended some college before coming out. It was a big decision for me. I am now happy to be serving on my mission and participating in the work."

Digby Heck, Brother Heck's teenage son, yawned. Sister Watson tapped her watch, indicating that I had taken enough time.

"In closing, I guess I would just like to say that I know participation is true, and—"

"Thank you, Elder Williams," Sister Watson interrupted.

I walked back to my companion. This time the gathering didn't split, so I had to sort of push my way through.

"Thank you, Elder Williams," Sister Watson repeated when I had settled back into my place. "I think we all need to remember that Elder Williams here is real new to the mission field. Anyhow, I was hoping for a larger crowd so that we could get the preparations for this pageant off with a bang."

*BOOM!*

I thought for a moment that my head had exploded. My ears vibrated and rang. I looked to the side of me and saw a man pointing a gun toward the sky.

"Yes, ma'am!" he hollered.

"It's a little early for firing that thing, Pete," Brother Heck said.

"Sorry," Pete replied.

"Normally you all know how I discourage Pete from shooting that thing off," Sister Watson said. "But I'm happy to see a little enthusiasm this morning."

Elder Boone leaned into me and whispered, "Pete loves guns."

I moved to the other side of my companion.

"As we all know, there has already been some arguing over who would play what in our sesquicentennial play," Sister Watson continued. "But I want you all to know that those people working behind the scenes and building the stage are just as important as those who play the leads. To make things easier, I've decided that when the time comes, my husband and I will play the two main parts, and we'll put the rest of the assignments in a hat and draw names. That way everything's fair."

No one protested.

"As most of you know, the celebration is about twenty months from now, on the exact date of our town's inception. We are starting preparations early because we want to make sure that we do things right. We have a lot of props to build, as well as a stage. The play itself, tentatively titled *'All Is Swell,'* should be completed in a few months, and at that point we will begin handing out parts. There will be songs to learn and costumes to make. I would have had the entire script finished by now, but Paul stealing the Book of Mormon has caused me to have to rewrite." Sister Watson took in air. "This isn't going to be as simple or as easy as our usual town plays. But don't get discouraged—we will have our ancestors on the other side pushing us around. Any questions?"

An older lady I didn't yet know raised her hand.

"Yes, Teddy," Sister Watson pointed.

"Will there be food?"

"Lots of it. This is going to be the celebration to end all celebrations. Plus we're going to open ourselves up to the world. All the surrounding towns will be invited, as well as anyone else who would like to come. This will put us on the map."

Pete Kennedy shot his gun off again.

*BOOOM!*

"Yes, ma'am!"

Roswell raised his hand and asked, "Do you have to be a Mormon to participate?"

"No," Sister Watson answered. "The only requirement is that you have Thelma's Way blood coursing through your veins."

Everyone looked down at their arms.

Brother Heck stepped up. "I'd like to say just a couple things, if'n that's all right."

Sister Watson nodded.

"Now, I never been a fancy word user. In fact, me and English just ain't real cozy. But I don't want some of you thinking that this is just another one of Sister Watson's silly plays. This is a pageant extra-ganza.

And just 'cause it's got a three-dollar word like *sesquicentennial* in front of it, is no reason to not take it seriously. That's why we voted to start preparing so soon. We want every stranger that comes to the celebration in two years to walk away with a dazed look on their face."

"Thank you, Brother Heck," Sister Watson said. Brother Heck stepped down. "Now, we here in attendance are the fortunate few. We're getting in on the ground floor of this. As the day gets closer, more and more people are going to want to get involved, and—"

*BOOOM!*

"We're on the ground floor!"

Everyone looked at Pete. Sister Watson held her startled hand to her heart.

"Anyhow," she continued, "as the time gets nearer there will be more and more to do. I hope I can count on all of you to do your part and then some. I promise you that if you do, this will be a pageant the people will never forget."

Everyone nodded, congratulating each other for getting in on the ground floor. I think I was the only one who was nervous. Thankfully, it was none of my business. Some other unfortunate missionary would have to deal with it twenty months from now.

I was deluded.

# 8

# IT'S A SMALL WARD AFTER PAUL

Week Four

I had been told by President Clasp that the Thelma's Way Ward was small, despite the fact that virtually everyone in the surrounding area was Mormon.

President Clasp had lied. *Small* is measurable. The ward consisted of Bishop Watson and his wife; the Heck family—Brother and Sister Heck, Narlette, and her older brother, Digby; Sister Teddy Yetch, an older woman who lived across the Girth River; Miss Flitrey, the grade-school teacher; Feeble Ford; and us.

"It's a small ward after Paul," Elder Boone sang as I sat there looking at our tiny congregation.

Paul Leeper was the infamous, dishonest, local apostate. Heavy on the *local,* heavy on the *apostate.* I had been briefed on him by my companion.

Six months ago Paul had won a free trip to Rome from the Savin' Town grocery store over in Virgil's Find. Paul was shopping for anti-lice medicine and ended up being the one-millionth customer, thus procuring himself a clean scalp, a one-week, all-expenses-paid trip to Rome, and a lifetime 20 percent discount on all nonsale items at Savin' Town.

Rome wasn't ready for Paul.

Paul spent the first half of the week there perpetuating every ugly-American stereotype the Romans had ever had of us. He demanded that his waiters and servers speak English. He took pictures in places that were off-limits, and when people tried to stop him, he screamed about his rights under the U.S. Constitution. He talked loudly, walked loudly, and made fun of everything from their dilapidated Colosseum to the stupid-looking currency the Romans used.

To make matters even worse, Paul had somehow confused Rome with Ancient Egypt. He became enraged when one of the local taxi drivers refused to take him to see the pyramids. Paul called the driver a couple of America's choicest words. In turn the driver ran over his foot, breaking all five of his toes and ruining his best pair of travel shoes.

While getting his foot worked on by one of the Roman doctors, Paul overheard someone talking about the finger of Thomas. Apparently the Vatican had the finger of Thomas the Apostle on display in its museum: the very finger that had once touched the Master after Thomas had refused to believe.

Well, Paul had his doubts. But he hobbled to the Vatican to see this finger for himself. There with his own two eyes he saw it, encased in glass and pointing toward him. It was an epiphany for Paul. It was a miracle, a life-changing event. Actually, it didn't really change him all that much, but it did afford him a whole new level of self-righteousness. He had seen the finger.

Paul was touched, and not like usual.

He was mugged by a couple of rough men on his way back from the Vatican. They took all his money and kicked him a few times. Paul saw this as a sign that Satan was personally trying to prevent him from making it back to Thelma's Way where he could testify that he had seen the finger of Thomas.

Penniless and stuck in Rome, Paul went to the American Embassy and demanded that he be given a few dollars for souvenirs and meals, seeing how he was a red-blooded American and all. The Embassy didn't give him any pocket change, but they did help him get an earlier return flight home.

Paul returned home to Thelma's Way two days sooner than he had planned and with an attitude that he was now better and more righteous than anyone there. Yes, he had stood next to the finger that had once touched the Master, and this, in Paul's mind, made him as important as any biblical figure, except maybe Moses or Abraham or that one guy who was in the fish.

The first thing Paul did was return to Savin' Town, the grocery store that had given him the trip, and demand some compensation for the two days of Rome he was forced to give up. Well, not only did the store refuse, they informed Paul that they had miscounted and he was not really their one-millionth customer. Their accountant, who was the owner's nephew, had been off by a couple hundred thousand. Savin' Town revoked Paul's twenty percent discount and threw him out the door. Paul stood in the parking lot and prophesied that Savin' Town would rue the day they had tossed out the self-made apostle. Three days later the Savin' Town dumpster caught fire, causing the store to close for four hours.

Coincidence?

Paul thought not.

In his mind, this proved he was a full-fledged prophet. He left the Church to strike it out on his own. The only thing he needed was a congregation. Sadly, he found one in the Mormons. He led almost all of the members away from the Church. In the past Paul had been known as a chronic liar. One of his most famous lies was that he was actually the top-secret, transfigured, fourth Nephite not mentioned in the Book of Mormon. There was also his claim that as a youth he had spent two summers harvesting cookies at the Pepperidge Farm. But unlike before, this time Paul had proof of his brush with greatness. You see, he had brought back a postcard of the finger of Thomas, a relic of his own. He used it as token of his authority and his Savin' Town prophecy as the proof of his power.

The members flocked.

The People of Paul began to construct a small chapel on the other side of the river. They organized a choir, bought a bell, and watched their congregation grow as the gullible locals and their fascination with the parable of the finger drove them from the ward. The heavens appeared to have smiled on the People of Paul. But fate served up the final snicker.

Before the big desertion, the Thelma's Way Ward was doing pretty well. It was good sized and relatively normal, despite its relatively abnormal members. Bishop Clem Watson and his counselors, Feeble Ford and Toby Carver, were moving the work along at a perfect pace for the area. Then along came Paul, and the ward fractured like clay pigeons in the sight of God.

Bishop Watson tried desperately to keep his ward together. He pleaded with the members to pray and stay focused, but they seemed to like the blur. People didn't want to focus; they were too swept up in the momentum of Paul's new church. Even Toby Carver, the second counselor, deserted the Thelma's Way Ward. Bishop Watson was devastated. He petitioned Church headquarters for missionaries to be assigned to Thelma's Way. He felt that with a little help, he could bring the deserting members back to their senses. The Church considered his request.

As Bishop Watson prayed for his wayward members' souls, Paul bad-mouthed Bishop Watson until he was red in the face. Then, during one of his tirades, Paul became bold enough to predict that bad things would befall the active Mormons. Two nights later someone broke into the church building (an act of minor difficulty, since it was never locked) and stole the Thelma's Way Ward community Book of Mormon.

At first I had no idea why these people were so concerned about a missing Book of Mormon. I was quickly informed that the stolen book was not your average, free, blue papercovered copy. It was in fact a rare first edition the apostle Parley P. Pratt had given the Saints when he had passed through Thelma's Way more than a hundred years ago. It was the most treasured possession in the entire town. It was the Mormons' stamp of approval—validating them, as it were. Parley P. Pratt had donated it to the town as a gesture of his appreciation for all the kindness and compassion they had shown him when he had become horribly ill from some bad meat, and the entire meadow area had helped nurse him back to full health. He had signed that Book of Mormon with the inscription:

*With sincere appreciation, Parley P. Pratt*

Not just appreciation, but *sincere* appreciation. It was quite a tribute to the backwoods town of Thelma's Way. The book was kept in the bishop's office and brought out to rest on the small table next to the podium each Sunday.

No longer. The book was gone. Someone had stolen the last thing the Mormons had to feel good about. The few members who had stayed faithful during the apostasy ordeal had always found additional strength in that old Book of Mormon. Now they didn't even have that.

The town was aghast. Thelma's Way prided itself on not having to lock its doors, on being able to leave a pie on the windowsill or a melon in the field without worry. What good was a neighbor if you had to keep an eye on him? Geoff Titter once left his good rake on the porch of the boardinghouse for a whole year before picking it up. No one ever touched it. That's the kind of people that populated Thelma's Way: mellow, Mormon, and honest to a fault.

Not anymore. The ugly crime of theft had appeared. And much like the mole on Tindy MacDermont's arm, the deed seemed to stick out and get attention. It was a big, hairy deal. Thelma's Way had its theories, or, more befitting, its theory, as to who had done it.

Everyone suspected Paul. They had found him to be a little too prophetic. They all figured he had done the deed so that his anti-Mormon prophecy would come true. As an ugly, final gesture he had stripped the Mormons and the town of their most prized possession. It wasn't enough that he had already driven everyone away—now he had, in a sense, stolen their soul.

Well, faster than they had joined him, Paul's people deserted him. They burned the bridge that spanned the Girth River and broke out the windows of the unfinished People of Paul chapel. No one wanted a leader who was a thief. He was completely dethroned, stripped of all the prestige his wacky prophecies had once afforded him.

Nowadays Paul spent his time in relative shame, working on his house in the forest across the Girth River. Neither Elder Boone nor I had as yet actually seen him. He still claimed his innocence, even though everyone knew he was guilty.

Since there was no real proof, Paul went unprosecuted for the crime, and the mystery of the missing Book of Mormon lingered like a goofy local legend. Paul's cabin had been searched, but the book wasn't there. Here in these hills there were a zillion places a person could hide a book. Most people figured he had either thrown it into the Girth River or burned it. Both possibilities were equally horrific and hideous.

Sister Watson took up with a couple of other civic-minded women and formed a small action group called M.A.P., Mothers Against Paul. It was a good name until Frank Porter, ever the wave maker, insisted on joining the group. Since he wasn't a mother in the true sense of the word, Sister Watson changed the group's name to P.A.P., People Against Paul. But then old conspiracy-minded Pap Wilson thought their group was out to get him personally. So Sister Watson changed the name once again, and P.I.G., Paul Is Guilty, was formally formed. Yes, young Digby Heck tried to make an argument for all the local sows, but his voice was not heeded. P.I.G. stuck.

So far, P.I.G. had made very little progress in its efforts. Its goal was to bring Paul to justice, or at least to give him a whipping or burn his house down. Justice worked differently in Thelma's Way.

Meanwhile, the Saints who had left the ward to join up with Paul never came back to our congregation. So now the hills were filled with less-active Mormons who were either too lukewarm, too lazy, or just too embarrassed to come back. Our job as missionaries was to rebuild the congregation. We were to find the ninety and nine who had foolhardily left the figurative one in this secret basin community filled with less-active Mormons.

Here it was, another Sunday service in Thelma's Way, and the enormity of the task ahead was giving me a headache. Elder Boone and I sat on the stand with Feeble and Bishop Watson. We were trying to make it look as if we had some sort of leadership authority.

Bishop Watson was a little old man. He stood just under five feet tall and walked with a limp. He had no hair and usually wore a shirt with sleeves that were entirely too long, and a tie that was too short. He had gray eyes and a big smile that made him look at least an inch and a half taller than he actually was. He was kind and spoke with a booming radio announcer's voice that didn't really match his physique. Everything he said sounded like an advertisement or news flash.

"Church at eleven."

"Don't miss out on tithing settlement."

"Be the first one to pick up your new manual."

Bishop Watson's wife was considerably taller and thicker than he was. She wore a dark wig over her light hair and spoke without really moving her mouth. It was actually a rather amazing and unnerving thing to witness. They made an interesting couple.

After church, Elder Boone and I had lunch over at the bishop's house. Sister Watson served up meat loaf, tossed salad, bean sprouts, peas, and some local delicacy called "ramp."

"It's the best thing around these parts," she bragged about the odd vegetable.

"One of the real perks of living here," Bishop Watson added.

I tried to smile as I ate.

"So, are you elders excited about the upcoming pageant?" Sister Watson asked.

"Well," Elder Boone answered, "it's still an incredibly long way off. I'm sure neither of us will be here."

"We're getting a real jump on this one," Bishop Watson boomed.

"I'll be finished with the script in a few months," Sister Watson announced. "The story is based on Parley P. Pratt coming here and getting nauseated. Of course there will be a lot of singing and dancing. Oh just think of it, Elders, our very own outdoor pageant. A pageant can really put you on the map, you know? Look at the Hill Cumorah pageant, look at Nauvoo, Illinois."

Bishop Watson looked around as if searching for Nauvoo.

The conversation drifted. Sister Watson began telling us in detail how she had helped birth the very cow we were now eating. Brother Watson provided color commentary. I found myself sculpting my portion of cow into the shape of Lucy with my spoon. It started half-heartedly but soon drew my attention. I glanced up nervously, but no one had noticed I wasn't listening. I pulled the table centerpiece in front of my plate to hide what I was doing. I stabbed a few pieces of lettuce from Elder Boone's plate when he wasn't looking and rigged up some clothes for my sculpture. I spied the peas across the table. They were green, but they would have to do for eyes. I asked Sister Watson if she would kindly pass them.

"Hand me your plate and I'll scoop some out for you," she offered.

I sat there for a moment, not sure what to do.

"Uh, actually, I like to scoop myself."

"Nonsense," Bishop Watson said, his radio announcer's voice

booming through their dining room. "Sister Watson will set you up fine; hand her your plate."

I decided to skip the eyes. I backpedaled.

"Well, to tell you the truth, I'm full."

They both stared at me for a few moments, but soon they returned to their meals. Things would have been fine if I had not noticed Bishop Watson's sprouts. They would make perfect hair for my Lucy. I just couldn't resist. I commented on an antique-looking clock on the wall. While everyone was looking the other way, I stabbed the sprouts from off of Bishop Watson's plate.

No one noticed.

It was not enough. Lucy had thick hair. I complimented the tole-painted watering can that was sitting on the shelf behind them. But before I could successfully extract any more of Bishop Watson's sprouts, everyone turned back around.

"What are you doing?" It was Elder Boone. I covered my plate with my hands.

"Is something wrong with your meal?" Sister Watson asked.

"No," I replied.

"Then why are you covering your plate?" Bishop Watson questioned.

I slowly moved my hands to reveal a mound of misshapen meat loaf adorned with a lettuce dress and stylish bean-sprout hair. I felt my face go flush. Any moment the Watsons would throw me out of their home for displaying such awful table manners. But Bishop Watson just went on and on about how lifelike the likeness was, and Sister Watson passed me the peas with new understanding.

I sheepishly applied the eyes.

Elder Boone shook his head in disgust. I realized for the first time that I just might fit in here.

Sister Watson served ice cream for dessert, and Old Bishop Watson, in the spirit of competition, made a snowman out of his portion.

My mission was taking shape.

9

# Drifting

Trust had been gone for more than five weeks but Lucy was adjusting. She shifted in her skirt and practice smiled at herself in the mirror. It wasn't often that her father set her up with dates, let alone a non-Mormon boy.

Lucy was looking forward to it. Gentile, beware.

Trust's letters were getting shorter. He complained less about the backwards people he was serving.

Lucy was concerned.

It was good to minister, but attachment could be catastrophic. What if Trust picked up unsophisticated mannerisms or a few awkward habits? He was supposed to grow up and out of his childish traits and ways, to come home ninety percent done, so Lucy could finish him off.

But Lucy's ability to refine, even by her own high estimate, could do only so much. Trust was a hardening ball of clay that needed to be molded further. Now, as his character stiffened, other people besides Lucy were there shaping him—people with names like Narlette and Feeble. It was all there in his letters.

Lucy furrowed her brow.

A mission was supposed to be regal and prestigious. It developed the finer arts of communication and persuasion. It was upper-class training, the first in an orderly sequence of steps leading to a foreign ambassadorship or overseas business appointment.

Lucy thought she would make a perfect ambassador's wife.

But stuck in Thelma's Way, Trust was about as likely to become sophisticated as she was to break out. Lucy had added the petition for his being transferred to her nightly prayer. So far, the request had gone unheeded.

"Oh, the trials I am forced to endure!" she moaned.

The doorbell rang—Lucy's blind date. The door opened. There stood Lance Fitzgerald with his square gentile jaw and dark gentile eyes. Lucy felt her body temperature rise.

Lucy was adjusting.

## 10

# One Up, One Down

### Week Seven

I realized in my first couple of weeks that Roswell and Feeble Ford were really the heart of Thelma's Way. It wasn't necessarily a healthy heart, but they seemed to keep the town exactly where it was at.

Both Roswell and Feeble were Mormon, but only Feeble was active. Roswell had been inactive ever since Paul showed him the picture of Thomas' finger and bid him follow. He left the Church and took up smoking all in the same week. Roswell felt a pipe made him look more mature, which was no small feat, given that he was over eighty.

Inactivity fit Roswell. He was tired of living under the substantial shadow of his hour-older twin. He liked the freedom and independence that inactivity provided. He liked to hear people say things like, "Feeble would never go inactive." It made him feel like a true individual.

Yes, at eighty-some years old he had finally found himself. Unfortunately, his inactivity helped foster the town's indecisiveness.

People felt better about not doing what they should be doing because Roswell wasn't. Roswell was old, you see, and supposedly wiser than most. If he wasn't going to church, then the rest of them could stay home, too. Roswell basked in the lukewarm glow of his newfound leadership position.

Of course, the few active Mormons used Feeble as their inspiration. Feeble had always been the good one, and smart. Feeble had read the Book of Mormon at least three times, the Doctrine and Covenants twice, the New Testament once, plus he had reread the Sermon on the Mount on at least six additional occasions. He had even started the Old Testament and gotten past First Kings. He was quite the scholar.

Feeble was definitely the more righteous of the two, what with his visions and all. Everyone felt that the only reason he had not already been translated was because he was so heavy. The heavens just couldn't heave him up. Most people believed that he ate so much just so he could remain overweight and stay here on earth to administer among the people. Such sacrifice. This theory, however, redefined the word *administer* to mean sit around and prattle. And it called attention to Roswell. After all, Roswell was so skinny that had God wanted him back, a slight breeze would have been enough to lift him home. His still being here in his eightieth year was a pretty good indication of where he stood with the heavens.

Roswell and Feeble were the last of the Ford clan to still be living in the state of Tennessee. According to Roswell, there was a cousin named Stubby who owned a pawn shop in Virgil's Find, but aside from him, they were it. What nice representatives they were. Roswell and Feeble spent all their time sitting on the front porch of their boardinghouse, Feeble commenting on the world around them, and Roswell making petty bets.

"Bet it'll rain this afternoon."

"Bet the raccoons'll be back tonight."

"Bet Tindy's sores take a good two weeks to heal."

"Five bucks."

"You're on."

The boardinghouse was a nice center of town, despite the fact that it wasn't much of a boardinghouse, or much of a town for that matter. There were a couple of rooms on the second floor that could have been used as a place for weary travelers to rest, but they were filled with old furniture, Roswell's collection of *Woodsman Weekly* magazines, and Feeble's "Great Men of the World" pewter figurine set, seventy-six four-inch figures in all. A complete set, all in perfect condition except for Thomas Edison's missing arm—on account of Roswell throwing Edison at a pack of noisy dogs one cold November night.

On the bottom floor of the boardinghouse there was a large all-purpose room and a small store that didn't have much to offer. You could buy bags of rice, beans, or flour and tubs of lard. There was also a glass cooler filled with soft drinks.

Feeble and Roswell had one of the few TVs in Thelma's Way. (Only about two-thirds of the homes in Thelma's Way even had electricity.) Their TV sat on a rolling cart in the middle of the store, and people from all over would come to watch football games and *Days of Our Lives.*

Feeble and Roswell were an institution, as close as Thelma's Way got to a Blockbuster Video or a high school basketball team. And to look at them rocking peacefully on the boardinghouse porch, you would never have guessed that their time had come.

It was early September and the seasons were beginning to rub up against each other. Elder Boone and I had just returned from the other side of the river where we had been visiting Sister Teddy Yetch for breakfast. She had a couple of new recipes she had wanted to try out on us. Her peanut-butter pork dumplings had not been too bad, but her fried widget recipe needed some tweaking.

Sister Teddy Yetch was about seventy years old. She was at the point in her life where her skin was turning from polyester to

100-percent cotton, wrinkling at every bend and crevice. She had thin gray hair and brown eyes that seemed to sag within their sockets. She didn't actually have a full set of teeth, but she did have most of the important ones in front. Teddy was kind, and she was the only active member who lived on the other side of the great Girth River. Apostate Paul lived across the Girth, deeper back in the trees, though to this day neither I nor Elder Boone had actually met him. There were a few other less-active members and Paul's abandoned chapel, but it was Teddy Yetch that we went to see.

To cross the wide Girth River you had to drag one of the community rafts to the part of the river near the high end of the meadow, right by the burnt-out bridge, and then paddle quickly with one of the community paddles across the strong current. However, if you used your head, you could manipulate the current to push you to the other side. If you didn't move fast enough, the river would pull you down past our place, past the back edge of the cemetery, through some rapids, and eventually down over Hallow Falls. It was quite a sight to see old Teddy cross the Girth. She put us young elders to shame.

Elder Boone and I had just dragged our raft back up to the starting point for the next user and were stomping across the meadow when we noticed people were running to the boardinghouse, shouting and crying. I looked at my watch to see what time it was. I figured folks were just holding another unnecessary meeting to discuss their pageant that was still so far away. Or maybe they were all throwing a fit over the current plot twist on *Days of Our Lives.*

I was way off.

I heard Feeble's name hollered a few times by different people. I thought then that he was just having another vision and people were talking about it. We picked up our pace and ran to the boardinghouse.

Feeble was lying on his stomach, his right arm stretched out, holding one of his pewter statues. His face was in the dirt, and it looked as if he had been in stride walking towards the meadow when he had simply fallen to the earth. Brother Heck was down next to Feeble searching for signs of life. Feeble's days of prophesying were over.

"What happened?" I asked as everyone else just stood around stunned, not knowing what to do.

"He's moved on," was all Brother Heck said.

Miss Flitrey's curiosity had gotten the best of her so she let her school kids out to see what all the commotion was. The horde of children joined the ring of folks that was now circling Feeble. The sky above clouded as if on cue. There was a heavy stillness in the air.

"Are you sure he's dead?" I asked in disbelief.

The entire ring of people nodded back, as if they too, by virtue of just knowing him, now knew him to be dead.

Toby Carver burst through the crowd and fell down beside Feeble. Toby was a kind person. He was always red cheeked and flustered. His square body was blocky and wooden, and he always had his sleeves rolled up, as if he were about to do something. He had a long thin beard and a pointy forehead that seemed to extend out past his nose. Toby was sort of the town's unofficial doctor. He had no medical training, but years ago he had twisted his ankle so badly, he had had to get it looked at by a clinic in Virgil's Find. The attending physician gave Toby a stretchy Ace bandage and a big bottle of pills for the pain. As things worked out, no sooner had Toby's ankle healed, than CleeDee Lipton hurt her wrist harvesting wildflowers east of the meadow. Toby trotted over to CleeDee's place, wrapped her wrist with his bandage, and gave her a couple of his pills. A week later she was fine. Well, from that point on, whenever anyone had an ailment or condition, Toby would hustle over and wrap it. He eventually ran out of the pills, but that bandage would be good forever. It had helped heal everything from Bishop Watson's pulled thigh to Digby Heck's swollen glands.

Toby knelt there next to Feeble's body, his Ace bandage clenched in his hand. It was too late. Toby cursed the heavens for not giving him more time. Toby could wrap Feeble from head to toe and it wouldn't make any difference now.

Then someone asked, "Where's Roswell?"

Everyone looked up.

Roswell rarely left Feeble's side. They were inseparable, everybody knew that. It had been difficult for Roswell to go inactive because it meant time away from his brother every Sunday. As much as he wanted to be his own man, Roswell needed his twin. Now here was his Feeble lying alone on the ground. It didn't look right. No one said it, but when it came to leaving this life, everyone had assumed the two would go together. Brother Heck and Digby raced into the boardinghouse. A few moments later they hollered for everyone to join them indoors. We all scrambled inside and into the bedroom, pushing and shoving for the best position.

There were two twin beds about six feet apart from each other in Roswell and Feeble's room. One was sagging in the middle, sheets untucked, pillows on the floor. The other looked almost new. It wasn't difficult to guess whose was whose. Roswell's pillow was indented as if a head still lay on it. His blankets were folded neatly back. Next to his bed was a pair of red slippers, ready for Roswell to step into.

One problem. No Roswell.

Brother Heck and Digby searched the rest of the house while everyone else just stood there staring at the beds.

No Roswell.

"I knew it," old Briant Willpts exclaimed as we stood there bewildered. "I had a dream 'bout it and I warned Feeble. He laughed me off. Thought he was the only one who could have any visions. Well I say to you all, look who's laughing now," he spat.

Everyone looked at Briant to see who was laughing now.

"Well, I'm not laughing, laughing," he covered. "But inside I'm a big wad of righteous snickery."

Briant Willpts was an orphan. He was one of the few residents of

Thelma's Way who had not actually been born in town. Because of this he felt he could misuse or make up words and then explain them by saying that these were words used in the outside world and people here just hadn't heard them before. Due to a bout with polio as a teenager, Briant walked as if he were trying out for the Hunchback of Notre Dame, his long arms swinging wildly whenever he stepped. He was about sixty years old, and used a cane whenever he needed sympathy.

"In my dream," he continued, raising his arms for dramatic effect, "I saw both Roswell and Feeble being lifted up to heaven on a liffy. I told Feeble to start preparing to lixidate this life. Pack your bags, Feeble, I says. Clean up your life and prepare to meet your creatoriums. Did Feeble take me seriously?"

Could anyone take him seriously?

"I'll answer on behalf of Feeble," Briant rambled, "seeing how Feeble is deceased and there is no way that he could properly respond to my incisive and indicament line of spectorial questioning. The answer is . . . Nope."

I couldn't even remember the question.

"Now, let me tell you all what happened," Briant waved his hands in front of himself, indicating that he would now lay things straight. A couple of people attempted to sit down on the beds, weary from standing and hoping to hear the explanation in comfort. Briant quickly scolded them and, as kindly and succinctly as he could, asked them please not to disturb the scene. So we all just stood around the beds while Briant spun one huge pile of yarn.

"Late last night after Roswell and Feeble retired to bed, a heavenly visitor came in a white robe. He came down and visited them here in this bedroom."

People looked around as if they were suddenly standing on holy ground.

"I know this to be an enveloping fact because around nine last night, I was walking past the boardinghouse and saw a strange glow coming from out of that window."

He pointed with his cane.

"It was a beautiful blue glow, brighter and more simshinery than any color I've yet seen before, and I've seen a lot of colors. Red, blue, green, brown, red . . . and some more I'm sure, I just can't remember right now. Anyway, I knocked on the front door but no one answered.

"I should have knocked longer," he added glumly.

"That heavenly visitor must have been informing Feeble and Roswell that they were about to be translated. He must have lifted Roswell out of his bed and tossed him up to heaven. It's obvious to the trained and scholaticable eye that this is what happened. Take a look-see. Slippers still neatly by the bed as if Roswell had never gotten out or up. Feeble, like we have suspected all along, must have been too heavy to yank topside-up. The way I see it is that this angel must have struggled with him, which would explain the messy bed. Then in frustration he must have given up. Feeble, desperatic to not be left without Roswell, ran outside in hopes of following this visitor. The visitor was so filled with compassion that he must have struck Feeble dead to end his heartache."

Everyone was nodding as if it all made sense.

"So you're saying that Roswell was translated?" I asked in amazement.

Everyone looked at me with one collective "Duh."

"That seems a little absurd," I observed, my blue eyes trying not to laugh.

Briant Willpts ignored me. He just stood there as if receiving fresh revelation. After a brief pause he opened his eyes and walked out of the room. He shuffled to the porch and then did the unthinkable. He planted himself in Feeble's good sitting chair.

Everyone gasped. They let out a collective murmur of approval. It was a sign—proof of Briant Willpts' authority as messenger. It was apparent to all, except me, that the spirit of Feeble had rested upon the hump of Briant Willpts.

"I don't think it's right," Brother Heck ventured. "You sitting on Feeble's chair as he lies there on the ground."

Leo Tip and Toby Carver, as if on cue, went to pick up Feeble and lay him somewhere more dignified. One tug, however, told them they weren't men enough to do it. Toby waved over Brother Heck and Pap Wilson.

One per leg. One per limb. Still not enough.

Gun-loving Pete Kennedy and Ed Washington joined them. They wiggled their arms underneath Feeble's belly, and locked hands. Then with one mighty heave, all six of them lifted him up off the ground. A pewter statue slipped from Feeble's grasp, making their load one pound lighter but still not easy by any means. With red faces and buckling knees they shuffled him over to the porch where they attempted to lay him down in dignity. Unfortunately the two porch steps got the best of them. Leo Tip, who was carrying the left leg and walking backwards, missed the second step and fell flat on his back. Brother Heck and Pap Wilson, literally at the head of this endeavor, pushed Feeble on top of Leo trying to keep their balance. Feeble's off-kilter weight twisted Pete Kennedy and Ed Washington's arms, giving the latter a burn he would complain about for years. The two of them fell towards Leo and onto the porch. Feeble's dead body rolled off of Leo and came to a stop in the center of the porch looking upward. Though deceased, Feeble wore the biggest smile I had ever seen him sport.

Everyone gasped. I guess folks had never seen Feeble smile before.

"He looks so happy," Sister Watson gushed.

"Downright peaceful," Bishop Watson added.

"Let there be no doubt as to what happened here today," Briant Willpts said, still sitting in Feeble's chair. "The heavens took two strong pillars from our community. One went in a golden chariot, body and all. The other? Well, see for yourself."

I wanted to cry foul, to stand up and make a protest. But as a missionary, I felt it wasn't my place. Thelma's Way had its mind set, and its mind was set on believing that Roswell had been translated and that Feeble had passed away in some sort of botched attempt by heaven to bring him home. Whatever the truth really was, that is what they wanted to believe.

Amidst the commotion, Toby Carver's youngest boy, Lupert, slipped away from the crowd and picked up the pewter statue still lying in the road where Feeble had dropped it. He examined it carefully, then ran off into the meadow, apparently unnoticed by anyone but me. The ring of people began to dissolve as folks remembered unimportant things they needed to tend to. Miss Flitrey tried to gather her brood and herd them back to class, but most of them were too hyped-up from all the excitement to heed her.

"It's a miracle, I guess," CleeDee Lipton whispered in disbelief as she turned to go.

"I'll say," Briant replied. "I'll say." Which, of course, he already had. And with that, Briant Willpts was silent.

11

# Close Enough to Touch

Grace had always liked Feeble considerably more than she liked that brother of his. Her heart sank when she saw him lying there on the ground. As the circle of townsfolk looked on, Grace looked away, her green eyes blinking back the hurt. Within her the seasons were already changing, and she could feel herself gearing up for a long, hard freeze.

As she glanced away she noticed the missionaries coming up from the river. She slipped back to watch. By now Grace had learned the newer one's name.

Williams. Elder Trust Williams.

She took his name as a good omen. With a name like Trust, he couldn't be all bad. From her vantage point in the hills, she had watched him closely over the last month. She knew he was struggling to fit in.

His brown hair and blue eyes were as familiar to her now as Lush Point or the Girth River.

Grace scolded herself for feeling like some kid with a crush. She wasn't going to fall for some missionary who would most likely leave in a couple months, never to come back. She was smarter than that.

The missionaries joined the circle of people looking over Feeble. Trust asked Grace's father about Feeble, and her father stated the obvious.

"He's moved on."

Grace followed the crowd as they walked into the boardinghouse. She stood behind Trust as he listened to old Briant Willpts prattle on.

She breathed in. Someone smelled nice. Pleasant body aroma was not something everyone around here had. She watched Trust as he listened to Briant stretching his story out long and tall. She could see Trust wasn't fooled.

She stepped a little closer. The ends of her red hair brushed against the back of Trust's arm. It was Trust who smelled nice.

She stepped back, turning to go. Maybe spring would come sooner than she thought.

## 12

# Half Empty, Half Full

There were no law officers in Thelma's Way. They had never really needed any. There had been no crime here until Paul pulled his stolen Book of Mormon stunt. I thought it would be good for someone in some sort of uniform to look into the missing Roswell, dead Feeble situation. But no one did. The closest thing was when Jerry Scotch, who worked at the Corndog Tent at the mall in Virgil's Find, showed up in his work outfit and pronounced the case closed.

Oh, the peace of mind.

I thought we should search the area for Roswell. People were offended, hurt, and confused by how disrespectful I could be of the so recently deceased. Elder Boone and I tried to get someone to toy with the idea that maybe, just maybe, Roswell had *not* been translated. Maybe he was alive somewhere, smoking his pipe or crying for his brother for all we knew, and that we should look for him. No go. In the big collective consciousness of Thelma's Way, Roswell had been lifted up just like Briant said, and his brother Feeble had died of a heart attack running to catch up. I wrote President Clasp and asked him if it wouldn't be better for us to try to get these people to join another church so we wouldn't have to associate with them anymore.

We didn't really have a funeral for Roswell and Feeble. We had a ward service project. It took us all Saturday to dig holes big enough for the two of them. Thanks to some foresight Roswell and Feeble had grave plots already picked out. Two nice sites, right on the back edge of the cemetery, touching the river. I complained a lot about making anyone dig a grave for Roswell, seeing how there really was no body to bury. Folks began giving me a hard time about my lack of faith.

"John was translated; Enoch was translated."

Roswell was hardly an Enoch or a John.

"I bet *they* didn't have graves," I quipped.

"If you want to have people join the Church you had better start showing some appreciation for the spiritual things," Sister Yetch scolded.

"Roswell is not dead," I stated bluntly.

"Hush," Brother Heck intervened.

I continued to dig.

As missionaries we had clocked in an awful lot of service hours in Thelma's Way. It seemed as if the only time people wanted us around was when they needed help around the house. Digging the graves was just such an occasion. Everyone professed to love and admire Roswell and Feeble, but the instant someone mentioned digging everyone suddenly had bad backs.

We finished the excavation (there's nothing else to call it when you're digging a grave for Feeble Ford), covered the coffins, and offered a dedicatory prayer. Instead of sending for headstones, Briant Willpts just had Roswell's and Feeble's porch chairs cemented to the ground at the head of their graves. A nice piece of granite can set you back a chunk of change, and besides, people would need a place to sit while visiting the twins. He figured he'd kill two birds with one stone. Pardon the expression.

Afterwards there was a small buffet in the boardinghouse for those who had known the deceased, which, of course, would be everyone in town—except for maybe Joey Carver, Toby Carver's nearsighted brother who lived with their sister behind Lush Point. Joey spent his days making beautiful leather wallets that his sister took into Virgil's Find to sell. Word was he didn't particularly care for people. Everyone left him alone.

As it turned out, even nearsighted Joey knew the twins. He stood in front of me in the funeral buffet line. Things would have been a lot neater if I could have served myself first.

After everyone had finished eating, Sister Watson stood and proposed a toast.

"To the twins."

We all toasted.

"And to our future sesquicentennial pageant."

Most toasted.

"And to me, for having to rewrite whole sections of *All Is Swell* seeing how Feeble is dead and won't be able to act."

Brother Watson raised his glass. Sister Watson sat down.

As I got into bed that night, I started to thank my Heavenly Father for everything I had. But then I got to thinking and decided I didn't have much. Maybe it was Feeble's death getting to me, or the town's refusal to believe Roswell might be alive. It seemed that my whole life I had planned for my mission. And now, here I was almost two months into it and I felt useless. I had hoped to be one of President Clasp's up-and-coming elders. I had hoped to be a district leader, or a zone leader, or a trainer. Instead, I was a big zero. I was lost in Thelma's Way. Lost and forgotten.

God needed to work with me.

13

# A Little off the Top

Week Eight

Six days a week we hiked the hills knocking on doors, teaching lessons to less-actives, and preaching to those who would lend us an ear. But every Monday was P-day. Preparation day. We would use our Mondays to do laundry over at the Watson house, go grocery shopping in Virgil's Find, and take care of all the things that didn't fall into our daily missionary routine.

It was Monday, and I was about to receive my first Thelma's Way haircut.

The last time I had gotten a cut was in the Missionary Training Center right before I left for Tennessee. A tall man with big hands had buzzed off any and all pieces of hair foolish enough to grow longer than a quarter inch. But now my hair was starting to look shaggy. Something needed to be done.

Wad, the barber, was short, dark, and so weathered that it looked as if life had gnawed on him and spat him out. His name suited him to a

"T." His barber shop was an old outhouse shell that he had dragged down from his home once he had gotten indoor plumbing. It was filled with scissors and brushes.

When I showed up for my trim, he pulled a folding lawn chair out of his shack, planted it in the grass, set me down, and went to work. He wasn't shy about his work. He hovered around me like a wrinkled fly—buzzing and clipping as if his hands were intimately acquainted with my head.

For the full cut I was the center of the community. Everyone who walked by commented on what a good or bad job Wad was doing. Out in the open like that, I was fair game.

"He'd look better with more off the top," Toby Carver said on his way to the boardinghouse.

"It's uneven on the left," CleeDee Lipton advised, passing through the meadow.

"Not entirely symmetrical," Miss Flitrey, the school teacher, said as I sat there getting pieces of hair all over myself. Wad quickly took her comments into consideration.

The big secret, or the best known rumor around town, was that weathered old Wad had eyes for Miss Flitrey. He cut her hair for half the price he charged Sister Watson, used big educated words when he spoke to her, and would spend what some folks considered to be an inappropriate amount of time dusting her neck off with his softest brush after the do was done.

The guarded affection was reciprocated. Miss Flitrey would bring baked goods to Wad and was presently tutoring him in math. Private lessons. Well, that is, if you consider the boardinghouse on a Saturday when the whole town is there watching television "private."

Miss Flitrey was a big, sturdy woman. She had taught school here in Thelma's Way for some twenty years. Her hair never looked the same, thanks to her frequent trips to Wad's scissors shack. She wasn't very tall, and her smile was like a comet—it appeared only once every hundred years and even then was difficult to spot. She was a workhorse and as stubborn a woman as I had ever met.

We had helped Miss Flitrey a couple of times at school by substitute teaching for her. It was a great way to give service to the community. Once when she had food poisoning, we filled in for a full day, teaching her schoolkids their times tables and alphabet. I would never forget how confused little Opie Wilford was as we sang the alphabet song. Every time we would sing the "l-m-n-*O-P*" part he would glance around nervously, thinking we were calling his name. I had the students sing the song a few extra times just so I could watch his reaction. Actually, his response had been the first indication to me that my heart was changing.

Don't get me wrong. I still wanted to be transferred out. But for the first time I was seeing these folks as the kind, simple, big-hearted people that they were. Maybe they didn't all have aspirations to own large homes. Maybe they weren't working towards owning a boat and a new pair of water skis. No, these people did things like put up chicken wire, chop wood, and shoot the breeze until the air was fatally wounded.

Wad snipped around my right ear.

"You liking it here?" he asked me.

"Sure," I replied. "What's not to like?"

Elder Boone was sitting on the ground next to the pile of old magazines Wad would put out for his waiting customers to read. He looked at me as if I were pulling Wad's leg.

"I like it here," I defended.

"Beautiful country," Wad said, "beautiful country. Makes a man want to take up painting."

I nodded in agreement. Wad jerked my head back, bothered by my moving it around.

"I've always dreamed of trying my hand at painting. I've got the artistic touch, you know. Right now, however, your head is my only canvas."

"Thank you, I think," I said.

"You've got such lovely hair, too," he went on. "So thick, so soft. My fingers love to touch it. Look at my fingers rejoicing," he said as his fingers celebrated within my hair.

I was about to tell him to please have his fingers rejoice elsewhere, when he set down his scissors and brushed me off.

"Well, you're done. What do you think?" He handed me a small mirror to look at myself.

My eyes were still blue, and my nose was still centered. Oh, and my hair was short.

Tindy MacDermont was strolling by as I stood up.

"Looks good, Wad," she complimented.

Wad sort of curtsied.

I offered to pay him, but he refused.

"I like to help out the missionaries," he blushed.

"How about coming out to church then?" I asked kindly.

"I sleep in on Sundays," he said, making his excuse and suddenly acting overly busy while putting his tools away.

"Church doesn't start until twelve-thirty," I rebutted.

"Like I said," he said, "I sleep in on Sundays."

Elder Boone and I headed over to the boardinghouse so I could use the shower and wash off all the tiny hairs that would otherwise stick into me for days. The town decided to turn the boardinghouse into a sort of co-op. Roswell and Feeble had left no will. Since the funeral, Briant Willpts had moved in to keep things going, but Briant had no objection to us using the facilities.

"We're never going to reactivate these people," I mourned, referring to Wad.

"Never's a long time," Elder Boone replied.

He was right.

14

# A-LOT-O-LANCE

Lucy liked Lance. Their relationship was so easy. It didn't require a lot of depth or thought for her to be with him. Lucy liked that. Trust had been so enamored with her that he was constantly trying to talk about important things, trying to sound more interesting.

Lance, however, didn't need to talk to be interesting.

Not that Lance wasn't as enamored with Lucy as Trust was, it was just that Lance expressed it so much more elegantly. With gifts.

Yes, in Lucy's eyes Lance was about as close to being perfect as a man could be. He had wealth, reputation, and stunning good looks. True, he wasn't a Mormon, but Lucy felt she needed to become a better person by looking beyond that.

"Didn't someone once say 'every member a missionary'?" Lucy asked herself.

Well, Lucy felt she was doing the lioness' share by continuing to be with Lance, and by setting such a high standard. Lucy made the Mormons look good.

*Trust would understand,* Lucy reasoned.

After all, Trust was also about the work. Lucy was simply doing her part. Could Lucy help it if Lance was right, and ready to harvest?

15

# The Road to Don't-Ask-Us

Three and One-Half Months

The path from Thelma's Way to Virgil's Find was remarkably unspectacular. For hundreds of years it had served as the towns-folk's only way in and out. And for hundreds of years no one had made a single improvement or upgrade to it. Despite the number of bare feet and dirty shoes that had traversed its dusty sprawl, it still remained nothing more than a skinny brown line that lay as a lazy guide from Virgil's Find to Thelma's Way, or more appropriately, to nowhere.

The people had petitioned the state for a road, but in the entire town there were only two registered voters: Sister Watson and Feeble Ford, now deceased. The state politicians didn't see Thelma's Way as a vehicle that would further their political careers. They saw it as an unknown pock concealed by forest, pleasantly forgotten by anyone who was anybody outside of Thelma's Way. Besides, turning the path into a road would require backhoes and dump trucks and risked offending the local environmentalists who wished to keep the parts of Tennessee that they didn't actually live in personally in their somewhat natural state.

Virgil's Find was a good-sized town with all the amenities that Thelma's Way was short on—movies, a mall, and plenty of paved main and minor roads. Its growth had covered what was once a big chunk of rural Tennessee, libraries replacing barns, banks replacing bars, and supermarkets replacing ranches and forcing the wannabe cowboys to spend their Friday nights sitting atop the grocery cart corrals, wishing for what once was well before their time.

We had to hike into Virgil's Find at least once a week. Thelma's Way just didn't have it all; in fact it hardly had any. It was a pain having to walk four miles to buy deodorant. The path was always either too muddy or too dusty. I wished for a road or a real trail. I wished for a legitimate out. I wanted a couple of well-marked exits, someplace where the ground was striped with black asphalt and orange dotted lines, with cars whizzing past me. Sure, Leo Tip had a car in Thelma's Way, but it didn't really count. Leo had built his car piece by piece, packing in old rusted parts from the Virgil's Find auto salvage yard, and assembling them in the dirt lot next to the school. Eventually, Leo had himself a real working automobile. Actually, what Leo had was four wheels hooked together by two bucket seats and a lumpy engine that ran only when it wasn't raining and if you greased the spark plug before you turned the starter over. It wasn't much to look at, but it did run, and Leo held his head high, perched in that bucket of bolts. It didn't matter that there were only about two hundred yards of actual dirt road in Thelma's Way. On a nice day Leo would drive that two hundred yards back and forth and around the boardinghouse again and again. At a cruising speed of five miles an hour he would wave at the local kids and nod at the occasional passerby who was usually walking faster than his piecemeal transportation could even go. If you were really lucky and caught Leo in an excessively unselfish mood he would pull up right next to you and pat the passenger side seat invitingly. I had yet to be invited.

I had less of a chance now then ever, seeing how Leo had cut back on his driving time ever since he had begun courting CleeDee Lipton. CleeDee didn't like the feel of the wind against her extra-sensitive face. CleeDee chapped easy. At five miles an hour, a stagnant breeze could suck every bit of moisture out of her chalky mug and leave her scaly and unable to smile. And, as even the most ignorant local knew, CleeDee's best and only feature was her smile.

The only other motor vehicle in Thelma's Way was Digby Heck's ancient dirt bike. Teddy Yetch had given it to him the year before on his sixteenth birthday. Teddy was too old to ride on it any longer—operating the clutch did a number on her arthritis, and the vibrating of the engine caused her teeth to slip out.

Digby loved it. There was only one problem: Digby had tiny ears. Sunglasses just wouldn't stay on his face as he rode. He tried taping eyewear on, but pulling the tape off all the time was making him prematurely bald.

Well, necessity gave birth to one odd invention. Inspired by a bowl of leftover casserole in his family's refrigerator, Digby went down to the Virgil's Find Shop and Save and bought him a couple of rolls of clear plastic Saran Wrap. A stroke of pure genius. Digby simply wrapped it around the top half of his head, covering his open eyes and voila, his sensitive peepers were protected. His mother even made him a little leather pouch that hooked onto the handlebars and held an economy-sized roll of the wrap. It was quite a sight to have Digby pull up next to you, his hair matted down by the wrap and his wide brown eyes pressed completely open.

At the moment, Elder Boone and I were on the path on our way to Virgil's Find to attend zone conference with President Clasp. I always liked getting out of Thelma's Way and meeting with other elders. Since the meeting would run late, Elder Boone and I had made plans to stay the night with Elder Gardiner and Elder Krammer in Virgil's Find.

We were about halfway there when we spotted an unknown person coming the other way. Having been in Thelma's Way for over three months, I thought I had at least seen most of the locals, but I didn't recognize this gentleman. He had dark black hair that didn't bounce or move as he walked, making it look like he was wearing a helmet. He wore a flannel shirt, blue jeans, and boots that topped off well above his ankles. His straight nose and tiny brown eyes looked silly the way they were placed on his face, as if God had decided to try something different and arrange his features unevenly. His big mouth gaped open to a smile as we came near to him.

He stopped in front of us, in the middle of the trail. He folded his arms in front of him. Not thinking much of it, Elder Boone and I broke to go around him, but he stretched out his arms to hold us back.

"Excuse us," I said politely as I tried to walk around.

"Do you know who you're talking to?" he asked, and without waiting for an answer, "I shall be recognized."

"I'm Elder Williams," I said, sticking my hand out.

"You are a child," he snipped, refusing to shake my hand. "I am an adult. Show some respect."

I think he wanted me to bow to him or something.

Elder Boone gave it a go.

"I'm—"

"Can't you see the light around me?" he interrupted. "Can't you?"

We both looked at each other and shrugged.

"Of course you can't," he sizzled. "You're numb to the Spirit, and withered on the bush. Lock horns and be gone."

The clear doctrine, the compassionate delivery, the feeling of utter and complete peace. I suddenly knew who I was talking to.

"Paul?" I asked. "Paul Leeper?"

"The truth has been manifest unto you. Drink and go home bloated," he blessed me.

This was Paul. I was standing before apostate Paul. The havoc-wreaking, Book-of-Mormon-stealing, town-splitting, lies-spewing, reason-I'm-now-in-Thelma's Way, archenemy Paul. Larger than life, yet at least three inches shorter than I.

Elder Boone gritted his teeth. "You're Paul?" he asked.

Paul sort of curtsied.

"The Paul that went to Rome?"

"Saw the finger," Paul boomed, pulling out a postcard from his back pocket and flashing it before our view. The postcard was worn and bent, but you could still see the finger, encased in glass, looking as if it were just floating in midair. Paul smiled smugly.

What Paul didn't know was that I had done my homework. About three P-days ago, Elder Boone and I had gone into Virgil's Find to do some grocery shopping, and we stopped by the public library to find out if they really did have the finger of Thomas on display at the Vatican. I found out that there was a finger on display, but that most real scholars didn't believe it was actually Thomas's finger. For all practical purposes it was probably some common schmo who had lost his finger dicing up beets and then discovered his loose digit could make him a few bucks.

I told this to Paul. Surprisingly, he was not at all grateful for having been enlightened. His face turned red and his hair actually seemed to darken.

"You're him," he said suddenly, holding his trembling hand over his big open mouth and pointing at me with the other. "You are the detractor I prophesied about."

"Now wait a second," Elder Boone jumped in. "When did you prophesy about—"

"Elder Williams," Paul interrupted. He had a hard time letting others get a word in edgewise. He looked at my name tag and gasped.

"Williams. Moments ago as I was walking, I was prophesying to myself, and voices told me to beware of a coming detractor for he would do the will of the underworld." He stepped back for dramatic effect. "Williams . . . Will . . . Will of the Underworld."

I tried not to smile.

"Will of the Underworld," he screamed, his misplaced eyes bulging from his head. Then again, more quietly, as if he were pronouncing a title upon me. "Will of the Underworld."

He kept repeating the phrase in a gradual crescendo as he scrambled off the trail and into the forest.

Elder Boone and I just stood there for a moment.

"Nice guy," Elder Boone joked, breaking the silence.

"Wow, I feel so important," I said.

"Will of the Underworld," he said, and he bowed.

We made it to Virgil's Find without any more incidents, unless, of course, you consider forty-year-old Ed Washington running past us wearing nothing but shorts and shoes and yelling for his mother, an incident.

# 16

# Geronimo

Grace had been fine with her life.

All right, that wasn't completely true. She had a few concerns. Growing up in Thelma's Way had not always been easy. There had been times she wanted to strike it out on her own. She dreamed about traveling to distant countries. She thought about college, out-of-state, anything that was a ticket out.

It wasn't that she was embarrassed by her heritage; she just wanted to try something new, something better.

On the other hand, Grace liked things simple. She sometimes felt it should be enough that God had given her a brain to think with, two legs for walking, the forest around her for beauty, and the Virgil's Find public library. Things could be worse and she knew it. She shouldn't be waiting around for handouts.

But Trust Williams in Thelma's Way was something like a handout.

He was different from the rest. Her whole life Grace had been able to see into people's heads, get vague impressions of their thoughts. Trust was a stranger; his mind was harder to view, but the slivers she caught glimpses of were promising. No doubt he sensed he had fallen off the back of the planet landing in Thelma's Way, and he was right. But there was something within him that cared, whether he knew it or not, something willing to learn. It was honesty. She was giving him the benefit of the doubt.

Grace had yet to meet Trust face-to-face. She knew he wouldn't be stationed in Thelma's Way for long, not if Paul could have his way. He was currently going about door to door with that nonsense about the "Will of the Underworld." Paul must have sensed it too. Trust Williams was a threat.

Grace had never really cared for Paul and his lying ways. Others in town seemed willing to let it slide. He had, after all, wooed away two-thirds of the local branch. Sure, they had deserted him after he stole that Book of Mormon, but Grace wasn't so sure he couldn't do it again.

She opened the door to her hidden cabin and walked inside. She placed some wildflowers in a vase on the table. She set her books on her chair. She had promised herself that she wouldn't go back to church until the missionaries were gone, but she was considering breaking her vow. She could get a better glimpse of Trust at church. She had to find out more about him before it was too late, didn't she?

Then she thought better of it. What possible future could there be for her with some rule-bound missionary from far away?

"Grow up, Grace," she scolded herself. "It's all or nothing with you. Only heaven can intervene."

And heaven has a way of taking its own sweet time.

17

# The Introduction of Grace

Month Six

Reports came in. Paul was using his "Will of the Underworld" prophecy to try to scare people into avoiding me. CleeDee had been walking across the meadow when Paul all but materialized from behind a clump of grass.

"Will of the Underworld," he told her, pointing to our cabin. "Will of the Underworld. Beware."

He was trying to scare us, too. He wrote threatening things in the dirt in front of our cabin and threw rocks at the outhouse when I was in it. He pinned notes to our door with hieroglyphic scribbles on them. I later found out from Pap Wilson that Paul was working on his own alphabet and language.

I could think of a few words I would like him to translate.

The town had held another sesquicentennial planning meeting a few weeks back. Things were still moving along slowly. Sister Watson had not yet completed the actual script. She claimed her work with

P.I.G. was really blocking the creative inspiration that this particular pageant required. Toby had finished the blueprints of the stage, and Patty Heck had begun sewing some costumes. I was starting to see the wisdom in allowing so much lead time before the actual play. This town moved slowly.

Summer had become winter, and winter was trying to outdo itself—flexing its cold, hard muscles and smiling its brittle teeth. The days had become shorter but felt longer. The nights had grown lengthy, and yet it seemed as if my head barely hit the pillow before morning poked its obnoxious nose around. Like the seasons, my soul was locking up. I didn't feel like I was becoming the missionary I should be. I needed to try harder. I felt as if the only thing I had to show for myself were my worn-out shoes and the beginnings of a backwoods accent.

Bishop Watson and Brother Heck were doing a pretty good job of holding our fifteen or so members together. They missed the Parley P. Pratt first-edition Book of Mormon that had sat as the ward's keystone and foundation for so many years, but they were coping.

Sister Watson and the members of P.I.G. had made a formal request of Paul asking for the book's return. They had offered to forgive him of all wrongdoing if he would simply give it back. They invited Paul over to the boardinghouse where they all gathered around a couple of long banquet tables. Sister Watson placed an empty basket next to a plate of cookies that Sister Teddy Yetch had brought for after the meeting. The members of P.I.G. told Paul they would turn off the lights and then, under cover of darkness, whoever had stolen the Book of Mormon could place it in the empty basket and be done with it.

Sister Watson turned off the lights. There were sounds of movement and shifting. She quickly flicked the lights back on. The basket was still empty and now Teddy's cookies were missing. Everyone sat there with full mouths as Sister Watson looked on in disgust. Well, if she had been disgusted by them all swiping cookies, she must have been even more grossed out when, moments later, everyone's taste buds told them to abort. People began spitting and coughing as they tried to obliterate the taste of Teddy's Spicy Raisin Mustard Snaps. Teddy, of course, went home offended, and the Book of Mormon was no closer to being back where it belonged.

One personal mission discovery so far was the realization that my mother had a weird flare for sending creative care packages. Mom and I were close, but sometimes I didn't feel like she really knew me. Part of the problem was that she was fairly timid and reserved. The moment any real emotion began to surface, she would scurry away like a frightened lizard. At last, it seemed, she had found a way to express herself.

She sent me new shoes, and old shoes other people in the ward no longer wanted. Forget the fact that most of them weren't my size. I guess she knew we were really hard on our footwear. She sent me cookies by the pound, and big posters with cute animals saying positive things. She sent me can after can of bug repellent, and notebooks filled with photocopied crossword puzzles and dot-to-dots for those times when I was discouraged. I had already completed most of the puzzles—discouragement was a familiar feeling these days.

We were finding work to do, but it was busy work, unproductive work. I had all my discussions down cold due to the fact that I had given them to every inactive who would lend an ear. Despite the distraction of Paul, people apparently still liked hearing me ramble. Time and time again they would invite my companion and me over to present the discussions. Then, when we had taught them and challenged them to commit to Christ and become more active, they'd ask us if we had any free videos (which most of them couldn't even play) and shoo us out the door.

Thankfully, we had one person in our teaching pool. We were working with automotive expert Leo Tip. He was twenty years old and had been raised in a Mormon home. His father had passed away years ago, and his mother had died just last spring. He lived alone in a rather large house up on top of Lush Point, a small hill that overlooked the meadow. His father had invented a twisty wire with which you could tie off rope or cord. The invention was called "The Pincher." Leo had shown me one once. I thought it greatly resembled a garbage-bag twist tie, but what did I know? Anyhow, Leo still received small royalty checks in the mail every month from the sales of his father's invention.

Leo had never been baptized into the Mormon church because his father was a rather large man who didn't feel comfortable getting wet in white clothes. He had petitioned the church to let him try sprinkling instead of immersion, but that didn't fly. And instead of getting someone else to baptize their son, the Tips just kept on postponing it until Father Leo lost weight. Well, the size of his grave plot in the Tip family corner of the cemetery stands in testimony to the fact that Brother Tip never did master the weight issue. After his passing, talk of Leo getting baptized never came up again—that is, until we were going over the ward records with Bishop Watson and discovered that, technically, Leo was still not a member—a real, live, honest-to-goodness nonmember right there in Thelma's Way. It was a glimmer of hope.

The glimmer was fleeting.

Leo humored us by letting us teach him, but really he had his heart set on waiting until the next life where he knew his father would be thin and then having him perform the baptism. I tried to explain that things didn't work that way, but there was no budging him. It was a family thing. I was confused.

On the personal side, things were equally confusing. Lucy was writing me less frequently, and in her last letter she had dropped the name of some guy named Lance.

*. . . my car is being serviced, but Lance has been kind enough to drive me to and fro. I don't know what I'd do without him.*

That was all she had said, but I was now in utter despair over her state of mind concerning me. Was this Lance some ninety-year-old uncle who had nothing to do but drive his niece around? Maybe he was a fifteen-year-old kid who had just gotten his driver's permit and needed someone to ride along with him as he gained experience. Or maybe it was some creep gaining experience of a different kind. Lucy was *my* girl. I knew that, and I had worked most of my life to get her to at least think about knowing it. I could feel our would-be relationship crumbling.

Things looked grim.

Elder Boone had obviously been living more righteously than I, because he had received a transfer out. It came; he went; and now I was companions with Elder Sims.

Elder Sims was short, quiet, and bossy. He had the charisma of a well-groomed dirt clod. He rarely spoke any louder than a mumble, and he insisted on never being more than a foot and a half away from me. He was from New Plymouth, Idaho, a town not too much bigger than Thelma's Way. I was having a terribly hard time getting along with him. He seemed to flutter around me like a mumbling pest.

It was late January in Thelma's Way and, I suppose, in the rest of the world as well. We had gotten a little snow and lots of cold. The ground was brown and white, but the evergreen trees and bushes kept their color all year long in Thelma's Way. The meadow was dead, blanketed only in snow and checkered with footprints and trails.

I looked out our front door at the dark meadow. It was late in the evening, and Elder Sims and I had just finished our companion study. We had read a potpourri of scriptures all with the common theme of enduring to the end. I was feeling discouraged. This was not how I had imagined my mission would be. I felt like I had been cubbyholed. Set aside. President Clasp had simply put me here and was now refusing to deal with me until later.

These people, bless their souls, were no more interested in coming back to full activity than I was in picking out a plot here and settling down. We had taught countless discussions and new-member lessons, eaten with these people, mended their fences, plowed their grounds, canned their food, and babysat their children; all with zero results.

People saw us as nothing more than two kind boys with way better clothes than they had. Besides, with so few nonmembers, it was hard not to feel we lacked real missionary purpose.

Bishop Watson was somewhat helpful, and Brother Heck was supportive to a point. But both of them were pretty much resigned to the fact that things would never get better.

"Let's wait until the Lord comes," Brother Heck said. "He'll straighten things out."

It was useless. I kept writing President Clasp and suggesting that perhaps he should close the area. We were doing no good. We could serve better someplace else.

Elder Sims came up and stood behind me as I looked out the door at the black night.

"It's dark," he commented.

"I'm going to go pray," I said.

Elder Sims frowned.

There was an old tree stump behind our house that I used to pray on. It wasn't the most comfortable place to kneel, but I could be alone. The little window at the back of our cabin looked out over the stump so my companion could keep a constant eye on me. Elder Sims would watch me go out the front door and then follow me so he could see me walk along the length of the cabin. Then he would run back inside and up to the rear window so that he only had me out of his sight for a couple of seconds.

I would pray for hours out at that stump just so I could have some space. And always when I would look up, there would be Elder Sims, his face pressed against the back window, keeping a constant vigil on me. It was unnerving, or comforting, depending on the definition of those two words. Elder Boone had been big on always getting up on time—that was his favorite rule. Elder Sims was big on the never-let-your-companion-out-of-your-sight rule. I knew it made him nervous to have me out of his view for even an instant. In his mind it must have been possible to do all the worst sins and a couple of the minor ones in a blink of the eye.

I walked out of our place and headed towards the stump, grateful just to be out of the house. Elder Sims followed me and then scurried back inside to watch me through the back window. It was a dark and cold night. A light snow had begun to fall. I had on my coat and gloves—I was bundled up for as long a prayer as it was going to take for me to feel right with the world again.

I knelt down and poured my heart out over the cold snow. The words came easily, even if they didn't make a lot of sense. I prayed for warmer weather, but thanked God for the cold that kept the bugs down. I thanked Him for the chance to serve, and begged for the chance to serve elsewhere. I prayed for patience to endure Elder Sims, but asked for a new companion.

There was a dull sensation of time passing. Every once in a while I would hear Elder Sims tapping on the glass, which did nothing but increase my resolve to lose myself in prayer. And lose myself, I did.

I can't remember falling asleep, but when I woke up my body was shaking. I was covered from head to toe with a two-inch blanket of snow, but through the snow muffling my ears, I could hear a voice.

"Wake up. You'll freeze out here."

I murmured, mumbled, and shooed.

The voice shook and spoke louder, a new sense of cold creeping over my sleeping body.

"Get up. You'll sleep yourself to death."

I opened my tired, cold eyes. My head was still resting on my arms. There were about two inches of snow covering me. I wanted to stand and shake myself off, but I could barely move. I had drooled into my arms and it was now frozen and sticking to my face. My legs were not only asleep, they had gone into hibernation. I tried to will them back to life.

"You've got to get up," the voice said again. "We need to get you warm."

I managed to move my drool-caked face a little to the right to see who was speaking to me. I felt like "Slobbery," the eighth and unknown dwarf, as I stared up into the moonlight.

It had to be about two o'clock in the morning. The snow had stopped, and a huge moon was hovering over the layer of clouds that were resting just above the ground. The moon lit the gray clouds with a soft white. Here and there a ray of moonlight had poked through and was kneading the new snow on the ground with its bright hands. One of those beams of light was resting on whoever it was that had woken me and perhaps saved my life.

From where I knelt she looked tall. She had on leather boots. She was wearing a big wool coat with a hood over her head, and red hair spilled out from beneath it in such amounts that I could barely see her face. The moonlight made her look like a ghost, or an angel.

"Who . . ."

She didn't let me finish. She grabbed me by the arm and pulled me up. My legs cracked in protest. She helped me brush snow off of myself. I suddenly remembered Elder Sims. I looked towards the window and there he was, staring at me with closed eyelids. I assumed he was asleep. Had he been awake, he would have already screamed and run out to rescue me from this girl.

She helped me walk back around our cabin and to the front door. She pushed open the door, and I could see that she wasn't wearing gloves. She had long fingers that seemed to flutter as she moved them. With the sound of the door opening, Elder Sims was instantly at attention. His mouth gaped large enough to cram a cantaloupe into it.

"Elder," he screamed, being more vocal than I had ever heard him.

I thought he was concerned for my health. I thought he was worried about my frozen condition. I thought he could see that I was mangled and shivering.

But all he could say was, "You're with a girl!"

The oil lamp was still burning, keeping the cabin nice and bright. I turned my head to get a better look at her. She stood just inside the door, her right hand holding my left elbow. Her coat was wet with snow, and her cheeks were red with cold. She tried to turn away as I gazed at her.

She wasn't beautiful, but she wasn't ugly either. She had dark green eyes, and her skin was pale, unlike anything I had ever seen before. She didn't smile. There was something mysterious about her. Maybe it was just that my neck was stiff and I was staring at her crookedly. Her large coat made her look big, but the tiny bit of shin showing just above her boots and below her coat told the real story.

"What are you doing with a girl?" Elder Sims asked. He was flustered and concerned. "No girls while serving a mission."

"I fell asleep while I was praying and she woke me up," I explained.

"You were sleeping," he moaned.

"It was an accident."

"Most sins are."

I turned to my visitor to say "Sorry, he's nuts," but she was gone. There was nothing but an empty door and the chill of the night.

"Where'd she go?" I said, almost to myself.

Elder Sims answered me by running and closing the door. He latched it, locked it, and then stood with his back against it as if he alone were keeping all evil at bay.

"I knew I shouldn't have let you pray alone," he mumbled. "I knew it."

I walked over to the stove, put two logs onto the dying embers, and then stood there shivering and trying to warm myself up. Heat slowly escaped the old iron stove as it sweated and crackled, the new logs giving it a fresh fire in the belly.

"I'm going to write President Clasp," Elder Sims informed me.

"Tell him hi," I said.

I knew that I should be kinder. I knew I owed him an explanation. I owed him an apology. I knew all this, but I chose to ignore it, at least until morning, maybe until one of us got transferred. I was cold, cranky, and intrigued by the mysterious girl who had just helped me. After about fifteen minutes, I crawled into bed. Elder Sims still sat there on his bed scribbling away. President Clasp was going to receive one long letter.

*Good,* I thought as I drifted off to sleep. Maybe my companion's concerns would get me transferred. It struck me, however, that I wasn't as gung ho to leave Thelma's Way as I had once been.

Odd.

Very odd.

I fell asleep seeing red.

## 18

# SEEK AND SEEK

In the morning, I sat down to a breakfast of cold cereal and bread. Elder Sims sat down next to me. He had already eaten.

"Who is she?" he demanded.

"I don't know," I answered.

"How long have you two been meeting?"

"I'd never met her before."

Elder Sims guffawed. "Come on, Elder," he said. "I *am* the senior companion."

This was true. I had hoped after Elder Boone had been transferred that I would get to be a senior companion, perhaps even train a new elder, but instead Elder Sims was sent here to be my big brother and leader. It was his position to call all the shots.

"I've known her for about four months," I lied.

"And?" Elder Sims prodded, ready for the sordid details he had already imagined.

"And that's not the truth. I just met her last night."

He *arrged.*

"What's her name?" he asked harshly.

"I don't know."

"Is she Mormon?" he demanded.

"I don't know."

He sat up in his chair.

"Holding back potential investigators?" he asked, even more furious. "Waiting until I get transferred so you can teach her and count her as your own?"

"What?" I asked, amazed. "Listen. I fell asleep while praying last night and she woke me up and brought me in. That's it."

Elder Sims watched me chew and swallow a big bite of cereal.

"So, is that your secret meeting place?" he finally asked.

"I've never met her before," I said, exasperated.

"Do you pull the blinds down over the window to signal her to meet you there?"

This was ridiculous.

"We don't have blinds on our windows."

"Do you stand in front of the windows then, and flash hand signals or maybe do some sort of love dance?"

"Elder," I demanded.

"At least I'm fit to wear the title," he said, standing up. "I'm now going to kneel and pray for you."

I watched him kneel beside his bed and ask for forgiveness for me. I tried to be appreciative. I had a lot of things I needed forgiveness for, but the situation last night was not one of them.

When he was done, he got up and wanted a hug. I refused. We read Doctrine and Covenants section 132 together and then headed out.

Snow had covered everything. Our shoes crunched as we stepped along. We stopped off at the boardinghouse to say hello to whoever might be there. Despite the cold, Ed Washington and old Briant

Willpts were sitting outside on the porch arguing about how many inches had fallen.

Elder Sims and I stopped and made a little bit of small talk with the two of them. Then I asked, "Are there many folks around here with red hair?"

Elder Sims shot me a dirty look.

"Now, let's see," Ed thought. "Toby's got red hair on his arms but black on his head."

"Other way around," Briant corrected. "Other way around."

"Don't mother me," Ed warned him.

Ed had a rather bad mother complex. Sister Washington refused to let him be his own man. Though he was about forty years old, he still lived at home and at her beck and call. Ed had thick hair that left him no forehead and no neck.

"What about women?" I asked.

"Don't know much about them," Briant admitted.

"No, what about women with red hair?" I clarified.

"I suppose they act similar to those with black or brown hair."

This was pointless.

Elder Sims grabbed my arm and pulled me off the porch.

"We've got work to do," he said to Ed and Briant.

We walked across the meadow to Bishop Watson's home. Sister Watson was the only one in at the moment. She was working on the infamous pageant script. The Watsons had no children and ran a little mail-order business out of their home. They sold handmade soap in fancy handmade packaging. Sister Watson made the soap, and Bishop Watson packaged it up and delivered it to Virgil's Find, where it was sent out around the world. Their house always smelled like lye.

Sister Watson invited us in and gave us a half a chicken that she and her husband hadn't been able to finish off. I took the wrapped chicken and put it into my backpack. We had been meeting with the Watsons and challenging them to pray for one of their friends so that the Spirit might soften their hearts and prepare them for us to come over and help reactivate them. Sister Watson was pretty nervous about forcing us upon one of her inactive friends. She claimed she was being more courteous than coward. I explained to her that her husband was the bishop and that it was their responsibility as well as ours to reactivate these people. She told me that she would feel more comfortable just waving at them when she walked by their homes. The ward was doomed.

"Maybe when you're talking to people about the sesquicentennial pageant, you could also encourage them to come out to church," I suggested.

"I never mix politics with religion," she replied.

"It's not really politics," I pointed out.

"I guess you don't understand all the behind-the-scenes work this pageant involves. There's a definite underbelly to it. Lots of lobbying and politicking. I had to give Mindy at the Virgil's Find library two free bars of soap in order for her to hang our flier on the community bulletin board."

As we were leaving Sister Watson's home, I worked up the nerve to ask.

"Are there many women with red hair around here?"

Sister Watson just stared at me. "Is that anything for a missionary to be concerned about?" she asked, her mouth open but not moving as she spoke.

"Well, I was—"

Interrupted.

"Forgive my companion," Elder Sims jumped in. "He had a rather late night."

Sister Watson adjusted her wig as if she were tipping her hat to us. Then we stepped outside and headed up the hill towards the Heck home. We were giving the lessons to Narlette. She was about to turn eight and be baptized, and her folks felt it would be good for her to have a better understanding of the gospel.

Brother Heck was doing all right. He had had a tobacco relapse about two months previous, but nothing since then. Elder Boone and I had had to stop him from digging his own grave in an attempt to bury himself alive. It was a close call.

We reached the Heck home and knocked on the door. Sister Patty Heck let us in. The Hecks had a nice house. It was clean, fairly modern, and big. Sister Heck worked for a laundromat in Virgil's Find. She did all of their altering and specialty mending. Once a week she would hike into town and pick up a bundle of clothes. Then she would haul them back home and work on them. She was a master seamstress. There was not a pattern she would not attempt, conquer, and then somehow improve. She made all her family's clothes, was in charge of the costumes for the sesquicentennial pageant, repaired the Thelma's Way official flag after it was struck by lightning, and stitched up Digby after their dog, Limpy, bit him.

She was a small woman with a big head, and she always wore a skirt and a determined look on her face. She had a way of looking past you. It was as if she were constantly looking over your shoulder at something far more interesting and important. She had long, dark hair and strong, tiny hands. She wasn't mean, but she wasn't necessarily nice. She was a neutral personality. She was Sister Patty Heck. She was asking us to sit.

Elder Sims and I sat down on their couch and waited for Narlette. Narlette was one of the many mountain kids who was homeschooled. Her parents took her out of school a few years back after Miss Flitrey suggested that Narlette's own relatives might have been descended from apes.

The very idea.

The Hecks felt personally insulted. Sister Heck waited by the phone for an apology, but it never came. (Miss Flitrey was not one to back down.) So now, thanks to a large amount of righteous indignation and her own hard-earned G.E.D., Sister Heck was homeschooling her children. The responsibility added immensely to her already hectic schedule, but she managed to find time between cuffing and mending. She also discovered that kids could learn while working. Narlette was improving her math by keeping her mother's books; and her older brother, Digby, had won first prize in the Heck family science fair for his assigned experiment of painting the porch to see if that would improve its resistance to rain.

Yes, homeschooling was working out just fine for the Hecks. Brother Heck even helped out when he could, his livelihood providing him with a rather flexible schedule. Brother Heck, like so many others here in town, did odd jobs. He fixed roofs for food, repaired appliances for clothes, and dug trenches for a little spending money. He sold eggs at the Virgil's Find farmers' market and blood at the regional blood bank.

Narlette came downstairs and joined us in the living room. The lesson went rather well up until the point when Narlette lost all interest and began singing to herself as we taught. She kept getting louder until we gave up. I closed with my testimony and a challenge for her to read her scriptures with her family. She said she would and would we care to see the scar she had procured by falling off the old burnt Girth River bridge.

Fair trade.

As Sister Heck served us an early lunch of peas and ham, I decided to probe just one more time for information concerning my visitor last night.

"So," I said, "you must know just about everyone around here."

"Pride myself on being familiar with the community," she replied, passing me a big bowl of white gravy.

"There are a lot of different-looking people around here," I declared, my observation sounding meaner than I had meant it to.

"God may not have put the best-looking folks here in the meadow, but he made them sturdy and simple."

Now she was on the offensive.

"What I mean is that there are a lot of different colors of hair."

Sister Heck, Narlette, and Elder Sims just stared at me as if I were dumb. I shoved a bunch of cold ham in my mouth, hoping to choke myself to death.

Sister Heck decided it would be best to change the subject.

"Do you elders think you'll have a baptism soon?"

My full mouth restricted me from speaking.

"Leo Tip is interested," Elder Sims replied.

"Leo will never go under," Sister Heck informed us. "He's permanently dry. Too much love for material things."

We took a few minutes to silently enjoy our meal.

"There's not a lot of people with red hair around here," I finally spoke up, hoping to steer the conversation back to where I wanted it.

Sister Heck eyed me suspiciously.

Narlette snickered. "Grace's got red hair."

"Grace?" I asked, feeling my heart rate quicken.

"Our daughter," Sister Heck clarified.

I had forgotten that the Hecks had an older daughter whom I had never met. She was sort of a local enigma. She was kindly spoken of, but in the last while she had become reclusive, adjusting to womanhood by pulling away. At least that was Toby Carver's assessment.

"Where is she?" I wondered aloud.

"Who knows," Sister Heck replied. "Silly girl keeps herself hidden up in the hills. Spends too much time in Virgil's Find."

"Doing what?" I questioned.

"They got that big library there. Books 'bout everything," Sister Heck informed me. "I think Grace is more comfortable by herself."

"Anyone else with red hair?" I asked casually.

"Not really anyone else," Sister Heck chewed. "Except old Randall down at Triplet Cove, below the falls. Of course, his hair is falling out faster than it's growing."

Digby came bounding down the stairs.

"I'm going out," he announced, ripping off a sheet of Saran Wrap and preparing to cover his eyes.

"Don't be gone too long," Sister Heck said. "You've got homework."

I guess there was something that still needed to be painted or repaired around their house. Digby blinked at us through all that plastic film and took off.

We left the Hecks and headed up to Leo's place on the top of Lush Point. Lush Point was so named because years ago Grandfather Leeper, apostate Paul's grandfather, had decided that the Word of Wisdom was an item-by-item restriction and it didn't list moonshine. So he set up a few stills on the hillside and brewed the stuff for about two years before the folks in town would no longer tolerate it.

It was a particularly boring time in Thelma's Way history. Pretty much everyone was doing what they should be doing—everyone except Grandfather Leeper, that is. With so many idle hands twitching about, they decided to stamp out Grandfather Leeper's stills. Done under the guise of a ward activity, they all brought bats and beat the heck out of Grandfather Leeper's equipment. Then they gathered down in the meadow for a light supper and poetry reading. The moonshine seepage made the grass grow wild and green and gave the place its name—Lush Point.

Grandfather Leeper had passed away years earlier, and his son had also gone the way of dust. Now the only remaining Leeper was Paul, and he had left Lush Point to live across the river. So far he, too, had not done the family name any favors.

Leo let us into his house and asked us to sit down. It was now around noon and obvious that Leo had just gotten up for the day. He wore a large nightshirt with a picture of Garfield the Cat on it, and his hair was sticking up and down all over. Leo had long blond hair and big teeth. He had blue eyes, the right one remarkably darker than the left. He was about two inches taller than me thanks to his fluffy hair, and he was missing the tips of his three middle fingers on his left hand. (Leo had learned early in life that squirrel traps are nothing to play around with.)

I could smell his morning breath from across the room as he lounged on one of his fake leopard skin couches. He was quite the picture of luxury.

Leo's mother had never allowed him to have a dog when she was alive, so at her death a year ago Leo mourned by going dog wild. He now had about twenty hounds that he let roam Lush Point and come through his doggy door all day long. Consequently Leo's place was always stamped with muddy paw prints and speckled with hair.

"Looks like you're doing all right," I commented to him.

"Ah, shucks," Leo replied. "I'm getting by."

We had been over a couple days earlier, and had challenged Leo to have daily scripture study. "Have you been reading your scriptures?" I asked, hoping to get an idea of how he was coming along.

Leo nodded. "It's been a while," he added.

"How long has it been?" Elder Sims seemed to demand. "Two days?"

"Few months," he replied.

I put my head in my hands.

"Do you remember last week when we asked you to read your scriptures every day?" I asked.

Leo nodded while one of his dogs came in from outside and began to lick him on the face.

"Do you remember saying yes?" I asked.

"Been meaning to," Leo replied, inviting the dog up onto the couch. "Shucks, CleeDee's been taking a lot of my time lately. You know how women are," he assumed.

"It doesn't have to take a long time, Leo," Elder Sims said. "Just try to read a few verses a day."

"I don't see what the gawl awful rush is," he pointed out. "I can't be baptized until I die anyways. Daddy's waiting in heaven to dunk me under. If I got baptized here on earth he'd be pretty sore."

"I think he wants you to be baptized here," I said. "He knows how important it is."

"Shucks, how do you know that?"

"I just know how he must feel."

"Seems awful bold of you to say so," Leo added.

"What about CleeDee?" I asked. "Don't you think she's looking for a husband who can take her through the temple?"

"Why, what have you heard?" Leo jumped up. "That girl's eyes wander like the birthmark on my back. I tell you I can't leave her alone for a minute without her looking at some other guy. Well, if I can't have her then no one can—"

"That's not what I meant," I interrupted. "Don't you think CleeDee is looking for *you* to take her through the temple?"

"Ah, shucks," Leo blushed. "CleeDee and I aren't serious."

I contemplated pulling out my hair strand by strand.

My soul had turned soggy and my existence was beginning to run down my leg, surrounding my feet with the muck of failure. I had to get out of Thelma's Way.

I slowly put my scriptures back in my bag.

"What's the matter?" Leo asked.

"We need to be going," I answered.

"But we're not done," Elder Sims said, pointing out the obvious.

"I don't feel well," I insisted while standing up.

"CleeDee's coming over in a bit," Leo said. "She could make you some soup."

"That's all right," I said, looking around for my backpack. It was not there. One of Leo's dogs had grabbed it and was dragging it outside. I guess he had smelled the half chicken inside. I tried to catch him, but the moment I advanced, he took off with my pack through the doggy door.

"Leo!" I complained.

"Shucks, don't worry none. Wanda will bring it back when she's done with it."

I could see out the back window that Wanda was on her way to being long gone—running swiftly, shaking my backpack in her mouth.

"That's all my stuff," I complained.

"Don't worry. Wanda will probably bury it someplace and keep it nice and safe," Leo informed me.

"I thought you said she'd bring it back."

"Dogs is fickle," he yawned.

Great, I thought. Just great.

19

# Half an Inch Deep

Lucy was far from flattered. There was a giant ring on her dainty finger, but that was to be expected. The diamond band looked brilliant against her tan.

Lucy and Lance had taken a vacation to the Caribbean to discuss the issue of becoming engaged. In the process Lucy's fair skin had darkened nicely, and she had procured herself a fabulous ring and a fiancé that most women would have died for. "Of course, they would have to die and then be lucky enough to come back as me," she mused to herself.

Lucy giggled.

"What a snot I am." She smiled. "And justifiably so."

She and Lance made one attractive couple.

Lucy did worry over Trust. She had mailed him the happy news a few days earlier.

She felt a tinge of guilt. She had sort of promised that she would be around when Trust returned.

Then she chastised herself, "Once again I'm thinking of others when I should be concerned about myself. Oh, poo," she swore. "I've got to stay focused on what's important."

She went back to matching color swatches.

## 20

# Fork in the Road

I was no dummy. I was not oblivious to the fact that Lucy and I had been sort of drifting apart. But I had thought that we would drift back together before the end of my mission. Certainly our relationship would be strained while I was gone, but I believed we would be stronger because of it. I had thought that no matter what, she would be there for me when I returned home. I was wrong.

Lucy was engaged.

I couldn't believe it, and I couldn't imagine a more coldhearted way for her to break the news to me. I searched every inch of my brain trying to remember if she had always been so cold. True, she put me in a fog whenever I was around her, but had I really been so blind?

She sent me a piece of paper with two pictures taped to it. One was of Lucy and me at a high school dance years ago. It had been my first such experience and I hadn't yet found a way to put the words "hair" and "style" together in the same place. My hair was parted down the middle and poofy, and my smile showed off my nice silver braces as they glimmered under the camera lights. Lucy of course looked perfect, even back then. The other picture on the paper was a photo of Lucy and this Lance guy on a tropical beach. They looked like a Club Med Vacation ad, like some fake ideal that no one could ever achieve. I practically got an eating disorder just looking at it.

Below the snapshots were two lines of Lucy's perfect penmanship.

"I think it's obvious why you and I are off.

The wedding is set for this coming April. Lucy"

I took one last glance at the picture of the two of us at the dance and then tore the paper into shreds. Enough was enough.

I pulled my suitcase out from under my bed and began throwing clothes into it. Elder Sims was frantic.

"Elder, this too shall pass," he nervously reasoned.

"I've been waiting over six months for this to pass," I moaned. "I'm going to Virgil's Find until President Clasp transfers me."

I fumbled with my shirts and socks.

"Elder, this is not the answer," Elder Sims whined. "C'mon, let's go to the boardinghouse and call the Mission Home."

I slammed the suitcase shut.

"I'm out of here," I declared.

"You're going to regret this."

I wasn't even listening anymore.

Elder Sims grabbed his backpack so that he could follow me. There was no way he was going to be left there alone. I was going to self-righteously storm out the door and over to Virgil's Find to wait for President Clasp to send me my marching orders, but as I threw open the door Brother Heck was standing there. He looked at the suitcase in my hand and shook his head.

"I heard you got some bad mail," he said, solemnly offering his condolences.

"Yeah, well," I huffed, knowing that since the mail came through the boardinghouse, all news was everybody's business here.

"Can I talk to you fer a moment?" he asked me.

"I actually needed to get going," I explained.

"Won't take but a tick."

What was a tick in the eternal scheme of things?

I looked from Brother Heck to Elder Sims.

"All right," I said, setting down my suitcase and letting my shoulders drop.

I followed Brother Heck over to the front of the cemetery. Elder Sims sat down against the side of our cabin so that he could keep an eye on me as I conversed with Brother Heck. Ricky Heck and I took a seat on a log next to the statue by the cemetery gate. It was cold and gray. Wind, like emotion, swirled up my arms and around my face.

"Do you know who that is?" Brother Heck asked me, pointing at the monument.

I had never really paid the statue much mind. I had been living by it for over six months now, and I still hadn't taken the time to get to know my bronze neighbor.

"I have no idea who that is," I answered.

"Guess."

"Your mother," I tried.

"Nah, my mother was a lot heavier."

"Not literally, I hope," I replied. "That statue must weigh a ton."

"Guess again," Brother Heck went on.

I shrugged my shoulders. The last thing I wanted to do was play games with Brother Heck.

"That's Thelma," Brother Heck said, pointing towards the statue and telling me this as if he were sharing the secrets of the kingdom.

"*The* Thelma?" I asked.

"Nope, just Thelma."

"As in Way?"

"Yep."

I took a real good look. The statue was about five feet tall, and it stood upon a big wood base. Thelma had her right hand over her eyes as if she were looking forward, and her left hand on her hip. She had a bronze bonnet on and reminded me of some of the more famous Mormon pioneer statues I had seen in pictures. I had never really thought about the origin of the town's name. I just sort of figured that it, like the locals, wasn't supposed to make sense. I had no clue there had been an actual Thelma.

Imagine my delight.

"Have you ever heard her story?" Brother Heck asked.

I shook my head no. I was beginning to cool down.

"Actually the big pageant play will be kinda based on her life," Brother Heck began. "Thelma was a brat. She was the only child of a wealthy Mormon family back east. Her full name was Thelma Fortsyth Palmer. Her parents and she had joined the Church when Thelma was only twelve. A year later they left New York state to join the Saints in Nauvoo. They set out with a big group of people. Called themselves the Palmer party. Maybe you've heard of them?"

I shook my head.

"Most of the Palmer party was poor, dirt poor. Done sold all their stuff to be able to afford the trip. But the Palmers weren't poor. Nope, not by a long shot. They had their servants make the trip with them. Thelma's own personal handcart was pulled by her butler while she fanned herself in comfort.

"Well, the trip became disastrous almost instantly. People's carts fell apart, the weather was bad, and there was lots of arguing as Sister Palmer bossed everyone around. They pressed on. Eventually, however, they got lost—somewhere in South Dakota, I think. Real lost. They made a camp and decided to hunker down 'til the bad winter was over. After three days of hunkering, Brother Palmer volunteered to go in search of assistance. They never saw him again. Sister Palmer assumed he had died in the cold struggling to find them help. Everyone else just figured he rode off to get away from her and Thelma.

"Well, Sister Palmer became real sick, and the party started to run out of food in their makeshift winter camp. So, they pulled up their stakes and commenced traveling while they still had strength. They traveled for weeks, not having a clue as to what point on the map they was occupying. They saw no one, no roads, no towns, nothing. Finally a brother Dan Biggy organized a party-wide fast. It wasn't hard to do, really, seeing how they was out of food, but at the conclusion of the fast Brother Biggy felt inspired to head in a different direction. Sister Palmer was too sick to protest, but young Thelma was livid. How dare a poor person tell a wealthy person which way to go. Thelma demanded that they go her way. She said Brother Biggy didn't know squat.

"The party split.

"Those interested in following the Spirit went with Dan Biggy, and those who were too frightened by Thelma's thirteen-year-old rage to disagree with her went Thelma's way. Months later Thelma's party rolled into this meadow. Thelma took one look around and declared, 'This is a disgrace.'

"But Thelma's mother died while they were encamped, so Thelma refused to leave. A couple of people struck out on their own, but most folks stayed and put down roots right here, accepting the consequences of going Thelma's way.

"Once things were settled, Thelma used some of her money to commission this statue. She died two days after it was put up, trying to cross the Girth. They found her body down river below the falls."

"How come I've never heard this before?" I asked, still not sure if I should believe him.

"It's not the kind of thing we tell just anyone. Shoot, the kids here would be so disappointed if they found out Thelma was selfish and spoiled. Most of them think Thelma is Santa's wife."

"Why do they think that?" I asked.

"I told them," he said, embarrassed.

I shook my head.

"She doesn't seem like a very good person to look up to," I observed.

"Maybe not, but you've got to promise me that you won't tell anyone else what I just told you. I could get in real trouble, you understand? Don't even tell your companion. It's a secret, okay?"

"So why did you tell me?" I asked, confused.

"Because if you listen to those loud voices in your head, you could end up in the wrong place. But if you take time to let God guide you, you could end up in a much better mess. Brother Biggy listened; young Thelma didn't. Take heed."

"What happened to the Biggy party?"

"They made it to Nauvoo. Brother Biggy opened his own cabinet-building business. Made quite a nice living. I guess Thelma was wrong after all; he did know squat."

I sighed. The afternoon was collapsing. The sky was folding in on itself as winter chalked up another day.

"I know Thelma's Way ain't exactly paradise," Brother Heck said after a couple moments of silence. "But it could be worse."

I thought about asking for proof.

"We're real glad you're here," Brother Heck said shyly. "We might get under your skin, but we're real fond of you."

"Me?" I laughed. "Will of the Underworld?"

"Ah, Paul's just plain nuts. We all know that. I tell you what, Elder, it's nice to have him pick on someone else for a change."

"Glad to be of service," I joked. Brother Heck was the most discombobulated, guilt-ridden person I knew, but he was wise in his own way, and I loved him for it. I couldn't remember my father ever taking the time to talk to me like Brother Heck just had. Any contact with my father had mainly taken place at the dinner table on Sundays, the one time during the week when we all got together. The rest of the week he was usually too busy to be part of things.

"There'll be other girls," Brother Heck said, referring to Lucy's letter. "I'm real sorry yours gave up on you, but the Lord will provide."

I smiled. It was hard to believe this was the same man who tarred and feathered himself with latex house paint.

"So, you gonna leave us?" he finally asked me.

"Eventually," I replied.

"Funny how life works, ain't it?"

"Funny," I said.

21

# Lather, Rinse, Repeat

One Year

It had been about six months since I had sat with Brother Heck in the cemetery. Six months. Pete Kennedy had grown a beard, let it go gray, shaved it off, and begun another. The winter had turned to spring, and the spring had given way to a beautiful summer that was now almost halfway over. Life was warm, green and rainy. I had been on my mission for over a year.

I was still in Thelma's Way, and surprisingly to everyone, especially me, I was okay with this. I no longer checked off the days till official mission letterhead informed me it was time to pack my things. In fact, there were things here that I knew I was going to miss whenever I did get transferred out.

Astounding.

I had had a premonition I was up for transfer a couple months back when President Clasp and the Virgil's Find stake presidency came to Thelma's Way to get a look at things. Instead I got a new companion, they released Bishop Watson, restructured the tiny Thelma's Way Ward to be a tiny branch, and put Yours Truly in as the new branch president. Brother Heck was called as my first counselor with my new companion as second.

I was in shock for weeks. I had been hoping for the chance to train a new elder, or be a senior companion. Instead I was given a handful of full-fledged responsibilities, and it required coming to terms with the fact that I would be traveling nowhere fast. I had not known that missionaries could serve as branch presidents. What a way to find out.

My new companion was Elder Jorgensen from Blackfoot, Idaho. He was almost seven feet tall and had the shiniest set of buck teeth I had ever seen. All his suits were too short for him, and his blond hair was wiry and abrasive-looking. He walked with a spring in his step, and was constantly talking about trucks and how to make them go faster. He was one of fourteen kids and the first in his family to serve a mission. Always up before dawn, he was the kindest, hardest-working missionary I had ever met. His parents were potato farmers who sent him boxes of spuds along with pictures of his truck, which they were washing regularly for him.

I had not heard very much more from Lucy. I assumed she was married and happy by now—while selfishly I hoped for neither of those things.

Months back, my mother had sent me a new backpack and a new set of scriptures to replace my lost ones. I guess I was grateful. The backpack had a big pink rainbow stitched on the back of it, and the scriptures were my father's set that he never used. Of course, the set was so old that it didn't have the new references or page numbers. Mom had also soaked the backpack in dog repellent, hoping that would prevent me from losing it again. The thing was too pretty, too stinky, and too small. But I carried it around in honor of my mom.

I never found my old backpack. Oddly enough, the morning after I had lost it, I discovered my wallet lying in the dirt in front of our door. Everything was in it except for Lucy's picture. It was a miracle. I figured fate had removed her photo for me so I wouldn't have to suffer any further. Out of sight, out of mind.

I had not clearly seen Grace Heck since our life-saving encounter in the snow. The first thing I did when I was put in as branch president was to set out to find her. My records showed that she was now twenty-one and, as her branch president, I felt it was my duty to make sure she was having success in life. But Grace was too elusive. Even her parents couldn't round her up long enough for me to talk to her. I had tried dropping in on the Hecks and surprising them at dinner or other points when I thought Grace would be there.

She never was.

We were having some success where reactivation was concerned. We had managed to get a couple of people back to church. Ed Washington and his mother were attending regularly, and Toby Carver had been out twice in the last two months. We had also found an older woman named Nippy Ward over behind the Heck home who was now coming out to church. Nippy was as old as the hills and almost totally deaf. She never really understood a word of what you said, but she nodded a lot and smiled enough to make you feel like you were getting through to her.

The big news was that Leo Tip had decided to be baptized. He was going to be my first baptism. The event that pushed him over the edge was when Sister Watson and the members of P.I.G. held their first annual hand shadow contest to raise money to take Paul to court—Sister Watson really wanted to get some closure on this Paul mess so as to be able to fully focus on the coming sesquicentennial pageant. They held the contest at the boardinghouse late one night using Tindy MacDermont's powerful flashlight. Practically everyone in Thelma's Way threw their hands into the ring. Competition was fierce. Digby Heck almost won with his realistic eagle hand shadow, but then he made the mistake of looking directly into the flashlight and temporarily blinded himself. Teddy Yetch's turtle with retracting head was also quite spectacular. But Philip Green ended up winning the trophy, he and his eerie beetle hand shadow impression. Of course, he had a tremendous advantage due to the extra finger on his right hand.

At the end of the event people milled around in the dark eating refreshments that the members of P.I.G. had brought. Young Narlette got hold of Tindy's flashlight and waved it around making scary noises. Well, the whole thing sort of spooked Leo, putting him into a reflective mood. That night he dreamed he was drowning in a baptismal font. He could see his father looking down through the water, but he did nothing to help.

Leo was unnerved. What if the dream was prophetic? What if it was his father telling him to get baptized now or suffer the consequences? What if it was the two dozen of Sister Teddy Yetch's pickle wheat cookies that he had eaten at the hand shadow contest making him hallucinate?

Leo wasn't taking any chances. He scheduled his baptism for July 4th. The town was abuzz. CleeDee Lipton started coming back to church and talked of eventually going with Leo to the temple. There were those who had their doubts about Leo's resolve, of course, but today was July 4th and unless my eyes were deceiving me, Leo was wearing all white.

Most of the active members of the Thelma's Way Branch were gathered around the river next to the burned-out bridge. It had been raining all day, and the extra water had given the Girth a bloated, angry-looking belly. We thought about postponing the baptism for a clearer afternoon, but Leo was ready now, and I didn't want to run the risk of having him change his mind.

Umbrellas were opened, slickers were pulled close, and mismatched boots stood in inches of mud. Just to be safe, Leo and I each tied ourselves to the frame of the derelict bridge before we waded into the Girth. The water was cold, especially for the middle of summer, and twice I felt the current almost knock my feet out from under me. We had to push out a good twenty steps to where it was deep enough for dunking. We then turned and faced the crowd. Everyone looked gray in the rain. Here and there a lit smile flashed, bright and cheery. Brother Heck and Ed Washington leaned out over the river to make sure Leo went completely under.

I said the words of the prayer and pushed Leo back. But his knees buckled as his head hit the water, and I fumbled to maintain my balance. It was no use, the water rushed over us and pulled us down river. Leo grabbed me and pushed me down, trying to climb above the water. The rope around my stomach went taut. I struggled to find my footing and stuck my head above the water, spitting and coughing. Leo was standing next to me breathing hard, his hands wrapped around his rope. We looked over at Ed.

"Sorry, it wasn't a complete dunk," he yelled above the noise of the water. "Leo's hand flew up."

I sighed, wiping the rain from out of my eyes. All that, and it didn't count. I thought back to when an older gentlemen named Myron was baptized in our ward back in my hometown of Southdale. No one knew he wore a toupee, but when he went down, his hair didn't go with him. Someone screamed that he'd been spiritually scalped. One of the little boys in the front row reached out to grab it. His mother almost fainted, thinking it was a water rat. But Myron's girlfriend cried the loudest, never having seen Myron without his fuzzy top.

The local priesthood leaders began to debate whether or not it was necessary for a person's toupee to be submerged. They consulted the handbook, but there wasn't a section on bad-looking rugs. Just to be safe, they baptized Myron once more with him holding his hair in his hand.

Now here I was standing in the pouring rain in the middle of a raging river, and Leo needed one more dip. We waded back upstream, feeling with our feet for firm footing. I tugged the rope around my stomach to make sure it still held. I wiped the rain from my eyes and pushed the short hair off of my forehead. Lightning crackled in the far distance. We needed to hurry. I threw a smile of encouragement to this branch I had grown to . . . love? Sister Teddy Yetch, her wrinkled face pinched in reverence to the event; Narlette, prancing on the shore with excitement; Bishop and Sister Watson, looking miserable in the rain; Digby Heck; Ed Washington and his mother; Nippy Ward nodding; and Grace Heck standing there next to the burnt-out bridge, her green eyes seeping out from under a yellow umbrella.

Her red hair was darkened by the wet air, and her white arms were cold and pale in the summer rain. I wanted to push Leo over and run back to shore. I just wanted to talk with her. She had been so elusive and now here she was.

I turned back to Leo. He was standing at attention, ready for baptism. I pulled my focus back to the moment and shut my eyes. I took his hands.

"Leo Tip," I said solemnly. "Having been commissioned . . ." I finished the prayer and pushed Leo under, holding on for all I was worth. This time Leo let himself go down. He came back up coughing and spitting water. We waded back to shore. I saw Grace slip away back behind the crowd. I almost called out to her, "Wait. Don't go." But I thought better of it, me being the branch president and all.

Folks congratulated Leo as they collectively stepped back from the crumbling river bank. Pete fired off his gun a couple of times in celebration and ruined his umbrella. Rain poured down through the holes onto his head.

"Do you think God's happy with my decision?" Leo asked, skeptical because of the rough weather.

Sister Heck handed him a wet towel to dry off with. "It's an Indian legend that God's happy when it rains," she explained.

"Paul says rain is a weapon God uses to smite the ingrates," Ed Washington chimed in.

Ed's mother flashed him a "be quiet" expression.

"I don't know no Ingrates round here, anyways," Toby Carver observed. "Less yore talking about them private folks next to Tindy's place."

"It's not a name, Toby," Brother Heck corrected. "Anyone can be an ingrate."

"Not me," Toby scoffed. "I'm German."

"I think all this rain is just Satan playing his fife," Sister Watson said as our group began to wander away from the river and back towards the boardinghouse. "He can finger some pretty tricky tunes," she went on. "Heard him play 'Battle Hymn of the Republic' as I was deciding whether I should go to church last week."

Leo and I quickly changed out of our wet white clothes. Then we all crammed into the boardinghouse for the celebration. We had planned for fireworks to celebrate the Fourth, but thanks to the rain, that was out of the question. Besides, someone had taken the box of fireworks outside and now they were soaking wet. Elder Jorgensen dragged them back into the boardinghouse where Digby fetched a blow dryer to dry them out. I told him it seemed like a bad idea, but he wouldn't listen until one of the fire flowers ignited on his lap and singed a hole in his shorts.

The rain stopped about two hours later. We set up lawn chairs in the mud and attempted to light the rain-soaked fireworks. We tried to *ooh* and *ahh* as wet wicks sizzled and dudlike sparks spit out of the only slightly airborne fireworks.

There was a big sheet cake made by CleeDee in honor of Leo's baptism. CleeDee sliced it up and passed out pieces on paper plates with plastic forks. Folks ate the lemon-flavored cake with big smiles and loud laughs, as night became late-night, and the day just a memory. Elder Jorgensen and I relished every minute of it. It was our first baptism and it had gone over Thelma's Way style. Not with a bang, but with a pop and sizzle.

At CleeDee's suggestion, Leo pulled his old jalopy close, turned on the headlights, and pointed them toward us so we could see to talk. We told stories long into the night. We talked about the crazy Tennessee weather. We talked about the branch and the litter of Mormons who still refused to come back to church. We talked about Paul. We talked about his problem with telling the truth. And we talked about how the members of P.I.G. almost had enough money to get themselves a lawyer and take Paul to court. We reminisced about Feeble and Roswell. We talked about the pageant, and how it was creeping up on us, and whether or not people would come.

Eight-year-old Narlette fell asleep on her mother's shoulder. Mosquitoes buzzed around us like bad thoughts. Bishop and Sister Watson finally left the group to go home, the bottom half of their legs covered in mud like the rest of us. Ed and his mother eventually bid us adieu, carrying their two lawn chairs off into the dark. Soon it was just the Hecks and Leo and CleeDee and us. Leo's headlights were getting dimmer as his car battery drained.

"I saw Grace there today," I ventured.

The Hecks nodded, Brother Heck scraping his paper plate with his fork and cleaning off the last bits of his third helping of cake.

"She and Leo go way back," Sister Heck replied, swatting at the mosquitoes near Narlette's sleeping face. "I think Grace was sweet on Leo for a while."

Leo blushed. CleeDee looked on with pride. She had won her man. They smiled in silence for a minute or two. Then Leo looked at CleeDee's watch, said something about not wanting to haul another car battery in from Virgil's Find, and the two of them slipped off together, leaving us in the moonlight. The sky had cleared and the night was ablaze with stars.

"Grace seems like a nice girl," I observed.

"She is," Brother Heck said. "She spends too much time alone, but whatcha gonna do? She can be stubborn," he went on. "If'n I tell her to go south, she goes up. If I tell her that today is Tuesday, she'll argue that it's Wednesday."

"But it was Wednesday," Sister Heck said, reaching over to touch her husband's arm.

"Sure it was, that one time," he huffed. "But I'm still her father, ain't I?"

Sister Heck rubbed her husband's shoulder with her outstretched arm. I looked closely at Brother and Sister Heck. Although they appeared different on the surface, they were worn to the exact same point. They were two peas in a rather weathered pod.

Sister Heck was proud of her man lately. Brother Heck had been doing so well controlling his addiction. So well, in fact, that I could see a point in the not-too-far-away future where he would be ready to assume responsibility for the branch. I know the idea of a twenty-year-old kid being over him was a blow to his backwoods pride. But he had handled things gracefully. As first counselor, he had stepped up to the plate.

Crickets moshed. Raccoons and critters were coming out of the woods. Every now and again eyes would flash in the moonlight. The meadow was ready to go to bed and we were keeping them up.

"Think Grace might be interested in coming out to church?" I asked, standing and picking up my muddy chair.

"I'm not sure," Brother Heck said. "She marches to a different pianist."

"Grace is just finding herself," Sister Heck defended. "If only she could find something to be interested in here," she said, heaving Narlette higher on to her shoulder and standing.

*If only.*

## 22

# Wet Your Appetite

Grace slipped down into the meadow with her umbrella overhead and stood behind the crowd of spectators. She owed it to Leo.

She watched Trust and Leo mess up the first time and almost float off downstream. Trust looked different. A full year in Thelma's Way had changed him. His shoulders seemed wider, and his smile easier. His brown hair, wet from the river, was almost enough to make Grace like him again. She slid right up next to the bridge to observe their second try.

Since that night in the snow, when Trust's companion had assumed the worst, she had put Elder Williams out of her mind. The last thing Thelma's Way needed was another church scandal. And, secretly, she felt she would be doing Trust a favor by staying out of his way.

Never in a hundred years did Grace think Trust would notice her standing there, but he did. And Trust's locked gaze was long enough to cause her to smile back at him.

Grace was no dummy; she was truly smarter than the entire town of Thelma's Way. The volumes of books she had digested made her a mental master on almost everything. She knew the whole idea of missionary romance was a contradiction in terms.

But she could not deny the feelings growing inside her. She ran off before Trust could climb out of the river, but she had seen how he was coming for her. So what if he was a missionary and, as such, just a fantasy. There was no harm in dreaming, was there?

# 23

# Door Number Two

Month Thirteen

Sister Watson had finally completed the pageant script. She called a town meeting in the boardinghouse and, with great flourish, she presented *All Is Swell: The Story of Thelma's Way.* Everyone applauded. She handed out copies to everyone interested in being involved. I took a copy and flipped through it. As I read a couple of the lines, I realized that the pageant would be even more ridiculous than I had anticipated. But knowing how important it was to everyone, I kept my opinions to myself. I slipped the script into my rainbow backpack, figuring it would make a nice souvenir.

Elder Jorgensen and I left to do some missionary work up in the hills. We had decided to investigate a particularly thickly wooded part of Thelma's Way that day. We had been systematically working our way through the woods, scouring every trail for lost locals. I kept having strong feelings that somewhere within these hills was someone no one knew about. An unknown nonmember. The Holy Grail.

We climbed over Lush Point and ran down through a ditch for a few hundred feet. We hiked up a small hill and into a clearing.

"This is where we left off last time," Elder Jorgensen said. It was only about three in the afternoon; we had hours before dinner. The trail stretched out in front of us, beckoning.

It was always surprising to me the number of homes hidden up in these hills. Most of the houses had been built years ago. According to Brother Heck, the community had really rallied together back in the good old days to help each other build.

Before long, we stumbled onto a house perched precariously on a small knoll next to a flowing stream. The place was old and looked to have been added on to about three or four times. It was the home of Corndog Tent employee Jerry Scotch.

Jerry was trying to be active. He had been coming out to church. Last fast and testimony meeting, he had testified about how he had almost lost his job. According to his testimony, Jerry had bought a candle for Jan, a girl that worked at the Teriyaki Carousel two shops down from the Corndog Tent in the mall. Jerry was kind of sweet on Jan and figured he would give her a scented candle because he had heard that people of Asian descent liked incense. Jerry bought the candle from a store on the upper level of the mall called Mr. Wick. Well, Mr. Wick charged three dollars for gift wrapping. Extortion! Jerry wasn't exactly getting rich working at the Corndog Tent. Luckily, Jerry thought up what he considered to be a fantastic idea. He took the boysenberry scented candle back to his work, dipped it in batter, and fried it up. He figured it would come out covered like one of his hot dogs.

Creative cornbread wrapping paper.

There were two problems with his plan . . . well, actually there were far more than just two, but the two most obvious were, one, just because Jan worked at Teriyaki Carousel didn't mean she was actually Asian. Jan, in fact, had been born in Virgil's Find to Inga and Swen

Swenson. Problem number two was that candle wax melts when put into a big vat of boiling oil.

Who knew?

Imagine Jerry's surprise when he pulled that present up to find nothing there. Jerry ended up giving Jan a discounted calendar from the year before. Jan didn't even accept it, informing Jerry that her parents wouldn't allow her to date until she was at least fifteen. Jerry's boss never found out about his mistake, and people enjoyed boysenberry-flavored corndogs until the oil was changed a few days later.

It had been quite the faith-promoting testimony.

Elder Jorgensen and I talked with Jerry for a few minutes at his home and then headed out to find somebody even less active. We hiked for another mile or so without seeing a soul. We were just about to turn around when Elder Jorgensen spotted a rock chimney hidden behind a thick wall of trees.

"Over there," he said, pointing like a happy dog.

I patted him on the back. "Good work, Elder."

We pushed through the trees and up to the cabin. It was small and weathered but cute. There were flowers in the window boxes and a front walkway that had been swept despite the fact that it was only dirt. The windows were clean and trimmed with colorful curtains. We stepped up to the door, feeling a little like Hansel and Gretel, our mouths watering over the possibility of teaching a first discussion.

I knocked. No one answered.

"Hello, anyone home?" Elder Jorgensen called out. He pushed his face up against one of the windows and peered in. "There's got to be somebody in there," he said, his buck teeth clicking against the glass as he spoke. "There's a half-eaten apple on a table and a book lying open on a chair." He knocked again, harder this time.

One thing I had learned while serving in the backwoods was that if people didn't want to be interrupted, they wouldn't be. And if you continued to bother them after they had made it clear that they wanted to be left alone, you could expect a brandished shotgun or a couple of loose dogs.

"We'd better go," I said, about ready to head back to town. But Elder Jorgensen looked deflated.

"When I saw that chimney," he said, "I thought for sure it was a sign. There's just got to be somebody out here."

I gave in. "Maybe we should hike back a little farther," I said. His face lit up, and he took off walking.

We had covered about a half a mile more territory when Elder Jorgensen hopped up on a fallen tree that was lying across a small crack in the earth. He proceeded to balance himself along, his arms outstretched, talking a thousand words a minute about back home.

"So Chet said, push the pedal harder. You'll get more torque if you just—" Elder Jorgensen was mid-sentence when I heard this huge snap and saw the log give way.

"Elder," I yelled, jumping down into the crevice where he and the tree were now wedged.

Elder Jorgensen was conscious, but his right leg was pinned by the folding tree—pinned and immobile, if not worse. His face was wrinkled by a grimace. He was in some serious pain.

"Can you pull me out?" he asked with the faith of one certain I could bring him back from the dead if I had to.

I pulled on the tree. I pushed on the tree. I kicked the tree until he began screaming.

"I've got to go get help," I said, wiping sweat off my forehead.

"But we're supposed to stick together," he moaned.

"Don't be ridiculous, Elder," I reprimanded. "This is an emergency. You're in real trouble."

"If I only had my truck . . ." he started to say.

I took off running before he could finish.

I'd never been great with direction. Standing next to the North Pole, I probably couldn't tell you which way was south without making at least three guesses. It was a serious flaw. I don't know why my perception was so bad. You could blindfold my mother, put her in an electric dryer for three hours, take her out, turn her upside-down, and she'd still be able to tell you exactly which way was north. My father was the same way. I don't think I had ever heard him use the words *left* or *right.*

"Look over there to the west, son."

"The fork goes on the east-hand side."

But my soul lacked direction, geographically speaking. This had been a real problem living in Thelma's Way. The forest and hills really threw me. I worked hard to establish a series of markers to help me stay oriented close to town. But deep in the woods, I was useless. I'd never make it back to the meadow alone.

I thought of the cabin nearby, the one with the unwilling occupant. It was my only hope. It took me a while stumbling around, but I finally spotted the cabin's rock chimney. I banged on the door begging for help. Nobody came. The handle was locked.

I considered trying to retrace my steps and hopefully find Jerry Scotch's place again. But I didn't think I'd be able to do it.

I took a deep breath. I forced myself to calm down, and then I did what I should have done earlier. Standing right there in front of that door, I prayed. I prayed for Elder Jorgensen. I prayed for his leg. I prayed for my mind to stop buzzing long enough for me to think clearly. I prayed for God to send help. I prayed that if he was not going to send help, he would at least let me know what to do. And while I was praying, I heard the door open.

It was a miracle. And it was Grace.

There she stood. She was the last person I had expected to see. And in the same moment that I realized I had discovered her secret hiding place, I also realized I had not been wrong about her. Her appearance was like the memory of an embarrassing pop song from my junior high years. I felt silly for being moved.

I stared.

Her red hair was long and loose. Strands of it were touching the right side of her face. She had on a summer dress and no shoes. She might have appeared to be just an average girl to anyone else, but I could see how the light rested upon her in the most unique way, giving her both sharp lines and soft curves. Not even Lucy had created such a visionary event for my simple mind. Don't get me wrong, Grace was no classic beauty. She wasn't the kind of girl you would see in a fashion magazine, or looking good in spandex at the gym. She was simple and complicated. It was as if she were a part of this lush landscape, her green eyes and pink lips being the best thing these hills had to offer. For me, it was kind of like staring at a psychedelic pinwheel.

Far out.

I was suddenly well aware of how companionless I was. Elder Jorgensen was in trouble and, by almost all measures, what I was now doing was against the mission rules.

I was alone. With a girl. The same girl as before, that night in the snow. I pulled myself together.

"My companion needs help," I stated.

"What can I do?" she asked calmly.

"Is there anyone else here?" I questioned.

"Only me."

Under normal circumstances Grace would be more than enough, but not at the moment. I needed a couple people to help me drag my companion out from under that tree.

"He's pinned down under an old tree," I began to explain. "His leg might be broken, and I don't know if he's bleeding or not."

"Did you give him a blessing?" she asked.

Good question. How dumb had I been? Here I was a full-time missionary and branch president and I had failed to do the one thing that could really make a difference. It took an inactive member to get me to even think of it.

"I didn't really think—"

"There's some rope inside," Grace interrupted. "We could hook it around a pulley and try to get the tree off of him."

I just stood there as Grace ran back inside collecting things that might be useful. Then we took off. The plan was to get Elder Jorgensen out from under the tree and make him comfortable. Then Grace would run into town and get further help. It was a pretty good plan, or would have been, had I been able to find him. We were lugging around the rope, the pulley, and some bandages. Our futile search soon became a pain.

"Can't you remember which direction you came from?" Grace tried to ask kindly.

"Over there," I kept trying to say with some confidence.

"What were you guys doing out here?" she asked.

"We were looking for investigators."

"No one lives out this far," she said. "The wells are bad."

I thought for a moment that she was saying the Wells family who lived a mile behind the boardinghouse were bad people. Then I realized she meant the water.

"So is that your family's cabin?" I asked, knowing already that it wasn't.

Grace didn't answer.

"I've been looking for you for quite some time," I huffed as we climbed up a small hill.

"Why?" was all Grace said.

"I wanted to thank you for waking me up all those many months ago. In the snow," I further clarified.

Grace just shrugged.

"Plus, I wanted to talk with you."

"About what?" she asked skeptically, stopping in her tracks.

I didn't have an answer for that. I had just always wanted to talk to her. It was my turn to shrug my shoulders.

We trudged on.

I thought we were headed in the right direction until we came to a stream that I knew I had not crossed before.

"Shoot," I said, embarrassed at being lost.

I screamed Elder Jorgensen's name but no one answered.

We stopped again.

"Tell me what the area looks like where he got hurt," she said.

"It looked like forest," I joked. "There were some trees, and bushes, and a short gouge in the earth."

Grace turned and headed in the opposite direction. I guess my poor description had been enough for her. A few minutes later, we were standing by the crack in the earth.

But Elder Jorgensen was gone.

"I don't understand," I said. "He was really trapped."

I craned my head around, but there was no sign of him.

"Don't be alarmed," Grace said calmly, sensing my panic. "I'm sure he's okay. He probably got himself out, or somebody found him. Let's head into town. Someone will know where he is."

"Which way is town?" I asked.

Grace answered with a point.

We walked towards Thelma's Way looking for Elder Jorgensen. We hiked up a few hills, across a few meadows, and down a few steep slopes. Neither Grace nor I spoke much. We were both uncomfortable. I started thinking about how this would probably be my only chance to talk with her. For over a year now I had been living and serving here in Thelma's Way and for all that time, Grace had remained hidden. Even though I was worried about Elder Jorgensen, I couldn't resist the opportunity to ask Grace a few questions.

"So you must like it here," I finally said.

She turned and looked at me like I was daffy.

"I mean, you grew up here."

She smiled at my poor communication skills. "This is home," she responded, her voice the sound of good news.

"How long have you been in Thelma's Way?" she asked me.

"Over a year."

"That's not normal," she observed.

I looked at her as if seeking clarification.

"Missionaries don't normally stay so long in one area," she added.

"Yeah," I replied wittily.

"Are you being punished?" she joked as we walked down through a small overgrown patch of ivy.

"Possibly," I replied, trying to keep up with Grace without appearing winded. "Heaven knows there's a long list of things I need to correct."

Grace smiled. "I find that hard to believe," she said, walking faster. "Do you think they'll keep you here until the pageant?" she asked.

"No way," I answered ignorantly.

Grace walked on in front of me, her bare feet stepping in all the right spots. I didn't know if I had romantic feelings for her or just feelings. I couldn't help but see her in a different light from the rest of the citizens here. It was as if she were purely an emotion with arms and legs. I had no idea how to voice my thoughts, even in my head.

Let me attempt, however.

I remember being a kid and going down to the toy store with my friends. We would stand in front of the display of action figures and talk about which one we would buy if we had the money. My friends always drooled over the mean-looking ones, the ones with rows of big teeth and huge muscles. I secretly liked the nice ones, the dad-looking ones with parted hair and smiles.

On one occasion when I actually had money, I cowardly bought a tough-looking one with flashy guns and karate-chop action just to save face in front of my friends. Had I been alone, I probably would have picked out the camping boy with working flashlight and first aid kit.

Well, that was Grace.

That's not to say that she was a boy, or that she carried a flashlight.

She was just the kind of girl I would pick out if I were totally honest with myself. She wasn't like Lucy with all her bells and whistles. Grace was like the science kit that most of us pretended to loathe, but secretly worked with in our rooms—fascinated by all the parts, and constructing worlds, but not brave enough to admit that learning was fun.

I was ready to learn.

And yet, how weird it was to have met Grace here. I would most likely be gone in a few months, never to return. And I could already see myself comparing every girl I met after my mission to Grace. I only wished that I could really get to know her. Of course, there was really no good way for a missionary to get to know a girl while serving a mission. At least, there was no right way. The fact that I was alone with her now was more than most missionaries should ever experience. I felt a little guilty.

"So do you ever *think* about coming out to church?" I asked Grace, trying to feel more like a branch president.

"I think about a lot of things," she replied.

"It would be great if you did," I said.

Grace sort of smiled.

"You have a nice family," I commented, desperately trying to make conversation. "Your father is a great help to the ward."

"I'm happy you approve," she teased.

I smiled, liking this side of her.

"What's your family like?" she then asked.

"Oh, two parents, a younger sister, and a brother," I answered as if I were being timed.

"Do they have names?" Grace asked, pushing aside a long tree limb so as to slip through a tight spot in the forest. She let go, and the limb swung back at me.

"My sister's name is Margaret, and my brother's name is Abel," I informed her while dodging the branch.

Silence ensued.

"You like to read," I finally stated bluntly, knowing she spent a good deal of time at the Virgil's Find library, and sounding like an idiot.

Grace smirked. Except it wasn't a smirk. It was void of any malice or sarcasm—it was a sincere smirk.

"I love to read," Grace answered.

Silence again.

"How about you?" she then asked.

"I read lots of things back home, but here I concentrate on just reading my scriptures."

Grace blinked, her long eyelashes giving me something new to concentrate on.

"I'm reading the biography of Martin Calypso," Grace explained.

"Oh," was all I said, hoping she wouldn't ask me if I knew who Martin Calypso was.

Grace stopped. "Do you know who he is?" she asked.

"No," I admitted with a sorry little laugh.

"He was a man who was unashamed of his family despite the fact that his debt-ridden brother eventually killed him."

"Mighty tolerant of him," I commented.

Grace laughed.

I recognized where we were now. A few minutes later the big meadow came into view. Kids were swarming over the rotted pioneer wagons, screaming and hollering as if they knew that summer was coming to an end.

The instant we stepped out of the trees and into the meadow, everyone looked up and took us in. I suddenly missed my companion more than ever before. Whether or not they were active, everyone in Thelma's Way knew that elders shouldn't be walking alone with girls, especially coming out of the trees.

A few adults gasped. Sister Teddy Yetch ran up to us as fast as her old legs could carry her. Briant Willpts shuffled right behind her. And

Paul, who was passing the afternoon arguing with members of P.I.G., came sidling up as well. He wouldn't miss this for the world.

"What's going on here?" Briant asked.

"I lost my companion," I tried to explain.

"How can you lose your companion?" Teddy asked. "He's bigger than you are."

"Yes, how?" CleeDee snipped snidely as she approached.

Grace tried to slip away from it all, but Teddy wouldn't let her go.

"Hold on a moment, young lady," she scolded, and she grabbed Grace by the arm. "I think you got some explaining to do."

"I knew it," Paul exclaimed. "I've been telling you all for months, and no one believed me. Will of the Underworld."

The little kids playing on the pioneer wagons stopped what they were doing to watch us adults act like children.

"My companion got hurt and Grace was trying to help us," I said, hoping to quiet Paul.

"How condental of you," Briant said.

"That's not a word," Grace retorted.

Briant's ears sizzled. In all his years, no one had ever been so bold as to correct him. He had heard tell of folks whispering behind his back about his made-up words, but before now no one had actually challenged him to his face.

"Why, you little. . . ." he said, stopping to think up a new word. But before his thought process could be completed, he was interrupted by Brother Heck.

"Leave her be, Briant," he said, stepping in front of us. "Where's Elder Jorgensen?" he asked me.

"Yes," Paul hissed. "Where is your companion?"

"I don't know," I replied. "I was hoping he was here. We had an accident and he disappeared."

"Disappeared?" Miss Flitrey asked in amazement. "Sounds like a story with holes."

"Holes," the children all said in chorus, as if they were still in school.

"I have been telling you people for months that your church is corrupt," Paul raged. "And here is the main corrupter." He pointed at me.

"Calm yourself, Paul," Brother Heck clipped.

"Really," I tried to explain. "I was—"

A low moaning broke out about twenty feet away from us. We all turned that direction to look. I saw a hand rise above the tall grass and sort of wave. It was Elder Jorgensen's. He was lying on the ground, completely hidden by the thick growth the untrampled parts of the meadow had to offer.

I ran over and propped him up.

"What happened?" I asked.

He gasped a few times and then licked his lips. "I was able to push the tree off," he explained. "You know the one that was on my leg, the one that cracked?" He asked me as if it were so far back and so inconsequential that I had forgotten about it.

I nodded yes.

He went on. "Then I made a splint for my leg and fashioned myself a couple of crutches out of dead branches. I hobbled all the way back. Right before I got to the meadow, I ran out of steam. Crawled to this point here. I hope you're not mad. You were gone so long, I thought you might be lost."

"Why would I be mad?" I asked.

"For me taking off like that."

Elder Jorgensen was one faithful missionary.

I saw Toby Carver take off running, most likely to fetch his Ace bandage. Brother Heck and I picked up Elder Jorgensen and helped him over to our home.

Amidst it all, Grace was gone.

"Shoot," I said aloud as I laid my companion down on his bed.

"I'll be all right, Elder," he comforted me. "Don't you worry about a thing."

"I'm glad," I replied.

His leg looked bad. It was bent at a funny angle. Toby came and wrapped it with his bandage. While he was wrapping, he questioned me about being alone with Grace.

"So you two were just helping your companion?" he asked suspiciously.

"Yes."

"I guess we'll have to take your word on that," he added.

It was no secret that the town talked about me and Grace occasionally, even though there was nothing to talk about. The story of her rescuing me all those months ago in the snow was a favorite to retell. I was okay with this, as long as no embellishment occurred. I had never done, and never would do, anything inappropriate in regards to Grace Heck. I was here to serve a mission. True, I had begun to refer to our mealtime prayers as "saying grace," but that was as close as I got to walking on the wild side.

Toby finished wrapping Elder Jorgensen's leg. Brother Heck and I laid him on a stretcher and carried him to Virgil's Find.

We only dropped him twice.

# 24

# Boo

Month Fifteen

Elder Jorgensen was looked over by a competent doctor in Virgil's Find. Prognosis: a bad break. We spent the night near the hospital with the two full-time missionaries stationed there, Elder Bess and Elder Jepson. The next day Elder Jorgensen was driven back to Knoxville to heal. President Clasp had done some quick shuffling to find me a new companion. Elder Weeble and I returned to Thelma's Way the following evening.

Elder Weeble looked like an egg. He was short and compact. His head was tiny and his feet were big, giving him a tremendous sense of balance. Weeble wobbled, but he didn't fall down—at least not physically. His spiritual balance was a different matter.

He spent all his time talking about how he wasn't worthy to be on a mission because he had done so many bad things before he came out. Oh, he was no real rebel. His pre-mission escapades consisted mainly of things like going to 7–Eleven during Sunday School and talking back to his parents.

I felt Elder Weeble was just looking for attention and a way out of actually working on his mission. He pined about his girlfriend back home. He agonized over basic Church doctrines, unsure of what he really believed. He didn't like climbing hills, couldn't teach a lesson if his life depended on it, and was horribly bothered by almost everyone in Thelma's Way. We didn't click.

Most irritating of all, he had the habit of asking ridiculous questions on a regular basis: "How come we have to work today? Why do we always have to wear white shirts? Do you think they accidentally left the page about afternoon naps out of the Missionary Handbook?"

Despite Elder Weeble, the branch was actually doing better than ever. I wasn't vain enough to think it had anything to do with my leadership, but ever since I was made branch president, Pap Wilson had started coming out to church. And Todd Nodd, the town wino—who used to come to church only because it was a warm place away from his vicious, alcohol-intolerant wife—had even attended once while sober. He sat in the front row and asked questions to the speakers during sacrament meeting.

Plus, as Wad and Miss Flitrey became more and more serious about each other, Wad began attending the branch with her. The two of them looked quite cozy each week as they cuddled in their pew.

Even Grace Heck had been making an appearance, wandering down from her hideout in the hills. Her presence made my Sundays more fulfilling, but whenever she got within three feet of me, everyone in the congregation watched us like hawks. She would smile, and I would nod, and the air around me would start to thin. I had told President Clasp all about her, and how I seemed to have these unexplainable feelings for her. I thought maybe he would play it safe and finally transfer me. He didn't. I thought maybe he would command me to never think of her. He didn't. He simply admonished me to do the job and serve as I knew I should. He also told me to make sure none of my subsequent companions conveniently broke their legs, giving me a chance to be alone with her again.

Snow had fallen by mid-October that year, making it more difficult for us to get around. It was particularly treacherous crossing the Girth to see Teddy Yetch, but Teddy liked to have the missionaries in her home, and we liked to check up on her at least once a week.

We were actually teaching Teddy's neighbor in the hope of reactivating her. Sister Lando and Teddy had been good friends for years. She was small like Teddy, but heavier, and at least ten years younger. It seemed physically impossible for Sister Lando to talk without using her hands. She had gray hair and perpetual bad breath. She had bright hazel eyes and a pointed nose that seemed to collapse into itself at the tip. Elder Weeble speculated that over the years she had overused the expression "right on the tip of my nose" and, thanks to her talking so much with her hands, she had poked the tip of it in. Whatever the reason, it gave her a distinctive look.

Sister Lando had been inactive long before Paul had ever gone to Rome and returned to tear the ward apart. Her reason for not coming out to church was simple: the Church didn't respect the fact that she came from a long line of supposed witches. Sister Lando could not understand how a religion that was so big on families being together could forbid her to wear her great-great-grandmother's pointy black hat to church. Sister Watson was allowed to wear her Easter bonnet, and Patty Heck received no reprimand whenever she donned her floral shawl. So why in the name of the good people of Salem couldn't Sister Lando wear her wide-rimmed, extra pointy black hat without getting guff?

Regardless of her ancestry, we wanted Sister Lando back at church. We needed her. I had told her that it still would not be appropriate for her to wear her hat in the chapel, but that she was welcome to wear it as she walked to and from the services. I even promised her that she could store it in one of the church closets for safekeeping. She found no comfort in this, seeing how Parley P. Pratt's first edition Book of Mormon had been stolen from right off the pulpit. I told her no one would be interested in stealing a musty old black hat. She told me to bite my tongue lest she be forced to turn me into a prune.

I laughed as if it were a joke. It *was* almost Halloween, after all, and everyone was getting into the spirit of things. The people of P.I.G. were leading the way. They had hit on a new money-making scheme and were busy making preparations for their first annual "Non-Satanic, Haunted Fun House."

Saints beware.

They had staked out a spot in the woods next to the Watsons' house. Toby Carver had hauled in some two-by-fours and rigged up a little maze. He stapled up plastic tarps for walls. For a week now the spot had been off-limits to anyone without a P.I.G. pass. I had cautioned all the people involved about not making it too scary, seeing how little kids would be going through and we didn't want to leave any of them emotionally scarred. Of course my words of caution did nothing but fall on deaf ears—except for Toby Carver, who asked if it was possible to make fake emotional scars out of relish and glue.

One good thing had come out of this non-satanic haunted house so far. Sister Lando had an occasion on which to wear her witch hat. Of course Pap Wilson put up a fight, arguing that her hat sort of watered out the non-satanic part. Pap was acknowledged and then ignored. Sister Lando also helped Sister Watson make some of the decorations and loaned P.I.G. a number of her best brewing kettles.

It was late afternoon that All Hallows' Eve when Elder Weeble and I went to the boardinghouse to check for mail. We stepped inside, shaking off snow and wishing winter were ending instead of beginning. Elder Weeble got one letter from his girlfriend, and I received a CD from my family. Pete Kennedy was working the counter at the boardinghouse. He was busy scooping flour from a big bag into a tiny container.

"You guys going to the fun house?" he asked, dusting his hands off.

"Probably," I replied.

Pete snickered.

"What's so funny?" I asked.

"Nothing," Pete giggled.

"Something's funny," my companion said, displaying his lack of patience for these people.

"I just hope you two don't get too scared," Pete explained.

"You're leaving your *gun* at home, right?" I asked.

"Yeah," Pete said mournfully. "Sister Watson said I'm not allowed to bring it to public gatherings any longer. I can't even bring it to the pageant."

Elder Weeble scoffed. "You mean that play you guys have been laboring over forever?"

"Yep," Pete answered with pride, oblivious to the sarcasm in Elder Weeble's voice. "Sister Watson just posted the parts. The rehearsals begin in the spring."

Pete pointed to the bulletin board. I walked over to take a look. Sister Watson would be playing the part of Drusa, and Bishop Watson was going to play a rather frail-looking Parley P. Pratt. Narlette was going to be Thelma, and everyone else was listed as "insignificants."

"How appropriate." Elder Weeble laughed.

We took our mail and went home to prepare for the night's festivities.

Our home was really coming along, too. We had new windows to keep out the cold, and the week before, they had finally hooked up the electricity. It was so nice to have electric lighting again. We found a secondhand microwave in Virgil's Find. It worked great. We even had a small refrigerator where we could store food and keep our condiments consistently cold year round. If all went well, in the spring we would get running water. I hoped not to be here for that.

I liked my branch president calling, and I really did have good feelings for this town, but I was becoming increasingly restless. I was feeling less like a missionary and more like a permanent fixture. I needed out of here and on to something else. It wasn't right, me being here for so long. I would have considered it all a big mistake if not for the fact that President Clasp wrote and visited so often. Always he would reiterate how strongly he felt that I should stay right where I was. I kept thinking that there had to be someone here that only I could touch. So I had written out everyone's name on a big sheet of paper and consistently prayed over them, hoping that heaven would show me the way. So far heaven had left me alone.

I just wanted to be somewhere where we rode bikes and tracted outdoors. I wanted my mission to have two parts: the unusual part when I was put here, and the after-the-unusual part when I was put somewhere to serve as I had once envisioned I would.

I hardly knew any of the other elders in the mission. I had seen nothing of Tennessee except for Thelma's Way, Virgil's Find, and a little bit of Knoxville. My after-mission pictures were going to be sorely lacking—"and here's another shot of the rotting covered wagons, this time in the snow . . ."

"Do we have to wear our ties tonight?" Elder Weeble asked as we finished up our soup.

"Of course," I replied.

"Why would we wear ties to a haunted house?" he whined.

"Because we're missionaries."

"But it's Halloween. The whole point is not to look like what you are." Elder Weeble was speaking slowly, as if I might have trouble understanding.

"Forget it, Elder," I said.

Elder Weeble put his soup bowl in the big tub of water we had by the refrigerator. "I don't see why there has to be so many rules. 'Men are that they might have joy,'" he said, quoting his favorite scripture, and the only one he knew.

"Take it up with President Clasp," I said.

"I just might," Elder Weeble said boldly. "This mission needs some innovators."

I took the dishes out to the river and rinsed them off half-heartedly. I brought them back inside and set them up to dry. We then headed over to the festivities. It was still light, and snow fluttered as the ominous clouds scratched themselves, sending dandruff-sized flakes down through the air. As we walked through the meadow we passed groups of kids dressed up for Halloween. It looked as if most of them had chosen the cop-out ghost costume.

Paul was in the meadow as well, heckling all those who were heading to the festivities. We waved politely. He didn't return the gesture.

We walked back behind the Watsons' house and over to the improvised spook alley. Sister Watson was standing out front with what looked to be a glass fishbowl, collecting money from the line of people waiting to go in and be scared.

"Are we going in?" Elder Weeble asked me.

"I'm not sure," I replied, stepping up to Sister Watson.

"Good turnout," I commented on the long line of anxious patrons.

"Folks appreciate the effort we've put forth," she proudly said. "Should put us over the top as far as P.I.G. money is concerned. We'll get that Paul Leeper yet."

So far no one had actually been into the tarp-covered structure to be able to fully appreciate all of their efforts.

"This isn't going to give kids nightmares?" I asked her.

"The kids around these parts are accustomed to fear." It seemed like a logical reply.

"Is it appropriate for missionaries?" I asked.

Sister Watson scoffed as if she would never take part in any activity that was not appropriate for missionaries. We paid her four dollars and took our place in line. A few minutes later Tindy MacDermont parted a portion of the tarp and started ushering people in. Lupert Carver was the first to go into the haunted house. I expected to hear screaming or hollering coming from inside as he entered. But there was not a sound. What seemed like only a few seconds later, Lupert came around from the exit in the back holding a small dish of something and complaining.

"Is that it?"

Ed Washington quickly whisked Lupert away before he could say anything else. The next child to go in and come out looked a bit more frightened but still seemed dissatisfied. Every child after that had the same expression when they came out. And always they were carrying a small dish of something brown and a folded piece of paper. For those kids who could get a word in edgewise before Ed hustled them away, it was always, "That's it? That's the whole haunted house?"

Finally it was our turn. We were the first adults—well, semi-adults—to go through. I parted the tarp cautiously and crept inside. It was pitch black for a few seconds and then, as the tarp closed behind me, a light flashed on and there was old Bishop Watson sitting on a folding chair handing out pamphlets for the John Birch Society.

"Corruption is everywhere," he booed. "Beware."

Around the next corner was Toby Carver covered in ketchup and lying on a table. I watched him lick and taste himself when he thought we weren't looking. Just past him was Miss Flitrey serving up chocolate pudding from a big kettle. The kettle was labeled "mud."

"Have some dirt, my pretty," she said. Sister Lando was standing next to her, sporting her hat and cackling.

For the grand finale, Jerry Scotch sort of barked at us as Pete Kennedy escorted us out the back tarp.

I stepped back outside and just stood there, wearing the same expression as everyone else. P.I.G. had spent a week on that haunted house and that was all they could come up with. I looked at my John Birch pamphlet.

"Do you really know who your friends are?" it said across the front in bold.

Obviously not.

Elder Weeble came out complaining about the pudding.

"This stuff tastes like tar."

"What'd you think?" Ed Washington asked us.

"It was short," was all I could think of to say.

"But scary, right?" he added.

"In a sense," I replied.

"Are you going to eat your pudding?" he asked.

I handed him my pudding and walked off with my companion.

*****

Those who had been through the haunted house already, and those who weren't planning to ever go through, had gathered at the Watsons' home to drink cider and socialize. I was pretty familiar with the Watsons' home, due to the fact that we did all of our laundry over there. We walked in and took a seat on their couch. People sat around talking about the haunted house, the John Birch Society, the coming pageant, and Paul, as kids smeared pudding over everything the Watsons owned.

I sipped my cider, enjoying the conversations and voices that had grown familiar to me. I was comfortable here. I would have helped myself to a second glass of cider, but Briant Willpts came into the room and informed us that they had used that same cider to play bobbing for apples earlier in the evening, and had anyone seen his teeth.

I stared into the empty glass in my hand with new horror when we heard Sister Watson screaming outside.

"It's gone!" she was yelling. "It's gone!"

Everybody ran out to see what was going on.

"What's gone?" Brother Heck asked.

"The money," Sister Watson sobbed, falling to her rear on the porch and beginning to cry. Her wig slid to the back end of her head. "All of the money we collected. Gone. Gone. Gone."

"Can't be," Sister Heck insisted.

"But it is," she insisted back.

Money missing was something to be concerned about. There was no one in Thelma's Way who took money for granted. Sure, Leo seemed to always have enough, but even he still seemed to respect the almighty bill.

Grace's brother, Digby, pulled up just then on his motorcycle and unwrapped the Saran Wrap from around his head.

"Are you sure it's gone?" Pap Wilson asked Sister Watson.

"I looked everywhere," she wailed. "We were keeping the proceeds in Sister Lando's crystal ball, and I set it down to help. We were just cleaning up, pulling down the maze. I turned around and it was gone. The crystal ball was right where I'd put it, but the money inside it was gone."

"Who could have taken it?" I asked.

A giant, dimly lit mental light bulb cracked on in unison above the crowd's head.

Paul.

Everyone turned around.

As if on cue, there he was standing about fifty feet from the porch. He had been pestering everybody earlier, now he was suspect. He stared at us all in disbelief.

"What are you all looking at?" he asked in disgust, taking a couple steps backwards and away from us. "I didn't do anything. Truth is the wind that lets me soar."

These people would show him sore.

"Thief!" Briant yelled in response to Paul's wisdom.

"Where's the money?" old Pap Wilson demanded.

Paul didn't stick around to answer questions or dish out any more confusion. He raised his fist in defiance and took off running down to the meadow and towards the river.

Everyone stood there as if they were helpless. It was one thing to be outraged by what Paul had done. It was something else to actually exert effort to try to apprehend him.

"I'll get him," Digby yelled, jumping back onto his motorcycle and kicking it to life. Smoke burst from its rusty pipe. The crowd parted like the Red Sea, providing a place for him to cycle through.

Digby gallantly whipped out his roll of plastic Saran Wrap and haphazardly rolled a bunch of it around his head to protect his eyes. He looked like a clear mummy out for trick or treat. He revved his bike, nodded to the crowd with his now-matted noggin, and took off across the snow.

The chase was on. It was almost impossible to see Paul and Digby in the dark.

As luck would have it, Tindy MacDermont just happened to have her powerful flashlight with her. She flicked it on and spotlighted the spectacle, bright against the snow.

Paul was well over halfway across the meadow before Digby had even gotten started. If Paul could make it to the Girth River and onto a raft by the burnt bridge, escape would be certain. We watched as Digby closed the gap.

Digby's rusted motorcycle was no speed demon. It had a top speed of somewhere just above the double digits. So now as he sped across the meadow trying to catch Paul, it looked rather surreal, like slow motion. From where we all stood, we could see the back of Digby and the back of Paul even farther off as he ran like the wind.

Digby was closing in.

Paul was heading straight for the bridge, his arms flailing wildly as he ran.

Digby was getting closer still.

Narlette began to chant.

"Go, go, go, go," she repeated over and over.

Everyone began chanting along.

Paul was getting ever closer to the river. It looked as if Digby might not be able to catch him. We saw Paul glance over his shoulder, see Digby, and move even faster. Digby was not about to give up. He needed to lighten his load. He reached over his shoulder, pulled off his backpack, and threw it down. Then, in one swift move, Digby lifted both feet from the pedals and kicked his boots off and into the air.

His load now lighter, he closed in on Paul. I don't know exactly what we all thought Digby would do when he got to Paul. I guess he could have run him over, or jumped off and wrestled him to the ground. Not knowing somehow made the suspense even greater.

"Go, go, go, go, go," we all whispered.

He was so close now. Paul wasn't going to make it. We all watched the back of Digby's head as he went in for the kill. Digby looked strong and heroic as he gallantly pursued Paul, his Saran Wrapped head shining in the light of Tindy's focused flashlight. He sat up straight on his motorcycle as he moved in for the grab. He put out his left hand, reaching. Then the back of his head began to wobble. His shoulders slumped as he suddenly put his hand back on the handlebar.

Something was going wrong.

Digby was slowing down! We saw him sort of bob from side to side as he decelerated. Then in one fluid movement he tipped over, bike and all. A patch of oil smeared against the snow marking his spot. Paul jumped down on the bank, grabbed a raft, and took off across the thickening Girth.

"What happened?" Sister Watson yelled.

I took off running with Brother Heck towards the spot where Digby had collapsed. Elder Weeble was right behind us. I could see instantly what the problem was. In his haste, Digby had plastered Saran

Wrap around not only his eyes but also his nose and mouth, cutting off all air intake. I quickly pulled the wrap off of his head. He coughed and took in a huge gulp of air. He looked up at me.

"I almost had him," he whispered.

"Paul's fast," Brother Heck said, leaning over Digby and me, his hands on his knees.

I helped Digby to his feet and then let him lean on me as we crossed back over the meadow to the Watsons' place.

"I almost had him," Digby told his father.

"I'm right proud of you, son," Brother Heck said.

Leo wheeled the motorcycle back to the Watsons' porch and leaned it against the rail.

"Good chase," everyone said, patting Digby on the shoulder.

"What about the money?" Sister Watson cried.

"It's gone for now," Brother Heck said. "We'll give Paul a visit tomorrow."

"It'll be too late," Teddy Yetch moaned. "He'll have hid it up by then."

"Well, I for one ain't going to go stomping over to Paul's place right now," Brother Heck said. "Paul would shoot me and claim he couldn't see who I was."

"And to think I was ready to re-believe in him," Pete Kennedy said.

Once again Paul had botched everything. Everyone besides Elder Weeble and I shuffled back into the Watsons' home. I guess they were hoping to salvage some sense of celebration. In my mind it was too late for that.

Elder Weeble and I left the crowd and headed into the night.

## 25

# Open Mouth, Insert Future

Elder Weeble and I walked back across the meadow to the boardinghouse and sat down on the porch. It wasn't often that the boardinghouse was vacant. Usually locals were strewn through it long into the night. But tonight the party was somewhere else. I could hear faint voices still coming from the Halloween celebration across the meadow.

"Why are we stopping here?" Elder Weeble asked, after we had settled onto the porch.

"It's kind of a nice night," I replied.

"It's Halloween and I'm cold," he complained. "If I were back home in Colorado I'd be hanging out with my friends."

I just stared at him.

"What?" he finally said self-consciously.

"After all that's happened today, that's all you can say?" I asked bluntly. "Why'd you even come on a mission?"

It was Elder Weeble's turn to stare at me for a moment.

"I don't know," he finally said stubbornly. "I guess my brother went to Russia, my sister went to Australia, and I'm stuck here."

I appreciated the family history, but his dialogue didn't exactly answer my question.

"So you went on a mission because your brother went to Russia?"

"No," he insisted.

"Because your sister went to Australia?"

"Don't be dumb," he said. "I came on my mission because I was supposed to."

"So why don't you try to like it here?" I asked. "These people aren't so bad, if you leave out Paul."

"This place is a dump," Elder Weeble said.

I looked at the black sky and the distant sparks of scattered houses lighting up for the night. I smelled the air as if it were a fine stew simmering in front of my hungry stomach. I looked at the porch steps and observed the knife etchings carved into its wood.

"Feeble was he . . ."

I assume it was supposed to say "Feeble was here." Feeble must have become distracted before he was able to properly mar the porch. I knew people who were dead here. That really made me feel attached.

I had barely gotten to know Roswell and Feeble, but I still missed them. Of course, in so many ways Feeble still was here. Thelma was still here. No one's spirit ever seemed to leave this place. The meadow seemed to trap the souls of all who wandered in. I already knew I would leave a large chunk of myself when I left. Elder Weeble just couldn't see it.

"This place really isn't so bad," I reiterated.

"Give me a break, Elder," he mocked. "You're just confused from being here so long. Besides, you like it here because of your weird girlfriend."

"What?" I asked sharply.

"Your girlfriend, the redhead," he explained. "Hope, Chastity, whatever."

"Grace?"

Elder Weeble snickered.

"What about Grace?" I asked.

"I've heard things. It's all through the mission."

"What kind of things? I hardly even know her," I protested.

"That's not what Elder Sims said," Elder Weeble went on. "He said you used to meet with her in secret. Even Toby Carver said you two were caught walking alone in the woods. Sounds awful cozy to me. No wonder you never want to leave. Although I can't see what you see in that backwoods horse."

I hated Elder Weeble.

It was an awful thing to feel, but I just couldn't stand him any longer. I don't know why my emotions boiled to the surface so suddenly, but I had a feeling that talk of Grace had something to do with it. I had never done anything wrong or improper. I had never even had an improper thought about her. But heaven be scorned, I did feel something for her, and in that respect I had been open and honest with President Clasp. I had done nothing to be ashamed of.

I had left Lucy, the most gorgeous girl in Southdale, and I had discovered that the world was bigger than her and her perfect smile.

Now, as I watched Elder Weeble sit, trapped in his box of pity and misunderstanding, I was sick. His mean words were both stupid and wrong. Grace was no backwoods horse. She was a confusing painting that took time and knowledge to truly appreciate. I was going to dispute what he had so callously said, but once again he opened his big mouth.

"Let's hear you stick up for your girlfriend," he slurred.

"She's not my girlfriend and you know it," I argued. "I'm a missionary, for goodness sake."

"Yeah, right," he said, standing up and wiping the cold from off his seat.

I don't know why I didn't tear into Elder Weeble. I wanted to throw him to the ground and make him take it all back. I wanted to call him names and maybe hit him a few times. I wanted to stand up and say, "Yes, I like Grace, and no, I do not like you." But I didn't do any of these things. We were companions. We were stuck together. I was the senior companion and consequently the one that should act with more maturity and reason. Elder Weeble was just confused. I needed to make this missionary experience good for him. I had a responsibility. It would do no good to drag things out. So I did the expedient thing and laid it to rest.

"Listen," I began slowly. "I do not like Grace. She's just another part of this crazy town. We're here to do a job and that's it. We can leave this place better than we found it, or worse. If we want it to be better, then you should at least act like you care."

Elder Weeble said nothing.

I stood up next to him.

"Happy Halloween," I joked.

Voices drifted from across the meadow as the snowy ground lay silent and clean. The festivities were still in full swing at the Watson house. I felt my heart slump as my tired feet and soul recognized the end of another day.

"I'm tired," Elder Weeble informed me.

We headed for home.

26

# Painfully Marred

Grace had not meant to hear. She had been walking through the cemetery when she saw Trust and his companion make their way back and sit down on the dark porch of the boardinghouse. She crept up to the wall and listened as they spoke. She couldn't resist.

Grace had been wrong about Trust. Very wrong. How had her heart permitted this to happen? Grace's one ally, her own intuition, had turned on her, betrayed her, left her alone. Grace could not explain the feelings she had for Trust, and she could not brush them away; she knew there was something more at stake. It had seemed at times as if Trust had come to Thelma's Way just to give her hope.

So much hope. So much hype.

"I do not like Grace."

Five words from Trust's lips.

Grace stood there, her back against the side of the boardinghouse, her heart lying cold with the snow.

"I do not like Grace."

Five words. Nothing else.

It was just that she hoped for something more.

27

# Sleigh Bells Ring. I Ain't Listening

Month Seventeen

Snow fell like shaved cheese—slices, wedges, and gobs—mixing together on the ground, and piling up as if God were Italian and earth was his lasagna. Just *grazie.* We wouldn't be going anywhere soon. I looked over at Elder Weeble. He scrunched his face up against the window.

"Great," he said, raising a fist and pretending to curse Mother Nature.

It was ten o'clock Christmas morning, and the prospect of spending my day cooped up alone with Elder Weeble didn't exactly excite me. The snow was at least a couple of feet deep and still coming down. So much for Christmas cheer this year.

I was still in Thelma's Way, celebrating my second and last mission Christmas. We had put up a tiny tree in the corner of the house, and a few small gifts sat beneath it waiting to be opened. We had planned to spend the day at the Hecks' home. They had invited us over for food and Christmas company. I couldn't help being excited about the prospect of possibly seeing Grace. Surely she would spend Christmas with her family. I had bought a little secondhand book in Virgil's Find to give to her. She had gone into deep seclusion the last couple of months, and I was simply hoping that my small Christmas present might make her feel welcome.

Yes, those were my intentions. Purely concerned.

The snow kept coming.

"Some Christmas," Elder Weeble whined, thrusting himself upon his bed in anger. "If I were home in Colorado, I'd be having a blast."

I pulled a chair up to the window and stared at the falling skies.

"Let's go do something," Elder Weeble complained.

The wind was really howling now, making the visibility about three feet.

"We can't go out in this," I replied.

"If I was in Colorado I would," he snapped.

I thought about starting a fist fight with my companion just for the sake of having something to do. Heaven knows he irritated me enough to bring me to blows.

I opened my backpack up and pulled out Grace's gift.

"Merry Christmas, Elder," I said, handing it to him.

"I didn't get you anything," he fumbled, suddenly gracious.

"No big deal," I replied, waving the whole thing off. "No big deal."

# 28

# SPRING RUNOFF

## Month Twenty

I had never seen a more beautiful time or place. This year spring seemed to bring more than just renewed life, it brought new colors and textures. Even the air seemed freshly pressed and packaged. The Girth ran stronger than ever, and the meadow was alive with tiny green limbs and speckled yellow faces. The children seemed older and wiser, and the adults less absurd. The dirt seemed richer, the houses nicer, and the season longer.

Oh, and by the way, I had been released as branch president.

I was now just a regular missionary again. My days in Thelma's Way were numbered. I had not actually received word concerning my transfer, but I knew it would happen soon. I had served in Thelma's Way for twenty months.

I was grateful for my time as branch president. It had taught me a lot. The Lord had allowed me to really care for these people. I hoped they would remember me. And I had reason to believe I had worked my way into the local lore thanks to the Nippy Ward Incident, as it had become known.

A little while back I had finally talked the mission into putting out the money to buy hard-of-hearing Nippy a hard-of-hearing hearing aid. Nippy had been faithful in coming to church every week, and I felt that we owed it to her to help her hear what was being said. The mission put up most of the cash, and the branch members got together and tossed in the rest. We bought her a really nice one—an unbelievably tiny device that was supposed to let her hear every interesting, and uninteresting, thing we said without hardly being visible in her ear. The Sunday after we had gotten it, we all met at church early to make the presentation. When Nippy came in we yelled "surprise." It was loud enough for her to hear. Then I approached her and presented her with the little piece of technical wizardry. I put the tiny thing in her palm and promised her it would help her to hear. Nippy smiled, nodded, thanked me profusely, and then, before I could stop her, she swallowed the thing. Hundreds of dollars down the throat. She thought it was some sort of super hearing pill.

I don't think Nippy ever fully realized what had happened, but she graciously pretended that the pill had had a positive effect. Now she nodded with much more vigor. I knew that incident would not soon be forgotten. That, and maybe the job fair that I had put on.

I had wanted to help the members better their lot in life by teaching them how to find work and instilling in them a desire to be self-sufficient. I invited some of the more established members from Virgil's Find to come and talk to us about work habits and share their secrets for procuring a good job. It actually went pretty well. Average-looking Jerry Scotch, however, interrupted the speakers a lot, butting in with suggestions. I guess he thought his steady job at the Corndog Tent made him an expert on the subject. His suggestion about taping a piece of licorice to your resume as a treat for whoever would read it was certainly a novel idea. Well, the long and the short of it was that Pete

Kennedy actually got a job as an exterminator in Virgil's Find. Later, of course, he did get fired when it was discovered he had been spraying the funeral home with his eyes closed, scared he might see something that would unsettle him. His indiscriminate spraying had killed a lot of expensive rose bushes and ruined a good portion of wallpaper. But the point was that being assertive brought results. I hoped he would remember the principle. Even if he never worked again.

Elder Weeble had given way to my latest companion. Elder Staples was from Texas, and he was big. His shoulders barely fit through our door. He had big hands, big feet, and a big voice. He had an appetite that an all-you-can-eat buffet would be hard pressed to fill. He was writing to about twenty girls back home, and talked realistically about how he would someday play quarterback for the Dallas Cowboys. He was constantly calling me "Sport." When I went over the "Elder" rule with him, he began calling me "Elder Sport."

He liked to look in the mirror. Actually, he liked to look at anything reflective. Polished shoes, silverware, glass, he wasn't too particular, as long as the image reflecting back was his own. He worked hard enough, but he also enjoyed playing dumb pranks on the locals. When we knocked on someone's door he would turn around so that his back would be facing them when they opened the door. He liked to tell people that he was from China and a member of the U.S. shuffleboard team. He liked to play games like "Got Your Nose," "Your Shoe's Untied," and "Button, Button." He had wavy blond hair and blue eyes that were shallow and gleaming. He didn't like the fact that I was senior companion and was rather vocal about it. We were working to make our partnership productive.

Grace's father was put in as branch president. He had come a long way. Toby Carver was his first counselor, and Leo Tip his second. They were a good team.

The work was going well. We still had not recovered as many inactive Mormons as I had hoped we would, but the ones who had hung around had grown stronger. On a sad note, Bishop Watson had passed away a few days after Christmas. He went peacefully in his sleep. We laid him to rest alongside his predecessors in the Watson family mausoleum.

Sister Watson mourned for an appropriate time over the death of her husband. Then she lost herself in preparations for the upcoming sesquicentennial pageant. With no husband to hold her back she was moving forward with great effort.

I had not seen Grace since before Halloween. She seemed to have disappeared. Brother Heck said that even he and his wife hardly saw her. She came by to help her mother with the costumes for the pageant, but that was about it. The Hecks didn't know what she did with the rest of her time. I was tempted to seek her out, but I knew that would not be right. Besides, with my poor sense of direction, I wasn't sure I could find her place again. Toby Carver had seen her a few times on the path to Virgil's Find, and Leo said she stopped by every once in a while to visit his dogs. When I thought about leaving Thelma's Way, my thoughts always circled back to Grace.

I had even written my mother and dropped Grace's name. I had mentioned that she seemed nice, and that I thought highly of her. Two weeks later I received a copy of *The Miracle of Forgiveness* in the mail. Mom wasn't taking chances.

With Bishop Watson dead, and the leading role in *All Is Swell* now up for grabs, Paul Leeper had taken new interest in the town pageant. Despite what Sister Watson might think of him, he demanded the right to star in the show as the only other male in town with the spiritual charisma and presence enough to represent Parley P. Pratt. He took it very seriously. He even said that since the lead male was Parley *P.* Pratt, the part should go to him, seeing how Parley's middle name was Paul. I informed him that Parley's real middle name was Parker. Paul insisted that in German "Parker" meant "Great Paul." Apparently he now saw the pageant as a way for him to get his message about seeing the finger to a wider audience than even he had originally conceived. The world was his stage, and he was ready to act on it.

But, of course, it was for naught. Sister Watson said there was no way on earth that she would ever consent to a thief like Paul having anything to do with such a sacred enterprise.

When it became clear that Sister Watson would not give in, Paul changed his tune.

"I wouldn't be caught dead in such a silly, stupid show, anyway," he said. "The real Parley P. Pratt would roll over in his grave to know you were representing his life in a pageant. May the winds of disgrace visit your commode."

Sister Watson stood her ground. Pulling her wig down over her eyes, she bore solemn witness that, on the contrary, outdoor pageants had served a critical role in Church history. Each of the centennial parades in Salt Lake City had featured pageants. And just because Parley P. Pratt or Brigham Young had never been in a pageant didn't mean they wouldn't have leaped at the opportunity had it been presented. Brigham Young was reportedly quite a dancer.

Paul said she was full of hot air and Sister Watson challenged him to a duel. Well, not a duel, really, but a public debate on the subject of pageants. Paul agreed, and a date was set.

The town was abuzz. Finally, Sister Watson and Paul would go toe to toe, tongue to tongue, and testimony to testimony in the middle of Thelma's Way. There was some concern about Sister Watson taking on so much so close to the big pageant, but she felt strongly that she must do it. The time had come to put Paul in his place, P.I.G. money or no P.I.G. money.

The afternoon before the big debate, Elder Staples and I slipped out to finish canvassing the very last section of Thelma's Way that I had not yet gotten to. It was a portion of forest between Thelma's Way and Virgil's Find. I felt like once I had really gone through this piece of land then I could leave feeling as if I had done all I possibly could.

Elder Staples led the way. We found a couple of homes. One was vacant, the other was occupied by a hermit named Melvin who claimed to have known Joseph Smith personally.

"Used to bowl together."

When I suggested that perhaps he knew another Joseph Smith besides the one who had restored the gospel, he got offended.

"Nope, knew the real one."

I kindly pointed out the fact that had he really known Joseph Smith then he, Melvin, would have to be at least a hundred and fifty years old. Melvin simply said that the little bit of extra weight he carried around helped push out his wrinkles and make him look younger.

Melvin wasn't interested in ever coming back to church. He claimed that Joseph cheated at bowling and that he wanted no part of a religion that condoned that kind of behavior.

We checked the back forest line of the area and found one more home. A young kid answered the door and invited us in. I recognized him from the meadow. I had seen him a number of times playing on the wagons.

"My mother's an actress," he said as we sat down.

"Wow," Elder Staples replied. "I'm impressed."

"Is your mother home?" I asked.

The kid ran off without answering.

A couple of minutes later the actress, his mother, came out. It appeared she mainly starred in parts requiring frumpy-looking backwoods leading ladies. She had a robe on and curlers in her hair. She sat down on the chair across from us.

We introduced ourselves and asked if she was familiar with the Mormon church.

She was. Her deceased husband had been a member.

"You're not a member?" I asked, seeking clarification.

"No," she answered.

"You're positive?"

She nodded.

I thought I was going to hyperventilate. Here, before me, sat a true-to-life nonmember—a real rarity in this hidden pocket of Tennessee. I think I was most jealous of other elders in this mission because they had so many nonmembers to work with. Well, we had one now.

"I'm a born again," she informed us.

Hallelujah.

We slowly questioned her making sure she hadn't simply forgotten that somewhere down the line she had been baptized a Mormon.

She had not.

Her nine-year-old son, Greg, was not a member either. Elder Staples had not put in the kind of time in Thelma's Way that I had. Consequently, he was not as overjoyed as me. Sure there was a chance she would never join the church. But at the moment, she was a possibility. She was a single nonmember mother. Her name was Judy Bickerstaff, and she worked part-time in Virgil's Find as a secretary for a small business. Of course, as her son had pointed out earlier, she aspired to one day be an actress. Her son, Greg, attended school in Thelma's Way. According to Judy, she and Miss Flitrey were fairly good friends. I couldn't understand why Miss Flitrey had never told us about this good nonmember friend of hers before.

Greg played with some toys on the floor as we got to know Judy. He set up action figures on my knees so that he could shoot them down with his dart gun. One figure caught my eye. It was a little metal man. I recognized it from someplace. I held onto it and studied it as we talked. There was a name etched into the bottom. "Martin Calypso."

"Where did you get this?" I finally asked Greg.

"Lupert gave it to me," he replied, snatching it back.

"Lupert Carver?" I asked.

Greg nodded. "He got it from a dead man."

Feeble.

I remembered seeing Lupert pick it up after Feeble dropped it in the dirt all those months ago. It was one of Feeble's "Great Men of the World" pewter figures.

"Martin Calypso," I said aloud. "It sounds so familiar."

"Whatever," Elder Staples replied. "It's just a toy."

Greg ran off, bored by us, and Judy invited us to dinner in three days and promised she would at least consider listening to the lessons. When we finally left their place, Elder Staples was properly excited. I was excited, too, but there was something about the name Martin Calypso that made me somber.

"Get over it, Sport," Elder Staples said as we walked back home.

It was early evening, the day before the big debate.

We had found a potential investigator.

Judy Bickerstaff.

Martin Calypso.

I hardly slept that night.

I woke up Elder Staples at four-thirty in the morning and told him to get dressed. We were going to Virgil's Find.

# 29

# Food Flight

By the time Elder Staples and I got back from Virgil's Find, Thelma's Way was primed for the afternoon debate. There was already a crowd gathering in the meadow.

Two long banquet tables had been set up in the meadow next to the rotting pioneer wagons and not far from the nearly completed pageant stage. One table had two chairs, one for Sister Watson and one for Paul; the other was covered with food that folks had brought for the potluck that would follow the debate. President Heck was actually wearing a tie and standing in front of the tables trying to look official. Sister Watson was working the crowd, shaking hands and patting backs. It was a big day.

Out in the meadow, Wad was sitting next to Miss Flitrey, CleeDee was lounging on a blanket with Leo, and Teddy Yetch and Sister Lando were selling extremely moist looking pre-debate pineapple brownies. I watched Digby Heck pull up on his motorcycle, unwrap his eye protection, then use the same sheet of Saran Wrap to cover one of the brownies for later. Kids ran around, and adults brought down lawn chairs and tree stumps to sit on. Old Pap Wilson and considerably younger Sybil Porter dragged out a couple of cinder blocks from the boardinghouse and made a few benches by laying boards across them. Nippy sat down in a folding chair and prepared to nod. The air filled with anticipation.

The scheduled starting time for the debate soon passed, and Paul had not yet arrived. Briant Willpts offered to play the part of Paul and debate Sister Watson himself. Sister Watson declined the offer. She would wait for the real thing.

The afternoon sun warmed the tops of our heads and shoulders as we sat ringed around the rosy looking at Sister Watson. Smugness seeped from her smile as she glanced about, feeling like maybe she had already won. President Heck shrugged his shoulders and looked to Leo Tip for the time. Leo didn't actually wear a watch, but CleeDee did. In fact, it was rumored that the real reason Leo had begun going out with CleeDee was simply because she wore a watch.

Whatever the reason for their first date, they were now the talk of the town. Word was they would be getting married in the Atlanta Temple sometime in July. That would be after my mission, but I had decided I would fly back if it happened.

Leo looked at CleeDee, and CleeDee glanced at her watch. Words were whispered and then Leo declared Paul officially late.

Ed Washington and his mother got up as if to leave. People shook their heads, disgusted with Ed's lack of patience. Ed's mother made his excuses for him.

"Ed's got some chores to do," she explained.

Poor Ed.

From the standing position Ed spotted someone down by the river coming their way. The crowd fell silent and parted to let him through. He was dressed all in black and strutting.

"It's Paul," Ed said, stating the overobvious.

Any and all wind died and the sun clicked things up two notches.

Paul stepped silently up to President Heck and nodded. President Heck answered with a similar nod. Paul took his seat at the table next to Sister Watson, and the circle of spectators closed in around them.

President Heck cleared his throat as Teddy Yetch popped open an umbrella for shade. Everyone glared at her, filled with shade envy. I saw Toby Carver try to scoot closer to her and procure himself some cover.

"A few rules," President Heck said. "There's no need to swear, 'ceptin someone says something really profound. In which case a respectful, 'I'll be darned' is perfectly acceptable.

"In the spirit of fairness," he continued, "we will let Sister Watson go first because she's a woman.

"Each person will be given a certain amount of time to speak their mind," President Heck said. Then he paused, using *his* mind to remember what amount of time that was. "I think a couple minutes a question is appropriate. Leo will be our official timekeeper."

Leo lifted up CleeDee's arm, showing all the watch he would be using.

"And just so as we're all in the know, the stated purpose of this debate is to find out if, given the chance, Parley P. Pratt would have acted a part in our pageant," President Heck explained. "I'm assumin' he would have played himself."

Sister Watson nodded her approval. President Heck signaled Toby Carver, who blew a whistle.

The sun was warm. The sky was clear. The debate was on.

Sister Watson turned to Paul and shuffled a few papers in front of her. She adjusted her reading glasses and sniffed through her nose. She pondered and looked as if she were going to ask a well-thought-out question.

Looks can be deceiving. She went right for the jugular . . .

"Why should anyone believe anything you say about pageants since you were the one who stole the Book of Mormon?" Her lips had barely moved.

Everyone sat there, stunned. The debate had hardly begun, and Sister Watson had issued what seemed to be a certain death blow.

Paul didn't flinch. "I didn't steal anything," he replied.

"That's a lie," Teddy Yetch yelled out from the crowd.

There was no rebuke from President Heck, our unbiased official. Sister Watson smiled.

"Why did you steal the P.I.G. money?" Sister Watson fired round two.

"I didn't steal your dirty money," Paul replied. "I never stole anything."

"That's a lie also," Teddy yelled out again.

I saw Toby Carver begin making a noose out of his ace bandage.

"Where were you the night the Book of Mormon was stolen?" Sister Watson probed.

"I don't know. That was well over two years ago," Paul sniffed.

"Funny how your memory is so selective," Sister Watson jabbed.

The crowd *woooooed.*

Pete Kennedy stood up in the third row. "Paul, you 'member when we caught that big deer that turned out to just be Geoff's dog?"

Paul nodded.

"That was seven years ago," Pete added.

"Ten, actually," Paul corrected.

"Well, if you can remember ten years ago then how come you cain't remember two?" Pete craned his head around, startled by his own insight.

The crowd began to murmur.

"Thing being . . ." Paul tried to explain.

Leo held up his hand indicating two minutes was up.

"Next question," President Heck said. "Paul?"

Paul tried to collect himself. He stood to speak.

"No fair standing," Jerry Scotch shouted out. "Makes Sister Watson look short."

President Heck knitted his brow. Paul sat down again.

"Thing is," Paul began. "I never stole nothing. Are these the hands of a thief?" he asked, gently spreading his palms before him. Sister Watson sort of opened her mouth, but Paul's words continued to fill the air. "True enough, these are the hands of an imperfect man."

Some of the spectators started licking their lips. Paul seemed ready for confession.

"But these imperfect hands," he continued, "have held infants that were sick, pulled friends out of predicaments, and paddled across the Girth in service. Take a good look at these hands. Respect the service they have dished up. Pull up a chair and feast from my sacrifice." Paul took out a hanky from his shirt pocket and started to wipe his eyes. "There is something I have not told you all," Paul continued, misty-eyed. "But I feel you have aged in wisdom."

The compliment melted like chocolate over the crowd.

"When I was in Rome," Paul went on, "all those years ago, I experienced something that I was told not to share. The heavens forbade me to share it with you. But it was revealed to me this morning as I was shucking corn that now is the time to let you know. I've been given clearance to impart the truth . . ."

Leo's hand went up.

"Next question. Sister Watson?" President Heck said.

Paul cursed himself, aware of how close he had come to swinging the crowd emotionally to his side. This two-minute time thing would be the death of him.

Sister Watson stood and looked down at Paul. She knew he had gained ground as it was. She pulled out all the stops. "Did you or did you not try to kill Digby Heck?" She was passionate, at least as passionate as a person can be without moving her lips.

The crowd started to murmur again and craned their necks looking back at Digby.

Paul's tiny, poorly arranged face puckered up.

"I . . . I never meant to hurt Digby," he claimed.

"Never meant to, meant to," Sister Watson repeated. "Just like Cain never meant to hurt Abel."

Folks wiped at their brows in awe of Sister Watson's powerful debating style. It was obvious from her last question that she had done research on the matter of murder.

Miss Flitrey raised her hand. "Do you really think it's necessary to drag the Bible into this?" she asked.

Sister Patty Heck, who was sitting behind Miss Flitrey and was still sore over her teaching her children about ape genealogy, shifted in her chair and knocked Miss Flitrey's legs out from under her. "Stop trying to remove the Bible from everyone's lives," Patty accused.

Miss Flitrey turned around with a raging face and said, "Nice skirt," snidely to Sister Heck, making fun of her homemade clothing.

Well, not everyone could afford to shop the Virgil's Find garage sales like Miss Flitrey. Her teacher's salary allowed her to live a little too comfortable for most folks. Besides, everyone knew that Wad was dropping a lot of his haircutting money on her these days. Yes, at the moment Miss Flitrey was the closest thing the town had to having its own Kennedy. Sure, Leo was well off, but he didn't flaunt it like she did. And yes, Pete actually bore the Kennedy name, but Pete was Pete, and Pete was poor.

Toby Carver bravely stood up for Sister Heck and her homemade clothing. "I think her skirt looks right smart," he said, tugging his beard.

"How would you know if anything was smart?" Miss Flitrey bit back.

"Hey!" President Heck yelled. "This debate is for Paul and Sister Watson. If you two want to schedule time to have your own argument, that's fine. Although I must say right now that my wife is right, and Flitrey is wrong."

Miss Flitrey looked at Wad, wondering if he was going to stand up and defend his woman.

Wad remained bunched down.

President Heck brought things back to the debate. "Paul's up. Next question."

"Wait a minute, he never answered my last question," Sister Watson argued.

"Your time's up," Brother Heck officiated. "Paul's turn."

"You can't count your wife and flighty Flitrey's squabbling as my time," Sister Watson protested.

"Rules is rules," President Heck snorted.

Sister Watson sat back, steaming like a bowl of blushing chowder. In the spring heat her wig was starting to slide to the back of her head.

"Can I speak now?" Paul asked, flicking the tip of his nose.

President Heck nodded.

"First off, let me say I would never harm Digby. He and I are kindred spirits. In fact, he reminds me of my trip to Rome."

Nice segue.

"Quick count," Paul continued. "How many of you here have ever been to Rome before?"

Narlette raised her hand, but she was ignored.

"I guess that makes me the expert," Paul bragged. "You folks have no idea what I'm talking about, do you?"

Touché.

"Now listen up," he said. "I am going to share with you what happened and those of you who are touched enough to understand will know I speak the truth." Paul paused and breathed deeply. He was going to say it all in one breath.

"When I saw the finger of Thomas I also had a vision about how you all would one day doubt my words and try and drag me down and have this debate and not let me be in the pageant and persecute me and then finally come to understand my position on heavenly and important and mystical things." He sucked in air. "So what I am about to tell you has been prophesied. The ghost of Thomas . . ."

Once again Leo's hand went up.

Paul was furious. "Why can't you allow a visionary man to properly prophesy?" Paul demanded, his big arguing mouth taking up the bulk of his face. "Blasphemy is your ally."

"The floor is now Sister Watson's," President Heck answered, motioning for Paul to simmer.

"So, Paul," she began. "Why did—"

"Maybe we should let Paul finish what he was saying," Ed Washington's mother interrupted. "Sounded sort of important."

We all stared at Ed's mom.

"Sister Watson has the floor," Jerry Scotch argued, as if he knew what having the floor meant.

"Don't you mouth off at my mother," Ed Washington demanded, showing more spirit than I had yet seen him have.

Jerry Scotch smirked. Ed lunged at Jerry, but his mother stopped him.

President Heck waved frantically at Toby Carver, signaling him to blow his whistle. Well, Toby was too busy offering Teddy Yetch money so he could sit in her shade to notice Brother Heck.

Paul pounded on the table. "Silence!" he demanded.

Everyone shut up.

"I have come down from my home," he huffed. "I have crossed the Girth River and taken the time to come to this farce. Your disrespect is a tube full of pasty ill will. I decree that I will be patient no more."

Paul stood.

"President Heck here," he pointed, "and his Mafia missionaries have had control of this valley for too long. Look at what they have brought you. The amount of Christian love contained in this meadow could be measured in a thimble's thimble."

Most of the crowd looked at their fingers, sort of pinching the size a thimble's thimble would be.

"Look at me," Paul blared. "I am an agent of prosperity sent to dwell among you. Your attention is necessary to your salvation."

Everyone now focused on Paul. In fact, they focused so intently that they didn't realize Sister Watson was not only standing up next to him, she was swinging one of Teddy's empty brownie pans at his head. I guess she wanted to speed up the debate.

"Sister Watson!" I yelled, pointing at her.

I had hoped to prevent her from hitting Paul. Instead, my pointing caused Paul to turn towards her. Sister Watson whumped Paul square in the face, the brownie pan ringing out through the meadow. Even Sister Watson was stunned by what she had done. Paul fluttered and then fell flimsily onto the table in front of them. President Heck ran to him and lifted his head. Because of Paul's already discombobulated facial features I couldn't tell if Sister Watson had done any damage. Toby undid his Ace bandage noose and sidled up to Paul. Paul stirred. He was all right.

I figured it was time for me to stand and tell the world what I knew.

"Paul didn't take the book," I yelled out.

"What book?" President Heck asked, the entire ring of spectators now looking at me.

"*The* book," I clarified. "The Book of Mormon that Parley P. Pratt gave Thelma's Way."

Everyone kept staring.

I walked up to the table. "I know for a fact that Paul Leeper did not take the Book of Mormon."

"Listen, Elder Williams," Toby said. "We like you and all, but I don't think this is really any of your business."

"Yeah," said Briant. "You're a good kid, but you ain't stock. Everyone knows it was Paul that stole the book. Just ask Jerry."

All eyes focused on Jerry. "*I* think he took it," Jerry said sheepishly.

"If he took it, then how come I have it?" I unzipped my rainbow backpack and pulled out the first edition Book of Mormon with the special Parley P. Pratt inscription—the very same one Paul was accused of stealing all those years ago.

Everyone gasped. Children cowered behind their parents. People covered their mouths.

"I told you!" Paul hollered. "I told you I didn't take it."

Pete Kennedy yelled out, "It was Elder Williams all the time. Let's get him." He reached for his gun, or at least where his gun would be had he been allowed to bring it.

I think they were considering a lynching, but Sister Watson spoke out. "Elder Williams wasn't even here when it was stolen," she said, staring at the book in amazement. "He wasn't even on his mission yet."

Everyone paused to think about this. It was worth considering.

Elder Staples tried to help me. "My companion didn't steal this book," he said standing. "I just saw him buy it."

"He bought it!" Pete yelled, still furious. "Let's get him."

President Heck held his hands up to silence the crowd.

"Maybe you have some explaining to do, Elder Williams," he said to me. The crowd hushed. I set the book on the table in front of me.

"I know that this will come as a great surprise and disappointment to all of you, but Roswell Ford took your book."

"Come on," Briant Willpts booed. "How dumb do you think we are?"

I prayed he wouldn't force me to say.

"It's true," I argued. "Roswell knew everyone would blame Paul, since Paul had prophesied that bad things were going to befall the Mormons, and Roswell needed the money. He stole the book and sold it to his cousin Stubby in Virgil's Find."

"Roswell's dead," Sister Yetch yelled out. "We shouldn't be speaking 'bout the rotted like this."

I hadn't considered that translated beings actually rotted.

"Teddy's right," Old Pap said. "Disrespectful through and through."

I threw out my next bit of news.

"Roswell's not dead," I shouted. "His cousin saw him last week. In fact, I have reason to believe he also stole the P.I.G. money."

Everyone's eyes turned red as they glared at me. Elder Staples stepped right up next to me and flexed his chest. I guess he was acting as my security.

"Now, Elder Williams," Toby cautiously said. "It's one thing to tell wild stories, but it's an entirely different deal to slander the translated name of Roswell and Feeble."

"You people have sinned," Paul spoke up. "You have misjudged me and now as the truth rears its big fat head you will see me as your superior."

Jerry Scotch had had enough. He jumped up and ran towards Paul, ready to grab his neck. Brother Heck held him back.

"People, listen up," he demanded, struggling against Jerry. "There has to be an explanation for all this."

"Yeah, Elder Williams is lying," Briant Willpts shouted.

"I'm telling you the truth," I insisted. "Roswell sold the book to his cousin Stubby for two hundred and fifty dollars. Stubby then sold it to a woman who collects old books so as to appear educated. I bought it back from her this morning."

The crowd fell hushed. I couldn't tell why until Wad spoke up.

"Two hundred and fifty dollars for that old thing. That's a fortune!"

"Two hundred and fifty dollars," I repeated.

President Heck picked up the book. "Let me get this straight," he said. "This thing's worth two hundred and fifty dollars?"

"Actually," I said, "this book is worth far more than that. A man back in my hometown bought a first edition Book of Mormon for twenty thousand dollars. And this one here's in better shape, and it's signed by Parley P. Pratt. I bet you could get a lot more for it."

Everyone was standing now.

"Twenty thousand dollars?" Sister Watson whispered in unbelief. "I thought all that book had was spiritual value."

President Heck set it back down on the table as if it were a hot coal. Then he reconsidered his actions and picked it back up. He held it tightly to his chest.

The crowd started to drool. I watched the gears in the noggins around me calculate what they could do with twenty thousand dollars. The wind picked up, blowing honesty, decency, and Christian consideration out of the meadow, replacing them with a triple helping of half-crazed greed.

Sister Watson moved first. She grabbed at the book, wrenching it from President Heck. By then, Briant Willpts was swinging his cane at Sister Watson. She dropped the book to put her hands up. The book had barely hit the table before Jerry Scotch clapped it up and turned to run. Sister Lando stuck one of her sturdy legs out and tripped Jerry. The book went flying though the air. It landed on Leo and CleeDee's blanket. For a moment, everyone just stared at it lying there. Then in one collective grunt they dove for it. Hands flew, hair whipped, and legs kicked. I stood there speechless. I turned to Elder Staples to see what he was doing to help calm the situation. He was no help; he had Paul on the ground trying to pin him down. He wasn't about to pass up this chance to wrestle an apostate.

"Elder!" I hollered.

I held up my hands foolishly, thinking it would help. And, just at that moment, Teddy surfaced from the pile of scrapping fighters with the book in hand. She only had a second. She had to get rid of it or get toppled. I guess she took my hands being up as a signal because she tossed it to me.

Frustrated and gunless, Pete Kennedy picked up a plate full of potato salad and launched it at me. Warm pieces of potatoes and eggs flew through the air.

"My salad!" Sister Yetch yelled, as if she had given birth to it. She broke from the pack and dove over the food table towards Pete. Everyone else dog-piled me. Hands, knees, elbows, and feet danced upon me like popping rocks. I was being kneaded like a ball of dough. Those who couldn't get to me and the book started throwing food at me and each other. The air was thick with handfuls of casseroles, cookies, and homemade confections.

For a good five minutes food and feet trampled and flew over me. Then one by one people dropped from the fight, falling to the ground to lie by me in exhaustion. A few people crawled off and away from us all. I watched Digby get hit in the eye and Leo get tackled by Paul. Old Pap Wilson beaned Wad with a few franks, and Frank Porter nailed Geoff Titter with a tin of Patty Heck's shortbread cookies. Eventually everyone was down.

I sat up and surveyed the scene. It looked like a battlefield, one big messy mound of people.

"Who has the Book of Mormon?" I asked looking around for it.

"Patty took it from me."

"I saw Pap with it."

"I never touched it."

"Just great," President Heck complained. "It could be anywhere now. I saw at least twenty people wander off when the food started to fly."

"So then why worry?" I sighed. "It will show up."

"Twenty-thousand dollars," Sister Watson whined.

"Well, I don't have it," Paul insisted, trying to pull some frosting from his hair.

"Just great," President Heck said again.

I lay back down and listened to the heavy breathing of my war-weary brothers and sisters.

"So Roswell's not dead," President Heck eventually said as he lay there recovering next to me.

"Nope."

"I thought I had seen him a couple months back in the deep forest," Toby muttered. "But I didn't say anything out of respect."

"He's somewhere," I replied.

Sister Watson was on her hands and knees looking for her wig. When she finally found it, it was covered in pudding. But the chocolate treat seemed to work well as an adhesive. So she slapped it back on her head and took a seat on one of the overturned cinder blocks. We all looked pretty ridiculous.

Sister Lando was the first to laugh.

I sat up and saw her body jiggle as she lay there violently snickering. Teddy laughed next, her old cackle filling the air like the food had previously. Ed joined in the jovial giggling, and then the rest of us.

We laughed for a good ten minutes, wiping our eyes and trying to catch our breath. We laughed and picked food off each other. Even Paul was enjoying the group snicker till Sister Watson shot him a wounding glance. It was okay for others to laugh at her hair, but not Paul.

We picked up the tables and cleaned up the meadow. I was wiping what looked to be some sort of jam off of my white shirt, looking down at the ground, when I noticed two beautiful feet step into my view. The feet were adorned by skimpy sandals that left little to the imagination.

Could it be?

I looked up slowly, hoping beyond hope that these two feet were connected to who I thought they were. My eyes stopped at the face of Grace. She wasn't smiling, but she wasn't frowning, either. Everything continued to go on around us as we stared at each other. Folks cleaned up and picked at themselves, oblivious to the two of us.

"You," I finally stated.

"Me," she replied, her red hair pulled back into a tangled ponytail.

I didn't know what else to say. She popped into my life at the most unusual times. I couldn't believe she had just walked up to me, planted her feet, and stayed there to let me speak with her. I was almost convinced that the feelings I had had for Grace were one-sided and unfounded. But here she stood, and the spring light made her appear more splendid than all the flowers nature could push forth. Her thin dress was long and blowing in the gentle wind. She looked taller than I had remembered. Her green eyes fluttered with the breath of life.

"Where have you been?" I asked.

Grace smiled by accident. She quickly corrected herself. "Why?" she asked.

"I just . . . well . . . I, you make me so nervous," I said, leaking more honesty than I had intended.

Grace took a step back.

"I make you nervous?" she questioned, putting her hand to her chest.

Maybe it was the springtime. Maybe it was the teasing of warm weather. Maybe it was the knowledge that I wouldn't be here for too much longer. Maybe it was Grace. Whatever the reason, for the first time in over twenty months, I felt completely alive. I had been relatively happy the last year or so. Thelma's Way had even felt like home a couple of times. But completeness had been fleeting. At the moment, however, my soul was a sanctuary, and contentment was grazing on the fields of my heart. I was a peg that Grace had hammered into the landscape, making me fit.

"Grace, I . . ."

I was too busy admiring the scenery to notice Elder Staples step up to us.

"So you must be Grace," he smiled coyly, sticking out his hand and interrupting us. "Sport here has told me all about you."

Grace's smile disappeared.

"Only nice things," I offered.

"The whole town knows he's sweet on you," Elder Staples blabbered.

I blushed responsibly.

Her green eyes let me know that she was on to me—in a good way.

"So, did you come to see the debate?" I asked, trying to sound sure of myself.

"No," she replied beautifully. "I just dropped off a couple of costumes I made for the pageant at the boardinghouse."

"Were they hard to make?" I asked, sounding like a fool.

"Not too bad," Grace responded kindly.

"Oh," was all I said.

"Like I said," Elder Staples butted in, "he's sweet on you."

Grace smiled, then she turned and walked off. Just like that she was gone. I couldn't tell if the conversation had ended well or weirdly. A little bit of both, I concluded.

"Way to go," I scolded Elder Staples. "I'm not sweet on her."

"What?" he asked. "I was just trying to help."

We went back to helping with the meadow cleanup until it was done. President Heck was the only one to ask me how I had figured all this Roswell, Book of Mormon stuff out. So, when everyone was gone, my companion and I sat down with him on the rotting pioneer wagons and we talked.

I told him how Feeble had passed away with the figure of Martin Calypso in his hand, giving us the ultimate clue. It had been Grace who had first informed me of Martin Calypso. We had gone to the Virgil's Find library that morning to research him out. It turned out that Martin Calypso was a gentle pig farmer who lived in the 1800s. He was best known for the saying, "Let man and pig fight for freedom as brothers."

"He wasn't real smart," I added. "Anyhow, Martin had been rather successful until his twin brother, Leonard, started gambling and depleting the family funds. In a desperate state, Leonard ended up stealing their rare family Bible and selling it to a Dutch sailor named Rugger. When Martin confronted Leonard, Leonard killed him.

"Well, I got to thinking how closely this resembled Roswell and Feeble," I said. "And the pieces fell together. I remembered that Roswell had told me about his cousin Stubby who had a pawnshop in Virgil's Find. I looked him up in the phone book. Elder Staples and I then went to visit him. I just wanted to find out if Roswell was still alive, and if Stubby by some chance knew where he was. I found out much more.

"When we entered Stubby's shop I simply asked him where Roswell was. He said he hadn't seen him in a couple of days, realizing immediately after he had spoken that he shouldn't have told me. It was too late. I knew Roswell was alive. I asked Stubby if he knew anything about an old book that Roswell might have had. Feeling that he had already said too much, he told us more. Yes, he knew about the book. He even gave us the address of the woman he had sold it to, there in town.

"I couldn't believe it. We headed over to her place, and she gladly sold it back to us, claiming that it didn't look as snooty as some of her other old books. She gladly took my out-of-state check. She obviously didn't know the value of the book.

"I was ecstatic.

"We raced back here, stopping only at the boardinghouse to check if the rest of Feeble's 'Great Men of the World' pewter set was still there. Of course, the figures were all gone. Roswell had probably been sneaking in and out of the boardinghouse, taking them to sell. I bet if we checked all the other Virgil's Find pawnshops, we'd find a few with a number of little metal men on hand."

"But why?" President Heck asked.

"For the same reason he stole the Book of Mormon. I guess it's like Martin Calypso," I said. "Remember how much Roswell liked to bet everyone?"

"I guess," he answered.

"Think," I said. "He was constantly saying 'I'll bet you ten bucks this, or that, will happen.'"

President Heck nodded.

"All I can figure is that he lost more bets than he won. He must have needed the money. And when Feeble caught on to the fact that Roswell had stolen the book, he probably threatened to turn him in. Feeble was pretty honest and, unlike his brother, an active Mormon. Maybe Feeble had a heart attack running after or away from Roswell that morning. Something must have happened."

"So he killed his brother," President Heck said, scratching his head.

"I don't know the whole story," I pointed out.

"Where's Roswell now?" President Heck asked.

"He can't be too far away," I said. "I figure he stole that P.I.G. money because he needed something to live on, or maybe he needed to pay some other debts. He must be pretty good at slipping in and out without being noticed."

Elder Staples yawned, bored with it all. "This is one goofy town," he commented.

"So Paul's innocent," President Heck said incredulously.

"Yep," I replied.

"Of course, he'll use all of this to build up his own religion again," President Heck pointed out. "He'll talk on and on 'bout how he was persecuted for the real gospel."

"Probably so," I agreed.

"We're right back where we started from," President Heck mourned.

The thought was thoroughly depressing. Any contentment I had felt earlier from the presence of Grace was suddenly gone. We got up from the old pioneer wagon and went home. Feeling that things were worse now than when I had entered the valley made me sick. I had turned this place back into what it always had been. Confused.

What was I thinking?

# 30

# HALF-BAKED

Sister Watson wasted no time. After getting permission from Ed's mother, she cast Ed Washington as Parley and called an emergency meeting to get him acquainted with the cast. Some folks thought she ought to have given the part to Paul after all, seeing as he didn't really steal the Book of Mormon or the P.I.G. money. But Sister Watson held her ground. Thief or no thief, anyone who claimed to have seen the finger was trouble. Besides, Paul had besieged her with hundreds of handwritten memos demanding changes to the script—changes that would emphasize similarities between Parley P. Pratt and Paul himself. They were both visionary leaders persecuted for their testimonies. They had both traveled to faraway lands, that sort of thing. It didn't work. Paul was banned from the planning committee for good.

The morning of the emergency meeting, everyone awoke to find a giant loaf of bread sitting right outside the boardinghouse, in the meadow. It was at least seven feet long and four feet wide. The sight of it was rather creepy and surreal. Having served in Thelma's Way for so long, I thought that there were few things that would surprise me anymore. This did.

No one knew where it had come from. Some speculated that it had dropped out of a plane.

"A really big bakery plane," CleeDee said.

Leo suggested that it was an alien loaf.

"Maybe other species travel in bread," he said, his eyes getting wide.

"I've never seen anything like it," President Heck said.

But Sister Watson was a voice of reason.

"It probably came from Teddy," she said. "Teddy's always making new things. I'm sure it's just her way of helping with the pageant. We should be right grateful, it seems to me."

Everyone agreed that seemed to make sense.

Lupert Carver walked right up to it and pinched off a piece.

"It's good," he declared, and that's all it took.

President Heck went to get his tree saw and stood there at the butt of the bread cutting off chunks for people. CleeDee fetched some honey.

After everyone had eaten, it was time for the meeting to begin. There was still about three-fourths of the loaf left, and people began talking about freezing the rest, and questioning each other as to who had a freezer. President Heck was about to start dividing the thing into sections when Teddy Yetch showed up.

"Thanks for the breakfast, Teddy," Ed Washington chimed. Everyone smiled and applauded until Teddy interrupted.

"I didn't make that enormous thing. Never been one much for baking bread."

"I wonder who baked it?" Toby asked.

Suddenly it was quiet. Sister Watson spat out the wad of bread she had in her mouth.

"What if it's Paul?" she said nervously. "What if it's poisoned?"

"It ain't poison," Toby said. "Poison tastes sour. Besides, if Paul had made a giant loaf of poison bread, you can bet he'd be around to watch us eat it."

Everyone looked about quickly, then all at once every eye, except for Tindy's lazy one, glanced back at the bread. People began stepping away from it.

"Paul, you in there?" Brother Heck yelled.

The bread remained silent.

Teddy Yetch took a stick and drove it into the center of the bread. Everyone gasped. Teddy pulled it out and positioned herself to do it again.

"Wait," I yelled. "If Paul is in there, you don't want to kill him."

Teddy thought about this for a second.

"Paul's not smart enough to bake himself in a loaf of bread," Sister Watson shouted. "Jab it again, Teddy!"

"Wait a second," President Heck said, holding his hands up. "Elder Williams is right."

President Heck walked up to the bread and jammed both his fists into it. He felt around in the middle for a few moments and then struck something. He looked like a breadenarian about to deliver a litter of loaves. He yanked hard and pulled out an ankle. Muffled protest began to emanate from inside the bread. Toby stepped up and helped Brother Heck pull Paul completely from the bread.

Paul lay on the ground coughing up bread for a few moments. He was completely covered in crumbs and mad about being discovered. He stood up and pointed at all of us.

"You and your secret meetings," he said. "I've a right to know what you're saying about me. I've a right to know about the pageant. But the joke is on you. I spent the last few months building a big hidden oven over beyond Lush Point. I knew it would come in handy. I wheeled this loaf out here and crawled up from the bottom and into it. And it would have paid off, too, if you'da just started your meeting on time 'stead of eating first. Greedy gluttons," he shouted, shaking his fist. He wiped some more bread crumbs from his face, turned around, and stormed off toward the Girth River.

We all just stood there. But Sister Heck was thinking clearly.

"Is the bread poisoned?" she called after him.

Paul turned back around and shook his head no before continuing on.

Elder Staples and I each had another slice before Sister Watson started her read through.

The pageant was coming.

31

# Practice Makes . . . If at First You Don't Succeed

About a week before the much-anticipated pageant, Elder Staples and I helped Toby finish the stage. This was no tiny structure. Toby had gone all out. The stage was on the far end of the meadow facing the boardinghouse. It was tall, wide, and fairly impressive. It had taken him almost the entire twenty months to design and construct it, but because of that, it looked as good as any meetinghouse stage I had ever seen.

With the stage completed, Sister Watson decided to do the first dry run of *All Is Swell* up on it. Elder Staples and I stayed around to watch. The play started with Thelma coming into the valley and settling. It then went on to tell the story of Parley P. Pratt coming to Thelma's Way and getting sick after eating the bad ham. A lot of the play focused on a woman named Drusa who helped nurse Parley back to health. Sister Watson also wrote the play to tell the full story of the missing Book of Mormon. She had even added the recent debate scene.

It was a hard production to watch. Not even Sister Watson's vibrato could cover up the awful lyrics she had written. People were still stumbling over lines and Ed Washington had a mild case of stage fright that made him wiggle when he spoke. I asked Sister Watson about alternates but she told me that the idea was ridiculous. No one would dare back out of such an important production. As far as she was concerned, the only way out of the performance was by death. She cited the example of her late husband.

As Elder Staples and I were sitting there, Frank Porter walked up. Frank was playing the part of the wicked ham. He had initially refused to be in the play. He said he didn't want that many people looking at him, but Sister Watson talked him into being the ham, seeing how the costume was a complete disguise. She guaranteed him that people wouldn't recognize him by his feet. Frank took the part knowing that his role would be crucial to the success of the show.

The ham stepped up to us and stopped.

"So what do you think, Frank?" I asked. "Is the show going to be a success?"

Frank grunted.

"Has the pageant committee decided on what food they will be serving?"

Frank grunted again.

The pageant committee consisted of Sister Watson, President and Sister Heck, Toby, Teddy Yetch, and Grace. Grace was basically a member by default. Since she had helped her mother with the costumes, Sister Watson felt it necessary to include her on the board.

"Have all the invitations been mailed out?" I asked Frank the Ham.

He didn't answer me.

"How many people have they invited to this thing?" Elder Staples asked me.

"I don't know," I answered. "At least a few thousand. Digby put posters up on telephone poles in Virgil's Find and at the mall in Collin's Blight."

"Do you think anybody will actually show up?" Elder Staples laughed.

"I sure hope so," I replied, looking at the huge stage and realizing just how much effort had been put into this thing. My gut told me otherwise. What were the chances that any outsider, let alone a crowd, would be interested in coming to see *All Is Swell*?

The cast on the stage broke out in song. They all sang along until Ed forgot one of his lines. Everyone stopped to look at each other.

"What's my next line?" Ed asked Sister Watson in frustration.

Sister Watson began flipping through her script.

"The work is moving forth," I hollered out, offering my assistance.

Sister Watson located the line in her script. "The work is moving forth," she said in amazement. "How did you know that?" she asked.

I shrugged my shoulders. "It's not that long of a script. I read through it a couple of times. It kind of sticks in your mind, I guess."

"Can we continue?" Ed demanded, his legs twisting under him. "The line just slipped away from me for a moment. It won't happen again."

"All right," Sister Watson yelled, "from the top."

Frank wandered off back behind the stage. We watched the next two scenes and then stood up to go to an early afternoon teaching appointment over at Judy Bickerstaff's home.

President Heck caught us as we were walking away.

"Have either of you seen Grace?" he asked.

We both shook our heads no.

"She put on Frank's costume to see if a person could walk with it on and never came back. I hope she didn't fall over and roll into the river. I think we're going to have to cut out a couple of arm holes in that ham. It's no fun falling over if you can't catch yourself."

Patty Heck stepped out from behind the stage and yelled at President Heck.

"I found her," she informed him.

"Never mind, guys," he said, walking off and away from us.

"So that was Grace in the ham," Elder Staples elbowed me.

"I didn't know," I pointed out.

"I'm sure you didn't, Sport."

"So, what did you think of the play?" I asked, changing the subject.

"I think it's even worse than some of the productions my sister used to stage in our backyard," Elder Staples answered.

"I hope this turns out to be a good thing," I sighed.

"Think of it this way," Elder Staples said. "Even if everyone hates it, at least it will finally be over."

I was comforted, I think.

32

# Live and Let Act

Two nights before the sesquicentennial pageant there was a knock on the door. I opened it up to find President Heck standing there, his face sober and long.

"What happened?" I asked.

"There's been a problem with the pageant," he replied.

I looked over at the huge completed stage on the far end of the meadow. It sat there, just waiting to be poorly acted upon.

"What kind of problem?" I asked.

"I think you'd better come with me."

Elder Staples and I followed President Heck over to Sister Watson's home. We entered without knocking. There was Sister Watson sitting on the couch. Next to her was Patty Heck, Teddy Yetch, Toby Carver, and behind Toby was Grace. I would have been happy to see her, I mean them, if it wasn't for the grave expressions on their faces. My heart shrunk to the size of a grape, then shriveled to a raisin. I suddenly felt guilty for something I had never done. It was as if I had been caught and dragged before a jury. How did they know that ten minutes earlier, I had had a quick, safe and fleeting thought about Grace?

These people were good.

It had caught up with me. I had tried not to let the presence of Grace be a distraction on my mission. I guess maybe I had failed. It was pretty tricky of President Heck to fool me into coming over by claiming there was a problem with the pageant. Everyone stared at me.

"I can explain," I offered nervously.

"You can?" Sister Watson asked.

"My mission president knows all about it," I fumbled, trying not to look at Grace.

"He does?" President Heck asked.

"I've kept him informed."

"Of what?" Toby asked.

I looked around. Everyone was obviously confused. I decided that now was a good time for me to shut up. Grace looked my way.

"You can explain about Ed?" Sister Watson asked in disbelief.

"What about Ed?" I questioned.

"Paul got to him. We don't know how, but now he's refusing to do the pageant unless we give in to Paul's demands," Toby said.

"You're kidding!"

"Wish we were," President Heck said sadly.

"What are his demands?" I asked, bracing myself for the worst.

Sister Watson picked up a piece of paper in front of her.

"These are some of the lyrics Paul insists we use," she said. "He claims they're very topical."

*God gave to all*
*The gift of Paul*
*So listen to his will.*
*The price of cheese*

*May rise and dip*
*But Paul is with us still.*

Everyone grimaced. Paul made Sister Watson's lyrics sound almost normal.

"That's why we got together as this committee tonight," President Heck added. "Grace and Patty have finished the costumes, Toby's done with the stage, and the others are ready to act. But we can't do the play without the lead male."

"Just find someone else," I reasoned.

"Where are we going to find someone at this hour?" Patty asked. "No one knows the lines."

"That's ridiculous," I scoffed. "Surely someone knows them. Even I know most of them."

Everyone smiled.

I had been tricked, all right. Except these people weren't calling me on the carpet because of Grace, they were calling me on stage due to Paul. It was all a setup. I had warned Sister Watson about having alternate actors, now here was my own forewarning biting me in the unthespian-like end.

"I can't—"

"Sure you can," Sister Watson said. "I think it would be only fitting to have you in our play. True, you're not blood, but you're the longest lingering outsider we've ever had here."

"I can't act," I pointed out.

"You just got to pretend you're someone else for an hour or so," Toby instructed. "It's real easy. I do it all the time."

"I think it's against my mission rules," I argued.

"We can call your mission president if you'd like," President Heck offered.

"There's going to be people from all over," I said, though I didn't really believe it. "You guys have invited the entire state. You don't want me going up there and doing a halfway job."

"If that's the best you can do," Patty said.

I looked at Grace, thinking that maybe she would help me.

"I think the people would love it," she smiled.

"The part requires singing!" I stated in a panic.

"All in favor say aye," Sister Watson sang out.

"Aye!"

"Don't I have a say in this?" I begged.

"Think of how this will help the missionary work," Brother Heck comforted.

"You've never seen me act," I said dejectedly.

"Well, I won't have to wait long to do so," he replied.

Sister Watson, Patty Heck and Teddy Yetch got up and went to the kitchen. Grace slipped out the back door, avoiding me as usual, and Toby laid down on the couch as if preparing for a late night nap on Sister Watson's sofa.

"I knew we could count on you," President Heck said, putting his arm around me. "I was the one that brought up your name."

"Thanks," I said.

"Don't mention it," he replied.

Elder Staples and I went home and read our scriptures. Then I took a few minutes to go over my lines. I couldn't believe that they were making me do this. But it looked as if the only way I was going to get out of it was to die. Maybe I'd die of embarrassment.

I had only one more day to live.

## 33

# Take a Seat

I had called President Clasp, and he seemed to think the idea of me acting in a pageant for nonmembers was a splendid one. In fact, he promised that he'd try to be there. We did a quick dress rehearsal the next day. It went pretty well.

Toby and Pete spent the day making sure that the big stage was in working order and adjusting the lighting. Leo and CleeDee went into Virgil's Find to pass out even more invitations. I was starting to believe that every person in the state of Tennessee who could read or hear would know about the play. Knowing and doing, however, were two very different things. I still couldn't imagine anyone who wasn't directly involved, taking the time to hike in.

After the dress rehearsal we set up all the rented chairs. It seemed as if there were thousands of them. If we filled one-fourth of them the following day, I would consider the pageant a smashing success. We wheeled the piano from out of the boardinghouse over to the stage.

Sister Heck brought out the curtain that she had made and Digby and Sybil Porter worked well into the night hanging it up. When all was said and done, things looked pretty good.

"This is going to be huge," President Heck said almost to himself, bursting with pride.

"Yeah, huge," I repeated less enthusiastically.

"Do you think it will bring people back to church?" President Heck asked almost reverently.

"Hey, anything's possible," I said, wanting to encourage him. Then I thought of Feeble and his vision, Roswell's translation, Paul's holy finger and the huge bread loaf.

"Anything's possible," I repeated with more conviction, "anything at all."

34

# Lights, Camera, Traction

The town was packed. I had never in my life seen more people gathered in one spot. Half an hour before the play, every chair was filled and people were spilling out onto blankets or lawn chairs they had brought themselves. There were at least seven different news teams, each with huge cameras waiting to catch this monstrous human interest story as it unfolded. A few extremely rugged looking trucks had even worked their way down the path and into our town. If I had been nervous before, I was now ready to choke up a lung. I had not signed on for this. I remembered quite clearly twenty months ago when I had shuffled into Thelma's Way. I remembered the small orange signs posted on the electric poles informing folks of the pre-planning meeting. I remembered thinking that it was absolutely none of my business, seeing how I would be so far away when the pageant was actually performed.

There were multiple tables set up with piles of food for all those in attendance. People milled around eating and waiting for the big show. I couldn't believe that this was happening to me.

President Heck, Leo, Pete, CleeDee, Toby, Frank, Elder Staples, and I all huddled behind the closed curtain on stage. We were all dressed in our costumes and trying to contain our performance night jitters. (All of us but Elder Staples that is, who was calm as a summer's day and looking forward to some good laughs.)

Every couple of seconds Toby would crack open the curtain and peek out into the darkening sky at the huge crowd.

"There's got to be over a hundred people out there," Toby whispered in fear.

"A hundred," I replied. "There's at least five thousand, maybe more."

"Wooo," Frank blew.

"What time is it?" I asked to no one in particular.

"We've only got a few minutes 'til starting time," President Heck answered.

"Where's Sister Watson anyway?" Pete Kennedy shook. I saw him reach for the spot on his hip where his gun would have been. He did it without thinking about it. Maybe it gave him comfort. "I haven't seen her around all day," he added.

"Patty went to fetch her," President Heck replied. "I guess she's been really resting up all day in preparation for tonight."

No sooner had President Heck spoken when Sister Watson appeared. She was with Patty Heck, Teddy Yetch, and Grace. I tried not to look at Grace for fear of losing it. I was barely holding myself together as it was. Patty Heck was the first to speak.

"Sister Watson has lost her voice," she said quite dryly.

"You've got to be kidding," I said.

"It's no joke." Sister Heck was very serious. "She must have lost it yesterday during dress rehearsal. She can barely whisper. She's been icing her throat all day, hoping it would get better. It hasn't."

"What are we going to do?" Leo moaned.

Sister Watson shook her head and began to weep.

Toby pulled his Ace bandage out of his pocket and began to wrap Sister Watson's neck. It was almost sweet.

"Does anyone here know Sister Watson's lines?" Patty Heck begged. "You've all been practicing with her, someone's got to remember what she says?"

"I was too busy trying to learn my own lines," Toby apologized.

"I could give it a go," Leo said, wanting to help.

"Thanks Leo, Toby, but I meant any of the ladies. CleeDee, do you think you know Sister Watson's lines well enough to do them?" Sister Heck asked.

"I've been too busy dating Leo to really pay attention," CleeDee replied.

"What about Miss Flitrey?" I asked.

"The costume won't fit her," Patty Heck answered matter-of-factly.

This was just great. For twenty months they had been planning this pageant, and now five minutes from showtime, the whole thing was falling apart. Sister Watson was the leading lady. Drusa brings Parley back to health. She sings four of the eight songs by herself. Her character is on stage alone for a third of the play.

"Can't we just leave her part out?" Pete asked. "You know, work around it?"

Sister Watson shook her head firmly.

"This is the most important part in the whole play," I said. "There is no pageant without it. I can't believe this."

"Five minutes 'til showtime," President Heck announced mournfully.

We needed a miracle. There were five thousand spectators to feed and not a single slice of talent to divide up. We stood there in shock.

Then Grace said softly, "I know the lines."

Everyone turned to look.

"I've heard Sister Watson say them a hundred times," she

explained. "I've also read over the script. I might not know them exactly, but I think I could get close."

It was a stunning moment. Grace was the town recluse. She hid herself up in the hills and avoided people like the plague. Was she really offering to walk out unrehearsed in front of thousands of people?

"Would you do it?" Patty Heck asked, disbelieving.

Grace nodded with confidence, even certainty.

"There's songs," President Heck informed his daughter.

Grace hadn't sung in public since she was eight years old. Toby told me she had sung at her own baptism and did such a terrible job that people actually covered their ears and hummed something else.

"She can't be worse than no singing at all." Leo tried to be practical.

"I don't know about that," Toby replied. "If you remember—"

"We have no choice," President Heck interrupted. "I'm certain Grace's voice has matured. Right, Grace?"

"We could just cancel the play," Grace offered, underwhelmed by everyone's confidence.

Sister Watson shook her head. "Places," she whispered.

We scurried off to our positions. My insides were beginning to knot up. I half-wished Pete had been allowed to bring his gun so he could put me out of my misery.

I was certain President Clasp would not have allowed me to be in this play if he knew it would be Grace that nursed my character back to health. The thought of being in Sister Watson's arms as she sang to sick Parley had seemed innocent enough before.

This was going to be some pageant.

The wind was beginning to pick up. I could hear the crowd growing restless and then Sister Heck started playing the introduction on the piano.

We were about to make history. One way or another.

I could barely see Digby up on the scaffolding above me. He pulled on the ropes and opened the curtain. Our narrator, President Heck, stepped to the middle of the stage where Pete flipped on a light and beamed it down at him.

The crowd was quiet.

Patty Heck tickled the ivories softly as President Heck spoke into his handheld microphone. He was only shaking slightly.

"On behalf of the Thelma's Way pageant committee, I—"

SRRRRRRREEEEEEEEEEPPP!!!

Feedback ripped through the air. The audience jumped in their seats. A startled President Heck held the microphone away from his mouth and continued.

"I would like to welcome one and all to the sesquicentennial production of *All Is Swell.* While it is based on a true story, we would like you to know that those historical figures being represented didn't actually sing."

The lights went off and Pete began to flick them on and around in dramatic sequence. It's hard to make a couple of colored yard lights look spectacular, but Pete was giving it his all. He swung the big swivel light through the air, finally resting it on President Heck, who was still standing in the middle of the stage.

"The history behind the land you're sitting on is not necessarily pretty," President Heck spoke. "In fact at moments it's been just plain ugly. As you will see tonight, it took much work and a handful of miracles to bring us to where we are. 'Where are we?' you ask. Well, this is Thelma's Way, Tennessee."

It was a big crescendo, but nobody clapped. President Heck coughed nervously.

"A hundred and fifty years ago," he hurried on, "on this exact day, a young, inspired girl named Thelma wandered into this valley with a host of worn-out travelers. Their only ambition in life was to be able to worship for free."

The lights slapped off for a second and then flipped back on. They were shining on Narlette, who was playing the part of Thelma, as she lead Leo, CleeDee, and Toby across the stage. Both Leo and Toby were pulling what looked to be two of the most modern-looking handcarts I had ever seen. In fact, if I didn't know any better, I would have sworn they were red metal wagons. Narlette stopped in the middle of the stage and spoke.

"I say this is a good place to stop," Narlette said haltingly. "The heavens have really, really, really, blessed us with blessings." Narlette stared at Leo, who was suddenly locked up with fear.

"I mean they have really blessed us," Narlette prodded.

Toby elbowed Leo.

"They have," Leo finally said.

"Perhaps we should give thanks to our Creator in song," Toby clamored. "Hymns are a way of praising."

My heart raced. I knew we were just moments away from the first song. Once they heard us sing, I expected half the crowd would pick up their things and try to sneak off.

"We shall call this place home," Narlette said, warming to the idea of performing in front of thousands.

*Da, da, da,* Sister Heck began on the piano. The cast on stage began to sing:

*We've found a piece of heaven,*
*tucked here in Tennessee.*
*We're waiting for the blessings*
*that we've been guaranteed.*

Ed stepped forward with flair,

*The Girth will give us water,*

CleeDee belted out,

*The land will be our friend,*

Narlette shouted,

> *We'll worship here in Thelma's Way*
> *until the bitter end.*

They all then danced and marched in a circle around the wagons. I counted sixteen circles before I gave up and said a prayer asking for mercy. The lights flicked off and everyone shuffled off stage. President Heck took front and center again. Pete lit him up.

"Two years after they entered this valley an apostle for the Mormon Church paid a visit. His name was Parley P. Pratt. He taught the locals many wonderful things. As a way of showing their thanks the town had a big dinner celebration in his honor. The dish served up was ham, and the ham served up was infected."

The entire congregation *Ewwwed.*

"Parley P. Pratt became very ill," President Heck finished.

The light flashed off of President Heck.

I was on.

I walked to the center of the stage. I could hear my heart beating. I could see Sister Watson off to the side praying for me. Pete shined the light on me. For an instant, I wished I were dead and heading towards it. All the extras gathered around as I stood on a small wooden box and pretended to preach.

"I bring you news from Zion," I began. "The work is moving forth."

"Let's have a dinner to celebrate," Toby recited.

"Why not?" Leo boomed. "We have earned this celebration. I'm certain that the heavens will not punish us for being too smug."

This play contained some really powerful dialogue.

"Let the celebration begin," CleeDee announced.

This was the moment I think I was most dreading. The play was bad enough, but this dancing ham scene was going to kill me. Tables were pulled out from the corners of the stage and all of us actors began to act as if we were enjoying a great meal. Sister Heck played the piano softly as some of the young local kids danced around us dressed as food. Lupert was potato salad, someone was gravy, and another kid was a bag of jelly beans. We had discussed the fact that the pioneers probably didn't have jelly beans, but Sister Watson had seen the idea of wearing a big clear sack and stuffing it with blown up balloons in a *Woman's World* magazine and just couldn't resist making the clever costume.

After the kids had danced around for a few minutes, Frank Porter emerged from stage right disguised as the giant ham hock. Sister Heck began to pound on the piano, the music growing louder and more sinister. Frank crept up on me. I pretended not to see him until he leaped, throwing his arms around me. The rest of the cast began to sing as I wrestled with the wicked ham.

*What is this meat that's got the man?*
*It looks like Satan's loose again.*
*How can we stand for what is true*
*When Satan tampers with our food?*

Frank stopped squeezing just enough for me to sing my solo.

*I've got a burning deep inside,*
*but not from honor, truth, or pride.*
*This current burning isn't great*
*because it came from what I ate.*
Everyone sang in chorus:
*Because it came from what he aaaaaaate.*

Frank Porter squeezed me even harder. He picked me up, shook me around, and flung me to the ground. I could hear my insides bruising.

The lights snapped off, and the curtains began to close. I caught a fleeting glimpse of the audience as I was lying there before the curtain shut. They looked moved, or stunned. I couldn't tell which. With us all behind the curtain, Sister Heck began to play the interlude. I picked myself up and helped change the scenery. In a moment the place was transformed into what looked to be an old log cabin. Grace came onto the stage. Everyone moved off leaving her and me standing behind the closed curtain. Sister Heck was playing something soft and sweet.

"Are you ready?" I asked Grace.

"I think so."

"How was it so far?" I asked. Grace had been watching from the side.

"It's a moving script," she joked.

"That bad, huh?"

I sat down on the edge of the bed now placed in the middle of the stage.

"When I practiced this scene with Sister Watson, she sort of brushed my forehead and pretended to comfort me," I explained. "But it might be best if you just kind of sat there near me."

Grace smiled as President Heck stepped out in front of the curtain and began introducing the next scene.

"Sadly, Parley P. Pratt was extremely sick because of the ham," President Heck recited. "He didn't move for a week. He just laid in bed moaning. The town began to lose hope. Until one day out of nowhere a woman wandered into town. Her name was Drusa. No one had seen her before, and no one knew where she had come from. But she was here, and she took it upon herself to nurse Parley back to health."

I laid down on the bed, and Grace took a seat in the chair next to it. The curtain opened, and the light shined down on her. I was pretty impressed. Grace's red hair was tied back behind her head, her green eyes so strong that I'm certain those in the back row knew just what color they were.

"Parley," she lamented. "If only there was something I could do."

It was time for Grace to sing.

The cast held their breath, except for Toby, who held his ears. I watched Grace as she opened her mouth. It was soft at first. In fact, I could see the entire five thousand lean in closer to get a better listen. But gradually it became strong and sure. Okay, so she was singing some of the dumbest lyrics I had ever heard, but with her voice she seemed to change the words into text worth tasting. It was beautiful, at least to me.

*I'm here to see your load is light*
*To see you through this longest night.*
*Through thick and thin, through poor or wealth,*
*I bid you Parley go to health.*

When she finished her song, everyone just stared at her. There was a kind of hush all over the meadow. Finally, Pete turned off the lights and the curtains closed. Sister Heck began to play the between scenes music. The scenery started to move about. I stood up from the bed and looked at Grace. Toby took his hands off of his ears.

"How was it?" he asked.

"It was . . ." I began to say in amazement.

"Places," Elder Staples whispered. "Places."

Suddenly Elder Staples was pushing me around, and Toby grabbed Grace and started hooking her up to a wire harness. I wanted to brag about Grace's singing a bit, but there was no time—this next scene was pretty crucial. It was to be the most visually spectacular scene of the entire production. It was where Parley gets better and Drusa is hoisted up like an angel on wires and appears to float while she sings. They had practiced it fifty times with Sister Watson. But it was all new to Grace.

I could hear President Heck in front of the curtains.

"Drusa saved Parley P. Pratt's life. Her kindness and caring helped bring him back to full health. Thelma's Way was blessed. Everyone thought that they had truly been visited by an angel. Heaven had opened its windows and dumped out Drusa. Sure, it turned out that she was actually just a midwife from one town over who had come here to get away from her unruly kids for a few days. Even so, her efforts were miraculous."

The curtains opened to expose Grace and me.

"How can I ever thank you?" I said while staring intently at her eyes.

*Da, da, da, da,* Sister Heck played loudly as the rest of the cast strode on stage singing and waving small sticks with tinsel glued to the ends of them.

*How can he ever thank you?*
*What could he ever say?*
*Where are the words to show you*
*You really saved the day.*

Grace sang her lines as she began to be lifted up.

*We must be ever willing*
*To help out our fellow man.*
*We must replace, "I will not,"*
*With the simple words, "I can."*

I looked up at Grace as she began to ascend above us all. I could see Digby up on the platform trying to wind her up. As soon as she was midway she stopped. I looked at Digby, who was desperately trying to get her moving again. The wire had looped and knotted, leaving her stranded in the air. Those in the audience couldn't tell that anything was wrong. People just figured this was part of the play. But all of us on stage knew full well that this was not what we had rehearsed. Grace was supposed to be lifted up, ending the scene. Digby tried to close the curtains but the knotted wire was binding the curtain pulley as well.

All of us were stuck below Grace, faced with the fact that we were going to have to improvise.

I was worried. This cast didn't exactly break records for spontaneous thought—unless there was a record for least amount. It was too much for Frank; he just took off running. Those of us left began to sweat and wing it.

"Parley, we thank you again for visiting," Toby said nervously. "It's not often we get someone like you that comes to visit us. It's really neighborly of you to visit us all."

"And I thank you all for sharing your town with me," I acted. "You have been the most sharing of towns. The Prophet would be happy with what you have done."

"What have we done?" Toby asked, confused.

"You have helped me get better, and stuff," I ad-libbed.

"I hope we didn't treat you too rough," Toby said, feeling that our conversation was supposed to rhyme.

We continued to act out pointless dialogue below the now-swinging Grace. The wind was beginning to really move her. I watched as she tried to remain composed up on the wire.

I saw President Heck climb up the scaffolding to help Digby. Once up there, he began to yank and pound on the wire. Leo, realizing that our improv was going badly, decided to break out in song. He marched around us singing words even more nonsensical than the ones Sister Watson had written. CleeDee became embarrassed by what Leo was doing and tried to slip off stage unnoticed. Her slinking away finally let the audience know that something was wrong. For a minute they laughed, and then they seemed to remember that they were supposed to be entertained. A couple of hecklers began to holler out.

Sybil Porter, who had been playing one of the extras on stage, raised her fist to the audience and taught them a couple of new words. The crowd began to boo. President Heck was still banging like crazy on the wire. I looked up and over at Pete sitting behind the light. I would have looked away, but I couldn't help noticing him pull a small gun out from a tiny holster on his ankle.

Pete aimed the gun at the wire.

Before I could scream anything he fired, snapping the wire and grazing Digby's left arm. Grace yelled as she fell on top of me. We both slammed down onto the stage and through the unnecessary trap door that Toby had insisted on building. Digby lost his balance and began to fall from the scaffolding. President Heck reached out to grab him but had to quickly steady himself by clinging onto the lights. Digby caught hold of the large net that was hidden above the stage and full of balloons for the finale. He ripped the net and swung down to the ground. Balloons whipped everywhere in the wind. President Heck followed after Digby, pulling the lights down and into the curtains. The lights exploded, and the curtains shot up in flames. The balloons caught on fire, flashing in the dark wind.

The audience went crazy. I couldn't see too much from beneath the stage, but I could hear sounds that both humans and chairs didn't usually make. I could also tell that the entire stage was falling apart, cracking, and breaking all over as fire consumed the entire thing. Grace and I crawled out from under just seconds before. Pete jumped off his perch and into the meadow. People were running everywhere.

It seemed as if everyone was heading for the path out of Thelma's Way. The few trucks that had made it into town were tearing away. I lost Grace in the mess of it all. I spotted Sister Watson, who was shuffling around looking dazed and confused. Her wig was hanging to the side, covering her right ear. Her pageant had gone haywire. We had not even made it to the fifth act.

President Heck grabbed me by the arm.

"Are you okay?" he hollered.

I looked around at the wild riot, not knowing if I could honestly answer *yes.*

"We've got to get this fire out!" I yelled.

Lit balloons were dropping all over. The crowd covered their heads in fear.

Elder Staples came running up and into me. He had a couple of trash cans that had been over by the once-erect food tables. He dumped the trash out of them. We started a chain from the river to the stage, passing the trash cans back and fourth until the fire was finally out.

By the time it had died down, the place was relatively deserted; not a single outsider had stayed around to help. Yes, a couple of the TV crews had remained to document the fire, but we sort of wished they hadn't. The meadow was a complete disaster. Chairs were everywhere, as well as food and paper. The stage was burned to the ground. Sister Heck picked up a charred piece of the curtain and shook her head.

"I don't think this night will gain us any respect," she hoarsely whispered.

"I don't know," President Heck replied. "I think it depends on how the papers handle it."

"We're ruined," Sister Watson coughed. She handed back the now slightly singed Ace bandage to Toby.

"I thought the small part of the play that actually got played was right neat," Toby offered.

"Yeah," Leo agreed. "Real fancy."

Sister Watson just sat there crying as we all tried to tell her it would be okay. Of course, I don't know that any of us actually believed it.

35

# Smeared

The papers murdered us. There was not a single kind thing said about the pageant or the tragedy. Words like *pathetic, backwards, ridiculous,* and *incompetent* were peppered throughout every report of the play. Sister Watson had wanted the world to attend; well the world had been there all right, and apparently they were sickened. I felt horrible. It was as if the entire planet was now in the business of putting down our town.

The meadow was a pit. It took us a couple of days to get things picked up. Even then it still looked awful. We tried to clear away the remains of the stage, but the kids seemed to enjoy playing in the big pile of ashes, so we decided to leave it and let Mother Nature take her course.

The disaster had worked out well for Paul. According to him, he had been at home reading scriptures and praying that we all might be forgiven for not joining his religion and preventing him from being in the play when the tragedy struck. He went on and on about how sad it was that it took these acts of heaven to show us all how wrong we were.

Sister Watson was probably the worst off. She felt personally responsible for it all. She seemed destined to live in an eternal funk until President Heck asked her if she would begin planning a Christmas play for the following year, stressing only that it be a little less elaborate than the last one. She went right to work setting up an agenda for the pre-planning meeting.

I hadn't seen Grace since she had fallen on me. My neck was still sore from the encounter. I actually wanted to thank Grace for putting the play out of its misery. The way I saw it, we were lucky the stage caught fire before the crowd lit it themselves.

President Clasp had not made it to the play and, consequently, had missed out on all the fun. When I called him to tell him what happened, he told me quite clearly that he would be to Thelma's Way in a few weeks to deliver the transfer news. It looked as if my days in Thelma's Way were numbered at last. I couldn't believe it. I only wished I wasn't deserting these people at such a painful time.

I tried to push the feelings aside. I tried to act as if it was really none of my business. I tried in vain.

36

# A Burning in the Bosom

Month Twenty-Two

A few weeks later, right before sacrament meeting, Elder Staples received a transfer out of Thelma's Way. He was out, I was still in. I was going to be serving the twenty-second month of my mission in the same place. President Clasp had come to town to speak at our ward and deliver the transfer news. He met with Elder Staples and me before church.

"But President," I had questioned after getting the news.

"You're not finished here," he smiled, his crooked teeth straightening as he tilted his head.

President Clasp had brought my new companion with him. Actual transfers were not for a couple of days, but my new companion, Elder Herney, had caused a few problems in his last area, and they had to get him out of there fast. He was an emergency transfer. Mission rumor was that he had been sneaking out to watch *Star Trek* movies at the midnight theater by himself. President Clasp thought Thelma's Way would be the perfect place for him to straighten out.

Elder Herney was not exactly a people person. In fact, he was one troubled individual. His parents had pushed him onto his mission hoping he would come back looking like some of the clean-cut elders they had seen in Church videos. It seemed to me he was moving in the opposite direction. He talked as if all wind entered and exited his nostrils. He had dark eyes that looked ringed, and thin skin that appeared blue under natural light. He was about six inches shorter than I and liked to pinch his lips as he spoke endlessly about science fiction movies and how they correlated with gospel principles. We had talked maybe fifteen minutes so far, and the entire conversation had been about the gospel accuracy of the Star Wars saga.

"The force is actually the priesthood," he explained. "And Yoda is the prophet."

I sat down glumly next to Elder Herney in the chapel. Elder Staples was still here, all smiles to be leaving. President Clasp sat up in front by the podium. Usually I blessed or passed the sacrament due to so few priesthood holders being in attendance. But today Toby Carver was blessing with Digby Heck, and Leo Tip was passing. I sat in my pew and sulked silently. I was hoping that to the naked eye sulking would look like reverence.

I didn't know what it was with me. Why was I still in Thelma's Way? I liked to pretend that there was some great cosmic reason for my being kept in one place. But the truth was probably something closer to the idea that President Clasp simply had it out for me. His smiling presence was just a funny front for a rather conniving nature. I had learned a lot in Thelma's Way. I really felt as if I had grown from my experiences, but I also felt I could use some rounding out. Couldn't I? I loved these people, but didn't a real mission require broadening? Shouldn't I be shifted around?

It had been a few weeks since the pageant, and things were still in confusion. Paul was claiming the failure of the pageant as proof that we all had been living in sin. He was currently promising people thicker hair, more energy, and three years longer life if they joined up with the People of Paul. So far Frank Porter was the only one to take him up on the offer. Frank figured if he had been desperate enough to smear Sister Lando's spotted frog larvae on his bald head in an attempt to overcome his baldness, then what could it hurt to take up a new religion as a potential cure? It seemed so much cleaner.

Paul wanted people to know that his being accused of stealing the Book of Mormon, and then being banned from the disastrous play, was the pattern God used to pull prophets out from among the rank and file. For the last two days, he had been over at the boardinghouse giving free workshops on how to recognize truth.

It was funny to think that a man who once claimed he had invented chicken cordon bleu and helped work out the bugs on the paper clip, could go into great depths about the importance of honesty. Paul wasn't keeping himself in check any longer. He had been falsely accused, we knew it, and we were going to pay.

The table next to the podium sat empty as usual. The Book of Mormon still had not been found. I focused on the empty table while listening to Elder Herney whistle through his nose as he breathed. I was tempted to reach over and pinch the thing closed. Sister Watson took a seat right in front of us. Patty Heck was sitting with Narlette across the aisle. By the time the meeting started we had about twenty-five members there. All told, our attendance was up by about fifteen people since the time I had arrived almost two years ago. Two years. Fifteen people. It was not an impressive record. I would read and reread the scriptures about the worth of one soul, and the importance of bringing just one person unto Him. But these were Thelma's Way souls we were talking about. It probably took about five of them to equal one ordinary spirit, right?

Possibly it was the other way around.

And where was Grace in all of this? Ever since the pageant, I had been overly hopeful that she would start coming back to church again. Not yet. I had ordered myself to stop thinking about her so many times that I was now having to tell myself to stop thinking about not thinking about her. She weighed more on my mind than my brain had strength to heft. I had told President Clasp after he decided to not transfer me that I was thinking way too much of her. He didn't fall for it. He simply told me I would be done with my mission in a couple of months and that I was welcome to come back and visit her then.

Some advice.

Sacrament meeting moved along slowly. And halfway through President Clasp's talk, I began to feel ill. It wasn't the normal queasy feeling that I sometimes got at church. It was something different altogether. I tried to brush it off.

I squirmed in my seat. I could feel beads of sweat running down my face. I loosened my tie just a bit and fanned myself with the hymnbook. The back of Sister Watson's head began to sway and contract. I needed some fresh air.

I looked over at Elder Herney.

"You don't look right," he droned.

I needed to get to the bathroom. I stood up to go, and Elder Herney and Elder Staples followed. It looked like I was taking half the congregation with me as I left. I went into the tiny church bathroom and splashed water on my face.

"I don't feel well," I said.

"You look awful," Elder Herney assisted.

I leaned against the wall and held my stomach.

"You were fine before you found out you were staying," Elder Staples accused. Then he threw a couple of pretend punches at me, wounding the air immediately in front of my stomach.

There was no way I could go back into the chapel. The wood walls of the building seemed to puff up, and the windows sort of slid down to the floor. I desperately pulled at my tie. I could feel my wrists turn slippery.

"I was fine just a . . ." I suddenly didn't know if I could stand for much longer. I stumbled.

"What do we do?" Elder Herney breathed at Elder Staples.

"He's your companion," Elder Staples said, no longer willing to take responsibility for me.

"I'll give you five bucks if you carry him home," Elder Herney bartered.

Elder Staples picked up my six-foot-two frame as my knees buckled and tossed me over his shoulder. My head knocked the door frame as he stepped outside.

"Owww!" I moaned.

"Easy, Sport," Elder Staples said.

He carried me back to our place and put me in bed. It would be quite some time before I got out again.

37

# Angel of Heresy

Month Twenty-Three

There are varying degrees of sickness. Forget them all. I had gone well beyond any known mark of discomfort. I lay in bed for weeks doing nothing but moan—slipping in and out of a vegetative state. At first folks thought I was faking it for attention. But after watching me struggle to keep my food down, they began to realize there were better ways to get noticed.

Toby Carver had attempted to heal me with his Ace bandage, but somehow a mere spandex wrap wasn't enough to lower my body temperature or calm my nausea. A real doctor (although we couldn't call him that to Toby's face) was called in from Virgil's Find to look me over. He diagnosed me with a rare strain of flu called Wilbur's Affliction.

Wilbur had been a woodsman who resided below Hallow Falls about a hundred years ago. He had lived out his days in obscurity until someone named an epidemic after him. He was a simple man who raised chickens and sold eggs. Every spring, in an effort to boost sales, he would take a bunch of his eggs and make a homemade spicy spread like a mayonnaise but with more kick. He bottled it and sold it to his neighbors from out of his wood shack.

One year the economy of the area went sour and in an effort to single-handedly restore regional prosperity, Wilbur whipped up an extra big batch of his concoction. But hard times equaled low sales, and he only sold half the goods.

Ever the savvy businessman, he packed away the excess supply in his warm attic and sold it at fire sale prices the following spring. The town never recovered.

Apparently, my doctor's great-grandfather had almost died of the dreaded affliction. That's how come he knew so much. Now anytime anyone came down with complications of mayonnaise, the diagnosis could only be Wilbur's Affliction (not to be confused, he said, with Briant's Curse, which was a whole different story.)

The doctor handed me some medicine for the pain and prescribed three weeks without eggs. The pills helped a little, but I spent my days in relative misery, tossing between the sheets. The one time I actually felt a little better, Elder Herney and I tried to go visit Judy Bickerstaff. I got twenty steps out the door before I knew I wasn't going to make it. I crawled back to my bed feeling worse than ever.

Thanks to the kindness of the townspeople, I always had visitors. Leo and CleeDee came by almost every day to show me neat-looking sticks or leaves they had found. Wad had been over a few times to sit by me and read me some of his old magazines. Teddy Yetch and Sister Lando brought food that I couldn't even look at, and Sister Watson came over twice to scrub our place sterile with her homemade bar soap. Even Paul came by to say he had foreseen my doom and wondered when I was planning to die.

Elder Herney had just about had enough of my being sick. He had not spent a single day with me outside the cabin. Occasionally he went on splits with Digby while President Heck stayed with me. He attended church thanks to Pete Kennedy sitting in. But when we were together, all we did was fight. We tried to have companionship studies, and we prayed a lot that we would get along, but it didn't seem to help. Both of us were at our wits' end.

It was Thursday afternoon, I think. I was feeling stronger physically, but mentally I was still fogged under. I was so stir-crazy I thought I would rather die than stay inside. But the doctor had told me to stay in bed for at least a few more days before attempting to go anywhere. I was wearing a long red nightshirt that my mother had just sent. She had made it for me in homemaking. It was about three sizes too big and had a rather silly-looking neck ruffle, but considering the trouble she had gone to, I felt duty bound to wear it at least once.

"You look stupid," Elder Herney commented.

"My mother made this," I argued as I shuffled across the room to get some water.

I had taken some cold medicine a few minutes earlier, and it was beginning to play on my brain. I had downed a double dose in the hopes of knocking myself out for the night.

"This isn't a mission," Elder Herney whined, "this is a babysitting job."

"Hey, I'm s-s-sorry I'm sick," I slurred, getting back into bed.

"This—"

Elder Herney was interrupted by a knock on the door. He jumped up, happy to have something to do. He answered the door, and President Heck came in.

"Could I borrow your companion?" President Heck asked me as I lay in bed. "I just need to talk to him outside." He was nervous about something.

"Sure," I said, beginning to really feel the effects of the medication.

"We'll just be out here," President Heck said, walking out the door with Elder Herney.

They left the door open so that I could see outside, but they had moved towards the cemetery and out of my view. I stared at the open door for a while, watching birds make tracers across the late afternoon sky. Wow. I began to hallucinate. From out of thin air, my mind conjured up Grace. I had seen a lot of weird things while I had been sick. My eyes had played so many tricks on me that I was beginning to doubt everything I saw. This vision of Grace slipped in the door and stood against the wall.

I sort of bobbed my head, squinting at the illusion.

The mirage smiled back.

"Nice pajamas," it said.

I patted my red nightgown. "Thanks," I replied, my voice echoing in the empty room.

"I just wanted to say good-bye," she fluttered, "before you go home and I . . . *we* never see you again."

"Grace?" I said, fathoming for the first time that it was really her.

She was still against the far wall.

"I'd better go," she said. "My father can only cover me for so long."

"Don't go," I begged, sluggishly.

She turned and paused.

"Do you remember last Halloween?" she asked with some hesitation.

In my present condition I couldn't accurately remember ten minutes ago. Last Halloween seemed like another life. I sort of nodded, toppled, and shook my head. I felt like a wino with bad rhythm.

"I heard what you said as you and your companion sat on the porch," Grace whispered, her soft voice barely carrying across the room. "Was it true?"

I had no idea what she was talking about. In my medicated state it sounded like a riddle. What had I said last Halloween? And was she happy or sad about it?

I just stared at her. She was beautiful then. Her red hair against the wood wall was poetic, moving.

"I've got to go," Grace said again nervously.

"What about . . ." I tried to ask.

But she was already gone. She slipped away like soap on glass. My heart peeled like an immodest orange, and for some reason my eyes were wet. Grace had come to say good-bye.

"Lutumt," I mumbled, my tongue feeling thick in my mouth.

Elder Herney came back inside complaining.

"I still don't know what President Heck needed to talk to me for. He just went on and on about how he thinks missionaries are good. There's a news flash for you—this just in, missionaries are good."

I looked up. The room was spinning.

"Why are you crying?" he snapped. "You're not that sick. Get a grip, Elder. My football coach used to always say, 'feeble of mind, feeble of body.'"

"Feeble," I giggled, the word sounding funny. "Feeble Weeble."

"President Clasp has got to get me out of here," Elder Herney continued. "I can't take being cooped up in this hole with you any longer. I feel like a lame horse."

The horse remark did it. It was like a revelation, except, of course, that it was drug-induced.

Feeble Weeble . . . lame horse . . . It all came back to me. That Halloween night, on the porch, Elder Weeble had called Grace a horse, and I had let it slide, not wanting to be confrontational. That's what Grace had been asking about. She probably thought I was a real idiot. She must have the completely wrong impression of me. I didn't think she was a horse. What I thought was that I might be in love with Grace Heck.

I had to talk to her—that couldn't be the end. My head pounded as sweat pushed up through my skin. My illness was toying with me again. I could feel the red nightgown my mother had made me sticking to my skin.

I watched Elder Herney pace back and forth across the floor, complaining about everything. I saw the walls move in, and felt the pressure of being cooped up come to a boil. The ceiling began to jiggle. I couldn't take it any longer.

I don't know what happened next, or what pushed me over the edge, but I jumped up and ran out. I had to get out of there. I couldn't take lying in that bed for one more minute. And since I was running, I decided that I might as well be running for Grace. I couldn't let those words she had whispered be our last good-bye. I had to find her and tell her that I remembered the porch conversation, and that I was sorry for not standing up for her. I had thought that Elder Herney would have the sense to run along after me as I took off. Nope.

I ran across the field, my red nightgown blowing in the wind. The sun was low in the cloudy sky as I scanned the horizon for Grace. But there was no one in the meadow, no one to witness the sick missionary who was running foolishly by himself. My head thumped as the exhilaration of being alone and out of our cabin made my heart swell. My sick limbs flew through the air, pulling my body behind. I knew that I had to catch up with Grace before she got too deep into the forest. My medicated mind and my poor sense of direction could be a deadly combination.

I reached the edge of the meadow and pushed on into the trees. The hill became steep as I scrambled through the foliage. The medicine in my blood kept signaling my brain to lock up. I had no idea where I was going. I just kept running, counting on fate to turn me in the right direction. My lungs filled with cool air as my legs found the strength to keep me going.

"Grace!" I slurred loudly. "Grace!"

Eventually I came to the spot where I thought the Heck house should be. It was gone. Either they had moved and taken their whole house with them or I was lost. I stopped to catch my breath.

"Grrraccce," I mumbled. My stomach was beginning to act up.

I turned around a few more times to see where I had come from. But each direction looked identical. The beautiful forest of Thelma's Way had become a mirrored fun house—I could almost see myself in the endless maze of trees. The low clouds seemed to rumble even lower, bringing Mother Nature's ceiling down. The sun was beginning to sink behind it, coloring the sky purple.

I was really lost.

I decided to climb to the top of a nearby hill and see if I could spot any houses or help. My mind was so goofy by now that I could barely put one foot in front of the other. I began to see things, and hear things. Trees shifted on me, and the ground bristled like a shivering dog. I tried to pray, but my mind was too muddled. I should never have left my companion. I tried to pray out loud, hoping that vocally I could pull it together. I reached the top of the hill and looked down. There were no houses in sight, but I could see someone walking. It took me a few moments to figure out who it was. It was Paul, striding across the landscape. He was the answer to my prayers.

He could help me back. We didn't get along, but certainly he wouldn't leave a sick man out to die. I stood at the top of the hill and waved my arms. The sun was setting behind me.

"Pauuuullll," I tried to say. "Pauuuuull."

Paul stopped and looked around. He put his hand to his eyes and gazed up at me. Then his face filled with fear. I probably looked ridiculous in my mother's nightgown, but he didn't need to be rude about it.

"PaIif eig eiitdkfeeeeffL," I tried to say, no longer able to construct words within my sick head.

Paul dropped the walking stick he was carrying and fell to his knees.

"Who are you?" he yelled back.

"Elllfienfld wilfjiggged," I answered.

He was trembling like crazy. His tiny, poorly arranged features ticked and popped. I could feel the sun setting behind me, and I looked down to see my oversized nightshirt rippling in the wind. The thin material my mother had used to construct it was glowing in the sunset, the fancy neck ruffle dancing about my head.

"Pawwl," I tried to explain.

"What have I done, great messenger," he yelled in fear.

"Paul I swump wa deee lop don." My tired tongue mangled the words as they came out.

"What do you wish of me?" he screamed.

"What?" I yelled.

"What do you wish of me?"

It suddenly hit me like a cannonball to the temple—the setting sun, my glowing nightgown, Paul shaking like watery Jell-O during an 8.8 earthquake. Paul thought I was something other than I was. It was too much. I couldn't resist egging him on.

"R-r-repent!" I managed to yell, amazed that I could get the word out clearly.

Paul held his skinny hand to his heart and let his big mouth gape. His chest was heaving.

"Repentafgr," I yelled again, feeling dizzy and rather full of myself.

I could see Paul begin to sob, his thick hair bouncing as he trembled. He really believed I was some sort of messenger. As much as I was enjoying myself, I couldn't keep up the charade.

"Paul, it's muflelf," I said, my tongue tangling again. I waved my hands and began to approach him.

Paul wasn't about to let a heavenly visitor get hold of him. He stood up and took off running.

"Paul!" I yelled, running after him.

I couldn't let him get away. I would never find my way back on my own.

"Pawwwul."

Paul ran like crazy, looking over his shoulder every few seconds. I tried hard not to think of anything but catching him. If I started focusing on how tired I was, or how sick I felt, I knew I would fall to the ground in exhaustion. We ran around through a stream, and then back up another hill and down into the meadow. I knew right where I was. I should have just stopped and waited for somebody else to come along. But I kept running. I think I was too sick to rationally realize that I could give up. I wanted to let him know it was just me.

He crossed the meadow, jumped down onto the bank of the Girth, and pushed out across it on a raft. I too crossed the meadow, still yelling after him. I jumped down onto the bank of the Girth and hopped onto a small raft that was lying on the shore. I pushed off and into the current. I knew in an instant that it was a mistake.

The Girth was moving swiftly this time of year. I paddled as well as a sick man could.

"Paul!" I tried again, realizing now more than ever that I needed his help. "Paul!"

I was running out of time. The river had pushed me past the meadow and beyond our place, water lapping up over the lip of my raft. I watched Paul make it to the distant shore. He didn't even waste a second to look back; he just kept on running. I paddled like crazy, but I was weak and my paddling was wimpy. In a few seconds Thelma's Way was behind me, the Girth having carried me past its border. The water became more and more rapid, rocky growths sticking up from the river's floor and teasing the water into a fury. My hand slipped, and my paddle dropped away. I was smack dab in the middle of the river.

Desperate and foolish, I jumped off my raft and tried to swim to shore. It was no use. The rapids had become higher and the water swifter. My tired legs and arms turned to mush. My body froze in the cold whipping water. The river dipped a few more times and then leveled out. For a moment it was flat and slick, dragging me along smoothly with speed. I watched the shoreline.

A horrible noise entered my head—a low roar that gradually began to get louder, piercing my heart and shaking my sick head sober.

Hallow Falls.

The roar increased. I struggled frantically to swim, my long wet nightgown feeling heavy and restrictive. I pulled it off over my head and pushed it away. I thrashed at the river. It was no use; I was going to go over the falls. I couldn't see it up ahead, but I knew it was there.

Hallow Falls was an eighty-foot drop. The previous summer, Elder Jorgensen and I had hiked down to it on one of our P-days. I remember being in awe of its massive weight. Looking up from below, the mist seemed to drift for miles. I had taken some pictures and sent them home to my family. How ironic that they would already have seen the scene of my violent death.

The roar became so loud that I felt my heart would stop. I made a couple more futile attempts to swim away from what was coming. I prayed like I had never prayed before. If God could part the seas, surely he could push a missionary upstream. I thought about all the things I had done wrong, and all the many legitimate reasons God had to not help me. I kept praying.

It was no use.

The Girth River pushed me along, impatient for my demise. The fear in my gut permeated my bones and seeped out of my mouth as I screamed. Then, with one giant push, I was thrust over the falls and into the air—flying through the sky, my arms flailing, the river below racing up to smack me.

I blacked out before I ever hit bottom.

38

# Pulled and Prodded

I opened my eyes to see the back of Roswell's head.

He was pulling me through thick trees. I was in a red wagon, dressed in some tattered jeans and a plaid shirt.

Suddenly I remembered the falls. I grabbed my head to make sure it was still there. I wiggled my arms and legs to test them out. Everything seemed to work.

Roswell looked older than when I had last seen him almost two years ago, before his supposed translation. If he was what a resurrected body looked like, I wanted no part. His head was puckered. His skin was gray.

I had to be dead, because I no longer felt sick. In fact, I felt pretty good. My head was clear, and my body felt healthy. I figured one of two things must have happened. Either the Falls had killed me and I had made it to heaven, where a translated Roswell was the only friend or family member who had come to meet me at the veil; or the Falls had killed me but I hadn't deserved heaven, so it was me and Roswell in outer darkness forever. Either way, things didn't look good.

"Where are we?" I asked Roswell.

I startled him. He jumped, dropping the wagon handle and cursing.

"You ain't supposed to get conscious yet," he informed me, holding his wrinkled hand to his skinny chest.

"Sorry," I replied.

"Just great," he ranted. "Now what the heck am I supposed to do with you?"

"Do with me?" I asked. "What do you mean?"

"You seen me," he ranted. "You know I ain't been translated."

"Oh, that," I said, coming to the realization that I was still alive. "I knew that weeks ago."

"You thought you knew that," Roswell corrected.

"I knew I knew it," I said, still sprawled out in the wagon. "Your cousin Stubby told me. He also told me you stole the Book of Mormon."

Roswell muttered something about his cousin under his breath. It didn't sound complimentary.

"What happened?" I asked, rubbing my head.

"To what?" Roswell questioned.

"To me."

Roswell took out his pipe and stuffed it.

"Found you in the river," Roswell puffed. "You're lucky them falls didn't kill ya. I seen 'em do worse. I dressed you up with some of my better threads. I'll need 'em back," Roswell insisted.

"So you saved me?" I asked, bewildered at the thought.

"Well, I couldn't just leave you there. Took you to my private fishing shack and tried to wake you up. I got tired of staring at your quiet face. So I decided I'd better take you home."

"How long was I out?" I asked.

"Three days," he snickered.

"You're kidding," I said, jumping out of the wagon. "Three days?"

Roswell grunted.

"My companion's probably going ballistic," I moaned.

"Look, kid," Roswell retorted, "we all got problems."

"I've got to get back," I insisted. "Right away."

"I was taking you back," Roswell pointed out. "But now that you're alive I think I'll let you find your own way."

"You can't," I snapped. "I don't know where I am."

"The forest is tricky," Roswell lamented.

"Take me back and I promise I won't tell anyone I saw you." I was prepared to barter.

Roswell thought about this for a minute.

"How 'bout we make a deal?"

"What kind of deal?" I asked.

Roswell sat down on an old tree stump. I sat back in the wagon.

"I'm tired of living all hidden up," he said. "Sick of having to keep myself tucked away. I'm a person's person. Like my neighbors to be curious about my doings. Found out I don't make myself very good company. I'm stubborn. Can't talk myself out of anything."

Roswell paused to puff.

"I'm a simple man—no skeletons in the closet, no demons to conquer," he continued. "Makes for lousy conversation."

"What about your brother?" I asked, begging to differ about the skeletons.

"I didn't kill Feeble," Roswell insisted. "My dear brother found out from Stubby that I'd taken the Book of Mormon and started having a fit. He began saying silly things like how honesty and integrity were more 'portant than money. Feeble found me out just two days before he passed on. He teased me with that dumb little statue. Kept saying I was an embarrassment to the family. He even said he was going to turn me in. I couldn't take it." Roswell paused to rub his eye. "I told him I was leaving and he chased after me."

We were both quiet for a moment.

"It wasn't much of a chase," Roswell finally said. "Feeble had a heart attack about ten steps into it. Figured I'd better hightail it out of there if I didn't want any questions asked. So I hid up in my fishing shack. I was eventually going to show my face, but I overheard Sister Watson talking about me being translated and all. Me, translated," he laughed. "It sounded so regal, I decided to stay hid. I'm a proud man," Roswell admitted.

"So why'd you steal the Book of Mormon?" I asked, staring at him and wondering how a proud man could wear two different pieces of plaid clothing.

"Had to steal it," Roswell replied. "I'd made a bet with Clove Timpleton in Virgil's Find that his newborn red cow was the heifer of prophecy. Turns out she was just dirty from birth. Washed up to be almost white."

I tried not to look dumbfounded.

"Take me back," I said, suddenly weary of Roswell's company.

Roswell made an offer. "You tell folks that I descended in a cloud from heaven to save your life, and I'll take you back."

"No way," I protested. That was too much to ask.

"You gotta give me something," he whined.

"Okay," I reasoned. "You come into town with me and I'll tell them you saved my life."

"And . . ." Roswell prodded.

"And," I continued, "you make up the rest."

That seemed to satisfy him, at least for the time being. We hiked for about an hour before I could tell where we were. I got back into the wagon, and Roswell wheeled me into town.

"Elder Williams, Elder Williams!" Sister Watson had spotted us. She was sitting on the porch of the boardinghouse. The meadow exploded with folks popping like popcorn. My buttery family. Roswell pulled me right up to the porch, a small cloud of dust puffing up as the wagon came to an abrupt stop. Sister Watson threw herself down by me, kissing my forehead.

"Crazy boy. Foolish kid."

President Heck was the next to maul me.

"Where? How? I can't believe it!"

Teddy practically cut off my circulation as she hugged me tightly, and Nippy nodded so violently that I became concerned about her head remaining attached to her body.

"We thought you was dead," they all said. Everyone was so happy to see me that they hardly even noticed Roswell. He just sort of stood there looking like he always had, content not to be the center of attention for the moment.

President Clasp came out of our cabin and ran up to greet me. I could tell he wasn't sure if he should hit or hug me, not that he would have really done either. He and Elder Herney had been in the process of packing up my stuff. I guess they and about forty law officers from all over the state had spent the last three days combing the forest of Thelma's Way. They had almost given up.

I called my family from the boardinghouse to tell them I was okay. My mom cried with joy. My father guardedly gushed. As soon as I hung up, President Clasp informed me we were leaving. This was it. He wanted both me and Elder Herney out of Thelma's Way. In a whirlwind we collected all of our stuff and briskly hiked out of town towards Virgil's Find. It happened so fast I barely had time to register what was going on.

My transfer had arrived, and the timing couldn't be worse.

I didn't want to leave. It was too sudden. I didn't even get a chance to properly say good-bye. I was just whisked away. Folks lined the path as we made our grand exit. These people were my family. I had endured and endeared them for the past two years. I scanned the crowd for a glimpse of Grace.

Salvation was out of sight.

Everyone stood there staring at me as if I were their son going off to war.

"God bless," Toby Carver said aloud, his Ace bandage waving in the air.

People followed us for a few steps, and then they slowly turned back. They would cope without me. I hoped the same of myself. I scanned the trees the rest of the way, hoping to see Grace.

From Virgil's Find we took a big van back to Knoxville. President Clasp tried to lecture and love me into understanding. I understood all too well. I spent the night in a real bed, in a real house, in a real town.

I couldn't ever remember being more uncomfortable.

39

# Knocks-Ville

## The Last Day

I spent the final month of my mission in Knoxville, serving with an Elder Jones. We had a baptism, and I learned what it was like to spend six hours a day knocking on doors in a suburban neighborhood. Elder Jones was probably the best elder I ever served with. He had a better sense of the gospel and a real sense of purpose. He lacked some of Elder Jorgensen's raw enthusiasm and wasn't quite as endearing, but he was solid.

This last month in Knoxville, I had been amazingly homesick for Thelma's Way, and Grace. My time had seemed too short there. I kept telling myself that I was just overly emotional because of how I had been ripped away. I knew, however, that my attachment to Thelma's Way was due to far more than a bad send-off.

As I packed my bags to leave the mission field, I thought long and hard about all that I had been through. This was it. I had made it the entire two years. I was considerably more melancholy than I had anticipated I would be.

At the beginning of my mission, I had thought constantly of how great it would be when I was finally able to fly home. To be done. I had imagined myself on the plane smiling over how fulfilling my time had been and how wonderful it would be to see Lucy and my family again. Now, as I packed to go home, the approaching plane ride seemed frightening. Every mile I soon flew, I knew, I would feel more and more distanced from the people I loved in Thelma's Way.

I met a lot of great people during my last month in Knoxville, but it wasn't the same. These people used Saran Wrap only to cover food, and Ace bandages were applied no more than once. Gatherings were civil and predictable, stripped of soul and commotion.

I closed my suitcase, looked around the room, and walked out to the van. We would be at the airport in no time.

My mission was over.

40

# JUSTIFICATION

Southdale in late October is a funny thing. People are so busy prepping themselves for the upcoming holidays that they fail to have any fall fun. The wide streets are cluttered with cars driving back and forth to this and that, for which and whatever. Things are busy but as empty as the once-bushy trees.

I missed Thelma's Way. I had gotten lost there and in the process been found. I tried not to be one of those ex-missionaries who spends all his time yearning for the past. I tried to distance myself from the people of Thelma's Way. I tried to find the positives in Southdale. Paved streets, large stores, cable TV—big deal. Where were the heart and purpose of it all?

College had been going well, but I was keeping to myself more than I probably should have. Often I would sit out on the benches watching the beautiful sun-kissed coeds and missing my Grace. Their tans would fade long before I was fully over her.

I had tried to talk about it with my father. He told me to forget about Thelma's Way. "Life is business, my boy, business," he had said. "You're polished past the point of worrying about those people."

I talked to my mother, hoping she would be kinder than my father. She too had little good to say. "Part of a mission is forgetting about those you served."

I wondered what manual Mom had been reading.

As October came to a close, I could feel my memories of Thelma's Way slipping. I had gotten a letter from President Heck about a month back. It was a long one explaining how CleeDee and Leo had gotten married in the Atlanta Temple on August eleventh. I had not been notified because Leo had wanted to test the branch's spirituality by not telling them about the wedding. He wanted to see if the Spirit would invite folks for him, prompting people to just show up. It was a lot cheaper than announcements, and it seemed to Leo to be a great barometer of local righteousness. Consequently, Leo and CleeDee got married without a single friend on hand.

Since Leo was now married, and had no need for his bachelor-mobile, he gave the car to Digby, who in turn gave his old motorcycle to Ed Washington. Ed was using it to commute back and forth to Virgil's Find, where he was taking a couple of college courses in business management. Ed had become a new man since he had moved out of his mother's place. And so had his mother. Apparently, she was using her newfound free time to make eyes at Briant Willpts. Who knew that all these years Ed had been cramping her style?

Sister Lando was coming out to church every week now with Teddy Yetch. President Heck had helped solve Sister Lando's desire to wear her witch hat by assigning his wife, Patty Heck, to be her visiting teacher. Patty Heck had tactfully offered to make Sister Lando a dress incorporating the hat material in it. Since then, Sister Lando showed up every week in her black and white dress, smiling as if she had fooled the system.

The town had no problem forgiving Roswell. These people were pros at forgetting. Roswell had even come out to church a few times in honor of his departed brother. Yes, instead of people being mad about what he had done, most folks viewed it as a miracle that he had returned. President Heck said it was kind of nice to spot him sitting on the porch like old times. Besides, he was old and wouldn't be around forever. Why argue his presence when time was not on his side?

The Book of Mormon still had not turned up. Folks were waiting for someone to start purchasing a lot of nice things—increased spending power would be a surefire giveaway if someone had hocked it for cash. As of yet, no one had purchased anything out of the ordinary.

While shopping for an engagement ring, Miss Flitrey and Wad had found an old-fashioned hearing aid at one of the Virgil's Find garage sales. It was an awkward thing that had an antenna and a thick head strap. It wasn't modern, but it worked, and it was too big for Nippy to swallow. She wore it everywhere now, walking around the meadow looking like a wrinkled space alien.

Since there were no longer any full-time missionaries in Thelma's Way, President Heck and Toby Carver were teaching the lessons to Judy Bickerstaff. She had been out to church once, and was willing to come again as long as it didn't interfere with any of her possible acting auditions.

Sybil Porter, Frank Porter's strong daughter, had moved in with Sister Watson. Sybil had wanted to get out on her own for a while. Sister Watson was presently teaching Sybil grooming and how to act like a lady. Sybil gave Sister Watson something to focus on besides the upcoming Christmas play.

It had been over six months since our exclusive one-night engagement of *All Is Swell.* The fallout had subsided—President Heck had even received a few letters from people around the state wanting to know about Mormonism. They figured any group of people who would go through so much trouble for nothing were worthy of investigation. President Heck sent them out what he called a "Thelma's Way care package," containing a Book of Mormon, a Church magazine, a complimentary bar of Sister Watson's soap, and a picture of the ward members at the Labor Day breakfast. I figured anyone who joined after seeing that picture would have to have been converted by the Spirit.

Amazingly, Paul had come around. According to President Heck's letter, Paul had had a vision of a red avenging angel who had scared him into coming back to church. He was so unnerved by the incident that true humility had finally gotten a chance to work him over. President Heck used words like *kind, submissive,* and *willing.* Paul was begging for forgiveness. It looked like the town would hold no grudge. President Heck also mentioned that once when Sister Watson showed up to church wearing a red dress, Paul had almost passed out.

President Heck had high hopes for the branch. He felt that Paul's new activity could help the meadow to mellow spiritually. Perhaps the numbers would begin to come back to where they were before Paul had pulled things apart.

Perhaps.

President Heck's letter had been great. Still, as I folded it and put it away for safekeeping, I knew he had failed to tell me what I most wanted to know. Forget all the other outrageous and quirky doctrines of Thelma's Way, I wanted to hear something about Grace.

He had written not a word.

I had tried writing to Grace once. I spilled out my heart. I told her everything. I tried to explain my feelings and my confusion. Did we have a future? I asked. Then I tore it up into little pieces and threw it away.

I had gotten a letter from Elder Jorgensen. He was still serving in Tennessee. His leg had healed, and he was currently companions with Elder Herney. He went on and on about how fantastic he and Elder Herney were doing. Elder Jorgensen's amazing attitude was just what Elder Herney needed. He had also included a picture. It was a snapshot of him and me at Leo's baptism. I got homesick every time I looked at it.

It was early afternoon. I had spent the day raking up leaves in our front yard. The big trees had shivered themselves bare, their naked branches ripping across the sky. I had raked the leaves into piles, tiny communities organized beneath the barky overlord. Leaves that had traversed the space from limb to soil, willing to rot and nourish the very trees that had let them go.

I cleaned up and drove to the local super-sized, bigger-than-necessary grocery store where, for your convenience, you could pick out new car tires while pinching tomatoes for freshness. When I finally found an employee to help me, he couldn't tell me anything except where the bathroom was and that the registers were up front.

I was perusing the more than one hundred brands of pancake syrup when I heard a recognizable voice one aisle over. Because of sky-high shelving I couldn't see who it was. I tried to place the voice, but I drew a blank. I walked around the aisle ready to say hi and saw them there. It was Lucy and Lance. Larger and glossier than life. They were trying to decide which self-tanning lotion to buy. I couldn't believe it.

I had wanted to see Lucy, thinking it would be such a big deal when I did. I had wanted her to know that I had grown up. I had turned out, despite her lack of confidence. I thought we would see each other and be blown away by all the sweet memories, the could-have-beens and should-have-beens.

That didn't happen.

They didn't notice me until I had *ahemed* a few times.

"Trust?" Lucy finally clued in.

Her skin was too dark for late October. Her hair was too shiny, and her lips were too thin.

"Hey, Lucy," I replied.

Lance sort of smiled, his big, perfect head tilting in condescension.

"So this is Trust," he *ho-ho-hoed,* his hands on his hips, looking like a poster boy for imitation humans.

Lucy struck a pose. I had caught her condescending to shop in a common supermarket, and that made her uncomfortable. She placed the tanning lotion back on the shelf like a hostess on a game show.

I wanted to say something to her but I couldn't. I couldn't find a single word worth wasting on her. I couldn't believe I had ever wanted what now stood before me. Lucy was a nice person, but she lacked soul.

"How was your mission?" she finally asked, needing to break the uncomfortable silence that had developed.

This was a great moment. True, I was no Lance, but I had never felt better about my appearance than now. Yes, here I was, looking better than Lucy had ever seen me look, and she looking like less than I had perceived she could possibly be. Most people would probably think she was perfect, not me. She was everything I no longer wanted. She was salvation by works.

"My mission was great," I replied.

"Did you ever get out of that weird town?" she asked, gazing at me curiously, as if I were behind glass.

I didn't answer. I just stood there thinking until she and Lance became self-conscious and walked off.

"Weird guy," I heard Lance say, as they carted themselves away.

I put my tomatoes and pancake syrup back, went outside, got into my car, and drove to the airport.

I had some unfinished business to take care of.

# 41

# Restoration

The path to Thelma's Way had never seemed so long. It had taken me just over a day to get to Virgil's Find. It was about two o'clock in the afternoon. I had made decent time, but couldn't help feeling I was months behind schedule. I picked up my feet and ran. The late October air filled my lungs.

When Thelma's Way finally came into view, my heart just sort of liquefied. It pushed through my veins and up into my throat. Still, I managed to stroll into town looking nonchalant.

There were kids in the meadow and folks hanging out on the boardinghouse porch despite the cold. I could see Leo walking hand in hand with CleeDee, and Digby in Leo's old car. As much as I loved each and every one of these people, they weren't the ones I had come to see. I walked with purpose to the old wagons and turned, heading towards the woods. For a few moments folks ignored me, not realizing who I was. But the second Narlette climbed up on one of the covered wagons, she recognized me. She then made the announcement I was longing to holler.

"Elder Williams is back!"

Folks froze. They put their hands to their hearts and mouths. I wanted to stop, to clap backs and give hugs, but I couldn't let them slow me down.

I was on a mission.

I watched people dive off the boardinghouse porch and chase after me. I'd never seen old Roswell move so quickly. Wad, who was giving Miss Flitrey a haircut, put down his scissors and rolled over to greet me. Kids clustered about me like bees on a hive. Narlette grabbed my hand as I walked.

"Elder Williams," she cried happily. "What are you doing here?"

Four words.

"I'm going for Grace."

The crowd burst into cheers and guffaws.

"He's going for Grace," they told each other, beginning to understand as they said it.

I walked quickly. The crowd fell in behind me. I had kind of hoped to do this on my own, but as I reached the edge of the forest no one turned back.

"What's going on?" people would ask as we passed them on our way. "He's going for Grace," someone would yell and they would join in, cheering and whooping.

When we got to the Heck house, everyone grew quiet to see what would happen next. I pushed back my longer-than-missionary hair and tried to calm down. I knocked on the door and waited. Practically the whole town was circled around me. My nerves were shorting out, and my fingers and arms felt loose and rubbery.

President Heck answered the door.

"Elder Williams," he said in amazement, his gray hair shorter than I remembered it, and his eyes more alive.

I spoke before I chickened out. "Is Grace here?" I asked.

"No," he answered, surprised.

The crowd behind me "ohhhhed" in disappointment.

"Do you know where she is?" I asked desperately.

Patty Heck came up beside him to see what was going on.

"I haven't seen her for a couple days," Brother Heck replied, acting like he was thinking extra hard for my sake.

Before he said another word, I stepped off the porch and marched further into the forest. I knew where I had to go. I had to find that cabin. Grace would be there. I just hoped I could remember the way.

President and Sister Heck joined our merry band. I heard Pete Kennedy fill them in behind me.

"He's going for Grace."

"Our Grace?" Patty Heck questioned.

My Grace.

We hiked over a couple of hills and down a ravine. More and more people gathered, all of them staying in my wake. As we passed Toby Carver's place I ran smack dab into Toby and Paul standing outside. They were arguing over the price of firewood, or some such thing. Toby, I was thrilled to see. Paul, on the other hand, still looked to me like the self-righteous apostate I had known so well. His face puckered when he realized it was me.

We stared at one another. Everyone hushed. I thought of a million things I could say to make him see the damage he'd done, and to check if he really had changed. But all that would take time, and I had an appointment to keep.

So I stuck out my hand, and he stuck out his. We shook and everyone cheered. I began hiking again. Paul patted me on the back, falling into step directly behind me, acting like we had been best friends for years. I was more than willing to let him feel that way. This, after all, was my town, and these were my people.

This was a big day.

Finally I spotted the rock chimney above the trees. Smoke curled from the top.

She was home. She was in there.

I thought I was going to pass out.

Softly, I pushed Narlette aside. Everyone stayed just where they were. The forest crunched beneath my feet. My blood turned from whole milk to skim.

I stepped up to the door and knocked.

No one answered, but I thought I heard movement inside. I knocked again and then tried the knob. It was locked. I felt the crowd step closer behind me.

"Grace," I hollered. "It's me, Elder Williams. Trust."

No answer. Pete Kennedy coughed.

"Grace, if you're in there, open up," I said.

Closed door.

Miss Flitrey sneezed.

"Gesundheit," Wad whispered.

I wanted to see Grace now more than ever. I wanted to look into her face like only a returned missionary could. I wanted to tell her the things that my mission had prevented me from saying. I wanted to say I remembered what I had said on the boardinghouse porch almost exactly a year ago. I wanted to say I was wrong. I thought about breaking down the door. I thought about climbing down the chimney.

I turned to face the crowd and shrugged.

These were the people I had come to love. These were the ones who had watched me become the man I now was. God had given me the patience to discover their secrets and their accomplishments. Like a pop-top, He had twisted my life and revealed my purpose—I could feel the guiding pressure of His palm. Now here He was pouring me back into the half-full glass of Thelma's Way.

Feeble had been right all those years ago. His prophecy had come to pass. Things had changed. The person I was today would hardly have recognized the reluctant boy who once wandered into this valley.

How could I have ever doubted a Creator who saw it all? He had changed me. I had been too busy trying to figure it out to notice. He had planted me here, provided the sun and water, and let me push my own way out of the seed. So often on my mission I had thought that I was doing God some great favor by serving. Now I knew that He had given me more in those two years than I could ever account for. He didn't mold me into some suave businessman. He carefully shaped me into a true son of God. He had sent me home safely and pushed me back here to see what the future could bring. I stood in front of that door smiling as the cosmos whispered its secrets into my ear.

I swatted away a small cluster of bugs and knocked again. I would knock all day if I had to. I would stand in front of that door forever, if there were the slightest possibility that someday Grace would open up and let me in.

I've heard it said that when God closes a door, He splits a crowd, or something to that effect. God was working His wonders. As I stood there staring through the window, I could hear the townsfolk begin to whisper.

"There she is."

"Move over."

"Here she comes."

I looked around and saw the ring of spectators shift, opening up for Grace to walk through. Grace had not been in the cabin, she had been about the forest as usual. She had small branches in her hands and wind in her hair. She looked at me as if *I* were a mirage—I drank her in as if she were an oasis. She was wearing jeans and a white shirt. Her red hair looked dark against the contrast of white, her deep eyes made the evergreens look dull. I watched her pink lips as they tried not to smile. I could see she was thinking. She was calculating me in. My feet turned to clay, my toes chipping off and rattling around in my shoes. I could feel the back of my neck fizzle, like cold water running over a hot pan.

She was calculating me in!

She walked through the crowd and right up to me. Afternoon light surrounded her like a heavenly aura. She stopped and looked into my eyes.

"You came back," she said softly.

"I love you," I answered.

"I thought you might," she replied, believing the words as she spoke them.

"I wanted to give us a try."

Grace smiled, giving bliss a whole new definition. "It might take a bit," she reasoned.

"I've got forever."

The entire town *Ahhhed.*

The low clouds dispersed with a burst, bits and pieces of them shooting off throughout the universe. The wind started to whisper, blowing beautiful thoughts around in a billion languages. Trees and bushes shook their limbs in jubilation, the rich ground singing the bass. Hats were thrown into the air and hugs were passed around like baby photos at a family reunion.

I looked at Grace and stuck out my hand as if to reach for her. She dropped her branches, breathing softly. I pulled her to me and held on for dear life. I could feel her shake.

"Are you okay?" I whispered.

I felt her hair in my face and her back beneath my hands. Gratitude streamed down my face.

From the corner of my eye I watched the crowd wipe their eyes. Toby's bandage would go home wet today.

Grace loved me.

All was well.

## 42

# Life and Limb

November 9th

I could hear Pete Kennedy breathing to the tune of "She'll Be Coming 'Round the Mountain" through his nose. My blue eyes gazed over at Leo Tip and President Heck as they crouched down together behind a fallen tree. President Heck was decked out in a safety-orange jumpsuit his wife Patty had made him, and Leo was wearing a pair of fake antlers he had constructed himself. I was baffled as to why we weren't currently surrounded by a horde of does who had been tricked into thinking Leo was some hot buck. Leo adjusted his antlers and picked up his rifle.

Pete suddenly stopped breathing. I looked up at him. He had on a small knit cap and a big faded flannel shirt. He looked like a grown-up gang member who didn't know how to properly wash and care for his colors. I watched his jaw drop and eyes grow big. Then quietly and with muted enthusiasm he pointed toward a huge buck that was wandering into our sights. It was the biggest animal I had ever seen. It walked slowly, radiating such confidence and self-esteem that even I began to feel inferior to it. The deer came to a stop in front of a tall thin tree and posed as if auditioning for a special-edition belt buckle. We had seen a couple bucks earlier in the day, but it would take the two of them to equal a single side of this one.

Leo, having the best shot and position, lifted his gun and pointed toward our huge prey. In the far distance a bird sang. President Heck nudged Leo, giving him both encouragement and the go-ahead. I watched Leo's hand twitch as he began to squeeze the trigger. Once again I just couldn't stand for this.

"Haaaawwwchhhewwww!" I forced out a fabricated sneeze.

The giant buck flinched and bounded away as Leo jerked and misfired. President Heck leaped from his spot and began shooting in hopes of hitting the dashing deer. Pete shot off his rifle a few times and then pulled a pistol from his holster and continued blasting. Leo, not one to pass up an opportunity to waste bullets, kept shooting as well. I covered my ears and watched in amazement. The buck was long gone—he had jumped away unscathed—but these three continued firing. Birds took flight from every tree. Small animals came out of hiding all around us and scampered away from all the noise. Not a single shot hit anything with feathers or fur. Nope, they just kept firing at the spot the deer had once occupied.

The tall thin tree that had been behind the buck was now being blown away by my trigger-happy companions. I assume that they would have eventually stopped shooting on their own, but that theory would never be tested due to the fact that the maimed tree was beginning to fall toward us. It cracked and screamed as it tore its wounded torso from its trunk. Leo and Pete stopped shooting so as to better be able to holler. President Heck kept firing in a panic at the thin pine as it came directly toward him. With a loud thud the tree hit President Heck on the head, knocking him to the ground.

It took a couple seconds for Pete's screaming and the echoes of gunshots to drift off and leave us in silence. President Heck lay there next to the fallen tree, his orange attire making the dark earth beneath him look black. We huddled over him, gazing down, until he opened his eyes.

"President Heck!" Pete said with concern.

"What?" he moaned.

"You okay?" Leo asked.

"I'm fine," he said, sitting up. A huge goose egg was growing on the top of his head and making his hair look as if it were doing the wave.

Leo gazed at the fallen tree.

"Is it dead?" he asked somberly.

Pete knocked Leo on the shoulder. "Don't be dumb," Pete said. "Trees don't die, they just . . ."

Pete paused, realizing that he had never really contemplated the mystery of where trees go. He scratched his head and remained silent.

"Darn it, Trust," Leo said to me, suddenly remembering that this was all my fault. "That's the third buck you've scared off today. The antlers on that one would have looked amazing over my fireplace."

"Wouldn't they," Pete agreed. "You coulda put them right above that picture of you and CleeDee at the fair."

"I've always liked that picture," Leo reflected.

"Me too," Pete agreed. "Those electric lights make CleeDee look fancy. I . . ."

"You know," I interrupted, "maybe I'll head back to the meadow. I've probably had enough hunting for one day. Besides, Grace and I still need to go to Virgil's Find."

Leo and Pete just stared at me.

"I'll head back with you," President Heck said. "This knot on my head might need some tending."

I helped him up from the ground. Leo took his antlers off and straightened out the left one. He put them back on.

"Come on, Leo," Pete commanded. "Let's go do some real hunting."

Pete and Leo walked off to find something to shoot at. President Heck and I turned toward the direction of town and started downhill.

"I guess hunting ain't your cup of stew," he said almost kindly.

"I guess not," I replied as we walked.

"I remember when I was just a kid," he reminisced. "I used to be all squeamish and cowardly about death, like you. Then my father took me out and made me smack our family pig over the head with a shovel. I felt real bad at first, but the bacon seemed to cheer me up. That's how life works, you give in to change and it feeds you."

"Actually, I have no problem with—"

"I'm glad you understand," he interrupted, not hearing me out. Then he began whistling to himself as he turned to walk downhill.

President Heck was a number of things to me. At the moment he was my branch president, my girlfriend's father, and my friend. He was closing in on fifty. His brown hair had finally surrendered, letting the gray invade in full force. He was actually quite distinguished-looking when he wasn't speaking (or wearing orange coveralls, for that matter). But his best asset by far was his oldest daughter, Grace. I had served my mission with these people and fallen in deep like with Grace. My mission had come to an end this last summer, but it only took me a few months to realize that I needed to come back to Thelma's Way—to find out if Grace and I had a future.

It was still too soon to tell. There was no doubt that Grace and I loved each other, but there were piles of issues and feelings and problems we needed to work through. I was staying at the boardinghouse while we sorted things out. In a way it was as if we had just met. Sure, I had served almost two years practically in her backyard, but we had never dated, or even really been alone together.

We had a long way to go.

I had hoped I could just come back, sweep Grace off her feet, and then the two of us could be one. It was still a possibility, but I could see now that it wouldn't be "for sure" without real effort.

My parents were livid that I had returned for Grace. In their view, I was jeopardizing my potentially affluent future for the sake of some unpolished Tennesseean. I had come back to Tennessee without telling them, and they now felt as if I had trampled on their plans of living vicariously through me. We weren't speaking, for the time being. Of course, for the time being, I was thousands of miles away from them, trying to keep up with a whistling orange.

My sense of direction was pathetic. I had lived and worked in this area for almost two years, and I still couldn't find my way around. My parents should have named me "Lost," or "Confused"—it would have been so much more fitting than "Trust."

President Heck stopped.

"You know, Trust," he said, "I don't think you belong here."

"What?" I asked, surprised.

"I was just looking up at those turtle-shaped clouds and I got the strongest feeling that you need to be back at home with your folks."

"That's silly," I smiled, somewhat taken aback.

"I know," he stated. "Turtle-shaped clouds. But if you look at that one right there you can see the . . ."

"No, not the clouds," I clarified. "Going back to *Southdale* is silly."

"I don't think so," he sniffed.

"What about Grace?"

"Well, the wife and I have been talking."

"And?" I asked.

"And I think maybe we could send Grace out your way to get some college in. She's always been wanting to further her education."

"Grace in Southdale?"

The idea was absurd.

"Sure," President Heck said. "It might be good for her to get away."

I had honestly never thought of such a thing. Taking Grace from

Tennessee was like taking the water from the beach, or the marshmallows from my favorite cold cereal. I couldn't imagine the Volunteer State drawing a single voluntary tourist without the lure of Grace Heck at its core. Sure, I was a little exaggerated in my thinking, but it still didn't seem right. Plus, as discombobulated as the idea of removing Grace was, it seemed even less plausible trying to fit her into Southdale. My hometown would eat her alive. I could see my parents now.

"Mom, Dad, this is Grace."

"Trust, I told you never to bring a girl from Thelma's Way into our house."

"Why don't you just put her outside, Son, so we can eat."

Grace had lived her whole life in Thelma's Way. She had spent her lifetime simmering slowly. I couldn't drag her into the seething, boiling ways of Southdale. There wasn't a single thing in my hometown that she would relate to. Even the gospel was faster there. My ward back home had just posted its own web page with announcements and pictures of the latest ward activity. Grace had grown up in a ward that thought the Internet was the extra stitching on the backsides of winter long johns.

She just wouldn't mesh.

"Do you think Grace would want to go to Southdale?" I asked.

"Sure," President Heck said. "Patty and I have put aside some money. We might be able to help her out a little."

"Grace in Southdale," I said softly.

"You don't really think Grace would be happy living her whole life here forever, do you?" he asked. "She's always tinkered with the idea of seeing the world outside. She could just try it for a while," he said, beginning to walk again.

"I honestly hadn't thought about it," I confessed.

"It might be good for the two of you to spend some time in your part of the country," he went on. "I know there must be a lot more things for people to do there than here. She could meet your folks, go to school."

"You think Grace would go for it?"

"Can't really see what you'd be tearing her away from."

"Well, what about her family, for starters?"

"Grace is ready for more," he winked. "It's time for her to start looking into a new family, if you know what I . . ."

President Heck tried to elbow me in a friendly manner, but he missed and lost his balance, falling to his knees on the ground. I didn't even have time to catch him. His head knocked against an old tree trunk. I tried really hard not to laugh. President Heck rubbed the new knot on his head.

"I used to like trees," he laughed, embarrassed, trying to stand himself up.

"Are you going to be okay?" I smiled, grabbing his elbow and lifting.

"I'll be fine," he fussed. "Toby will wrap my head when I get back."

Sister Watson was wearing Toby's bandage at the moment. She had procured a really deep splinter a couple days back while stacking wood. Her fear of tweezers prevented her from having the sliver removed. She was hoping that by keeping the finger wrapped the splinter would just disappear. I'm sure Toby would ask for the bandage back, claiming that head injuries receive first priority.

We walked on in silence, with me thinking about Grace and Southdale. After a while the meadow came into view.

"I'd have a hard time leaving," I said, almost to myself.

"Things are easier if you just don't think about them," President Heck replied.

I could see the boardinghouse off in the distance. A speck of red moved across the porch as smoke twisted up and out of the chimney.

"Do you want to talk to her?" President Heck asked. "Or would you like me to?"

"I'll do it," I replied. "I'll do it today."

43

# Ready, Set, Go

November 11th

The next day I called my parents from the boardinghouse and told them that I had partially seen the light and was coming home. They said they were partially happy, but wanted to know what the catch was. I told them the catch, in every sense of the word, was Grace, and that she was coming home with me. Surprisingly, my parents were okay with this. I think they saw the opportunity of picking her apart on their turf as somewhat of a blessing.

"Mom, I'm not bringing her home so that you and Dad can make her feel uncomfortable and unwanted in person."

"We'll see," Mom replied sweetly.

"You'll see what?" I asked, bothered.

"Trust, why don't you talk to your father?"

I could hear Mom hand the phone to my father. He cleared his throat.

"Son?" he questioned, as if there were a possibility that I had morphed into someone else while my parents were making the phone hand off.

"It's me, Dad," I said.

"Son, we feel . . . well, we're encouraged by your change of heart. But we can't pretend that we are delighted about your feelings for this person."

"Grace is her name," I helped.

"Son, I just don't want to see you thumbing your nose at all the opportunities that lie ahead of you."

"Thanks, Dad," I said, hoping to end the conversation.

"Son, this is an important time in your life. Our community won't let you drift forever. People expect more from a Williams child."

"I'll try not to let you down, Dad," I rolled my eyes. "I promise to only drift a little."

"Good to hear, my boy, good to hear. Now here's your mother."

I could hear my father whisper, "We're reaching him," to my mom as he handed her the phone.

"He always did respect your opinion," she whispered back as she took the phone from him.

"Trust? Are you there?"

I couldn't imagine what my parents thought happened to people waiting on the phone over here.

"I'm still here, Mom."

We talked for a few moments more, making arrangements and trying hard not to say things that might get someone upset. Sybil Porter tapped me on the shoulder and informed me that she needed to use the phone to place an order for makeup. Sybil had been working really hard on getting in touch with her femininity. She had spent her life under the many shadows of her older and manlier brothers, but now under the tutelage of Sister Watson, Sybil was slowly turning into a lady.

Sybil tapped me a little harder.

"I'd better go, Mom. But if someone could pick us up from the air . . ."

Sybil pushed me and "Grrrrred." I turned to look at her. She glared at me for a moment and then frowned as if she were remembering how to act.

"Sorry," she scowled. "It's just that if I call in the next fifteen minutes I save twenty percent on all eye and lip liner."

"Mom, we've got an emergency here," I said into the phone. "Grace and I will see you tomorrow. Bye."

I hung up the phone and moved aside so Sybil could use it. I walked out of the boardinghouse and down the porch. Grace was outside watching some of the local kids play on the rotting pioneer wagons in the meadow.

She had her long red hair tied behind her neck. A couple thick strands hung in front of her face as she looked on. I watched her push them back behind her ear. She was more beautiful to me than a thousand wordy poets could ever describe, her presence a previously undiscovered chemical compound—one that supplied huge amounts of oxygen to my brain. I hoped that I was doing the right thing by taking her away from Thelma's Way.

Grace noticed me and smiled as I approached.

We were going to Southdale.

# 44

# Open Harms

November 12th

As our plane descended, I held Grace's hand and watched Southdale grow big around us. Each foot we lowered left my insides feeling even more knotted. Like taffy in the hands of a nervous pessimist, I was being twisted and pulled. Bringing Grace back home was a big deal.

From out of the plane window Southdale appeared brown and unspectacular. I could see the Dintmore Hills, and the Southdale River. The hills rippled across the landscape, flattening out a few miles away from the city and making the earth appear as if it were having a cellulite problem. The now shallow Southdale River slowly pushed through the middle of town, dividing the city. A recent drought had thinned the river out something terrible. From high above, it looked no wider than a road, but covered bridges spanned its water in stripes, and the new Wedge Freeway cut across it downtown, wide and topless. Southdale itself seemed to bleed even more in every direction than it had just a few months ago—homes and neighborhoods where once there was nothing. New malls and shopping centers were rising from the ground like blocky weeds.

Southdale was supposedly named for Dale Wedge, a Scottish immigrant who helped settle what was then called Weaver's Claim. According to legend, Dale had taken two bullets in the head while arguing with a cousin over water rights. Both bullets got lodged between his right ear and brain. Amazingly, they seemed to cause nothing but a few days of pain. Well, with little discomfort, and fantastic bragging rights, Dale decided to leave the bullets in his head. They didn't seem to affect him mentally. (Of course, he was no cerebral wizard in the first place.) After the shooting, people noticed that Dale seemed to lean south just a bit. Some reasoned that it was due to the extra two ounces of silver embedded behind his ear. Others figured it was the magnetic pull of the earth on the metal. Of course, it could just have been that Dale's right leg was shorter than his left. Whatever the reason, Dale leaned, and in doing so earned himself the nickname, "South Dale," or so the story goes. Shortly after his mysterious death, the town voted to change its name from Weaver's Claim to Southdale. Sure, there were still some who insisted the town got its name from the fact that it was one of the southernmost towns in the state. But those folks were labeled crackpots and invited to settle farther west.

I liked Southdale—I always had. I liked the small hills that surrounded it. I liked the people and the pace. I liked the warm, mild, year-round weather. It was an almost perfect American city. Crime was low, wages were up, and a national magazine had just ranked it seventh in its "Great Places to Raise a Family" poll. I had to agree. True there were moments I had begun to wish that it was a little smaller or more green and hilly, but that was my only real complaint. And now with the addition of Grace, my city had everything. The fact that I felt this way made me wonder why I couldn't relax.

"Are you ready for all this?" I asked Grace as our plane approached the runway.

"I hope so," she answered softly, her green eyes taking in the big city below us. "This certainly isn't Thelma's Way, is it?"

"You'll do great," I said, wanting to reassure her.

"I think you have more to lose than me."

Grace was already coming around. She had been a mystery my entire mission, staying away from town, hidden from view. She had kept her distance, and in doing so, had laid claim to my heart. Now here she was, sitting next to me, about to meet my parents. I stared at her shamelessly for a few seconds.

"What?" she asked self-consciously.

Her white skin and red hair stood out against the horribly busy fabric that was covering the seats on the plane.

"What is it, Trust?"

Her long fingers closed as she pressed a hand to her chest.

"Trust?"

Her pink lips teased me.

"What are you looking at?" She smiled.

"Nothing," I replied, wanting more than anything to make this work.

My father, Roger, picked us up from the airport. He was all smiles. He shook both of our hands and asked Grace how she spelled her name. (He had read in one of his many business books that this gesture let people know you were truly interested in them.) He treated Grace as he would a client. He tried to be clever and funny in a sterile sort of way. It seemed more pathetic than personal. We took a detour on the drive home, stopping off at a nice restaurant for a light lunch and a heavy lecture. Once Grace and I were trapped in a booth, he started talking at us.

My father was an interesting person. He was tall and fairly fit due to all the tennis he played. He had thick dark hair that he insisted wasn't dyed. But by the end of each month Dad's hair would fade, only to turn jet black a day or two later. He had become very successful in the last few years with his investment company. In the process, however, he had found that he no longer needed the gospel. Oh, he didn't mind my mother taking us to church and participating, but he wanted no part of it. He had come to think that all religion was silly unless it could make you money. It was a humble outlook.

Dad wasn't really too involved with us kids anymore, either. In the last few years we had been mainly raised by our mother with Dad checking in on us mostly during Sunday dinners, and never in depth. I loved my father, but I longed for the father I remembered from my childhood.

I wanted so badly to talk to him about my mission and what I had learned. I wanted him to tell me how much I had grown. But unless I could present it in a portfolio, with a spreadsheet showing my increased value during those two fiscal years, he just wouldn't be interested anymore.

At the restaurant, Dad went on and on about when he was a kid and all the wonderful things he did to make his parents proud. The entire conversation was peppered with innuendo showing his displeasure at Grace and me. He just couldn't see how marrying a poor girl from Tennessee could benefit my future professional life. He told us about his courtship with my mother, and how things were so rosy due to their similar backgrounds. Then he told us a story about a Canadian boy who married a Hawaiian. "Ended in a bitter divorce," he said dramatically. "Ruined both of their reputations."

I had warned Grace about my parents acting a little weird toward her. But now there was no denying it—they were hoping that Grace was a phase and not a destination.

"Actually, Dad, Grace and I are just going to date. We only want to see if there is something between us."

Dad tried to smile. The waitress dropped off our food and we all started picking at our plates.

"Grace, what does your father do?" my dad asked bluntly.

"He works in Thelma's Way."

"Doing?"

"Dad," I argued, knowing full well that he was aware of what Grace's father did and did not do.

"How about your mother?" my father asked while picking up his glass to take a drink.

"She's a seamstress," Grace answered. "And she teaches school to my brother and sister at home."

Dad spit out what he was sipping. In the Franklin planner of life, *homeschooling* was a four-letter word. He could think of nothing more repressive or achievement-stunting than isolating a child in the home.

"Homeschool?" Dad clarified.

Grace nodded and took a bite of her sandwich while trying to look unaffected by my father's arrogant attitude.

Dad didn't say another word the rest of the meal. When we were done he took us home and dropped us off, claiming he had somewhere else to be.

Our home was located on the east side of Southdale in a nice neighborhood that lay low against the river. The houses in our area were big three- and four-floored models with large double-acre yards around them. In the summer the yards were lush and green, with lawns spilling about like dark green paint. At the moment, however, the scenery was bare, brown, and colored as if God owned nothing but rust-colored crayons. The homes had all been built a few years back, giving our neighborhood more character than any other spot in Southdale. I had loved growing up here.

Mom greeted Grace on the front porch so she would be able to warn her about not wearing shoes in our home. She hugged Grace like she would a thorny cactus.

"It's so nice to meet you, dear," she tried.

"It's nice to finally meet you, Sister Williams," Grace said graciously.

"Call me Mrs. We're not in church," my mother said pettily.

My fifteen-year-old sister Margaret told Grace she would be happy to help her with her hair, and my eleven-year-old brother Abel's only words were, "She doesn't look that weird."

All things considered, I thought things were going rather well.

# 45

# Close Proximity

November 13th

Grace and I had thought long and hard about where would be the best place for her to stay while she was in Southdale. We both agreed that it wouldn't be right to have her under the same roof with me. Her parents had offered to pay for an apartment, but there really weren't any inexpensive ones in our part of town. So we decided to hit up my longtime neighbor, Wendy.

Wendy was a widow, in the loosest sense of the word. There had been a man she met a few years ago on the bus. Henry, she thought his name was. He had said hello to her for two straight years, only to up and disappear on her a couple of years back. The bus driver claimed Henry had retired, but in Wendy's mind, he was dead. She wore black for a month afterward, which made sense in a backward kind of way, not because she was mourning the loss of someone she had never had, but because black was slimming, and Wendy had put on a few pounds while grieving.

Wendy had lived next to our family forever. She had inherited her home from her parents after they passed away. Her folks had also left her enough money that she would never have to worry about working. She didn't worry. Not only did she not have any employment, she also didn't bother to lift a finger around the house. Her place was a mess and her yard was the topic of many neighborhood association meetings.

Wendy was heavyset and short. She had the driest eyes I had ever seen—her eyelids squealed every time she blinked. She kept her hair short and had a long nose that hung over her top lip. Wendy wasn't a member of the Mormon Church, nor did she ever plan on being one. She claimed the doctrine was too restrictive. I couldn't imagine what she thought our beliefs would keep her from. All she ever did besides ride the bus back and forth to her book club was stare out of her front window and make calls to the other neighbors whenever something or someone looked out of place.

Well, Grace and I thought that since Wendy had the whole house to herself, maybe she wouldn't mind having a little company. And surprisingly enough, Wendy liked the idea. So Abel, Grace, and I helped Wendy clean out one of the bedrooms on her top floor.

Abel was big for an eleven-year-old. He was as tall as some of the priests in our ward, and would soon pass up those who were taller. He had the perfect little-brother personality—smart, funny, and always entertaining. He had changed from being a pain to being a peer within the two years I had been away. What impressed me most at the moment was how kind Abel was to Grace. Both he and Margaret seemed to be happy for us. It was nice to have my siblings on my side.

We finished cleaning out the bedroom and then worked on the bathroom next to it. When that was done, we all stood around in Grace's room acting as if we had accomplished something impressive, and wishing there were someone around to tell us so. The bedroom was big, with a large window that looked out and across the yards and down into my window.

"You won't mind me looking down at you?" Grace asked.

"Thank goodness for curtains," I joked.

"Isn't that the truth," Wendy said with a passion, creeping us all out.

Saturday night as I lay in bed, I looked out my window toward Grace. The night air looked still and heavy. My window seemed to buckle under the weight of it. The light in Grace's room went off, causing the silhouette of Wendy's home to completely disappear.

I searched for stars but found none.

46

# Debating the Odds

November 14th

The moment we walked through the chapel doors the whispering began—like air leaking from obese tires, the hissing spit about. I watched Sister Fino almost throw her back out bending over the pew to blab something to Sister Johnson. Brother and Sister Treat held their hymnbooks in front of their faces to hide their gossiping lips, and Leonard Phillips actually pointed at us. I squeezed Grace's hand. This was not going to be easy for her. And part of me was struggling with it too. These people were polished, refined to the point of bland. This, after all, was the ward that had spawned my once-girlfriend Lucy. I couldn't help worrying people would look down at me because I was taken with Grace. Of course, I felt horribly guilty for even thinking such a thing.

We walked down the aisle and took a seat next to Brother Leonard Vastly. He looked at us as if to say "Why me?"

Sister Morris was pounding on the organ keys and spreading

prelude music over the whispering parishioners—her large fingers struck too many notes, as usual. I could see Sister O'Shawn six benches back, telling her husband something with great animation. Then she shoved him up out of their pew and across the aisle toward Grace and me. The O'Shawns were the Clearview Ward irregulars. No matter how hard they tried they just didn't seem to fit in. Brother O'Shawn worked for a computer company writing math software. He was tall, and walked with a sort of "I've not yet mastered gravity" swagger. He had extremely dark hair with a perfectly round bald spot, which from any distance greater than two feet away made it look as if he were wearing a flesh-colored yarmulke. He wore a cell phone clipped to his belt even during church. I suppose he was just being prepared in case someone needed some emergency math software. Sister O'Shawn was a homemaker, but admittedly, not a very good one. Her kids always wore pajamas to church, even when our schedule shifted to the 1:30 meeting cycle. She was constantly talking about how much laundry confused her. She dreamed of Southdale getting a temple so she could work in a laundry room where she wouldn't have to worry about sorting whites from darks.

Brother O'Shawn stuck out his arm to shake my hand.

"Trust," he said sweetly. "How nice to see you here. So, this must be the girl that we've heard so much about."

Grace took Brother O'Shawn's hand and gave it a gentle shake.

"Can she understand what we're saying?" he asked me with his other hand to the side of his mouth.

"I can understand you perfectly," Grace answered for herself.

"Wonderful," Brother O'Shawn replied awkwardly. "Does everyone talk like you back home?" he asked, referring to Grace's Tennessee accent. He spoke a little too loudly and a little too slowly, as if Grace were some rare native that didn't have a clue.

"Most people do," she replied kindly.

"Well, I'm sure it will wear off eventually," he remarked, still too loud, reminding me of just how socially inept all those hours of designing software had made him. "So, are you just visiting?"

The entire congregation seemed to lean in, waiting for Grace's answer. Sister Morris decreased the volume of her prelude music.

"I'll be going to school here for a semester," Grace informed him.

"How nice," Brother O'Shawn smiled, scratching his forehead. "So where will you be staying while you are here?"

All around us, ears perked up.

"I mean, certainly you're not residing at the Williams' home."

"Certainly not," Grace smiled.

"She's staying with our neighbor Wendy," I answered.

"The nonmember?" Brother O'Shawn said, leaning closer and allowing us to see that his white shirt was tinted pink, evidence of his laundry-challenged household.

"Yes," I said.

"So you met Grace on your mission?" he asked, as if I were on trial.

"Yes."

"Well, the circumstances are not entirely appropriate, but we welcome you here anyway," he said, looking directly at Grace and speaking to her as if he were bestowing some great blessing. "Now, would you two classify yourselves as a 'couple'?" he asked, making quotation marks in the air, "or just 'good friends'?" again with the fingers curling like bunny ears.

"Somewhere in the middle," I answered.

"Be careful or that fence might give you splinters."

"Excuse me?" I asked.

"The heavens don't like fence-sitters. I'm speaking figuratively, of course."

"Of course," I replied.

Brother O'Shawn's cell phone rang. He snapped it open as if he had watched far too many *Star Trek* episodes. "Talk to me," he said. Then, "Oh, it's you, dear . . ."

I looked back at Sister O'Shawn. She was six rows back with her own cellular device clutched to her ear. I could almost hear her talking into it from where I stood. Brother O'Shawn "Okayed," and "Rogered," and then signed off, flipping his phone together like a phaser and hooking it to his belt.

"Well, I need to return to my family," he said, as if we were just begging him to stay. Then, looking at Grace and remembering to raise his voice, he added, "It's nice to meet you . . . uh . . ."

"Grace. Grace Heck."

"Oh," he said. "In our home *heck* is a sloppy word."

"I'm sorry to hear that," Grace replied.

Brother O'Shawn smiled awkwardly and stumbled off. Apparently, the congregation had eavesdropped on enough of our conversation to re-stimulate their own, because they all turned back to their neighbors and began whispering again. Sister Morris picked up the volume on the organ, and Bishop Leen stood up to walk toward the pulpit. I looked over at Leonard Vastly. He had scooted about as far away from us as possible. I spotted my mother and sister coming in the far chapel doors.

The whispering spiked as others noticed them too.

Mom looked as if she wanted to pull her scarf up over her head to shield herself from recognition. It was as if she were a criminal being whisked into the courthouse; as if my bringing Grace back from Tennessee had besmirched her good name.

My inactive father had worked long and hard to bring our family to a position of respect within the community. Both he and my mother had hoped my mission would turn me into a bilingual, well-polished, go-getting, ladder-climbing, shiny, young Republican. Instead I had gone native. I had come home with a slight accent and a local girlfriend.

Horror of horrors.

Dad was not happy. And if Dad was not happy, then Mom was red-ring-around-the-eyes miserable.

My mother had never felt that she lived up to the image my father's position demanded. She tried, mind you, but it was an impossible goal. So she filled the supposed gaps by trying to raise children that Dad could feel completely smug about. Now her oldest boy, the chip off the old block, had ruined things for her. They had been so happy about my pre-mission dating. Lucy Fall would have been the ideal daughter-in-law for them—blonde, tan, and oozing with better-than-thou. Now this? Apparently, Grace just didn't measure up.

The prelude music stopped and Bishop Leen tapped the microphone. Nelson Leen had been the bishop for six years. He was a short, light-skinned man with a long neck and thinning blond hair. His skin was so fair, in fact, it was almost translucent. From anywhere beyond the fifteenth row of the chapel, his features started to fade. He liked to say he was proud of the Norwegian blood coursing through his veins, and that if you looked real hard, you could see it.

Bishop Leen owned a successful landscaping company called "Leen's Lawns." Consequently, all of his gospel analogies had to do with landscaping: "We must combat the weeds of Satan," or "Let us roll down the lush lawns of truth." He was passionate about the parable of the olive tree in Jacob, chapter 5.

He started the meeting with a few words of welcome, and then announced that due to ward conference the previous week and Noel Miller's mission farewell the week before, our ward was having its fast and testimony meeting a couple of weeks late.

Today.

My heart skipped a beat. I couldn't believe it. Why hadn't my mother warned me? Sure, we weren't on the best of terms, but she owed it to the ward to let me know. You see, to say that Mormons don't condone gambling wouldn't actually be completely true in Southdale. Sure, we frowned upon slots and roulette like everyone else—visiting Vegas for the buffets and amusement parks alone. But I'd wager my last copper penny that there wasn't an active member of the Clearview Ward who didn't feel fast and testimony meeting was a proverbial roll of the dice. It was like open mic night with nobody to screen for the content of what anyone might blather on about.

One month we might be edified past the point of realizing that we were sitting in a pew, surrounded by people who knew altogether way too much about us. Then, the next month, it took every ounce of willpower to keep from bolting from the room to flee the droning boredom. Standard fare in most sermons, I realize, but in our ward the stakes were much higher, thanks to Brother Rothburn.

There was an unwritten rule in the Clearview Ward: no visitors or investigators on fast Sunday. If someone unknown to Brother Rothburn showed up, he always took it upon himself to stand. He always bore powerful testimony of the prophet Adam, but after that his thoughts would start to wander—and I mean wander, like a picnic napkin on a windy day.

I had just broken that unwritten rule by bringing Grace.

Pleading ignorance would get me nowhere. Had I known that today would be fast and testimony meeting, Grace and I would have attended another ward in town. But it was too late for that. I considered taking off my coat and throwing it over Grace's head but figured she wouldn't go for that. I looked around for Brother Rothburn and spotted him on the third row. He was sitting at the end of the pew, near the aisle, next to the Cummings family. Poor Sister Cummings was aware of the problem. She was taking evasive action. She appeared to be asking him questions about the tie he was wearing to keep him from looking around.

Everyone sitting anywhere between where Brother Rothburn was and where Grace and I were suddenly sat up taller, hoping to block his view if he were to start scanning the congregation. I put my arm around Grace and tried to push her down.

"Trust," she protested, "what are you doing?"

"Believe me, it's for the best . . ."

We sang the opening songs and sat nervously through the ward business. I felt some peace during the sacrament when I could pray and all heads were bowed, but before I knew it, Bishop Leen was back at the pulpit inviting one and all to share the microphone.

Sister Johnson was the first member up. Once again she had drawn her eyebrows in a little thick. She no longer had real ones thanks to an accident at a ward picnic about five years ago. You see, Sister Johnson wore extremely thick glasses. Her vision without them was as poor as a bat's in bright daylight. Well, at the picnic she fell asleep in her lawn chair. About ten minutes into her nap, her large lenses caught the sun and magnified its rays, setting both her eyebrows aflame. She woke up fast enough and ran around screaming before she found a punch cooler to dunk her head into. Her life was spared, but it was too late to save her brows. Now she had to draw them in. But apparently, she had to take her glasses off to do it. They never looked anywhere near normal.

Sister Johnson told a nice story about a nephew of hers who had made some bad decisions in life. He ended up marrying a girl that couldn't cope with motherhood. She used it all as some sort of analogy for the life of the Savior, but it seemed so out of place.

Next up to the pulpit was Janet Laramie. Sister Laramie was a polished woman. She lived her life in peach-colored suits and big self-adjusting sunglasses. Her mouth constantly smacked from the thick coat of glossy lipstick that covered her thin lips. She always held her left hand up as if she were continually hailing a waiter or a staff person of some kind. Sister Laramie owned two small poodles, Minty and Shoo-nu, and was often out of town attending dog shows. She had blonde hair that was so poofy that it was perfectly round. It created a halo-like effect with the choir lights behind her. I had always liked Sister Laramie, but I began to wonder if she felt the same.

"Now, I'm not up here to make friends," she said, looking directly at me. "But I felt impressed to stand before you all and relate a story."

Grace looked over at me with concern.

"All of you here know the Williams boy, Trust."

There was a silent gasp from the congregation. Speaking my name directly could prompt Brother Rothburn to turn around and take a gander, causing him to spot Grace.

He began turning his head to look our way. A desperate Sister Cummings handed him one of her toddlers to distract him.

It worked! Brother Rothburn took Isaac Cummings on his knee and began whispering a story into his ear.

Poor kid, I thought. Sacrificed for the cause.

"Well," Sister Laramie continued, "I taught Trust in Sunday School for two years, and I know that we must have covered some lesson concerning the importance of honoring your parents." She stopped to pull a Kleenex from the box next to the microphone. She lifted her glasses and wiped at the small eyes on her taut face. She smacked her lips and sniffed directly into the microphone. "I want to add my testimony of the great job that Sister Marilyn Williams is doing to keep her family active and strong. I hope we can all learn from her sterling example. I also hope that it isn't too late for her children to come around."

I didn't hear the last part of Sister Laramie's testimony due to the fact that Leonard Vastly had decided to make a move for the pulpit. He stepped on Grace's and my toes as he tried to slip past us out of the pew. He accidentally elbowed the head of Sister Barns who was sitting right in front of us. She turned around and gave me a dirty look. I pointed at Leonard, but she just turned away.

We should have stayed away today. We should have gone to another stake, another state for that matter—maybe even have tried out a different religion. I knew that my mother wasn't happy about my dating a girl I had met on my mission. I imagine that there were those who couldn't resist speculating on how Grace and I had grown close when I was a missionary and supposedly unaware of the opposite sex. At first I didn't really care what others might think or say, but it was getting old.

I had done nothing wrong. *We* had done nothing wrong. Why couldn't anyone see what a great thing Grace was?

Then Brother Vastly walked up to the pulpit. He talked for ten minutes about being physically prepared for the Second Coming. He bragged about his closets full of beans and Spam, and warned us all that he had also piled away ammo and wasn't afraid to use it on anyone who tried to take away his stuff.

He witnessed to the fact that in his opinion, all prophecy—except that moon turning to blood one, unless you counted last weekend's spectacular sunset—had been fulfilled and that at the first of next year the angels of retribution spoken of in Revelation would come to burn the wicked.

He spoke of a man named Noah Taylor, a visionary guru of emergency preparedness, a veritable fountain of lamp oil for foolish virgins—allegorically speaking, of course. He thanked the Clearview Ward Relief Society for bringing Brother Taylor to town to help us all get ready. He also reminded the ward to keep praying for rain. Southdale had been going through a horrible drought over the past year, and if God didn't bless them with some moisture soon, Brother Vastly feared for the safety of his topsoil.

Leonard Vastly was our resident misunderstood. He lived alone in a long single-wide trailer down by Southdale Falls. He was short, spongy, and had big bushy eyebrows. He wasn't exactly heavy, but he was one of those people who refused to let go of his old wardrobe even though he had grown a couple of sizes from when he was younger. Everything he wore was tight—uncomfortably tight—both for him and for us. I felt pity for his belts and buttons.

Brother Vastly had not always been a Saint. He had joined the Church years ago after he had broken into someone's car and stolen what looked like a purse, but turned out to be a leather tote with scriptures inside. After his initial anger at being cheated out of a purse, he read the Book of Mormon and joined the Church. He was the fabled convert that Church members always hoped would be the result of their stolen Mormon goods. He blamed his criminal past on the fact that his brother used to put straight mayonnaise in his bottle when he was a kid—all that egg had made him rambunctious and deviant.

I had always kind of liked Brother Vastly, despite his many annoyances. He was such an interesting person to look at and listen to. His lessons were off the wall, his ideas were absurd, and his insights were consistently way right of center and unbelievable. He gave our ward color and comical confusion.

After Brother Vastly finished speaking, he came and sat down two benches in front of us. He must have sensed conspiracy in the presence of Grace.

Lonora Leen, the bishop's wife, got up and bore her testimony. It was like a peaceful intermission during a confusing play. She simply testified to the fact that the Lord had helped her through each day. There was no mention of disobedient children or ill-advised marriages, just gratitude and answers to prayer.

For a few moments after her no one got up. Tension grew thick as faces started to wander. The Saints between us and Brother Rothburn sat up again in their seats and Sister Cummings started knocking her kids' books on the floor and asking Brother Rothburn if he'd mind picking them up.

A chair-sitter coughed. Sister Lewis psyched us all out by standing up only to take one of her twins out to the foyer. Someone had to break the suspense. I thought about getting up and bearing my testimony, but judging by Grace's reception so far, I wasn't sure how it would go over.

Someone caught my eye, moving up the aisle to the front.

My relief was short-lived.

It was my mother, Marilyn. She was already moving up the platform stairs. Mom never bore her testimony—I was in for it now. She must have felt a great burning about something to actually get up the nerve.

Mom patted her set blonde hair on the sides and smiled weakly. She was wearing a lime green dress with a lace doily collar. She seemed ill at ease, but that wasn't surprising—Mom dreaded public speaking. She had refused to speak at my farewell, let alone my homecoming. It was stage fright. She liked the people in the Clearview Ward fine; she just didn't like the idea of talking in front of them.

My mother wore glasses and had a small button nose. She smiled a lot, but it never looked easy for her to do. She had been a good mother, a little more emotionally timid than I felt I needed at times, but kind and concerned about her children.

My mother bore her testimony, sounding like she had lost a child to war. She thanked the ward for their support. She asked them all to pray for her. It was heartfelt. She worked her way around the story of the prodigal son, mixing up important aspects of the story with the tale of David and Goliath. The part where the prodigal son sold his slingshot for food was particularly interesting. At the end she paused, as if she feared she had gone too far. Changing the subject, she thanked Noah Taylor for his insightful and timely instruction at enrichment meeting last week, and challenged the ward to give him their full support. "December seventeenth is just around the corner," she added in strangely cheery tones. "I'd hate to be caught short."

"Who's this Noah Taylor?" Grace whispered. "And what happens on the seventeenth?"

"I have no idea," I replied.

Mom paused awkwardly again, suddenly said "Amen," and sat herself down. Though I was glad she was through, it occurred to me that she had ended at the worst possible moment. If she could have gone on for just a few more minutes then time would have been up and the bishop could have closed the meeting. Now, however, there was still a five-minute window for Brother Rothburn to work his magic.

I know it was dumb to be so bothered by Brother Rothburn and his never-ending oratory style, but no one could truly understand unless they had actually suffered through it. Brother Rothburn's nickname was Brother "Oh, that reminds me." After almost every sentence he would make some odd connection and go off on some completely unrelated subject. Unfortunately for all of us, he always went off on the *same* unrelated subjects. He rarely said anything new. In fact, I'm certain that, if pressed, a large portion of our ward could recite much of his testimony by heart. For my entire life he had stood up whenever there was a visitor, and gone on and on about everything from Church history to modern-day appliances. He would tell how the golden plates were translated. How the Saints came west. How when he was in the army, his friend Ryan Hinkle was saved from a bullet by a Book of Mormon in his breast pocket. Of course it always took him two minutes to recall Ryan's name. It was something to watch—everyone biting their tongues, dying to shout "Hinkle! Hinkle! Okay? His name was Hinkle!" though no one ever did, it being sacrament meeting and all.

The big hand on the chapel clock moved a minute. Still no one moved. I watched Brother Rothburn notice that there was dead air in the building. He looked at the clock, then at his watch. His head began turning my way. I pushed Grace down as far as I could. Sister Cummings tugged hard on Brother Rothburn's sleeve. He paid her no mind. He was going to take a look around, even if it killed us.

It just might.

Bishop Leen's wife tried to wave her husband up to the stand. She must have been hoping he would close the meeting a few minutes early. But we all knew that wouldn't happen. Bishop Leen was actually part of the problem. He refused to ever end fast and testimony meeting early, but he didn't mind if it ran overtime. He didn't have the guts to tap anyone on the shoulder and tell them to sit down. Sunday School teachers assigned to teach the first Sunday of the month knew to prepare summaries of their lessons, never knowing how much time they would have.

Brother Rothburn began to glance over the crowd. Like a rickety old lighthouse searching for wreckage, his worn eyes skimmed across the reeflike rows. Systematically, he picked his way over the pews, looking for an unfamiliar face. He knew all the regulars rather well. People made it a point to talk to him often so that he would always be aware of the fact that they were supposed to be there. If anyone changed their hairstyle or lost a significant amount of weight they always kept him up to date. No one wanted to take a chance.

I tried not to look nervous as his glance got closer to Grace and me. I didn't want to give it away. Then, like someone else's bad breath, I could feel it slowly wash over me. I stopped breathing. His gaze brushed right past us and moved on, without so much as a hitch. I breathed out. I could see shoulders relax throughout the gathering. But just as his gaze reached the Chavez family, Brother Rothburn glanced back our way as if something had caught his eye. Somehow, he was peering his way over shoulders and around hair.

Bishop Leen began to stir on the platform. He leaned down to pick up his things. He grasped the armrest on his chair to lift himself up.

It was a little too late.

Brother Rothburn had spotted Grace. He smiled as if he had just eaten something buttery. I had been foolish to think we could get away with it. There were only two other members of our ward with red hair. Slowly, like crust-topped lava, Brother Rothburn began to ooze up and out of his seat. Bishop Leen saw him and shifted his weight back into his chair.

Brother Rothburn stood and straightened his tie. He pulled out a hanky and blew into it. He carefully folded the hanky, placed it back into his pocket, and began to amble up to the pulpit. It seemed to take a full five minutes for him to make it up to the stand. He shook the bishop's hand. He shook his counselors' hands, one by one. He stood at the pulpit and instructed the bishop to raise it a bit. Then he asked him to lower it again.

Too high.

Down just a little.

Nope.

Up a little bit more.

Tiny bit more.

Bit more.

Nope.

The bishop gave up in frustration. Brother Rothburn adjusted his microphone to compensate.

Brother Rothburn was old. He had already turned ninety before I left on my mission. His second wife had passed away about ten years earlier and he had lived alone ever since. He didn't do much besides go to church. He went to every scheduled function there was. It didn't matter if he wasn't invited—he went. I couldn't remember a single meeting in my entire life where he had not been in attendance. He had thick gray hair and a big rubbery nose. His eyes had been blue once, but age had washed them out to a shade that matched his hair. He was tall for a ninety-year-old man, and still got around amazingly well.

"I wasn't planning to come up today," he began. "But I thought, seeing as there is a fresh young face among us . . . Oh, that reminds me of a situation. What was his name? It's slipped my mind, but he was always real outspoken about modesty. Well anyway, I was at the big mall just recently looking for a part to my phonograph, that's a record player for you youngins. They don't seem to make many of them anymore; can't understand why. To me there is nothing more exciting than the scratchy intro on a new 45. We used to get stacks of them and play as many as twelve songs right in a row. Anyhow, I couldn't believe some of the outfits that these kids wear to the mall these days. It seems modesty is outdated. When I was a young boy we used to get dressed up for such things. I hardly went anyplace without a coat and tie. A person wouldn't dream of going to the movies or taking a plane ride in jeans. But I suppose I'm just old and out of it these days. Oh, that reminds me of the story of the stagecoach driver. It seems that this gentleman was interviewing potential applicants for his stagecoach company. The question he asked was how close to the edge can you get? So the first driver, he . . ."

This was terrible. This was worse than terrible. Brother Rothburn was on a long roll and it was all my fault. Every chance they could, ward members turned in their seats to scowl at us. There would be no forgiveness for Grace for coming today, or for me for bringing her. This would last half an hour if it lasted a second.

" . . . And do you know who he picked? The man who could drive the farthest away, that's who. Anyhow, what do you get when you cross . . . now let's see, what was his name. None of you probably remember him, and of course I'm dating myself by bringing him up, but he was a great leader with sort of a salty mouth. Bishop, can you recall the name?" Brother Rothburn turned toward the bishop.

Bishop Leen put his head in his hands.

"Regardless, a lot of people frown on profanity, and well they should. But if you ask me a well-placed swearword can make the impression of twenty plain ones. But I guess you didn't ask me. . . ."

I put my head in my hands.

Fifteen minutes later he began to wrap up. Twelve minutes after that he said something about "In conclusion." And four minutes after that he closed with, "And that's why bonnets were originally called head wraps. Amen."

It was finally over. Heads began to pop up all around like prairie dogs. Brother Rothburn exited the podium and Bishop Leen once again gathered his stuff together by his feet. I was in rapture. I hardly noticed Grace stand and begin to walk to the front. I hardly noticed the bishop sit back down. Before I knew it, however, she was standing at the microphone looking as if she had something to say.

What was she doing? Had she lost it? Didn't she know the patience of these people had already been pushed beyond the breaking point?

I sat stunned in my pew wondering how I would ever live this down.

Bishop Leen was as surprised as anyone. We were already running half an hour over. I heard someone moan out loud.

Grace began. "Brothers and Sisters, I've never been one to know just what the heavens are thinking. It's always been kind of a guessing game with me. But I know . . ."

I don't know how you would describe my relationship with Grace. I knew that I loved her. She said she felt the same for me. But everything between us seemed so discombobulated. In a normal relationship, people date, they cope with uncertainty, and after a while things get clearer. If they're made for each other, they come to the conclusion that love is in the air, in the water, and in the food. They talk about getting married.

Things were running in the opposite direction for us.

I had known of Grace for most of my mission. I was intrigued by the bits and pieces of her she let me see. By the end of my two years I knew I couldn't live without her. But lately, I wasn't so sure.

It was like seeing an intriguing new board game that you instantly want. You fall in love with the colored box and the concept, but when you crack it open you realize that you've got a whole book of instructions to wade through and understand before anything worthwhile is going to actually happen.

That was us. Except our instructions seemed to be written in Spanish.

*No hablo eb panola.*

Had I asked the people Grace had grown up with to describe her, they would more than likely say she was shy, hard to track, perceptive, an enigma with red hair. Of course they wouldn't have used the word *enigma,* but stick in "kinda confusing" and you get the idea.

But I had seen Grace differently. I had seen her use her determination in the most self-assured ways. It was as if Thelma's Way had been holding the real Grace back. I had gone there to find myself. But it seemed Grace had needed to get away to discover who she was.

In the two days since we had arrived in Southdale, I had already noticed a difference. She was coming through loud and clear. In fact, I was a little frightened by it. I didn't want to get left behind.

Grace bore her testimony. She talked about how wonderful it was to be in such a huge ward. She said all the right things in all the right ways and by the end of her testimony, the feeling in the room was entirely different.

I just stared at her. She came down and sat next to me. She smiled.

Bishop Leen closed the meeting.

A couple people came up to Grace afterward and welcomed her to the ward. Sister Barns apologized for what she was thinking about Grace at the start of the meeting. Brother O'Shawn informed us that he just remembered that he had a nephew who married a girl he met on his mission and that so far, things had worked out okay.

"You're amazing," I whispered to Grace between well-wishers.

"I'm glad you think so," she whispered back.

It felt as if most folks were suddenly willing to give Grace a chance—most folks besides my mother, that is. She slipped out the back without saying a word.

I mentally notched off week number one.

## 47

# LUCY

Lucy Fall was miserable. For the first time in her life she felt absolutely helpless. Still, she couldn't decide if she was more upset about what she was going through, or by the fact that what she was going through had caused the natural blush in her cheeks to fade. Pale was not on her color wheel.

It had been three days since Lance had walked out on her. He had simply packed his bags and stepped away. That was it. Lucy had known that the marriage was strained, but she never imagined Lance would leave her for someone else.

She threw off her robe and slipped into the bath. Even the warm water didn't cheer her.

Where was her mother?

Where was her father?

How could her folks be in Europe at a time like this? Weren't parents supposed to have some sort of intuition thing going on? How could they not have known that their daughter would need them?

Need them. Lucy needed them.

It was such a demeaning thought.

Lucy had thought Lance was perfect. Sure, he wasn't Mormon, but she had married him knowing that her power of refinement could produce the desired results. Lance had come out to church a few times, but he had ultimately decided that fishing and boating were a lot more fulfilling than church. Apparently, he had also come to the conclusion that marriage was a little too confining. He claimed to have tried, but in truth the marriage had gone downhill right from the honeymoon itself. Lucy had wanted to hold things together for the sake of their image, but it hadn't worked.

And now it was too late. Lance was gone.

She began to panic. Something was happening to her. Her insides were pushing up inside her and tears were streaming down her face. Lucy hadn't cried since the day Sally Moss punched her in the stomach for liking Billy Wheeler. That was the third grade.

Her shoulders shook, her throat released, and she moaned. A sudden anxiety wrapped around her, squeezing the air from her lungs. She noticed the mascara dripping into the tub. Things were going to get messy before the night was out.

48

# Fact-Finding Feast

That night at family dinner my father tried to keep the conversation light. He asked my sister Margaret twice how school was going, and told us all the score of the high school basketball game three times.

"Forty-seven to thirty-two. Can you believe that?"

All the while, he never once made eye contact with either Grace or me. Dad had been avoiding us ever since he had dropped us off from the airport. Clearly, he didn't know how to handle the situation, and life seemed to go better for Dad when he just ignored the things he couldn't change.

"So, Margaret, how is school going?" he ventured again.

Margaret had just turned fifteen. She was a pretty girl with way too many clothes. I had never seen her wear the same outfit twice. She changed clothes more often than most people brushed their teeth. The Gap had personally called her on her birthday to wish her well, and to inform her that the new jumpers were in. She was short enough to be nervous about her height, constantly praying for a growth spurt, and skinny enough to make all the other girls mad. She had blonde hair, blue eyes, and a smile bright enough to make every young man in our ward simultaneously woozy.

"You've asked Margaret about school two times already," my brother Abel offered.

"I'm just interested," my father defended, while buttering one of his dinner rolls. "Just interested in my little girl. Isn't that right, princess?" he winked.

"School's fine, Dad," Margaret replied.

"Good to hear," my father said, "good to hear. Is there any more jam in the kitchen?" he asked nobody in particular.

My mother got up to check.

"So, Dad," I dared. "Do you know if there are any jobs available at your office right now?"

"You never know what kind of strings your old man can pull for his son."

"I already have a job," I said. "But could you pull a couple for Grace? She'd like to work until the semester starts."

"You already have a job?" my father questioned.

"I'll be working for Brother Barns again starting next week. But Grace could really use some help."

Dad sort of huffed and shifted in his seat. "Well, I'd need to find out a little bit more about this Grace. I can't just hand out a job on the spot."

"What do you need to know?" I asked.

"Well, for starters, what can this Grace do?"

I looked around the room, wondering why he was talking about her as if she weren't there. "Dad, you can talk directly to her. She's sitting right in front of you."

Grace opened her mouth to speak, but before she could say anything, my father hollered, "Marilyn, how's that jam coming?"

My mother came out of the kitchen and began spooning jam onto everyone's plates.

"So, Margaret, how is school going?" Dad asked.

"This is stupid," Abel said, frustrated. "Trust, are you and Grace going to get married?" he asked bluntly.

"What?"

"Dad thinks you're going to get married and ruin your future."

"Out of the mouth of babes," my mother sang as she sat down.

"Now, Abel, that's not exactly how I phrased it," my father backpedaled.

"I know," Abel said, "but I didn't want to hurt Grace's feelings."

"This is ridiculous," Margaret snipped. "Who cares who Trust marries?"

"Wait a second," I tried to say, "why don't—"

"There are certain things that are expected of us, young lady," my mother interrupted, waving her fork at my sister. "If you were doing drugs, do you think your father and I would just turn our backs?"

"Margaret's doing drugs?" my father asked in shock.

Abel began to laugh. I saw him smile at Grace as if to say sorry for all this. Grace smiled back.

"Margaret's not doing drugs!" my mother shouted.

"Good going, princess," my father congratulated.

For a second there was nothing but the sound of chewing.

"Dad, what about that job?" I tried again.

"So how was church today?" Dad asked, ignoring my question.

It was obvious that my father didn't want to talk about a job for Grace. Painfully obvious—Dad never talked about church. He sort of skirted around the fact that he was inactive by never talking about anything related to the gospel. The fact that he had just brought it up was proof positive that he was getting desperate.

"Mom bore her testimony," Margaret informed him.

"This roast is better than ever," was my father's only reply.

"Sister Barns brought an old Book of Mormon to class," Abel tried.

"Patty Barns has really lost weight," my mother commented. "I hardly recognized her in that waisted dress."

"How old was the Book of Mormon?" Grace asked Abel.

I looked at her, thinking about how nice it was to hear her voice at our dinner table.

"I don't know. Old. But not real old, fake old," he answered. "Sister Barns said it was just a copy of the first one."

"I wouldn't mind getting my hands on a real first edition," my dad said, happy to have landed on a less threatening topic. "That's quite a piece of American history. Remember Jack Shaw?" he asked no one in particular. "He had that first edition. Boy, he thought he was something else."

"They had a real first edition in Thelma's Way," Grace ventured.

"Where's that?" he asked.

I shook my head. Forget the fact that his own son had lived there for two straight years, or that one of our dinner guests was born and raised there—Dad still didn't recognize the name.

"Thelma's Way," she said, unfazed. "It was a nice copy. It was even signed by Parley P. Pratt."

"You're kidding," my dad said, actually looking at Grace and showing genuine interest for the first time in the entire conversation.

"Nope." Grace smiled. "It belonged to the branch."

"Where is it now?" he asked quickly.

"Who knows?" I piped in. "Someone took it."

"Who knows?" my father said, turning to me. "Did someone sell it?"

"I don't think so. Folks are kind of just waiting for the guilty party to admit they did it."

"Do they know how much it's worth?"

"I told them about fifty thousand," I said.

Dad took a big bite of his roast beef and chewed thoughtfully.

"One sold at a New York auction for over seventy thousand last week," he finally said.

"Well, that wouldn't matter in Thelma's Way. Whoever has it will probably trade it for a couple cows, or a piece of land. Actually, they'll be lucky to get that. People don't have much use for old books. I'm sure whoever has it would be willing to let it go for something shiny or new-looking."

My father turned back to Grace and smiled.

"Tell me more about your hometown," he said.

Grace knew he had ulterior motives, but she was happy to oblige. She told him about the winding path from Virgil's Find and the chapel where the branch would meet. She told him about the debate the town had had, and how after the food fight the Book of Mormon turned up missing again. She told him how the whole town was waiting for some-one to begin spending a lot of money, so as to give away the fact that they had secretly cashed it in. She told him every single thing she knew about the lost Book of Mormon, and all about Thelma's Way.

My father listened to Grace as if she had a doctorate in conversa-tion from Yale (instead of a letter of recommendation from her father concerning homeschool).

Two days later, Dad flew out of town. He wouldn't say where he was going, only that it was very important and that he would be back in a week or so. My mother insisted it was a routine business trip, and that his leaving had nothing to do with the huge fight the two of them had had the day before over Margaret wearing makeup (Mom for, Dad against).

"He has business trips all the time," my mother told Abel and me defensively.

We had no reason not to believe her—at least not yet.

49

# Be Prescared

November 17th

As luck would have it, we didn't need my father's name to find Grace a job. Wednesday evening, Brother Victor, the Clearview Ward employment specialist, showed up at our house to let Grace know what jobs were available.

Brother Victor was a tiny man. Although he was many years my senior, I always felt tempted to pick him up. He was just so compact. He looked like a miniature human, like one of God's trial-sized samples. He was also one serious ward employment specialist. He had held the position for as many years as I could remember and apparently desired never to be released. Thanks to him, almost no one in our ward stayed out of work long. A few years back, when Brother Treat had been laid off from his job at the carpet factory, Brother Victor worked day and night to find him a job. Brother Treat was actually kind of enjoying the lazy rush of drawing unemployment, but he soon found out that it was more work avoiding Brother Victor than holding down a regular job. He took a position driving one of the city buses that went down our street.

Brother Victor informed Grace that Brother Noah Taylor, the emergency preparation guru from Manti, was looking for someone to answer phones and do the billing for his food storage warehouse. The job would only last until the end of December. It was perfect for Grace.

"I thought it might be," Brother Victor smiled.

Grace called up Brother Taylor and was offered the job on the spot. It was a nice wage with good hours. She was very relieved.

"My work here is done," Brother Victor whispered as he left.

My mother was actually pretty impressed that Grace got the job. I guess she thought it was a socially enviable position—Brother Taylor was the out-of-towner to know.

Later that evening, I walked Grace back to Wendy's for the night. We stood on the unlit porch pretending that it wasn't as cool as it actually was.

"How are you doing with all this?" I asked.

"It's a slight adjustment," she shivered. "But I like it here."

"You do?" I asked, surprised.

"Your family's nice . . ."

"They are?"

Grace slipped her arms around me and put her head on my shoulder.

"That's kind of nice," I said, trying to sound calm.

"Trust," was all she said.

I kissed the top of her head. She pulled back just a bit so that my lips could meet her on the forehead. Her body shifted and suddenly her soft mouth was on mine. I didn't really know how we had gotten there, but I was not about to complain. I could feel her fingers on the back of my neck. Suddenly it was way too dark out and I couldn't see anything except me kissing her forever. The night spun around me like cotton candy, making my senses sticky and sweet. Grace touched me on the cheek and brushed my right ear with her hand. Then she placed her head back on my shoulder and sighed.

"What was that for?" I finally asked.

"I want to make sure that we're turning into more than just good friends."

Grace kissed me again and then slipped through Wendy's front door. I walked home with a windy soul under a clear sky.

My mom was in the living room pasting pictures into photo albums as I came in.

"Trust, is that you?" she asked, too busy to look up. "You know, I think Grace is real lucky to land that job with Brother Taylor. I hope she's grateful, but then I guess those natural people usually are."

"Natural people?" I asked.

"You know, free-spirited. She'll learn a lot under the tutelage of Brother Taylor."

"So what's the deal with this Taylor person?" I asked, curious to know more about this man everyone spoke so highly of, that Grace would now be spending time with on a daily basis.

Mom smeared glue stick onto the back of a photograph and slapped it on an empty page.

"Brother Taylor is an important person," she raved. "He's a direct descendent of some important Church leaders."

"John Taylor?" I asked, making a stab at it.

"No, Tony Taylor," my mother thought. "I believe he was a stake president in Manti. Anyhow, Noah Taylor is going to be the one who saves our whole town."

"From what?" I asked.

"Oh, Trust," Mom replied. "You have so much to learn."

"No, really," I tried. "What is this Brother Taylor going to save us all from?"

"Well, for starters . . . oh, look at this picture of your father," she said, becoming distracted. "I tell you he could turn heads. He had a real sense about him."

"Mom?"

"Yes, Trust?" she asked nicely.

"Brother Taylor, what's he saving us all from?"

"Well, Sister Barns felt that we sisters in the Relief Society should make sure that our food storage was up to date. Times are awful crazy and we need to be prepared in case. . . . Look at your father in this one." She held up another picture. "He used to love to fish. He would take me out all the time. He could catch any fish. But he always threw them back." Mom sighed. "That's the kind of man he was—compassionate. He used to be so compassionate."

"And?" I prodded.

"And moral. Why, your father was so considerate of my standards while we were dating."

"Mom," I complained. "I meant, and what else about this Taylor person?"

"Well, he's really helping us out. We thought he would come and tell us what to buy and what to store. But then he told us how hard it can be to find places for all that food and water. That's true, you know. We have one of the biggest houses in the ward, and I can't think of an extra foot for storage."

"What about the garage?" I asked.

"Brother Taylor says the temperatures are all wrong. Foods can become stale, or lose their flavor. Now that's funny," my mother paused. "I remember this picture, but I didn't remember your father wearing that shirt in it. I wonder if this photo has changed colors, or maybe someone doctored it up. They can do that now, you know. So who could have slipped into my old photos and changed his shirt color?"

"Maybe you're remembering a different photo," I offered.

"No," she insisted. "This is the one I'm remembering."

"Mom, no one snuck into our house to change the color of Dad's shirt on that photo."

"It's just odd, that's all," she observed.

I'll say.

"So where does this Brother Taylor think you should store your food?" I asked, thinking that perhaps he was a temperature-controlled shed salesman with objectives of his own.

"That's the wonderful part. He's taking care of all of it for us. He's renovated that old warehouse right there on Frost Road to be a climate-controlled food storage wonderland. Oh, here's that picture of Margaret that she hates so much. I don't know why she fusses so. Anyone can tell that's a skin-colored turtleneck and not her chin."

"Ralph couldn't."

"He still would have stopped writing her if I hadn't sent him a copy," Mom said defensively.

"They'd been pen pals for eight years."

"It wasn't my doing."

"He never wrote again after that."

"Germans can be a little touchy."

"So anyhow," I said, trying to pick up the conversation someplace near where it had dropped off. "You take your supplies to Brother Taylor's warehouse and he keeps them there for you?"

"Sort of. Look at your father in this shot. I can hardly remember him looking this relaxed," she said sadly.

"Sort of?"

"We pay Brother Taylor and he buys everything for us," she said, picking up a new stack of photos. "It's really lightened my load not to have to bother with it. It's sort of like time-share food storage. You know, like with the condo."

"What good is food storage if it's down the road?" I asked, starting to feel weird about Brother Taylor. "Besides, aren't you supposed to rotate food storage? What's this guy going to do when his entire warehouse begins to expire?"

"Oh, Trust," my mother cooed. "Look at you. I remember your birth so vividly. I'm sure glad the shape of your head snapped back."

"Mom, I don't know if keeping your food storage at a distant warehouse is what the prophet had in mind."

"Trust, don't be so cynical," she scolded. "Brother T's from Manti. I'm sure he would know if the prophet disapproved. Besides, Noah Taylor has been blessed with a foreknowledge of when things will begin to fall apart."

"He has?" I asked.

"I guess he had a vision or something—December seventeenth."

"December seventeenth? You mean of this year?"

"Of this year," she said, unconcerned. "That's why everyone's operating in such a huff. Noah's got us all on fire. He's a dedicated man," my mother complimented. "He's even rented an old farmhouse to live in out past the Dintmore Hills because he can't stand to be away from his farming roots," Mom paused to turn the album page. "Now just what is your father doing in this picture?" She laughed. "He had a silly streak, you know. He wasn't always so business oriented."

"I remember," I said. "He was so different when I was small."

"I can't believe it's the same man today," my mother said, suddenly sad.

Mom was silent for a few minutes.

"Are you okay?" I asked finally, feeling as if I should say something.

"I'm fine," she replied. "I just can't get over how much things change, that's all."

"Mom, I'm in love with Grace," I said out of the blue, unable to hold it back.

"Things change," she said again sadly.

I left Mom to her memories.

## 50

# Hollow

November 18th

Lucy couldn't remember ever being happy. She knew that she had grown up pain-free, but that was not happiness. She knew that now. She understood that now. She looked at herself in the mirror and tried to smile.

People were supposed to smile.

Her blonde hair looked lifeless and dull, almost as if she had been using a generic-brand shampoo. She couldn't believe that the blue eyes staring back at her were the same ones that had once made Lance weak in the knees.

Lucy hadn't been out of the house in days. She had passed the hours cutting up everything that belonged to or reminded her of Lance. Her home looked like the scratching post of a cat with powerful paws. Lucy knew she needed to begin again, but she just couldn't find a way to let go of the hurt. She sat on the couch and thought about all the horrible things people would soon be saying about her:

"She must have driven him away."

"I guess he had to find companionship elsewhere."

"What kind of failure loses her husband to a waitress?"

She went to the window and adjusted the blinds. Light slipped through, striping her bare arms with contrasts. She thought about summer, and how much easier all this would be if it had happened during a greener month. Even nature seemed against her.

Lance had stopped by the day before to pick up a few more of his things. He seemed so unbothered by everything that was happening. Lucy had locked herself in the bathroom until he left.

"I hate him," she said as she raised the blind to peer out the window.

A white car drove by on the street below. Lucy wasn't sure, but she thought it might have been Trust's. She had bumped into him a few weeks back at the grocery store while shopping with Lance. She remembered now how good he had looked.

What had she ever seen in Lance? Lucy's mind drifted back to life before they had ever met.

A vague memory settled over her, and she smiled.

She could remember being happy.

51

# Spinning Cookies

November 20th

Saturday morning my father called to inform us that he'd run into some trouble with his business negotiations. He wouldn't be back for at least another week. He still didn't say where he was. Mother didn't push it.

Grace had begun her job the day before, and was enjoying it. She, like the rest of them, seemed to think that Noah Taylor was an outstanding guy. I had yet to meet him and form a favorable opinion. The two times I dropped her off he had not been around. All I knew was that he was a widower from Manti who wanted to prepare the world for its end.

Southdale was growing even more hectic than usual. The fact that Thanksgiving was less than a week away made everyone feel as if they needed to act a little busier. Stores were hanging Christmas decorations and promoting Christmas items in their usual gloss-over-Thanksgiving fashion. Southdale never did get very cold, but it wasn't usually this dry.

The November ground was dry and porous, giving Southdale a ruddy complexion and making us all pray for rain.

I was sort of just kicking around, waiting for this week to end and the next week to begin, when a surprise visitor showed up. I was outside fixing the garage door for my mother when I heard a loud vehicle turn onto our street and tear toward our house. I looked up to see a truck that looked vaguely familiar turn into our driveway.

It stopped a couple feet away from me. The driver turned the engine off, opened his door, and climbed out. As he pulled in, I didn't recognize who it was, due to the sunglasses, but the moment he was standing on the ground there was no mistaking Elder Jorgensen for anybody other than himself.

The last time I had seen Elder Jorgensen was right after he had broken his leg. We had been knocking on doors out in the Thelma's Way woods when he had fallen and snapped his lower leg. It was his accident that provided Grace and me our first chance to be alone when she helped me go for help. There was no doubt in my mind as to why he was my favorite companion.

"Elder," I said, excited to see him.

"Not Elder anymore," he exclaimed. "Just plain Doran. Doran Jorgensen. Of course there's a P there in the middle. P for Peter. But I don't mention that much, seeing how I was named after my uncle Peter who *was* a good guy before he left his wife and kids for a girl half his age. I usually just go by Doran Jorgensen."

I stared at him until he felt further explanation was necessary.

"Doran was the name of my great-grandmother's business."

"Wow," was all I could say.

"She made brooms," he further explained.

I almost said "Wow" again, but I had used that up already.

"I remember your first name," he bragged. "Honor."

"Actually it's Trust," I laughed.

"Those virtues confuse me."

I hugged Doran and then stood back an appropriate distance.

"So what are you doing here?" I asked.

"Just got done with the mission," he said proudly. "Finished honorably, of course."

"Of course."

"My folks were kind of smothering me so I thought I'd take a road trip and visit some of the ex-companions. Wanted to show you guys my truck."

I walked slowly around his vehicle, pretending to admire it and know exactly what I was looking at.

"It's just like the pictures," I observed.

"Yeah," he sighed proudly, following me around. "So, you want to go for a spin?"

Not really, but I said, "Sure."

Doran looked at the dirty work clothes I was wearing. "Maybe you should change."

"Really?" I asked, thinking that he had to be joking.

"I just steam cleaned the upholstery."

I changed clothes and we drove through Southdale acting like we owned the place. Doran took a corner quickly, throwing me up against the passenger-side door. I looked for a seat belt and was informed that he had just removed them.

"Why?"

"They were old and fraying," he hollered. "I special ordered some new ones but they won't be in for a few weeks."

I hoped I would live to see them.

"Isn't this great?" he asked.

"Yeah," I yelled over the engine roar.

He stopped abruptly at a red light, causing my knees to press up against the dashboard. The small plastic elk head he had hanging from his rearview mirror dangled wildly.

"Hey, whatever happened to that girl in Thelma's Way?" he asked.

"Grace?" I asked back.

"Yeah, Grace. Too bad about her doctrinally incorrect name."

"We believe in grace, Elder."

"Doran."

"We believe in grace, Doran."

"So what happened to her?" he asked, apparently not wanting to get into a gospel debate at the moment.

"She's here," I informed him.

Doran looked around the cab of his truck. "I'm sure she is, Trust. You always did act a little funny about her."

"Not here in . . ."

The light turned green and we sped off noisily. Doran spotted an empty parking lot with hundreds of speed bumps. He turned sharply and began bouncing over all the long asphalt lumps. Our heads knocked against the roof of the cab as he swerved and plowed over more of them. Doran laughed as if this was as fun as life could possibly get.

"Listen," I tried to reason. "Could you slow it down a little?"

"Watch this," was his reply. He pulled into a dirt field next to the parking lot and began spinning circles, his big tires grinding loudly as I became wedged against the passenger door. Dirt was spraying everywhere. He honked his horn and "Yee Hawed," in celebration of diggin.' The thought struck me that Elder Jorgensen and I really were very different. When I had served with him, I thought the talk about his truck was kind of folksy and endearing, and I had seen his enthusiasm as a positive missionary tool. Now those two things combined were going to kill me. I held onto the door handle and tried to act as if I were having fun. I could see other cars along the road staring at us as we spun donut after donut in the dirt. I was surprised that Doran wasn't too dizzy to drive. He had obviously done this before. He kept on turning, picking up speed.

I was just about to suggest we move on to something less noisy and mind-numbing, when I shifted in my seat and accidentally pushed the handle on the door. Like a Pringles can, it popped open, blowing me out. I flew through the air and onto the hard dirt ground, crumbling into a six-foot-two bent-up heap of human.

My head hurt. Earth exploded all around me as my mind began to grow dark. The last thing I remembered was the sound of Elder Jorgensen's musical truck horn playing "La Cucaracha."

52

# Kicking 'Em When They Fall Down

November 25th

The person who invented hospital food must have been a patient himself, admitted because he was an abnormality of nature and had no taste buds. I pushed my piece of turkey away in unsavory disgust.

This was the worst Thanksgiving ever.

I had attempted to be gracious by telling Grace and my family that they should not bother about me and to go on and celebrate at home.

The nerve of them to listen.

I had been in the hospital for over four days now. The concussion that I had sustained by falling out of Elder Jorgensen's truck left me in pretty bad shape. Today was actually the first day that I had begun to feel almost normal again. After I had been thrown out of the truck, Doran rushed me over to the hospital where I had lain unconscious for days. When I had come out of it, Doran was leaning over me, shaving the hair on the right side of my head.

"What are you doing?" I whispered.

"Don't worry," he said. "Just rest."

I should have worried. When I really came out of it a day later, one side of my head was bald. I would have been completely bald if it hadn't been for a nurse stopping him mid-strand. Doran claimed he was just trying to help, shaving my head in case they needed to perform surgery.

I was so glad Doran had come to Southdale to visit me.

Grace had spent all of her evenings by my bedside. She read to me and talked to me even though my side of the conversation was often lacking. She would tell me all about her job and how Brother Taylor, or Noah, as she had taken to calling him, was really working hard to get this town up to speed.

Doran felt so bad about everything that he had decided to stick around until I was completely better. He had also been kind enough to volunteer to take Grace to and from work each day.

According to my sister Margaret, Grace was beginning to fit in. The ward had really come around ever since Noah Taylor had given her a job. The only person who was still having a hard time was my mother. She just could not accept the fact that Grace might someday be her daughter-in-law. I'm sure my father would have been struggling with it too, if it weren't for the fact that he still wasn't around. He would call my mother every few days to let her know that he was all right, but he wouldn't say what he was up to, and he wasn't rushing home. It wasn't that big of a deal to my mom; business was business, and if providing for the family meant that he had to be away for a couple of weeks, then so be it. That was all well and good, but I couldn't help thinking it was awful strange for him not to come home for Thanksgiving.

Thanksgiving afternoon, Doran brought Grace over for a visit. Then he left us alone so we could speak.

Grace looked great. Southdale seemed to sit well with her. She was wearing faded jeans and a smile that seemed to suggest she still liked me, regardless of my half-missing hair and attractive gown.

"You look good," she said, sitting down on the side of my bed.

"Not as good as you," I replied.

Grace leaned over and kissed me. Despite my hospital breath we both seemed to enjoy it.

"I'm sorry about all this," I offered. "I was supposed to be helping you adjust to Southdale."

"Doran's helping," she said.

"Doran's the reason I'm here."

Grace's red hair looked so dark that day. She had also cut it a few inches shorter. The way the ends of it lay across her dark T-shirt had me fixated. A sense of something washed over me. Grace was changing on me, and it was no longer subtle. Like a dam that was bursting after years of a slow leak, she wasn't holding back anymore. A personality, a presence that had been stored away all these years was emerging in full force. She wasn't the same person I had known in Thelma's Way. It scared the heck out of me—she was already more than I could comprehend, and the possibility of where she could end up blew me away. At the same time, it thrilled me beyond words.

"Well, I shouldn't stay long," Grace said. "Your mother wants me to help her with something, plus Doran needs to speak to you for a moment alone."

"He's not carrying any razors is he?"

Grace laughed.

"Have they told you yet when you get to go home?"

"Hopefully in a couple days."

"I can't wait," Grace smiled, her pink lips causing my monitors to jump.

She leaned over and kissed me again.

"I think I love you," I said.

"I thought you might," she whispered, giving me her standard reply.

Grace slipped out of the room and Doran came in. He shut the door and pulled up a chair beside me.

"Hey," he said, straddling the chair backwards, his long legs pushing his knees up to his chin.

"Hey," I said, wishing that I was still talking to Grace.

"You feeling better?"

"A little."

"Sorry about the hair," he apologized.

"It'll grow back."

"That's where you're lucky," he tried to joke. "Mine's thinning out, never to return."

I pretended as if I hadn't noticed.

"You okay?" I asked him, noting that he seemed a little nervous.

"Actually, Trust, there is something I wanted to talk to you about."

"All right."

"I don't think you'll think so."

"What is it?"

"Well, I feel real bad about what happened to you. Real bad. You know you were my favorite companion and everything. I learned more from you than anyone else."

"Thanks."

"You're welcome. Now here you are in the hospital because of me. I shouldn't have taken those seat belts out."

"These things happen," I consoled.

"I'm glad you feel that way. Anyhow, I really do think that things happen for a purpose. God doesn't stir something up for nothing. I had an uncle that got hit by lightning and lost his sight. Two weeks later he got hit by a car and passed away. My mom's always thought that God took his sight away so he wouldn't see it coming. Do you understand what I'm trying to say?"

"I think so," I lied.

"Good," he said with some relief. "Well, I think something good might just come out of all this."

"Are you thinking of something specific?" I asked.

"Actually, now that you mention it, there is one thing. You know I've been wanting to help you out," he rambled. "I just feel awful about all this."

"You said that."

"I helped your mom with that garage door you were fixing."

"Thanks."

"Don't mention it," he said with a faint smile. "I took Abel shooting with his BB gun. We didn't hit anything, but there was some bonding going on."

"He's a good kid," I said, wishing he would get to his point.

"I've been driving Grace to and from work."

"That's great."

"There's more. It seems as if I have fallen in love with her," he said quickly. "I didn't mean for it to happen, but what could I do? Her, me, driving back and forth in my truck. I'm only human."

I couldn't believe what I was hearing. It was like Donald Duck saying he now liked Minnie Mouse. He had no right—Minnie belonged to Mickey. The analogy wasn't that great, but I was on a lot of medication at the moment.

"Did something happen between you and Grace?" I asked, dumbfounded.

"Oh, no," he insisted. "I haven't even touched her."

"Have you talked to her about this?"

"Nope. She's usually too busy talking about you."

I breathed a sigh of relief.

"Well, I'm glad you brought this up," I exhaled dramatically. "I guess it might be best if you just went back to Idaho before your feelings get too strong for her. I'm sure my mother can get Grace to and from work. Besides, I won't be in here that much longer."

Doran just stared at me.

"You *are* leaving?" I asked.

"Trust, I don't know how your parents raised you, but my folks have always told me to follow the prophet. And the prophet has said that every young returned missionary shouldn't waste any time getting married."

"But he didn't tell you to marry my girlfriend."

"Maybe not exactly."

"Doran."

"I love Grace, Trust. I didn't come here right now to bow out, I came here to tell you of my intentions. I plan to marry Grace in the Idaho Falls Temple as soon as she says yes."

"Is this a joke?" I asked, beginning to get a little bothered by it all.

"This is no joke, and those are my intentions," he said, standing.

"Grace is my girlfriend," I debated. "She came here so that the two of us could figure out our future together."

"Things change," he said firmly. "I just thought I had better be honest with you about all this. I'd better go."

"But . . ."

He was gone. It was the most ridiculous thing I had ever heard. Elder Jorgensen and Grace. The idea was so absurd that I wanted to laugh. The phone in the room rang. I picked it up to find my mother on the other end.

"Trust, is Grace still there?" she asked.

"No," I answered. "She just left with Doran. Why?"

"Nothing really," she answered guiltily.

"Mom, what is Grace going to help you with this afternoon?" A growing sense of concern was coming over me.

"I suppose I can let you know now," Mom gave in. "The

missionaries in our ward are looking for people to practice their discussions on. I thought Grace would be perfect. They should be here in a few minutes."

My mother was so sneaky.

"Mom, just because Grace fell for me while I was serving a mission doesn't mean she's going to fall in love with one of those elders."

"Trust, I'm just trying to help Elder Nicks and Elder Minert learn their discussions."

"Mom, they've both been out for over a year and a half," I argued. "I'm sure they know their discussions by now."

"Elder Nicks is from Arkansas."

"What's that supposed to mean?"

"All I'm saying is that Arkansas is a lot closer to Tennessee than here."

I'm sure that in my mom's mind this all made perfect sense.

"Grace is going to know exactly what you are trying to do, Mom."

"Trust, I don't think it's very nice of you to second-guess your mother."

"So where are they going to teach her?" I asked.

"I thought I'd let them do it in the den; it's much more private."

"Mom."

"I'll keep the door cracked," she defended.

"You're not going to sit in with them?"

"Oh, I'd just be a fourth wheel."

"Mom, I'm in love with Grace."

"I'm sure you think you are. I'd better go," she said. "I wanted to warm up some leftovers for the elders. Happy Thanksgiving, Son," she added.

Click.

This was just perfect. First Doran was staking claim, and now my mother was throwing our poor missionaries into the pot.

A nurse came in and messed with my IV for a bit. I asked her for extra drugs and she didn't even smile.

The world was a cold, cruel place.

The nurse left, and a few moments later I heard a soft knock on the door.

"Come in," I said dejectedly.

In walked Lucy Fall.

If Moses himself had come to visit I could not have been more surprised.

"Lucy? Is that you?"

"Hello, Trust," she said, her demeanor softer and more subdued than I had ever remembered. "Can I come in?" she asked.

I should never have said yes.

## 53

# CONTRITION

Lucy Fall moved through the hospital doors and out into the November cold. She pulled her wool scarf tightly around her neck and breathed in deeply. Thanksgiving had turned out a little different than she had predicted. Of course, the entire month of November had not gone as previously planned. For the first time in her life Lucy was having to adjust to change.

The divorce was already going through. Lance didn't want to waste any time getting it all over with. Apparently he had other matters on his mind. Brunette matters. Lucy was as anxious as he was to finish it. She wanted nothing more than to be done with Lance. He had been a bad decision, with a costly outcome.

Lucy found out from a friend about Trust's accident, and that he was staying at the Southdale University Hospital. For the last few days she had wanted to stop by and visit him, but it had never felt right until today. She wanted to tell him how sorry she was about all that she had put him through, and apologize for the way that she had treated him in the past. Her intentions were forgiveness.

Bare trees twisted in the wind as Lucy crossed the street and approached the parking lot. A few leftover leaves swirled around her feet like they were connected with string. She reached her car and got inside quickly. The wild air howled, angry over her getting away.

Even in the hospital gown and with a half a head of hair, Trust looked good. He represented everything Lucy had given up and now wished to have back. He had been glad to see her, fumbling even.

Lucy had forgotten about the effect she had on him.

Lucy hung her head as she sat there in her car. Once again the tears came. Her shoulders shook and her eyes poured. As she had done so often in the past weeks, she just let it happen, feeling better after it passed.

Things were changing for Lucy, and this time possibly for the better. It seemed as if for the first time in her life she was recognizing a real soul within herself.

Was that possible?

Lucy had no real intention of taking Trust back. She had heard that he was interested in a red-headed girl named Grace whom he had met on his mission.

Funny, Lucy thought, Trust had not even brought this Grace girl up tonight.

Lucy started her car and slowly pulled out and away.

## 54

# Infiltration

Roger passed the potatoes and smiled. He had never seen so much food in his entire life. Mounds of it rolled over the table like foamy waves. Bowls the size of bathtubs were bursting with cheese-covered confections and piles of meat. His eyes sized it up as his stomach trembled. This was his third Thanksgiving dinner for the day.

"Are you certain no one else will be joining us?" he asked Sister Watson for the second time.

"Certain." She smiled. "Just you and me. Now, where was I? Oh, yes, when I turned twelve my mother changed my name from Cindy to Melinda."

"I thought your name was Mavis?" Roger asked.

"That's a whole other story," Sister Watson replied. "We'll go into that later."

Roger Williams tried to remain calm. These last couple of weeks had not been easy for him. He had thought that it would be so simple to just walk in, find the Book of Mormon, and walk out. That had not been the case. It had taken him two days just to locate Thelma's Way.

And now here he was after weeks of combing the town with nothing to show for it. He had had some success in convincing the locals that the book really wasn't worth that much and that they had been misinformed about its real value, but that was it. He could not comprehend how his son Trust had managed to live so long among these backward people. There had been moments when he even considered just giving up his quest, but he wanted that first edition Book of Mormon. And he felt confident that once he located it, he could talk whoever had it out of it for next to nothing.

He could afford to hang on a little longer.

The locals had allowed him to use an upstairs room in the Thelma's Way boardinghouse. It wasn't too bad a setup from which to operate. He had drawn out maps and prioritized the people in town most likely to help him find the elusive first edition.

Most everyone in the area believed the Book of Mormon was still around. Roswell Ford had informed him that the entire town was watching each other closely for clues. But President Heck thought maybe the heavens had taken it back, just like they did the golden plates.

Roger was betting on Roswell's theory.

The search continued. Information wasn't hard to extract because these people loved to talk. Plus, Roger had made it even easier for them to do so by tearing a small piece of paper up, writing the word "Press" on it, and sticking it in the brim of his hat on his way into town.

Everyone bought it.

Roger claimed he was a reporter from out west, one who was looking to chronicle the history of Thelma's Way in a book. Not a single person in Thelma's Way was shocked by this. Most folks wondered why it had taken the west so long to come around.

He had made no mention of the connection between him and Trust. He didn't want to complicate things by having people get sentimental and nostalgic on him. It was obvious, however, that Thelma's

Way loved his son. Roger found himself growing proud of the boy he had grown so distant from.

" . . . I think you should dedicate an entire chapter—no, section—to the pageant that I wrote and . . ." Sister Watson was blabbering.

A sudden knock at the door silenced her for a moment.

"Well, who in the . . ." Sister Watson mumbled as she got up, more than mildly bothered by the interruption.

Sister Watson was decked out. She had on her nicest dress and her best-fitting wig. She was also wearing more makeup than a non-circus performer should be allowed to wear. Her attempts to impress Roger Williams were going unnoticed, however, and now someone had the gall to disturb their conversation.

She stepped to the door and flung it open. Framed by the weather-worn doorjamb was Toby Carver, holding a plate of food and wiggling his neck to look around her into the house.

"I've got company, Toby," Sister Watson insisted.

Toby ignored her by stepping inside. "Thought I might bring something by for Mr. Williams here," he explained.

Roger turned in his seat to face him.

"We've plenty of food," Sister Watson scolded.

"Well, I also just thought of something that might interest Mr. Williams."

"What is it?" Roger asked, setting his fork down.

"Well, you was asking 'bout that Book of Mormon, and where to find it."

"Yes," Roger said with excitement. "Did you find it?"

"Sort of," Toby bragged.

"Sort of?" Roger demanded.

"Well, not that exact one, but I went down to the church in Virgil's Find and borrowed one of their extra copies for you. Them's the same words inside."

Toby Carver handed an inexpensive blue-covered Book of Mormon over to Roger.

"I marked a couple of my favorite parts for you," Toby said proudly.

Roger forced a smile. It took everything he had inside not to blow up in Toby's face. The last thing he needed was a worthless modern copy of the Book of Mormon. These people were impossible.

"Thanks," he managed to say. "But it would really make my history of your town complete if I could see, or maybe take a picture of, the real first edition."

"It's lost," Toby informed him.

"I know that," Roger said, frustrated. "But I'm sure someone could find it."

"Yes, Toby," Sister Watson said. "Why don't you go look for it and leave Mr. Williams and me alone."

"If I found it, could I hold it up for the picture?" Toby asked.

"Of course," Roger brightened. "In fact, you tell everyone that whoever finds it, I'll put their picture on the front of the book."

"The front?" Toby asked reverently.

"The front," Roger punctuated.

Toby Carver smiled, slowly took two steps backwards, and raced off.

"That book will turn up now, sure as rain," Sister Watson said. "Who in their right mind wouldn't trade a dusty old book for the chance to be on the cover of a new one?"

Roger Williams smiled. Things were looking up.

# 55

# Dizzy

November 26th

The next morning the doctor informed me that I should be able to go home within 24 hours. I was ecstatic. I had been a little concerned about the whole Doran-and-Grace thing. Not that I thought she would actually leave me for him, not that he was a real threat, but it just made me nervous to have a gung ho returned missionary spending all his time in pursuit of my girlfriend while I was chained to an IV.

Grace dropped by Friday afternoon after work. She sat on the edge of the bed and read to me from the newspaper for a while. It was one of the nicest moments of my life. Then she proceeded to bring me up to speed on the ward's current events.

Noah was continuing to drum up sales for his food storage time-share, and Grace was beginning to speak about him in far too glowing terms. Apparently everyone was really happy he was around. Everyone except Leonard Vastly, that is. Two weeks ago, Leonard Vastly had been singing Noah Taylor's praises—not anymore. Word on the ward was that Brother Vastly was beginning to feel Noah Taylor was encroaching on his status as the number one hoarder in Southdale. Brother Vastly did not like that. He had worked long and hard to be known as "That crazy man with all the food." Too hard to let some yahoo from southern Utah with a fancy warehouse come in and bump him from power. So, in an effort to one-up his new rival, Brother Vastly had completely sealed off his single-wide trailer with heavy clear plastic tarps and duct tape, vowing not to come out until the first phase of his food storage ran out. After a couple of hours, he had been forced to cut an air hole, but aside from that minor glitch he had completely cut himself off from the world. He called it his "Bio-Doom." He was funding his little project by collecting his retirement ten years early. He hated to give up his livelihood, but some things were worth it—this was for the betterment of society. Grace told me he kept the curtains on his bay window open so that scientists and interested civilians could study and watch him in this great endeavor of self-reliance. No one had complained about him taping up his house, but a couple of his neighbors protested the open-curtain policy. Now, by order of the mayor, his curtains were to remain closed after six in the evening. No one wanted to know *that* much about him. Brother Vastly communicated to the outside world via ham radio and hand signals.

"Won't come out at all?" I asked in amazement.

"That's what he signaled," Grace replied.

Grace told me all about the missionaries who had come over to practice their discussions on her. According to her, my mother could not have been more obvious about her intentions if she had tried. She had played soft music on the home stereo and served hot cocoa with chocolate mints while they taught Grace the discussion. Elder Nicks and Elder Minert were a little embarrassed, but they had been good sports.

"So, I guess they won't be coming back?" I asked.

"Actually," Grace said, "I was hoping I could hear the rest of the lessons. With you by my side, of course. I don't know if Thelma's Way really afforded me the chance to learn much about the Church."

"How about if I teach them to you myself?" I offered.

"You'd get too distracted," she smiled.

"Hmmm," I mused, staring at her.

Grace stood up, signaling that it was time for her to go.

"How are you getting home?" I questioned.

"The bus."

"So did Doran tell you?" I asked.

"About being in love with me?" She smiled.

I nodded.

"Not in so many words, but this morning at six o'clock he was outside my window singing."

"You're kidding?"

"No," Grace laughed. "Wendy threw one of her cats at him. He got pretty scratched up. Then when he drove me to work, he kept playing country slow songs and looking over at me. I thought maybe it would be best if I learned how to use the bus system."

"Sorry about him," I apologized.

"He's harmless enough," Grace brushed it off. "He kind of reminds me of Leo back home."

I hadn't thought about it, but Doran and Leo Tip did have a lot in common.

"You just have this effect on men," I smiled.

"Boys," Grace joked while leaning over to kiss me.

She kissed me longer than usual. I'm sure I would have resisted, but I was a helpless patient strapped to a hospital bed.

Saturday morning I was released from the hospital. For insurance purposes, I had to ride in a wheelchair to the front door where the nurse then dumped me out and wished me well.

My mom and Grace had come to pick me up. Grace helped me into the car as if I were an invalid grandfather.

"I'm really okay," I insisted.

"Let me help," she said, slipping her arms around me.

I obliged. I was happy to be going home.

# 56

# Signs O' Stress

That night, before bed, I sat in the kitchen watching my mother re-iron my father's shirts. She carefully went over each one. She would take one from its hanger, lay it across the ironing board, and press down on it as hard as she possibly could.

"They get wrinkly just from hanging," she fussed.

"Mom, are you going to be all right?" I asked.

"I'm fine," she insisted. "Happy as a . . . happy as a clam."

"No news from Dad?"

"Oh, I'm sure he'll call when he gets a chance." She pressed so hard with the iron that I thought she would rip the shirt. "You know how busy he gets."

"Busy doing what?"

"Business stuff."

"Where?"

"Honestly, Trust, what's with all the questions?"

"I just think it's weird that Dad's been away for so long. He missed Margaret's recital, and Abel's play, and Thanksgiving."

"He was there in spirit," Mom pointed out. "Besides, if I recall correctly, a certain someone else missed those things as well."

"I was in the hospital," I defended.

"And your father is on business."

"Mom, who are you trying to protect?" I argued.

She set the iron down and steam hissed out angrily. "Trust, there are things about marriage you can't yet understand," she said harshly.

"I'm not fifteen," I pointed out.

"You just don't understand how your father and I operate."

"So tell me."

"This isn't the time, Trust."

"You know, I can remember a time when you and Dad were different," I told her.

"I'm ironing," my mother said, as if she were eating a good meal and I had just begun to talk about some graphic surgery.

"I really thought Dad would come around while I was serving my mission," I said reflectively. "Do you know that he only wrote me four letters the entire time?"

"He works very hard to keep this family comfortable," she defended.

"You don't look so comfortable," I observed.

"Trust!" she said, slamming down the iron. "I don't appreciate you talking to me like this."

"I just meant that with all the things you and Dad can afford, our family still seems lacking."

It was no use. I had lost her. Mom had slipped into her "I'm not going to talk about anything emotional" mode.

"So how is Grace liking the missionary lessons?" she asked.

"Actually," I sighed, "I wanted to talk to you about that too."

"Abel's getting tall, isn't he?" she said, blatantly changing the subject again and focusing only on the shirt in front of her.

I stood up, kissed my mother on the cheek, and went to bed.

57

# The Problem with Widowers

November 28th

Sunday morning we all rode together in my mother's van to church. Grace had even talked Wendy into coming with us. She and Wendy had really gotten along well, despite their age difference. I think Grace was happy to have a woman to talk to, and Wendy was thrilled to have anyone to talk to. The only other time Wendy had ever come to church with us was for my mission farewell over two and a half years ago. I had forgotten what she looked like in a dress. Common courtesy prevented me from laughing.

When we pulled up to the building, the parking lot was already full. Cars and minivans covered the ground like bulky sequins on a black rug. As we were walking into the building it became obvious that folks no longer feared or felt bad about Grace. Everyone would greet my mother, comment about my half-shaved head, and then trip over themselves to say hi to Grace. I couldn't believe it.

"What did you do to these people?" I asked Grace quietly.

"They just feel sorry for me," she brushed it off.

Wendy didn't really want to go into the chapel, so she decided to stay out in the foyer and sit on the soft, boxy couches. When I told her that the foyer was sort of reserved for parents with fussy children, she told me she loved kids. When I reminded her that she really didn't like children, she told me that her opinion of children had changed ever since she saw that one movie about that one kid that saved that whale. I decided not to reason with her any further.

Grace and I entered the chapel and picked out a private pew on the side. It would have been a nice place to observe the meeting, but Sister Cravitz walked over and insisted that we join her.

Sister Cravitz was the Clearview Ward's unofficial mother. She watched over and kept track of every part and person within our fold. She felt most comfortable with her big nose wedged forcefully into everyone's business. She wasn't a pretty woman, but she wouldn't have made a completely ugly man. She styled her hair in a tight bun that was flat and perfectly round. She wore huge orthopedic shoes and the same skirt every week, alternating it with her rose-colored blouse that matched, and her orange-colored one that didn't. Sister Cravitz had celebrated her sixty-ninth birthday about a month ago. She had no kids, and her husband was buried in the Southdale Memorial Park right next to the maintenance shed. Although Sister Cravitz made it her business to be involved in others' lives, it was generally understood that she didn't like people.

Now here she was, doing an uncharacteristic thing like inviting Grace and me to sit next to her during church. I was shocked. Two weeks ago she had acted as if Grace were a virus sent to infect us, and now she was letting her sit closer to her than she had usually allowed her husband to sit. It must have been because she felt pity for me and my recent accident.

It's fun to pretend.

I knew full well it had everything to do with Grace. I was amazed.

It had taken me almost the entire two years of my mission to recognize the effect Grace had on me, and here she had been in Southdale for only a few weeks and people were already falling all over themselves to get to know her. After we were seated, Sister Cravitz pulled out her change purse that was filled with white TicTacs, and offered us some. I took only one, not wanting to appear greedy. Once again I was astounded—Sister Cravitz didn't share her TicTacs with just anyone. The only time I could even remember her doing so was when she had been forced to sit by Brother Vastly in Sunday School during one of his garlic health blitzes. Of course she didn't actually give him TicTacs—she threw them at him.

Sister Cravitz took a TicTac for herself and then snapped the clip shut on her coin purse. She sucked the marrow out of the mint, and then turned toward Grace.

"I hear you're doing wonders for Brother Taylor," she said. "I'm not quick to hand out compliments, but I'm usually first to say 'job well done' when the task at hand is accomplished properly."

"Thank you," Grace said.

"Being prepared is a mighty task," Sister Cravitz lectured. "A mighty task indeed. This city has got a real leg up on adversity thanks to Noah Taylor. What are you most frightened of, dear? Drought, or fire?"

"Both," Grace answered politically.

"How about you, Trust? What do you fear most?"

I paused for a moment to give the appearance of contemplation.

"No need to answer," she insisted. "I can read your mind."

I was just about to apologize for what I was thinking when she guessed . . .

"Fire."

"You're right." I played along.

Sister Cravitz smiled and pulled out her coin purse again. Suddenly we were her best friends.

Sister Morris began to wrap up the prelude music and Bishop Leen stepped up to the pulpit. He ran his light fingers through his faded hair and pushed his skin-colored lips to the microphone.

I looked at my program to see how the meeting would run today. There was one youth speaker, Jeffy Smith; a musical number by the Rose kids; and a non-youth speaker, Noah Taylor. I looked up at the stage to see if I could spot Grace's employer, but from our position, I couldn't see anyone sitting on the other side of the pulpit. I wanted to meet Brother Taylor and thank him for everything he had done for Grace. I still wasn't convinced he was as honest as everyone said he was, but the positive effects he had had on my girlfriend were worth setting aside any personal misgivings.

Doran came in the far doors and sat down across the room from us. Coming in five minutes late had allowed him to make something of a dramatic entrance. He was still pursuing Grace. It was as if the heavens had commanded him to persevere. He was that committed. The fact that Grace had made her feelings for me clear made no difference to him. In Thelma's Way, with him as my junior companion, I had been so happy about the strength of his will. Now it was beginning to make me uncomfortable. Doran had moved into a small apartment across town and sent Grace a copy of his personal mission statement. I couldn't remember the whole thing, but a couple of lines still stood stiffly in my mind.

" . . . I will better myself by loving you. I will seek to find resolution by committing myself to the idea of being eternally proactive with my lady . . ."

Doran was wearing a gray suit that accentuated his gangly figure. He had on a cowboy tie and boots that he had tucked the legs of his pants into. His spiky hair was gelled down and parted perfectly in the middle. He looked at us from across the room and sighed. I felt sorry for him. I knew what it was like to love Grace from afar. I could only imagine how hard it would be to know that she cared for someone else. I needed to be more compassionate with Doran.

After the sacrament was administered, the youth speaker, Jeffy Smith, talked about honesty and how his aunt was in jail for mail fraud. I watched Sister Smith hide her head as her boy aired their dirty laundry without a thought. At least we knew he had written his own remarks. Jeffy then reported on the Scouts' last campout and announced that anyone who may have ended up with an extra mess kit needed to return it before his big brother found out he had borrowed it.

Amen, I think.

The Rose children sang "In My Father's House Are Many Mansions." It was a lovely number, but as it progressed I could hear Brother and Sister Carp growing angry in the pew behind us. It was no secret that the Carps and the Roses didn't really get along. The Roses were a very well-to-do family. Brother Rose was a partner with one of the largest law firms in the state. He was also the school board president, and had been elected Father of the Year twice. His family drove the nicest cars, had the nicest house, and were constantly talking about their huge summer home in Wyoming. Well, Brother Carp didn't have a summer home. In fact, thanks to a bad business deal, he and his family were back living with his parents in their duplex. Brother Carp claimed it was temporary and that they were only going to stay with his folks until he could get his financial feet back on the ground. Well, that was two years ago. Now, instead of looking for work, he chose to pick apart those who actually had some—Brother Rose being his favorite target. The Roses had tried to get along with the Carps but whatever they tried seemed to backfire. So Brother and Sister Carp continued to grow more and more bitter, biting at the Roses whenever possible and finding offense in nearly everything they did. Now here were the young Rose children singing "In My Father's House Are Many Mansions." Brother Carp missed the analogy completely, thinking that the Roses were simply bragging about their summer home. He stood up and stormed out.

I took a moment to self-righteously contemplate how someone could possibly be so offended by something so simple.

The Rose children finished singing and sat down. I watched someone get up and walk to the podium. I watched that same someone claim that his name was Noah Taylor and that he was happy to be speaking today. There had to be some kind of a mistake! This man didn't look like a Noah Taylor—he looked more like a Mr. "I'm everything every woman could ever want in a man and then some." The Noah Taylor I had imagined was a gray-haired old man from Manti, Utah. A widower with a bad hip, a long beard, and a tendency to go on and on about how rotten our society had become. You know, Noah . . . Noah Taylor. What stood before me was something altogether different.

"That's Brother Taylor?" I whispered to Grace, hoping the answer would be anything but what I knew it was.

"That's Noah," Grace said without taking her eyes off him.

This was just awful. Noah Taylor was a good-looking man. He had short brown hair that seemed just clean-cut enough to indicate that he was orderly, and just tousled enough to show that he wasn't worried about what others thought. He wore a sweater with a tie that only a woman would pick out. He looked to have a few years on my twenty-three. I suspected he was pretty close to thirty. He smiled and made a bad joke about food storage that every member of the congregation laughed at.

I didn't think I liked Noah Taylor.

"I thought you said he was widowed," I said.

"His wife died a year and a half ago." Grace frowned. "Isn't it sad?"

I was grieving.

Noah talked all about the last days, and how God was hoping that we were watching for Him. He laughed, he cried, and he convinced even me that he was too good to be true. He pitched his effort to prepare everyone, pleading with the members to let him help organize them.

After sacrament meeting was over, Grace insisted that I meet Noah personally. She dragged me up onto the stage to wait at the end of the line. I ran my fingers though my half-missing hair, hoping he would think it was some sort of cool new style and knowing that he probably wouldn't. Every woman in the ward was frantically trying to thank Brother Taylor for his inspiring words. Our neighbor, Sister Lewis, was talking with such animation to him that she seemed to spit all over everyone. Sister Cravitz hugged him twice, and Sister Johnson spent a good four minutes questioning him about the shelf life of chocolate drink mix vs. fruit punch. Eventually the adoring throngs thinned out and Grace and I approached.

"Grace," he said with far too familiar an inflection. "How'd I do?"

"Great," she replied. "I wanted you to meet Trust."

I stuck out my hand to say, "Hey."

"It's nice to finally meet you, Trust," he said as if on cue.

"Likewise." I nodded.

"Grace has sure been a lifesaver at the warehouse," he complimented. "Thanks for bringing her out here."

"I thought you were old," was my only response.

"Well, I feel old," Noah said, looking at me queerly.

"Probably not as old as I thought you were," I said kindly.

"How old did you think I was?"

"I don't know," I said, sincerely trying to sound friendly. "I sort of pictured you looking like Moses, or Colonel Sanders."

"The chicken guy?" Noah asked. "Is that how Grace has been describing me?" He laughed.

"Trust really hit his head hard when he fell out of that truck," Grace playfully defended me.

"Well, I'm glad to see you're feeling better," Noah said perfectly.

"I'd better run now," he added. "Sister Treat wants me to look at her wheat."

He was smooth.

Noah walked down from the podium, shaking people's hands and patting them on their backs. The confidence the guy radiated couldn't be contained on the North American continent, let alone in the room. I couldn't believe that someone with the first name of Noah could be so suave. Grace smiled at me knowingly.

"Colonel Sanders, huh?" She laughed.

"What?"

"You're not jealous, are you?"

"Me jealous of him? I mean, just because he's good-looking and sort of stylish. . . ."

"He does look nice today, doesn't he?" Grace reflected.

Darn that sweater.

"I'm just wondering why you never mentioned what he looked like before."

"I didn't think it was important," she teased. "Besides, you know I'm not really into good-looking guys."

"Thanks," I martyred, as we began to walk down from the stand.

I was going to go on and on about how hurt I was, milking it for all it was worth, when suddenly there was Lucy. I actually hollered, making myself look guilty.

"Ahhhhh!"

"Hello, Trust," Lucy said, obviously pleased by my reaction.

Lucy looked great. No, better than great. She looked as if she had tossed aside her old self and was now emerging as something completely new and fascinating. Her blue eyes had been so shallow, but now they looked deep and cloudy. I could tell that the last little while had really worked her over and was forcing her to look at life differently.

"Lucy, what are you doing here?" I asked, still startled and standing in front of Grace as if to hide her. It was a bad move.

"I'm back in my parents' home," Lucy informed us. "They'll be out of the country for another month still. I wanted to come to church so badly. Lance didn't really approve of me going."

Grace squeezed my arm harder than necessary as she stepped out from behind me.

"Oh, yes," I fumbled. "Lucy, I would like you to meet Grace Heck. Grace, this is Lucy Fall. She's an old friend of mine."

"Nice to meet you," Lucy said dispassionately.

"Nice to meet you, Lucy," Grace replied kindly.

I thought now would have been a good time to end this discussion, but Lucy felt otherwise.

"Well, Trust, you look better than you did the other day," she commented, digging my grave by big, huge shovelfuls. "Your hair's growing back nicely."

"The other day?" Grace inquired.

I tried lamely to cover my tracks. "Didn't I tell you about Lucy stopping by the hospital?"

"I don't remember you mentioning that." Grace smiled.

"I just stopped by to say hi to Trust," Lucy explained. "Ever since Lance left, I've been so lonely. When I heard that Trust was in the hospital, I thought it might help me feel better to visit an old friend."

"Who left?" Grace asked.

"My husband, Lance," Lucy said sorrowfully. "Or I guess I should say my ex-husband. The divorce has already gone through."

"I'm sorry to hear that," Grace consoled.

"It's better this way," Lucy sighed. "Well, I should get going," she added. "I just wanted to say hi again, and thank you for cheering me up."

"No problem," I lied.

"It was nice meeting you, Grace."

"You too, Lucy. I hope things work out for you."

Lucy managed a smile.

Grace stood there still holding my arm tightly as Lucy walked away. I was in for it. I had meant to tell Grace about Lucy, but it had slipped my mind. There was no way I could ever be interested in Lucy again. She was just an old friend who needed some comfort. It would be wrong of me to simply abandon those in need because they were beautiful ex-girlfriends that I used to obsess over.

"She seems nice," Grace said coyly as we both watched Lucy wander off.

"I meant to tell you about her stopping by the hospital," I tried.

"I'm sure you did."

"Seriously."

"I believe you," Grace toyed with me. "That's too bad about her marriage."

"Isn't it?" I said, trying to sound sincere.

"She sure is pretty," Grace observed. "She's even more beautiful than her picture."

"I hadn't noticed," I said, quickly adding, "and what picture have you seen of her? I don't remember ever having shown you one."

"There was one in your house."

"Where?"

"That's not important," Grace insisted.

"Seriously," I persisted. "I didn't know we had one around."

"There's that one," Grace said. "On that table by the nook."

"Oh," I said, not realizing that we had a nook.

"So were you trying to hide me from Lucy?" Grace asked accusingly as she moved on. "You're not embarrassed by me, are you?"

"No," I said, slower than I should have. "It was just a reflex. Like a spasm or something."

"A spasm?"

"Or something."

"Oh."

"Really, I get them all the time."

"How attractive," Grace joked.

"I mean they're not real noticeable."

"We'd better get to Sunday School," Grace said, changing the subject. "Wendy's probably still waiting in the foyer."

As we walked out of the chapel, Wendy was nowhere to be seen, but Doran was waiting for us. He stepped up and addressed Grace.

"Hello, Doran," she replied.

"Grace, I was wondering if you would accompany me to Sunday School?" He stuck his arm out eagerly for her to latch on.

"Actually—" Grace began to say.

"I know you're still seeing Trust," he interrupted. "But I'm just asking for thirty minutes of your time. If you don't feel differently about me after that, then I'll try another approach."

"Doran, don't you think this is a little—" I was interrupted.

"You know," Grace said, "maybe I'll take you up on that, Doran. Trust needs a little time to think about his reflexes."

Grace took Doran's arm and walked off down the hall. I stood there in the now-empty foyer feeling like a pair of glasses on a blind man—worthless. The two full-time missionaries, Elder Nicks and Elder Minert, came down the hall and walked up to me.

"Have you seen Grace Heck?" Elder Minert asked.

"No, why?" I asked despondently.

"My companion wants to get her address so he can write her when he gets home."

Elder Nicks blushed.

"She went that way." I pointed.

The two elders skipped off toward the Relief Society/gospel doctrine classroom. I walked outside of the church building, across the street, and all the way home. When everyone got back from church, Grace went directly to Wendy's house without even stopping to check in on me. She also skipped our family dinner, not even bothering to call to inform us that she wasn't coming. When I walked over to her place later that night, Wendy gave me some lame excuse about Grace already having gone to bed.

I was beginning to worry.

58

# A Little Closer

Few things had ever stirred up Thelma's Way as much as the offer of having their picture put on the front of a book did. Everyone was trying frantically to locate the missing Book of Mormon.

By default, Roger Williams was actually doing the town a great favor. For so long most of the members in the area had been inactive. Now everyone was asking President Heck for forgiveness, and begging him to be assigned to as many home teaching and visiting teaching families as possible. To the locals this seemed like the best way to get into people's homes to take a look around. People were showing up at each other's houses with pies and bread and lessons that required them to stay for a while. Folks were even teaching those that had already been taught, bringing the home teaching percentage to 140 percent, and visiting teaching to 112. In two days the attitude of the entire valley had changed. And in the process everyone was forgetting why they had stayed away from church. Sure, they all knew that the reason people were visiting them was because of the Book of Mormon, but they didn't care. It was just so nice to be getting along.

Sunday morning sacrament meeting was packed. The branch presidency had to call upon the members to bring lawn chairs and grain drums for people to sit on. They lined the aisles with makeshift seats and large quilts. They were sprawling out on the floor and sitting on each other's laps. Even the seats up around the podium were filled. President Heck sat with Toby Carver and Leo Tip looking out at the biggest crowd they had ever drawn. And Roger Williams sat on the other side of President Heck as the branch's guest of honor.

President Heck stood up and began the meeting. "Brothers and Sisters," he said. "Never in the history of Thelma's Way has there been so many members at one sacrament meeting. Now I ain't so backwards as to pretend why you're all here, but I'm sure God is happy to see you, even if it's greed that brought you in." President Heck cleared his throat and sniffed his nose.

"Now this last week was Thanksgiving," President Heck continued. "It's a time to remember the pioneers. I hope that while you were all eating you took just a tick to think about those poor people that founded this great country. I know I did. I also took time to think about each of you, and be thankful for your company. But I suppose I'm most thankful for my family. The wife can harp a bit, and Digby ain't doing as good in math as I'd like him to. But they're blood, and I'm grateful to 'em," he said elegantly.

"We miss Grace," he continued. "She didn't actually hang around the home as much as we'd like her to done do, but still we miss her. Why just last night Narlette was talking about her. Isn't that true, Narlette?" President Heck asked out to his daughter in the crowd.

"Yes, Daddy," she hollered back.

"Kids can be so sweet sometimes," President Heck pointed out. "And I'd be mighty neglectful if I didn't say that we miss Elder Williams. That boy did more for this meadow than I care to recap. I don't think there is a soul here that didn't have some conversation or interaction with Elder Williams. He was good stock."

Roger Williams tried to stare passively out at the crowd. There had still not been a single person in Thelma's Way who had made the connection between him and Trust.

President Heck put both hands on the pulpit and straightened his arms. "I feel inspired to be honest with you," he went on. "This Book of Mormon thing makes me a little jittery. Not since I gave up smoking for the final time have I been so shaky about something. I don't really like us all smiling at each other just so that we can peek up our neighbors' knickers. But I feel a comfort knowing that this book-writing Roger Williams has the same last name as our Elder Williams. I know we're not supposed to be sniffing around for signs, but this one smells right. I figure if the Williams name has done us right once, then the Williams name will do us right twice."

The congregation began to whisper amongst themselves, commenting enthusiastically about how much sense this made.

After the services, Roger Williams headed back to the boardinghouse to rest in his room. He had a couple of hours before he needed to go over to Sister Teddy Yetch's home for dinner.

Roger's shoulders hung heavy as he walked. This whole thing was taking way too long, and each hour longer seemed to make things more complicated. He hoped with all his heart that it wouldn't be someone like President Heck, or Sister Watson, or Toby Carver, or Narlette, or CleeDee, or . . . he hoped that whoever found the Book of Mormon would be someone that he had not begun to grow attached to. Roger didn't know if he could honestly look them in the face and take it away.

This Thelma's Way was one strange place.

59

# FOREWARNED

November 29th

Monday morning I called Grace at 7:00 only to find out that she had caught the bus to work an hour ago, and that Wendy didn't take kindly to being woken up any hour earlier than eight.

Then I called Brother Hyrum Barns to see about the job he had promised me two weeks ago.

"Actually the position's filled, Trust," he explained.

"But I thought that—"

"I needed someone a week ago, and well, you were all banged up," he rationalized. "I didn't know if you would be able to handle the workload when you did get better."

"It's only paper filing," I laughed. "I could do that with my eyes closed."

"I'm just nervous about having someone who busted his head alphabetizing my files. I've already given the job to that tall boy from Idaho."

"Doran?"

"Don't blame me, Trust," Brother Barns pleaded. "I had an opening and Brother Victor filled it for me."

I didn't blame Brother Barns or Brother Victor—I blamed Doran. I hung up the phone and began to think about other possible jobs and how much Doran was complicating things. I could hear the doorbell ring downstairs. A few moments later my mother hollered at me to come down.

Bishop Leen was in the living room tapping his foot and glancing about.

"Hello, Trust," he noticed me.

"Bishop."

"I was wondering if I could visit with you a moment?" he asked.

I nodded and we sat.

"Normally this kind of thing would be handled by your elders quorum president, but he was scared to tell you."

"That bad, huh?" I asked, my blue eyes clouding.

"Well, it all depends on how you look at it. You see, Brother Leonard Vastly needs a home teacher to visit him monthly, and no one's willing to do it. It seems that everyone sort of feels like Brother Vastly and Noah Taylor are enemies. And well, no one wants to give the appearance of siding with Leonard Vastly."

"And you think I do?" I asked.

"Well, Sister Cravitz said you seemed a little jealous of Noah Taylor yourself. You and Leonard would have something in common . . ."

"Why would I be jealous of Noah?" I asked.

"Now, I'm not saying jealous exactly. I'm just saying that you're mad because he seems to have more going for him at the moment. Big business, great personality, plus he's been spending all that time with Grace. She really is an exceptional girl, by the way."

"Thanks."

"Anyhow, by your helping Leonard Vastly you would be showing Noah that you're not afraid to take a stand."

I couldn't believe what I was hearing.

"Bishop, I'd be glad to home teach Brother Vastly, but I'm not doing it to spite Noah. He seems like a nice enough guy."

"All right," the bishop winked. "That's what we'll tell the others."

"Really, I have nothing against Noah."

"I read you loud and clear."

"Actually, I don't think you do," I said, frustrated. "I'm happy that Grace is working for him."

"Denial's a hard pit to climb out of," Bishop Leen counseled.

I put my head in my hands and sighed. "Is Brother Vastly still living in his 'Bio-Doom'?" I asked.

"Unfortunately, yes," the bishop said, standing. "And he still vows to not come out until Noah Taylor is proven wrong. Of course, Sister Morris swears she saw him at the dollar movies the other night wearing a wig and fake glasses."

Things just kept getting better.

"So, will you accept the assignment?" the bishop asked.

"Of course," I replied.

"Good," he said, verbally slapping me on the back. "Now, is there anything else I can do for you?"

"Actually, yes."

"Shoot."

"Well, I was—"

"Hold on a moment," he interrupted. "Is this going to take real long? I'm due over at the planetarium for some indoor pruning."

"It shouldn't."

"Shoot."

"Well, Bishop, everything aside, doesn't this Brother Taylor thing bother you just a bit? I mean, should we really be putting ourselves into his hands? Food storage time-share? How much do we even know about this guy?"

"Listen, Trust," he said kindly. "I understand why you're worried. But I talked with Noah Taylor for a long time when he first came to town. I e-mailed his father who used to be a stake president. This December seventeenth thing is more of a gimmick than a genuine scare."

"That's not how the ward is acting."

"Trust," he tisked. "I've seen this before. Young men returning home from their missions to discover that everything running exactly the way it was before they left is suddenly wrong."

"It's not that," I protested. "I just don't think we should be putting our fate in Noah's hands."

"Nothing will happen on the seventeenth—nothing except for everyone in our ward being completely prepared for what may actually come later on. Is that so bad?"

"I guess not. But don't you think people should have their stuff in their own homes?"

"Noah Taylor is only going to be around until the end of December," he lectured. "Southdale isn't his permanent home. He'll go on to some other town that's in need of preparation. I suspect right now he's just organizing our supplies in that warehouse for the time being. When he leaves, people will have to find a new place to store their stuff. This is a good thing, Trust."

"I hope so."

Bishop Leen looked at his watch. "I should be going. Good luck with Leonard Vastly. He's really a good guy, just a little weedy between the ears."

Ten minutes after Bishop Leen left, Sister Barns, the Relief Society president and wife of my would-have-been employer, showed up to ask for permission for Grace to participate in their date auction coming up on December the ninth. All the proceeds would go to help those in our area who couldn't afford to pay Noah to get themselves prepared. The auction was actually a farce, a big setup, where folks would simply bid on their wives or girlfriends in an effort to help the needy. Afterwards, all those who had successfully bid would get to participate in a big group date in the cultural hall.

"I thought we weren't allowed to have fund-raisers," I questioned.

"Well, we've invited all the Scouts so that we can call it a Scout activity."

I told Sister Barns that the decision to be bid on was Grace's, and that I would bid high if she agreed to it.

"I think you'll have some competition," Sister Barns smiled. "That boy who's working for us sure is sweet on her. And Brother Treat seems to think that Grace would make the perfect girl for his Leon."

"Leon's only seventeen," I laughed.

"That's old enough to group date," Sister Barns chirped.

"Sister Barns, Grace is twenty-three."

"Love can fill tremendous gaps."

Something was wrong. The entire city of Southdale had gone goofy. I should never have brought Grace back unmarried. We should have gotten hitched back east and then come west. Better yet, we should have gotten married and stayed back there. Her presence here was making everyone, including me, crazy.

"I thought this auction was just a setup?" I questioned. "Don't we all know at the outset who will take whom home?"

"In theory," Sister Barns clucked. "But the potential for someone to outbid you is always there."

I shook my head.

"Leon's been working at the Shoe Stop, after school," she added, hinting that Leon might have money to spend on Grace.

"Sister Barns, Grace and I are loosely engaged," I explained. "We just haven't set a date yet."

"Satan looks for the cracks," she said. "Then he wiggles in and destroys the foundation."

"What?" I asked, wondering what she was talking about.

"Long engagements are a first-class invitation to failure. Don't R.S.V.P., Trust. Don't R.S.V.P.!"

"We're not actually engaged," I tried to explain. "Just loosely engaged."

"Well, then I see no harm in Leon or Doran staking claim."

Sister Barns stood, thanked me for the nice conversation, and left.

I spent the next hour trying to call Grace at work. No one ever answered. After twenty-four attempts, I gave up.

I was not feeling good about things.

60

# Applying Stucco

Monday after work Grace came straight home and found me. She apologized for not coming over to Sunday dinner. She apologized for going to Sunday School with Doran. She apologized for not calling me earlier in the day. And she told me I was all she had thought about for the last twenty-four hours.

It was a start.

"Let's take a drive," she suggested.

We drove up into the Dintmore Hills and parked above the Scarsdale Meadow. There were literally thousands of hills there. Some of them were tall and rolling, others were jagged and flat. Each one of them had an official name—an early settler had gone to the trouble of labeling them all. It would be impossible to remember all the names, but we were now parked on top of Georgia, one of the best-known mounds. Georgia was high and rounded at the peak, and she also provided the nicest view of the largest meadow within the hills.

The afternoon was turning to dusk, and tiny clouds slid across the sky like ice on an iron. Grace held my hand in silence. She looked great at night. Her dark red hair and deep eyes were more mesmerizing than a single flickering flame against the blackness.

Pale stars began to appear in the fading blue.

"Sister Barns came by today," I said, starting the conversation.

"I bet I know what she wanted," Grace replied, gazing at the sky. "Nothing like an auction to make a woman feel important."

"So she called you?"

"Yep."

"Are you going to do it?"

"I guess so," Grace replied. "After all, I know who will win me. Plus, it will help Noah out."

"Oh," was all I said.

"It still bothers you that Noah's not some old prophet-looking guy, doesn't it?" Grace poked.

"Not really," I said, mentally crossing my fingers behind my back.

"You're a poor liar." Grace smiled, turning to look at me.

I looked into her eyes and forgot all about Noah Taylor. In fact, I forgot everything I had ever known except for how to form this next sentence.

"So, are you glad you came?" I asked her.

"Here?" she asked, meaning the top of Georgia. "Or here?" she said, putting out her hand and indicating Southdale.

"Here," I replied, with my hand as well.

"Umm hum," she said, biting her lip. "This has been the best time of my life."

"Do you miss Thelma's Way?"

"A little," Grace admitted. "The sky out here is too open, and your river doesn't hold a candle to the Girth. I miss the meadow and the miles of trees. And I . . ." She laughed at herself. "I guess I miss Thelma's Way more than I thought."

We both sighed.

"Do you actually think anything will happen on the seventeenth?" I questioned.

"Noah does," Grace answered.

"Do you think he's an honest guy?"

"I guess so, why?"

"I don't know," I answered. "I just think it's kind of creepy, him acting like he knows something that no one else does."

"The important thing is that he's getting people prepared," Grace defended him. "Back home in Thelma's Way, folks wouldn't dream of not having decent food storage. Everyone's always out of work, or struggling, but they always have food put away. Here these people . . . well, they . . . I don't know."

"We're too comfortable to care," I said for her.

"Exactly."

We sat on top of Georgia and watched some animals run across the dark meadow. The headlights of our car gave them definition for a brief moment.

"You know, we should probably talk," I pointed out.

"I thought we had been," Grace said knowingly.

"I mean about the more important things. Sister Barns said that long engagements were a personal invitation for Satan to crack our foundation."

"I didn't know we were engaged."

"That's sort of what I meant by talking."

"Are you asking me to marry you?" Grace questioned with a little less enthusiasm than I felt the moment deserved.

"I don't know." I blew it.

"Well, let me know when you've made up your mind."

"I don't want to rush this," I said defensively.

"I see."

"I'm just thinking of you."

"Thanks."

"I thought maybe you needed more time."

"Maybe I do."

Daylight faded completely, turning the sky from denim to dark. Grace and I sat together quietly listening to the night. I thought about Lucy, and how up until two years ago I had always imagined myself marrying her. Now I couldn't see myself with anyone besides Grace. It didn't matter if my mother objected. It didn't matter that she wasn't rich, or socially influential. The only thing that made sense was us. But we still had not set anything in stone. For some reason it was hard for us to verbalize what we both believed to already be.

"You know," Grace said softly after a few moments of silence, "I've never driven a car before."

"Never?"

Grace shook her head. I don't know why I was surprised by this. There were no roads in Thelma's Way and no cars besides the homemade one that Leo Tip had built. I guess I just figured she would have driven in Virgil's Find at some point in her life.

"You want to learn?" I asked.

I had barely gotten the question past my lips when Grace began crawling over me to switch seats. We struggled with each other as we changed places.

"We could have used the doors," I pointed out.

"That was a lot more fun."

I had to agree.

I showed Grace where all the pedals were and how the stick shift worked. She started the car, pushed down the clutch, and pulled the stick shift into reverse.

"Let up slowly on the clutch," I instructed.

The car bucked, rocked, and then sputtered out.

"What did I do?" she asked.

"Nothing really. It just takes practice."

So we practiced for the next few hours. Eventually, Grace got the hang of it. She flew down the dirt road in utter bliss, spraying rocks and dirt behind us. The Dintmore Hills were actually an ideal place to practice driving. There were hundreds of dirt roads and very few other vehicles around. I was just about to suggest we begin making our way home when the car coughed and died. Grace coasted to a stop at the side of the road.

"What happened?"

"I'm not sure," I replied. "Try to start it again."

Nothing.

"Switch places with me," I suggested.

Grace climbed over me, kissing me as we passed. The car wouldn't start. I flicked on the car light to better read the gas gauge. Empty. We had been so busy having fun that I had forgotten to pay attention to how much fuel we had left.

"We're out of gas," I said plainly.

"Sure," she said seductively. "You're obviously not the gentleman I thought you to be."

"You were driving," I pointed out. "I'm the victim here."

"So what should we do?" Grace asked, smiling.

"We could stay here for a while and wait for help," I suggested.

We both looked at each other, taking in our intimate enclosure.

"That's probably not a wise idea," Grace said, blushing under the dome light.

"We could walk."

We both jumped out of the car. Grace buttoned up her sweater and took my hand.

"At least it's not raining," she said optimistically.

"Doesn't your Noah live somewhere out here?" I asked.

"*My* Noah?" Grace glanced at me.

"Well, he's not mine," I guffawed.

Grace laughed to make me feel funnier than I really was. "He lives somewhere out here in an old farmhouse," she said, "but I have no idea where."

"Good," was my only reply.

The dirt road shifted beneath our feet like dry cereal, each step crunching loudly. Grace leaned her head against me and talked—about life and love and the amazing things that had brought both of us to this point. At the risk of sounding unflattering, time with Grace reminded me of my old bike.

My family had not always been so well-off. As a child I remember my parents struggling to make ends meet. We had lived in a little house across town right next to the Southdale Dairy. It seemed like I never had the things other kids did. I remember wanting a bike so badly for Christmas one year. I begged and begged, knowing that the best way to get Santa to cough up the goods was to strong-arm my parents. Christmas morning I woke up to my worst nightmare. I had gotten a bike, but it was a used one—a girl's model with a long seat and a low middle bar. I could tell that there had once been pom poms on the handlebars, but in an effort to appease me, Santa had trimmed them off. It was purple, white-wheeled, and bigger than any of the bikes my friends had.

My world crumbled.

Mom and Dad tried to make Santa look good by saying nice things about the bike. They acted like there was absolutely nothing wrong with it. Afraid of tarnishing their opinion of the fat guy, I kept my feelings to myself. My friends, however, let their opinions be known, teasing me like mad. They called me "Tricycle Trust," because they couldn't come up with a nickname that rhymed with "purple two-wheeled girl's bike."

One evening after a particularly heavy teasing day I returned home crying. My father sat with me on the front porch and tried to cheer me up. He told me not to worry about what others said, and that my big bike was actually faster than any of my friends'.

Dad was right. The next day I discovered that I could outride any of the neighborhood kids. There wasn't a single bike that could touch me. In one afternoon, everything changed. I went from "Tricycle Trust" to "Trucking Trust, the Fastest Kid on the Block."

As we walked, I told Grace about my bike and how she sort of reminded me of it. What had once been viewed as out of place became the envy of the town.

Grace stopped walking. It was so quiet and so dark.

"You know, you're a weird guy," she said. "You really are."

It wasn't quite the reaction I had been hoping for.

Then she kissed me, setting things right.

We walked a while longer. Half an hour later when we finally spotted headlights, we were both a little disappointed. Two teenagers in a beat-up pickup stopped and gave us a ride. We rode in back with a big dog named Glue. They dropped us off at a gas station on the edge of town. It was past eleven o'clock. When I called my mother, she acted bothered but agreed to come get us after she went to the trouble of getting dressed again.

As Mom drove us home, she went on and on about how Elder Minert and Elder Nicks had been by to schedule a time to teach Grace the second discussion. Mom asked Grace if Wednesday evening at around seven would be okay.

"That would be fine," Grace answered.

"Oh, and Trust," my mother chimed, "I volunteered you to help Sister Barns set up the stage for the auction on the ninth. I hope that's okay."

"That's fine," I said. "When does she need me?"

"I told her you'd be at the church Wednesday around 6:45."

I should have guessed.

Grace squeezed my hand and offered her condolences in the form of a long stolen kiss. Mom spotted us in the rearview mirror and coughed wildly. We then listened to her talk about morality the rest of the ride home.

## 61

# SINKING

The big empty house made Lucy even more depressed. She listened to the clicking of the clock and the barking of a dog somewhere far away. Things were only getting worse. It seemed to take everything she had simply to crawl out of bed in the mornings.

She had called her parents in France, desperate for some counsel and compassion. But Lucy's mom and dad were far too busy traveling to pick up on the dire straits their daughter had coasted into. They seemed to have little advice. They told her to buck up and move on.

Life had turned into one giant bruise.

Lucy had been pleading with God to help her. She had even tossed out her standard prayer phrases in exchange for words so honest they made her weep. Her knees were tired and her head was throbbing. She didn't want to be alone anymore with who she used to be. She didn't want to go on.

She would have called her parents' home teacher to ask him for a blessing, but their home teacher was Leonard Vastly, and according to the lifestyle section in the local paper, he had sealed himself up in plastic sheeting for the time being. Lucy didn't know where to turn. She glanced over the ward list, looking for someone whom she would feel comfortable getting a blessing from. Truth be told, she had not actually been the kindest person to most of the names in front of her.

*Abraham, Ronald and Lynn*

Lucy had made fun, more than once, of Sister Abraham's choice in clothing. Her wardrobe made it so easy. The white shoes after Labor Day had been too much for Lucy to overlook.

*Aston, Kim and Mary*

Lucy had been fairly clear about how she felt concerning a man having the name "Kim."

*Baull, RoyAnn*

Lucy had talked both behind and in front of RoyAnn's back. Words like "spinster," "old maid," and "loser" came to mind.

The list went on.

Lucy had been such an awful neighbor. She pushed her head into her pillow. The expensive cover and imported goose feathers did little to comfort her crumbling self-esteem. A small twinge of inspiration fell upon her as she wept. She sat up and turned to page three of the directory.

*Williams, Roger and Marilyn*

In God she would trust.

62

# Bio-Doom

November 30th

Tuesday morning I got up early, grabbed a gas can, and went to pick up our stalled car. I gassed it up and drove it home for my mother to use. With no employment yet, and little will to look, I decided to go pay Leonard Vastly a visit. My mother had already gone for the day and I couldn't find my father's car keys, so I decided to take the bus—it seemed so socially conscious. Grace had been using the bus on and off for the past week, and if it could take her where she was needed, then I felt certain it could serve me just fine.

I found a few dollars and walked down the road to the bus stop. Fifteen minutes later, I was almost to Brother Vastly's place. Brother Vastly lived about five miles straight up the street from us. But his home was about a half mile away from where any bus would go, so I had to make the last leg of my journey on foot.

Leonard lived on the edge of an upscale subdivision. He owned the only mobile home in this part of town. He had brought his single-wide in about fifteen years back, inspiring the locals to make more restrictive zoning laws. Luckily for Brother Vastly, such laws couldn't touch what was already in place. His single-wide stayed, making him the king of the only factory-manufactured castle anywhere in the area.

When I first spotted his place I was amazed. The entire mobile home looked like a huge wad of trash. It was wrapped in plastic and streaked with duct tape. I spotted the bay window and the open curtains through the cloudy plastic. It looked as if Brother Vastly were sitting at a desk typing something. I watched a couple cars pass and stare. Someone honked, prompting Leonard to raise his hand and wave politely.

I sauntered up to the window and knocked on the glass. Leonard turned and peered out at me with excitement.

"Hello, Trust," he hollered through the plastic layer covering his window. His muffled voice was hard to make out.

"I came to visit you!" I hollered back.

"I'm sealed in," he signaled.

"Me, your home teacher." I motioned to myself.

The heavy plastic made Brother Vastly look distorted and fuzzy, but I could see him scratching his head as if in thought. Then he looked out the window to see if anyone else was around.

The coast was clear.

Leonard signaled for me to come around the back side of his trailer. I walked around, finding nothing but a sealed-up single-wide. I looked about as if I were missing something. I was just about to return to the window when I felt someone pulling on my ankle. I looked down to see one of Brother Vastly's arms reaching out from under the plastic at the bottom of his home. He pushed apart a metal section of the underskirting and stuck his head out.

"Brother . . ." I started to say.

"Shhhhh," he said quickly. "Crawl in here where we won't be observed."

Happy no one was around to see, I got onto my knees and crawled under the plastic and through the skirting. We scooted on our stomachs for a few feet, and then popped up through a trapdoor that Leonard had made out of a huge linoleum square in the center of his kitchen floor. Once we were up into the house I looked around at all the food rations he had stored. I had never seen so much food and supplies crammed into one place. It looked like the complete inventory of at least two grocery stores. And the place smelled like garlic mixed with kitty litter.

"Whoa," was all I could say.

"I've spent years getting things just right." He beamed.

I looked around and once again settled with just, "Whoa."

"Now, in here we're a fully functioning sphere," he began to inform. "Break your leg? I got you covered. There's a fully stocked infirmary in the master bathroom and two satellite first aid kits located in here." Leonard pointed to the cabinet above his refrigerator as if he were a stewardess giving safety instructions, "and here." He signaled to a drawer underneath his kitchen bar. "Hungry?" he continued. "Enjoy one of thirteen kinds of grain I've got stitched into the fabric of the couch."

I looked over at the lumpy sagging couch and tried to act impressed.

"You think Noah Taylor's thought of things like that?" he asked determinedly.

"No," I replied in all honesty.

"Thank you. Now, say the government's gone mad," he spat, "the computers are down, and there's a foreigner with a hungry family at the back door."

Brother Vastly caught his breath.

"Open the oven," he demanded.

I was actually scared to.

"Just open it," he insisted. "The energy's off. I stopped being a victim to electricity days ago."

I slowly opened the big oven door to discover that he had removed all the insides and hollowed the entire thing out back into the cabinets. I could see a couple of boxes of crackers and a small pillow in there.

"It's my hiding place," Leonard explained. "Who'd ever think to look in the oven?"

"Don't you . . ." I began to ask.

"Save the praise for later," he said, holding his hands up. "There's more to see."

Brother Vastly led me down the hall to the master bedroom.

"So you've got a house full of food, your couches are stuffed with grain, your walls insulated with soup mix, and most of the crawl space beneath your abode is filled with dehydrated bananas and apricots."

Brother Vastly paused for effect.

"Big deal. What separates the men from the morons in the competitive field of food storage is water. That soup mix is going to go down awful dry unless you have some $H_2O$ to bring it to life. Look away," Leonard instructed. "Look away."

I turned my head, but I could hear him punching in a code on the door lock leading to the master bedroom. I thought it rather silly to have an expensive door lock on a cheap particleboard door. A chime sounded and he opened up the door. I turned to find myself staring at a big, above-ground swimming pool. The pool was filled with water, the weight of which was so great it had broken the flooring out beneath it and was sitting a good foot and a half beneath the rest of the mobile home foundation.

"She's resting on cases of apricots," he informed me. "Floor gave way right after I filled her up. Luckily I had already put my cans underneath it. God cares for the sparrow."

"That's a lot of water," I said, expecting he'd like me to say so.

"Think Noah Taylor's got that kind of liquid holed up?"

"I couldn't say."

"Well then, let me do it for you. No. Plus, we're on a well here. Water's pumped into this pool, continually restocking me. If times get real hard I can even bathe in it. Don't tell a soul about this," he insisted.

"I won't."

"I'd hate to have people begging me for sips."

I figured he could put an end to that just telling them he swam in it.

"What kind of water storage do you and your family have?" Leonard asked me.

"I'm not sure," I said ignorantly. "If we have any I'm sure my mom's storing it with Brother Taylor."

Leonard shook his head sadly. "Our ward is wading into some dangerous territory. I'd hate to have the lights go out and *my* fruit and date bars be ten miles away."

"Wouldn't we all," I tried to joke.

"I like you, Trust," Leonard approved. "I like your attitude. Your good looks make me a little skittish, but you seem to have a solid head. Although I must admit I don't care for the radical hairstyle," he said, referring to my shaved head. "Come here," he continued, waving me back down the hall.

"How's the carpet feel?" he asked.

"Fine," I said, although I realized for the first time that it was a tad lumpy.

Back in the kitchen, Leonard leaned over and pulled back a section of the carpet where it met the linoleum. I could see hundreds of Ziploc baggies filled with what looked to be red licorice.

"A lot of people are saying to themselves, 'I've got twenty cases of wheat, and four cans of elbow macaroni, I'll live off of that,'" he said dramatically. "More power to them. But what good is living if you can't soothe the sweet tooth every so often?"

"Pointless," I said, playing to his vanity.

"Pointless indeed. That's why I've lined the entire low-traffic areas of my carpet with red licorice. Don't like the black, never have, leaves a real pasty taste in my mouth." Brother Vastly smacked his lips, acting as if he had just ingested something pasty.

"Now, the heavy-traffic areas are lined with beef jerky," he continued. "Your walking around is actually tenderizing my beef. Of course, I got turkey jerky in the laundry nook, but the traffic isn't as heavy in there."

Leonard's wrinkly, dirty clothes stood as witnesses to the truthfulness of his last statement.

"Any questions?" he asked.

"Where do you sleep?" I wondered, knowing that the master bedroom was filled with a pool, and the other bedroom was the bedless bay window room I had stared through from the outside.

"Sleep," he guffawed. "Sleep is nothing but a weak man's mandolin."

I had no idea what that meant, but I left it alone, asking only, "So you don't sleep?"

"I take fatigue prevention every three hours. I sprawl out on the bags of wheat flour I have stored next to the couch there."

"Why don't you just sleep—"

"Fatigue prevention," he corrected.

"Why don't you prevent fatigue by lying on the couch?"

"Trust, you've got a lot to learn," he said, shaking his head. "Why, even a tenderfoot must know that flour is softer than grain. Better back support too."

"Well, you certainly have gotten prepared," I complimented.

"The way I see it is there are no real emergencies for those who are fanatic," he espoused. "I read that somewhere. Any other questions?" he asked.

"Actually, do you have a bathroom I could use?"

"I'd love to let you, but I took the toilet out of the master bathroom to make room for the infirmary, and I've unhooked the guest room toilet so that I could plant wheat in the bowl."

"So where do you . . ."

"I've got a solar compost behind the fire wall in the infirmary."

I didn't want to know any more, so I said nothing.

"So then I guess you have a message for me?" Leonard said, changing the subject.

I could think of lots of things I would like to tell him, but I had no prepared message.

"Not really," I replied.

"Didn't you say you were my home teacher?"

"That's true, and—"

"Have a seat then. I'm spiritually weak due to the fact that I can't come out to attend church. I asked Bishop Leen if I could get someone to bring the sacrament to me, but he said no. It's a real shame when people who stand for a cause get overlooked."

"Pity."

"I gotta do what I gotta do," he insisted.

"So how long do you really plan to stay in here?"

"However long is necessary."

"And what determines that?"

"Noah Taylor. If his December seventeenth doom date is accurate, then maybe I'll come out soon after the carnage and destruction die down. But if he's wrong, which I'm thinking he is, I'll just stay here for a spell to prove my point."

"And your point is?"

"People don't need people."

"So would you rather I leave?"

"Actually it's kinda nice to have someone around."

"Well, if it makes you feel any better, I think everyone is wrong to put so much stock in what Noah Taylor is saying. He's just a man like you or me. He has no right or privilege to know the future for us."

"Sister Cravitz told me you'd fly off on him," Leonard said.

"What?"

"She radioed me a while back and told me about you being jealous of Noah."

"I'm not—"

"We're the only ears here," he said, pointing to his.

"Really, I'm not—"

"Listen, Trust, lying to yourself is the same as lying to another."

I was being chastened by a man with licorice-lined carpet.

"I guess this Grace girl you brought to town is really stirring things up," he went on. "You know, Southdale really needs a little mixing. Especially the members here. We get a little stale stuck out here away from all the other western Mormons. It's nice to have Grace waking us up a bit."

"She's not really doing anything," I said, baffled.

"Exactly," he replied. "Exactly."

"No really, she just works for Noah."

"You know, I used to have a sister-in-law with red hair," he reminisced. "She was the most exasperating person. She was all about money. Couldn't get enough of the stuff. Her husband, my brother, was working three jobs and had an adult paper route. That's different than a juvenile route. The adult routes usually cover a large area and require a car. Anyhow, she left my brother about three years back, no, no I take that back. It was right after Ned had that work done on his teeth, so it would have to have been about six years ago. My goodness, how time flies."

I was glad he thought so.

"Left him for a car salesman," he went on. "I'm sure she drives a nice vehicle, but does she have the amount of food security I do? I don't think so. So, Trust, what's your message?"

"Well, I really just wanted to make this first visit a get-to-know-you kind of thing. I actually didn't think I'd be allowed to come into your 'Bio-Doom.'"

"I am a self-contained ecosystem, but if I need to bend the rules to help out my new home teacher, then so be it."

"Do you think you might bend the rules to come to church?"

Brother Vastly laughed. "You know, that sense of humor of yours might be just the thing to help you hold on to Grace."

"My relationship with Grace is doing just fine."

"Remember, a lie to yourself . . ."

"I know, I know."

"Trust, this is awkward, I understand," Leonard said, putting his left foot high up on a crate of no-name green beans and making it almost level with his belt. "It's unnatural for a home teachee to teach the home teacher, but I'm going to give you a little advice. Put your personal safety first."

"I'm not sure I agree with that," I replied.

"Line upon line," he saged. "Line upon line."

"I'm pretty certain the Savior would want us to put others before ourselves."

"I'm sure He would," Leonard defended. "You've missed my point completely."

"What's your point?"

"I don't want to get into specifics." He shifted uncomfortably.

"I'd better get going," I said, standing up.

"Listen," he insisted. "Before you go, I want you to try something I made. It's an all-natural dried fruit bar I call the 'Lenny' because it rhymes with 'skinny.' If you ate these all the time you'd be pretty skinny—cleans the body out completely. Not that you need it—you've actually got a nice shape considering you've only been back from your mission a few months."

I wanted to list all the reasons why I didn't want to try a "Lenny," as well as point out that "Lenny" and "skinny" didn't actually rhyme, but I felt it was my priesthood duty as his home teacher to indulge him in this wish.

Leonard rushed off down the hall and into the pool room. He went inside. I heard splashing, a door open, a door close, more splashing, and a fairly mild swearword. A few moments later, he emerged with a plate of unwrapped fruit bars, the bottom half of his pants wet. I didn't dare ask. The fruit bars were brown and abrasive-looking.

"Take one, and shove another in your pocket for later if you'd like."

"One's fine."

Brother Vastly picked up a second and pushed it into one of my pockets for me.

I bit into the bar in my hand reluctantly. It was worse than I had anticipated. It was like eating a piece of pulpy chalk.

"You know, a while back I heard this story," Leonard said. "This woman made a cake at the start of every month and then would serve it to her home teachers when they came over. If they came at the beginning of the month, it was fresh. If they came near the end, it was stale."

"I just got assigned to you yesterday," I complained, wondering why I had to eat a twenty-seven-day-old date bar because of it.

"These aren't a month old," he said merrily. "I made these about four years ago. I haven't had a home teacher since the boating incident. I'm sorry, I can't see why a seven-year-old kid should get a life jacket before me."

I just stared at him.

"My last home teacher owned a boat," was all he said by way of explanation.

"Do I have to leave the same way I came in?"

"Excellent question, and yes. I'll also need you not to tell the others that I let you into the Bio-Doom. I don't want folks thinking I'm some sort of non-committed freak."

Heaven forbid.

"I'm here for the long haul," he said. "Of course, if you showed up for your next visit with a couple cases of soap, I wouldn't be sad."

Brother Vastly picked up the linoleum-square trapdoor and waved me over. Then he waited for me to finish my fruit bar. I shoved the whole thing into my mouth and swallowed. He gave me the okay sign.

"Thanks for coming by, Trust. I'll remember these kind acts when I'm enjoying my mansion on high."

"Thank you," I said, wanting only to get out, and maybe get a drink. I would have asked him for one, but I was afraid he'd retrieve it from the pool.

I crawled across the dirt, out the skirting, and through the plastic. It was nice to smell the open air again. I walked through the neighborhood and to the bus stop. There was no one else waiting at the moment, so I just stood there patiently by myself. When the bus arrived, the doors opened to reveal Brother Treat behind the wheel. Brother Treat had driven a bus ever since Brother Victor had found him the job. I had never actually ridden on his bus, but he had talked often of how hard he worked to keep this town running smoothly.

"Brother Treat," I said, happy to see him.

"Trust," he replied coldly.

I stepped up to get on and he drove forward a couple feet. My foot knocked into the side of the bus, the door no longer directly in front of me. I stepped over and looked at Brother Treat. He motioned as if to say, "oops." I tried again, and once again the bus moved forward. I tried again, this time a little more quickly. He moved the bus up six feet. I ran to try to get on, and he moved it a good twenty feet. I walked slowly up to the bus, the people currently riding on it staring at me. I'm sure that they, like me, were wondering what was going on.

Right before I got to the door I hollered out, "What's the matter?"

Brother Treat didn't answer.

I stepped toward the open door, and once again it started to creep forward.

"Brother Treat!"

I didn't know Brother Treat that well. He and his family were "overflow Saints," meaning they sat in the folding chairs at the back of the chapel. Years back when there had been a fuss between the bench sitters and the chair sitters, it had been Brother Treat who had been wounded by Sister Cravitz, prompting him to pour bleach all over her prizewinning azaleas. Brother Treat had a nice face and bad hair. He was tall and unusually thin for a bus driver. Due to a bet involving a skateboard and stairs in his youth, he had false teeth—teeth that he would occasionally take out and publicly clean. Actually, he was a rather quiet man who, aside from the bleach episode, had never shown much gumption. Excluding, of course, the time he accidentally stepped on another Scout's pinewood derby car—a car that was in competition with his son Leon's.

Leon.

I had forgotten that Sister Barns had mentioned Leon's supposed crush on Grace. Certainly this strange bus episode couldn't be about that, could it?

"Brother Treat," I hollered, the bus doors about eight feet away from me at the time. "This isn't about Leon and Grace is it?"

I had barely gotten the words out before the bus doors slammed shut and Brother Treat took off for good, exhaust billowing into my face.

I couldn't believe it. I waited around for another bus but none came. I began walking home, stopping only twice: once to get a drink and use the bathroom at a small business along the way, and once to see an early afternoon movie about a spy with a lisp.

What? I had nothing else to do.

When I arrived home, it was already beginning to get dark. I looked over at Wendy's house and saw that Grace's bedroom light was on. I thought about going directly over and visiting her, but I decided to wash up from the day's activities first.

The second I walked through the front door of my house, my mother yelled at me to call Sister Cravitz. I did so, only to find that Brother Vastly had just radioed her to tell her that the date bars he had served me were actually small fire-starter bricks he had made, and that he was terribly, terribly sorry. I held my stomach and pulled the one he had pushed into my pocket out. I had thought they tasted rather woody. I flipped it over and over in my hand, contemplating the day I had just completed. Then I called Grace and invited her over for dinner.

We ate in the living room in front of a roaring fire, compliments of Brother Leonard Vastly.

63

# Who Would Have Thawed It?

Thelma's Way was driving Roger Williams mad. The town had turned into one happy batch of Mormons, partly because of him. Who would have thought that an uninterested member such as he could be so instrumental in bringing souls back into the fold? Folks had often told him about how hard Elder Williams had worked to beef up the branch. And yet, Trust's efforts had yielded little fruit. Now here, with a few lies, Roger seemed to have brought most of the flock back home.

Roger wasn't sure if this strengthened or weakened his newly rekindled testimony. He was also having a hard time not getting frustrated about the still-missing Book of Mormon. His efforts, despite reactivating the members, had produced nothing. Roger had done everything he could think of. He had even considered praying for help. It was a thought he pushed quickly away.

Roger sat himself upon one of the chairs on the boardinghouse porch. Paul Leeper emerged from around the corner and bid him good afternoon.

"Paul," Roger greeted.

Paul Leeper was the once-famous once-apostate who had caused the town so much trouble. He was a skinny man with a thick helmet of hair and scrunched up facial features. Whereas Paul had once been a loudmouthed troublemaker, he was now just a loudmouthed local.

"Any luck finding the book?" Paul asked.

"Nope," Roger stretched. "Not even a decent clue."

"I just saw it over at . . . nope, that's not true," Paul caught himself.

Paul was working hard these days to stop his habit of perpetual lying. It wasn't easy. This, after all, was a man who had once claimed to have invented grease. He had also bragged about being at the Council of Nicaea where he had helped pick out and edit the original books of the Bible.

"I think that old Book of Mormon might be lost for good," Roger sighed.

"These are some big woods," Paul added.

Lupert Carver came toward the boardinghouse from across the meadow. He appeared to be dragging something behind him on a leash. As he got closer, it became obvious that what Lupert was pulling was a stiff dead dog.

Paul leaned against the porch rail and looked out at him. Roger raised himself from his seat and gazed as well.

"Lupert Carver," Paul hollered. "What are you up to?"

Lupert slid the dog up to the boardinghouse and stopped.

"You remember Bushy, here?" Lupert asked.

"I thought he died years ago," Paul gaped, stepping off the porch and crouching down by the dog. Roger stepped down as well.

"He did," Lupert shrugged. "I couldn't stand to bury him so I stuck him in my mother's deep freeze. Mom found him this morning while rummaging for some frozen sausage. She's not real happy with me."

"I suppose not," Paul sympathized.

Roger lightly kicked the frozen dog with the toe of his shoe.

"My father saw a movie where they froze someone till they found a cure to fix 'im," Lupert explained.

"Movies ain't real life," Paul lectured. "I guess you'll need help burying him."

"Maybe," Lupert answered. "But I thought I might prop him up in the sun and see if he thaws out alive."

"Now Lupert, boy," Paul said sternly. "Once a dog is dead, no amount of sunning is going to bring him back to life."

"That's what my pa said," Lupert lamented. "A course, he wasn't positive about it. He went to Virgil's Find to look up if it's true."

Roger Williams simultaneously shook his head and smiled. Lupert Carver was a great representation of what he was up against here in Thelma's Way. It was as if these people remained in a constant state of slow, childlike innocence.

Roger watched as Lupert walked over to the middle of the meadow. The ground was snow-covered and dirty. Lupert propped Bushy up in the center of the clearing. The dog stood frozen stiff, staring at the boardinghouse as if it were a fat pheasant. After Lupert had stood the dog up, he turned and walked back toward Roger and Paul. The moment his eyes were off of Bushy, two of Leo Tip's wild dogs tore out of the woods, ran up to the frozen dog, and quickly and almost silently dragged their once-friend out of the meadow and back into the trees—like a hand playing jacks, they had swooped down and taken what they wanted.

Roger and Paul stood there with open mouths. Lupert stepped up to them unaware.

"Maybe if he thaws just right," Lupert said hopefully, turning around to gaze at his dog that was no longer there.

"Where's Bushy!" Lupert yelled in a panic. "Where'd he go?"

Paul put his hand on Lupert's arm and tried to think of something honest to say. Roger helped out.

"He's gone to heaven."

"No kidding?" Lupert smiled.

"No kidding," Roger answered.

Lupert bowed his head in reverence. "They sure took him quick," he observed.

"Heaven knows a good hound when they see one," Paul comforted.

"I knew God was up there," Lupert wowed. "I just knew it. I gotta tell Mother." He beamed, turned, and ran off.

Paul put his hand on Roger's shoulder.

"Our secret?" he asked.

Roger nodded. He would have said more, but for some reason his heart was doing flips and turns within his chest. It pumped wildly. He tried to rationalize what he was feeling. Thelma's Way had tossed him around like a bin full of lottery balls. The tragic (or magic) nature of this place was overwhelming. To think that an accomplished man like himself could be touched by a thawing dog and the faith of an ignorant child was baffling.

True, he had witnessed one miracle after another while staying in Thelma's Way. He had been there when Annie Holler had given birth to twins. He had watched Janet Bickerstaff get baptized in the freezing Girth River and witnessed Frank Porter regrow hair after applying a new salve that Sister Lando had concocted. Memories came crowding in on him both hard and soft.

Roger Williams sat down.

64

# CONVERSATIONS WITH THE COMPETITION

December 1st

Wednesday evening I left Grace at my home and drove my mother's car to the church building. The Southdale chapel was rather spooky looking at night. Actually, it was rather spooky looking during the day. It had been built before the Church started using molds. The east side of it was brick, while the west end was wood siding and stucco. As far as buildings go, it had the personality of a pudgy toddler. We loved it, we were happy to have it around, but we wished it would photograph better.

In front of the chapel there was a steeple which stood alone, circled by a rose garden and rising incredibly high above the ground. The steeple had been added to the chapel grounds about five years ago. Before that, we had been a steepleless people, relying only on the pitched roof to point us toward heaven.

The steeple was supposed to be half the height it actually was, but someone had messed up during the installation of it, ordering and installing one that towered high above all the other steeples in town. The Lutherans had complained, and the Baptists had written a letter to the local paper pointing out our poor taste in putting up such a blatantly offensive edifice. I think I agreed with the Baptists. The tall metal steeple looked like a radio tower sitting in front of our house of worship—a radio tower with hair. You see, the top of our tall steeple was flat and round, providing a perfect place for a single bird's nest. Well, a not-so-single bird had built one years ago. That bird had lived there until it was struck by lightning. The bird itself caught fire and toppled out of the nest, its feet tangled up in the fibers of its own creation.

There the dead bird dangled. Many tried to knock it down, but nobody was successful. Marcus Leen, Bishop Leen's youngest son, had even chosen the task of removing it for his Eagle Scout project. He had made elaborate plans to extricate it, building scaffolding around the tall steeple and crafting a very long stick to push it off with. He got close, but the winds at that altitude made it too dangerous to proceed. A few of the priests at the time had tried to knock the bird down by throwing rocks. That effort ended in two broken windows and a stray cat that didn't think too kindly of Mormons.

So the dangling bird had stayed until nature concocted its own remedy. One morning it was gone, the wind having dislodged it and carried it away. If you squinted, you could still see bits of nest up there, but no fowl had chosen to build since.

I walked into the building and straight to the cultural hall. Sister Barns was already there bossing a couple of the young women around.

"Trust," she said as I walked in. "I'm so glad you came."

"Thanks for asking me," I replied, unable to think of anything else to say.

"Listen," she squeaked. "I need this ramp to be solid. There's going to be a number of single women walking on it and some of them, well, let's just say that a few of these choice women, well, what I'm trying to get at . . . God doesn't make everyone petite."

"I'll make it strong," I smiled.

"Good. Now, I asked Noah Taylor to help you out. I hope you don't mind."

"Not at all."

Sister Barns looked around and then leaned in toward me. "In my opinion you've got much nicer shoulders than he does," she whispered, as if I needed some bolstering up.

"Thank you," I whispered back.

Sister Barns blushed.

"Noah's in the Relief Society room, picking out support beams," she informed me and turned back to what she was fiddling with before I arrived.

I walked to the Relief Society room and found Noah leaning against one of the tables talking to a rather mature seventeen-year-old girl who looked in need of a strong lesson on modesty. He was making jokes and complimenting her on her nice smile. He was wearing another sweater.

I cleared my throat.

"Hello," Noah said, startled. "I didn't see you there. You could have given this old man a heart attack."

"You're not so old," the young girl teased.

"Not according to Brother Williams here," he smiled, referring to my Colonel Sanders remark.

"So is this the wood we'll be using?" I pointed, wanting to get the project over with.

"That's right," Noah clapped. "I hear that you and I are a team tonight."

"I heard the same thing," I said back.

"Well, this will be great," he smiled falsely. "I've been wanting to get to know the guy Grace calls 'Trust' a little better."

The young girl finally realized she wasn't going to get any more personal attention from Noah and wandered away. Noah and I picked up a couple pieces of wood and carried them into the cultural hall.

"So how is Grace doing at work?" I asked.

"She's great, Trust, a real gem. I don't know how I would get all of this together without her."

"I'm glad," I said honestly.

"Listen, Trust, I'm not going to pretend that I don't hear all the whispering," he said softly to me. "I know that people here are talking about all the time Grace and I spend together," he said in a friendly tone. "I just want you to know that I have absolutely no interest in her whatsoever."

I didn't know what to say. A couple moments ago I was bothered about the possibility of him liking Grace. Now I was bothered by the reality that he might not.

"Excuse me?" I asked.

"She's a nice girl, but I would never pursue someone like her. So, set your worries aside."

"I wasn't worried," I insisted.

"Trust, when you've been in the business as long as I have, you get used to these girls that see you as more of a hero figure than just a regular guy."

Noah Taylor was one pompous person.

"I'm not sure I understand what you're saying," I said, giving him a chance to reword what he had just worded.

"How old are you, Trust?"

"Twenty-three."

"I'll be thirty in June."

"What does that have to do with anything?"

"Southdale is fine," Noah patronized. "It's a nice city, but it's not the real world. Live a year in L.A. or New York. Then you'll know what I mean."

This was the dumbest thing I had ever heard.

"I've been to both those places," I said defensively, adding to the stupidity of the conversation.

"Great," he said mockingly. "Now let's get this walkway done."

We scooted under the walkway on our backs and began to work with the wood to shore things up. There was cloth skirting all the way around, leaving Noah and me in relative privacy.

"So how did this date of December seventeenth come about?" I asked while shoving wood up into the underside. I expected some great larger-than-life story, but instead I got the truth.

"Well, as I've told the people here, I had a dream where the heavens parted and showed me. But I like you, Trust. You seem like you've got things figured out so I'll level with you. I made the whole thing up. It's a nice way to make some money and, if you like, I could figure a way to include you. Get people spooked and they'll pay through the nose, if you know what I mean."

There was a moment of awkward silence while the words I had just heard sunk in.

"What?" I asked in disbelief.

"Come on, Trust, you're smarter than that. Admit it. It's a way to get them off their duffs. They get excited about something for a change and it doesn't hurt us any either." He turned his head and smiled. "In fact, December seventeenth is perfect timing, really. It sets me up to take one of those less expensive winter cruises when I'm through here. A penny saved is a penny . . . well, you get my point."

"I can't believe you're saying this," I said, anger beginning to build.

"Oh, Trust, you should be happy," he offered. "There's no way I could ever be interested in some pale redheaded girl when I can have my pick of all the bronze women in the Caribbean, or maybe Tahiti. That would be nice. What the heck, I'll be loaded. I'll just spend a month at each." He chuckled and went back to wedging wood supports into place.

I was absolutely dumbfounded. If someone had just informed me that in a matter of minutes all my limbs would fall off and everyone I ever loved would leave me, I couldn't have been more shocked. Sure, I didn't like Noah, and yes, there had been twinges of jealousy, but I had never suspected that under that tousled hair and big sweater there lurked such a truly horrible person. This was fraud to the highest degree, and somewhere in the last mound of garbage he had spit out, my subconscious had heard fighting words.

Poor Noah.

I'm not sure what it was. Perhaps it was all the stress I had gone through in the last few weeks. Maybe it was Elder Jorgensen and his relentless pursuit of Grace. Maybe it was Southdale and their gullibility to buy into Noah's plan. Maybe it was all the pent-up emotions I had held back on my mission—the companions I had bit my lips and counted to ten for. My mother, my father, my half-shaved head, my most recent concussion. Maybe it was the drought, or the season. Or perhaps it was the fact that I had still not fully digested Leonard Vastly's fire-starting brick. Or maybe, just maybe, I was flashing back to Thelma's Way, and the time Elder Weeble had bad-mouthed Grace on the front of the boardinghouse steps. I had wanted so badly to stick up for Grace, to wrestle Elder Weeble to the ground and demand him to take it all back. I had restrained myself due to the fact that I was a missionary at the time, and that I needed to act the part.

I was no longer a missionary.

I sat up quickly, banging my head on the underside of the walkway. Then I lunged at Noah. His smug smile quickly vanished. He was obviously a man who was used to little resistance. I jumped on him, hitting him in the face as he desperately scrambled to get out from under the walkway. I pulled on his pretty sweater, dragging him back under. Then he screamed and kicked at me like a sissy grasshopper with huge lungs. I could hear footsteps running into the cultural hall. I grabbed Noah's arm and pushed it up behind him. He screamed again, ripping his arm out of my grasp and frantically crawling out from under the walkway. I followed right behind him, not yet satisfied with the amount of damage I had caused. There was a small crowd of onlookers now. Sister Barns rushed up to the fleeing Noah and grabbed his hand.

"What's going on here?" she demanded.

Before Noah could answer, I pulled my right arm back and threw a punch directly into his right eye. Noah seemed to fly backwards out of Sister Barns's grip. He fell with a thud to the ground, his rear end sliding across the gym floor until he came to a stop against the wall. I stood there with everyone looking on in astonishment.

The young woman who had been talking to Noah earlier ran to his side. She then yelled at one of her friends to bring her a wet towel. Noah stood, embarrassed about what had happened and by all the attention he was receiving in the wake of it.

"I demand to know what's going on here," Sister Barns stamped.

"Ask him," I said, cooling down, already beginning to regret what I had done.

"Well?" She turned to Noah.

"I'm not sure," he said innocently. "I told him that Grace was doing such a good job and he went ballistic."

"That's not true," I tried.

"Trust, I think it would be better if you left now," Sister Barns said, pointing toward the far door.

"He's duping you all," I insisted. "He told me so himself. Said he's going to enjoy spending all the money you're foolishly giving him in the Caribbean."

Noah looked shocked.

"Trust," he said calmly. "Lying about this isn't going to make it any better. I forgive you for hitting me. There's no need to make this situation even worse."

"Tell them what you said about Tahiti," I demanded, not sounding like I made much sense.

Everyone just stared at me, pity and shame painting every self-righteous mug in the room. I looked at Sister Barns, who was still pointing toward the door.

"Sister Barns," I tried.

She replied by pointing with even greater fervor.

As I walked from the cultural hall, I could see everybody begin to huddle around Noah Taylor. I picked up the pace, hurrying from the building and out to the parking lot.

I needed to get to Grace before Noah did.

# 65

# Swapping Wounds

By the time I had arrived home, Noah had already called and spoken to Grace. Grace met me in the entryway of my house, leaving the full-time missionaries who had been teaching her tucked back in the den. She claimed that Noah had called to apologize if he had done anything wrong, and that he felt just awful.

"Tell Trust I'm sorry if I said something that offended him. I thought we were just having a friendly conversation," Noah had weaseled.

"Grace," I groaned. "He's a phony."

"Trust."

"I'm serious," I went on, taking off my coat and setting my keys down in the small dish by the door. "He told me he's only doing this for the money."

"He said that exactly?" Grace asked, obviously torn between believing Noah and believing me.

"Those weren't his exact words, but he's out to make fools of everyone."

"I just don't—"

"Believe me?" I finished for her.

"I've worked with him, Trust. He's not like that."

"What's he like?" I asked in frustration. "Cute? Handsome? Funny?"

"You're being stupid," Grace said boldly.

"I'm trying to tell you the truth, but you just want to take 'sweater boy's' side of the story."

"Let's talk about this later," Grace said softly.

"Why? So you can go to work and get all the details from him?"

"Trust, have I ever given you reason not to trust me?" she asked firmly.

"No, but . . ."

I was interrupted by the missionaries. Apparently they had heard enough from their listening point back in the den to sense that it might be best for them to leave. They came slinking down the hall, hoping to slip out unnoticed.

"You guys don't need to leave," Grace told them.

"Well, we just remembered . . . uh . . ." Elder Nicks said, unable to conjure up what he had just recalled.

"Yeah," Elder Minert tried to help. "We just remembered."

"I'll call you tomorrow, Grace?" Elder Nicks asked forlornly.

"That'd be great," Grace said. "I'm sorry about tonight."

"Will you be okay?" Elder Nicks asked, looking at me suspiciously.

"She'll be fine," I insisted.

The two elders took their cue and cleared out.

"Listen, Grace," I tried to reason once they were gone. "You have to believe me. Noah is in this for himself and no one else."

"I'm sorry. I just don't believe you."

The words hit me harder than anything in my life ever had. I felt like a crash test dummy that had been shot from a cannon directly into a cement wall. My head collapsed as my ego tucked and folded. How could Grace not believe me? How was it possible that in such a short time Noah Taylor could cause her to turn on me?

"You don't believe me?" I asked incredulously.

"Trust, I just know that Noah . . ."

"No way," I cut her off. "Don't give me the 'I just know' line. For a year I've loved you. Now Noah walks in here and you instantly decided that he's right and I'm wrong."

"He told me, Trust," Grace said soberly.

"Told you what?" I asked, angry.

"He told me how you threatened him into leaving town."

"Ha," I laughed. "And you believed him?"

"We should talk about this later," Grace said.

"Much later," I replied, so disgusted with all of it that I wasn't thinking straight. "Maybe I'll be back tomorrow. Maybe." I turned and stormed out, slamming the door behind me. I stood on the front porch waiting for Grace to come out and stop me.

She never did.

My coat and keys were inside, and there was no way I was going to put my pride through the kind of pummeling that going back in would induce. I stormed off into the night, having absolutely no idea where I was going.

# 66

# Be Thou Bumble

I wandered around Southdale until about eleven o'clock. I refused to go back home, confident that Grace would be watching out of her window for me to come slinking back. I had no money, no credit cards, and the cold was only getting stronger. I thought about going to another member's home and asking for shelter. But I figured word of Noah's and my disagreement had already been properly spread around. I didn't think anyone would agree to shelter a known miscreant.

At 11:30 I finally gave in and decided to do the one thing I had been avoiding all night. I made my way over to Leonard Vastly's Bio-Doom. I knew that Leonard didn't have an extra bed, but he did have a vacant couch, and I had remembered his home being warmer than the naked outdoors.

I walked quietly through the posh neighborhood surrounding Leonard's bubble house. Then I approached the plastic-covered monstrosity and tapped lightly on the window that I believed was closest to where Leonard slept. I was worried about making him mad by awakening him from his fatigue prevention, but I was now tired enough not to really care.

I tapped louder.

Nothing. I walked around to the bay window and knocked some more.

"Psst! Leonard, it's me, Trust."

No answer. I walked back and down to the master bedroom window and tried rapping there, thinking that perhaps he was taking a late bath in his water supply. Not a single sound came from within. I looked around at the dark night and decided that now would be a perfect time to break the law. I snuck over to where Leonard had let me in before. Then I dropped to the ground and crawled under the plastic covering and beneath the mobile home skirting.

It was pitch black below. I tried to feel my way around, finding cans and buckets blocking almost every way. Eventually I felt the trap door and pushed up and into Leonard's kitchen. It was almost as dark inside as underneath. I located the couch and sat down. Then I called out Leonard's name a few times, hoping he would answer.

I would have walked around and searched the house for him, but I guess I was too tired. The thought occurred to me that he may have been balled up in his oven hideout. If that was the case, I could wait until morning to find out. I leaned back on the grain-filled couch and fell asleep.

What seemed like only moments later, but in reality must have been a couple of hours, I was awakened by the sound of the hinged linoleum swinging open. My eyes were adjusted enough to the dark to see that it was Leonard. He came up through the floor pulling what looked to be a couple of grocery bags. Then he closed the floor and opened the refrigerator door. Light flooded the room, silhouetting Leonard as he stood in front of the fridge looking in. From this perspective, I could tell that he had put on a few pounds while living off his low fat fruit bars. I was also surprised to see that his refrigerator had electricity. According to Leonard, he had shut off all current so as to not be a servant to energy.

Brother Vastly began to unload groceries into the refrigerator. Then he shut the refrigerator door and walked right past me. He picked up a huge cardboard box to reveal a TV set. He turned it on and backed up toward me to take a seat on his couch.

"Hey," I warned as he bent to sit.

"Whoaaa!" he screamed, throwing the soda he had in his hand into the air and jumping on top of the bags of flour lying on the floor. In the light of the TV, I watched him scramble frantically for something.

"Brother—"

Before I could finish my sentence, gunshots began to ring out wildly. I slid off of my seat and pushed my back up against the base of the grain-filled couch, thinking about what an absolutely pathetic way to die this was. I could see the headlines already: "Local boy buried by bullets and barley." After a couple of seconds, however, I realized that I was still alive. I looked up just as Leonard threw something across the room at me. I jumped up, running out of the way and knocking Leonard into a huge bag of flour. The bag ripped and exploded all over the two of us and the TV. Brother Vastly slipped away from me and fell to the floor. He folded into a fetal position mumbling something like, "Must protect the soft innards." I rolled him over and stared at him.

"Brother Vastly, it's me, Trust."

He slowly opened his eyes and gazed at me in astonishment.

"Trust?" he asked as bits of flour continued to flutter to the floor.

"Yes," I said with great relief.

"What the heck are you doing in my dome?" he whined, straightening himself and sitting up. Then he leaned over and pressed the stop button on his home stereo. The sound of gunshots ceased.

"Clever," I observed, indicating his method of home security.

"I never much cared for guns," Leonard said, embarrassed.

"I won't tell a soul," I promised.

"So, what are you doing here?" he cleared his throat, trying to act tough.

"I had no place to go, so I came here. When you didn't answer I crawled in the way you showed me. I'm so sorry."

"'Sorry' is nothing but a lower form of flattery," he said, leaning over and pushing himself up.

"Well," I tried, "I didn't mean to break into your beautiful palace."

"Thank you," Leonard nodded.

I stood up straight and dusted myself off.

"So why can't you just go to your home?" Leonard asked.

"Grace and I sort of got into a disagreement, and . . ."

"Say no more," Leonard insisted. "We've all been there."

Falling flour shimmered under the light of the infomercial now showing.

"I'm sorry about the mess," I apologized. "I didn't think you'd react so hastily."

"I'm a pro at reacting," he pointed out.

"What about your neighbors?" I questioned. "I'm sure they heard the fake shots. Won't they call the police?"

"Don't worry about the police," he piffed. "I've been through this before."

About two minutes later, as we were picking things up, we heard a car pull up outside Leonard's home. There was a loud rap on the front door.

"Leonard," a male voice called out.

Leonard unlocked the front door and pushed it open as far as the plastic covering would allow. Through the four open inches I could see flashing red and blue lights, as well as the blurry profile of a big man. Leonard flipped on an inside light, once again giving away his current power connection to the local electric company.

"What seems to be the problem, officer?" Leonard yelled.

"Could I come in for a moment?" the cop asked.

"It's best that we don't corrupt the bubble," Leonard insisted.

"Leonard," the cop seemed to pleadingly whine.

"Everything's okay," Leonard comforted. "I thought there was an intruder. Turns out it was just someone from my church."

Even in the dark outside I could see the cop shake his head.

"It was only a recording," Leonard added.

"We went over all this before, Leonard," he said mournfully. "We can't have you waking up the neighborhood every time a noise worries you."

"I know, I know," Leonard said, bothered. "But aside from some scattered wheat flour things are in order."

"Leonard," the cop begged.

"Sam," Leonard whined, apparently more familiar with this lawman than he had let on.

"Just no more noise. Promise me?"

"I promise," Leonard said begrudgingly.

"And finger crossing doesn't count this time," the cop said, frustrated.

I looked down at Leonard's hands just as he was uncrossing his fingers.

"All right," he consented.

Leonard shut the door and turned to me.

"Sam was married to my sister Tina for a couple years. They broke up when Tina and my two older sisters went into business together. The business went bust about three months into it. People just aren't interested in competitive hopscotch or the gear that goes along with it. Anyhow, now Tina won't talk to either Nina or Linda. My younger brother Fidel did manage to get us all together for a family picture, but I'd be a dishonest man if I didn't admit that Tina's smile looks a little strained." Leonard pointed to a big family photo hanging on the wall behind him.

"You sure have got a lot of family," I commented.

"Mother loved children," he said solemnly.

"Well," I sighed. "I've caused enough trouble for one night. I should probably just leave."

"Nonsense," Leonard huffed, the flour on his skin making him look like a frosted cookie. "You're in need, and I'm an enabler. I've got a spare couch with your name on it."

I looked over at the empty couch he was referring to. It was covered with flour and sagged above the floor like an exhausted sumo wrestler.

"We'll throw a blanket over it and it will be as good as new," Leonard said optimistically.

We both worked for a few minutes cleaning the place up to the point of being sleepable. Leonard then retrieved a couple of blankets from the back room and handed me two of them. I spread mine out over the couch and then lay down. Leonard reclined on his sacks of flour eating ice cream out of a small carton and watching some TV show with an elderly detective who was able to see into the future. I probably would have drifted off if it had not been for him constantly interjecting, criticizing, and picking apart the show he was watching:

"That's impossible."

"A real detective would never leave his gun lying around."

"Oh, how convenient."

"Who wrote this drivel? I could have written a script ten times this good. In fact, I just might. Where's my pencil?"

I wanted to fall asleep so that I could wake up and have this night be ended, but Leonard was just too vocal. I had never seen a grown man get so worked up over a TV show. Except for maybe when the locals in Thelma's Way would watch *Days of Our Lives* and argue over story lines and plot closures. After listening to Leonard complain for a while, I sat up and gave in.

"Not tired, huh?" Leonard asked.

"I guess not."

"Grace worrying you?" he questioned.

"A little."

"Women," he spat, sending flecks of ice cream across the room and onto the TV screen.

The store-bought ice cream he was eating reminded me that Leonard had not been around when I arrived. I decided to stick my nose into his business.

"So where were you earlier?" I asked. "I thought you never left the dome."

"What do you mean?" he asked back.

"When I got here you were out."

"I must have just been in the back room," he said defensively.

"I saw you come up from the floor with groceries," I laughed. "I helped you put the last of them away."

"Trust," he said calmly. "A lot of people are counting on me. You wouldn't want to be the one to let them down, would you?"

"I'm not going to tell anyone that you went out."

Leonard *Whhheeewwwed.* "I appreciate that," he said. "You're thinking of the greater good."

"If you don't want to stay in here then why don't you just quit?"

"And look stupid?"

I bit my tongue.

"Noah Taylor would have a heyday if I gave up," Leonard continued. "He's just looking for a chance to make me look bad."

"Noah Taylor is a fake," I added.

Brother Vastly looked at me with pride. "You've really turned out to be a fine young man."

"Seriously," I ignored him. "The whole reason I'm here now is because of him. He told me in confidence that this December seventeenth thing was all just a big scam. And when I confronted him in the open he claimed I was just making it up because I was jealous."

"He does have that hair thing going on."

"I'm not jealous of Noah Taylor," I said, frustrated.

"It's just you and me, Trust. You and me."

"He's a crook."

"I believe you."

I suppose I should have been comforted by this, but there was surprisingly little personal fulfillment in the knowledge that Leonard Vastly was mentally aligned with me.

See, everyone? I told you I was right. If you don't believe me, just ask Leonard Vastly, the man over there in the plastic-covered single-wide.

"Thanks, Leonard," I lamented.

"I'll tell you what," Leonard said, setting his ice cream down. "What would you say if we helped each other out. We could make it our mission to expose Noah Taylor as the fraud that he is. You and I could be like a team of do-gooders righting this horrible injustice."

I must have done something incredibly bad in my premortal life.

"I don't know," I said. "I don't think we really are the most believable witnesses at the moment. No one's going to listen to a single word we say."

"You've got a good point." Leonard hummed.

"I shouldn't have walked out on Grace," I scolded myself.

"We all live with regrets," Leonard agreed.

My list was growing longer and longer.

67

# Dial Tone

It had taken a few days for Lucy to work up the nerve to call Trust. She had debated every point and position that she could think of, only to come to the conclusion that she had nothing to lose. Her father was still out of the country, her home teacher was locked up in a mobile home, and there was simply no one else she would feel comfortable receiving a blessing from.

The phone rang and Abel answered.

"Hello," he said.

"Hello," Lucy replied, willing herself to go on. "Is Trust at home?"

"Nope," Abel said flippantly. "Who's this?"

"Do you know when he'll be back?" Lucy asked, ignoring his question.

"Can't say for sure. He stormed off about two hours ago. I don't think he's coming back."

"Ever?" Lucy asked, distraught.

"Well, he's got to come back sometime," Abel duhhed. "I just don't think he'll be back tonight."

"Is your mother at home?" Lucy asked, desperate.

"She went to sleep an hour ago."

"Oh."

"Is this that girl that Trust used to date?" Abel asked bluntly.

Life was just too much for Lucy at the moment. Here she was, the bitter taste of swallowed pride still in her throat, and hitting up against little brother syndrome. With each rise and fall of emotion, God was becoming more and more distant to her. She could see little purpose in a creator who relished the slow discomfort of his children. What good was a world where those in need were victims of petty particulars like schedules and missed opportunities? Why would a fair God put her in such a hopeless place?

"Hello," Abel said sarcastically. "Are you still there?"

Lucy hung up the phone by throwing it across the room. It slammed up against her vanity, smashing it into a dozen pieces.

The irony was completely overlooked.

68

# Fit to Be Tied

Roger Williams was becoming increasingly concerned. He was no closer to finding the Book of Mormon, but he was starting to . . . no, it couldn't be. Not a single decent tip had come from the promise of being on the front cover of his fictitious book, but he still . . . it just couldn't be. He had interviewed dozens of people, visited too many homes, and the only thing he seemed to have discovered was . . . it was too unbelievable to admit.

Roger Williams was beginning to care for these people.

He didn't know what it was. Maybe it was the water. Maybe it was the air. Whatever the reason, the valley of Thelma's Way had seemed to soften his heart and leave him less polished than he preferred to be. Out of fear he packed his bags and planned his exit. The first-edition Book of Mormon wasn't worth losing his sense of identity for.

Before he could escape Thelma's Way, however, he had promised to help Ed Washington get his motorcycle across the Girth River.

The Girth River ran along the far side of the Thelma's Way meadow. It was thick, deep, and relatively bridgeless. There had once been a usable bridge, but it had been burned down years earlier after Paul Leeper led most of the Mormons astray. The burned bridge now spanned the river like an incomplete and charred set of Lincoln Logs. The only way across the Girth these days was to use one of the community rafts. You had to take your raft to the head of the river and paddle furiously across before the current washed you out of town completely. In his quest to find the Book of Mormon, Roger Williams had crossed the river many times. He had actually become quite good at it. So good, in fact, that now that Ed Washington wanted to get his motorcycle over to the other side, he looked first to Roger for help.

Foolishly, or fatefully, Roger agreed.

Ed owned one of only two motor vehicles that the town had to its name. He had been given the old motorcycle by Digby Heck after Leo Tip gave Digby his piecemeal car that he had built himself. There were no real roads for Digby to drive on, but he liked to circle around the boardinghouse acting better than all the poor people on foot. The motorcycle was actually a far more functional mode of transportation for this town. Ed rode it daily down the thin footpath that connected Thelma's Way to Virgil's Find. Ed was currently enrolled at the College of Virgil's Find, taking mostly electives until such a point that he could decide what he wanted to be when he grew up. Most folks felt that Ed had better hurry up and figure it out, seeing how he had just turned forty-five and wasn't getting any younger, or smarter, for that matter.

Well, today was Wednesday, and Ed had no classes. He decided to fill his time finding a way to get his motorbike across the Girth River so he could try out a few of the trails over there. To the best of anyone's knowledge, which really wasn't saying a whole lot, no one could remember any motorized vehicle being driven on the other side of the river.

Ever.

Ed sensed a personal challenge.

Unfortunately for Roger Williams, Ed's personal challenge required the help of others.

"Why don't you just ride around in the meadow like usual?" Roger asked. "There's plenty of ground to travel here."

Ed shrugged his shoulders. "I don't know. I suppose the urge to go where no man has gone before and all is getting to me."

"But folks have actually gone there before," Roger informed Ed.

"Sure they have, on foot."

"Actually, Ed, I was sort of heading out for a bit. I've got some things to do."

"Please," Ed begged him. "Pete said he'd help, but you know how Pete is. He's not exactly an expert on things like this."

"All right," he relented. "I'll help you, but it'll need to be quick."

Roger and Ed headed out across the meadow. Ed walked his motorcycle and theorized about how best to get a heavy piece of machinery across a swollen river.

"I was thinking catapult," Ed said enthusiastically.

"I think you're thinking too big," Roger replied.

Ed smiled happily, taking it as a compliment.

"How about just going real fast and hoping the motorcycle will skim across the top of it," Ed suggested.

Roger grinned. "That's impossible, Ed."

"Yeah," Ed shrugged. "That's what I was thinking."

Roger and Ed reached the banks of the Girth near the burned bridge. Eighteen-year-old Digby Heck was there, throwing a long rope with a rock attached to the end of it into the current.

"Digby," Roger acknowledged him.

"Mr. Williams, Ed." Digby looked up from his rope, then pulled the rock back in and tossed it out across the river again.

"Do you mind if I ask what you're doing?" Roger asked.

"Mind? Shhheeesssh, why would I mind? I'm just dragging the

river looking for the Book of Mormon," Digby shrugged. "I figure if we ain't found it on land, then maybe I'd find it under the river."

"Actually," Roger said, "if someone had put it in the Girth, it most likely would have been washed downstream by now."

Digby laughed. "That's a good one, Mr. Williams."

"Listen, Digby," Roger said, using his deepest, most authoritative voice. "Do you think Ed and I could borrow that rope for a moment?"

"I suppose I can stop searching for a few secs."

"What'd you got in mind?" Ed asked Roger.

Roger answered by laying the motorcycle on one of the bigger rafts and tying it down with the rope Digby had been using. Ed and Digby just stood there as if their hands and arms were painted on.

"Think it will float?" Ed asked after Roger tied the last knot.

"There's only one way to find out," Roger replied.

Together Ed, Digby, and Roger pushed and pulled the raft to the edge of the river. But just as they were about to test it out, Roswell Ford approached them, drawn over by his own curiosity.

"Now just what is you three dinking 'round with?" he demanded, his old head wobbling as he spoke.

"Ed wanted to get his bike over to the other side," Roger explained.

Roswell spotted Pete Kennedy and Toby Carver across the meadow. They looked to be pushing around a dead squirrel with a long stick. Roswell whistled loudly.

"Toby, Pete," he hollered. "Head over here 'fore Ed and Digby kill Mr. Williams." Roswell then wagged his wrinkly right pointing finger in Roger's face. "You can't put me on the front of your book if you're dead," Roswell said, sharply reprimanding him.

Toby and Pete scurried over to the bank.

"Ed's wanting to get his motorbike over to the other side," Roswell informed them.

Toby and Pete looked at each other.

"He could use your help," Roswell spat.

"I was thinking that we could tie this raft onto another and then paddle the both of them across," Roger suggested.

"Now, in a perfect world, that just might work," Toby mused. "But the Girth would pull both rafts downriver before either made it."

"That's true," Pete said.

"Well then, we could stretch a rope across the river and try pulling the thing over," Roger brainstormed, getting caught up in the challenge of it.

"That'd be a mighty long rope," Ed said.

"It could work," Toby commented with excitement. "Teddy's got that rope she used to hang dry all them towels she found at the dump."

"It still doesn't sound right," Pete said.

"Why don't you just ride your bike over here in the meadow?" Roswell questioned Ed. "You're always going 'gainst the flow. Does your mother know you're doing this?"

"I'm over forty years old," Ed said defensively, his dander flaring at the mention of his mother.

"Well, does she?"

"I'm my own man," Ed argued.

"All right, you two," Roger arbitrated. "Let's not get ourselves all worked up. It shouldn't be too hard or too big a deal to get this motorcycle across the river. Doesn't anyone here have a rowboat or a canoe?"

"Jerry Scotch bought a real nice one a few years back," Toby said.

"And?" Roger asked.

"He forgot to tie it down and it floated downriver and over the falls. Splintered into a million pieces."

"It takes two weeks to count to a million," Digby Heck chimed in.

Everyone just stared at him.

"Learned that in homeschool," he explained.

These people were impossible. How Roger could have ever grown to care about them was beyond belief. This was the laziest, most backward place he had ever visited. There were probably lost tribes in Africa that would find this place repressive and slow.

Roger was about to throw in the towel and leave the task at hand to Ed and the others while he slipped out of town. His resolve was thwarted, however, when Ed suddenly slapped himself on the forehead. Ed's eyes lit up as an idea of gigantic proportions rumbled through his brain.

"Now, why didn't I think of that before?" Ed asked excitedly. "Toby, does Wad still have that big piece of pressed wood?"

"Of course," Toby answered as if it were ridiculous to think of someone ever giving up such a thing as a large piece of pressed wood.

"You got them big bricks still?" Ed asked Pete.

"They're over behind the boardinghouse," Pete reported.

"Good."

"What's the plan, Ed?" Roger asked.

"You're all gonna feel real silly that you didn't think of it first."

"Spit it out," Roswell demanded.

"I'm going to jump the river," Ed beamed. "We'll build a little ramp, and then I'll sail over to the other side."

Everyone *oohhed* and *ahhed,* embarrassed that they themselves hadn't thought up such a solution. Everyone except Roger Williams.

"Ed, you can't jump the river," Roger said. "That's no different then just riding across it. It's impossible."

"This is a time for support, not mutiny," Roswell scolded.

"Think about it, Ed," Roger pleaded. "This motorcycle can't go over ten miles an hour. And even if it could go a hundred, that still wouldn't be fast enough to fling it across the Girth."

"We'll see," Ed insisted.

"Yeah." Roswell slapped Ed on the back. "We'll see."

"Say something, Toby," Roger begged, knowing Toby was a tad more levelheaded than the others.

"I'll spread the word," Toby said. "I bet we could get a right nice crowd to witness this."

"D'you think?" Ed smiled excitedly.

"You'd better bring your bandage," Roger said, disgusted, referring to the Ace bandage that Toby doctored the entire town with.

"Oh, you of tiny faith," Toby commented as he ran off to alert everyone about today's spur-of-the-moment festivities.

Within half an hour, most of Thelma's Way had gathered down by the river. Pete and Wad dragged out his big flat board and Digby, with the help of his little sister Narlette and sturdy Sybil Porter, brought out a few big cinder blocks. Then they constructed a makeshift ramp and aimed it toward the river. Roger Williams had thought about just leaving town. Getting out while the getting was good. But he felt compelled to stick around and witness the outcome of this man-made tragedy.

To make things even more spectacular, Ed tied several pieces of long rope to the back of his bike. He figured once he was airborne and flying across the river, the ropes would flap around in the wind creating a visual wonder like few in these parts had seen before. Folks lined both sides of the path leading up to the ramp. Toby tried to get everyone to hold hands and form a sort of course-marking fence, but Roswell refused to hold hands with Jerry Scotch, claiming that Jerry had never really cleaned up since the taffy pull the town had put on a week back. And Sister Watson was not about to give widowed Frank Porter any ideas by putting her mitt in his. So no one held hands, except for Leo and CleeDee, Wad and Miss Flitrey, and Philip Green, who held his own—but that was mainly to hide the extra finger on his right hand that he had only recently become ashamed of. It's funny how something can be neat at age seven and awkward at age sixteen. Paul Leeper was on hand, taking lots of pictures so he would have proof of this occasion when and if people ever doubted it.

Ed revved up his engine and rode over toward the boardinghouse so as to be able to get the necessary speed required to help him make it across. Everyone watched Ed work up the nerve to make the run. He drove in a few circles near the boardinghouse. He waved at all those standing near the river and across the meadow. Then he faced his motorcycle toward the ramp and gunned it. The bike took off from underneath him, went a couple of yards by itself, and then fell to the ground. Ed picked himself up and ran over to it. He waved to everyone to indicate that he was all right. Everyone waved back.

Roger Williams was sick in the stomach.

Roger figured there was no way Ed could come out of this unscathed. He hadn't even gotten near the ramp and already he had fallen over. Ed got back on the bike and started it up again.

This was it.

The rusted old motorcycle choked and coughed as it tried desperately to get above ten miles an hour. The crowd held its breath as Ed closed in on the ramp. When he finally got there, the motorcycle barely made it up the incline. It reached the top and sort of rolled over on its side, flinging Ed onto the river bank. Well, not actually flinging him, but it was far fancier than saying he rolled limply off of the bike and landed in a goofy-looking heap in the mud. The motorcycle itself splashed in the water near the shore. Everyone just stood there speechless. Ed floundered around on the banks of the river, moaning and flapping like a sea lion who had just been harpooned in the ego.

Everybody ran to Ed's aid. All the fuss really wasn't necessary, seeing how Ed had sustained no more than a couple little scratches and bruises. Roger Williams stepped back from the crowd to watch. Toby and President Heck disassembled the ramp and carried the large flat board over to Ed. They laid it down by him and rolled him onto it. A number of men and boys grabbed hold of the edges and lifted him up, carrying him about like an open-faced sandwich. The entire crowd marched off toward the boardinghouse. Roger just stood there staring at the motorcycle that was still lying in the water. Young Narlette Heck was the only soul around. She wandered up to Roger.

"Ed's not real smart," she commented.

Roger just smiled. Two weeks ago, this girl had been a bothersome pest. Now, however, he found her almost endearing. Although she was at least five years younger than Roger's daughter Margaret, he saw a lot of similarities.

Roger needed to get home. It had been too long.

"The motorcycle's slipping," Narlette said, pointing to the bike that was now beginning to be tugged by the current.

Roger looked around him, wishing for someone he could send to grab it. Not a soul was in sight. Everyone was inside the boardinghouse by now helping Ed dress wounds that didn't need dressing. Without a word, Narlette ran to the bank and tried taking hold of one of the ropes that was tied to the back of the bike. It was no use, she wasn't strong enough, and the motorcycle kept sliding forward.

"Help," Narlette struggled. "It's slipping."

"Just let go," Roger hollered.

"Ed needs it for school," Narlette yelled.

Roger shrugged in frustration. He ran to help. The motorbike seemed to be floating—the large foam seat and gas tank seemed to make it more buoyant than anyone could have predicted—but it was being dragged in the current at a pretty good clip now. Roger couldn't help thinking as he got his shoes wet that this whole day could have been salvaged if Ed had only known of the floatability of his bike.

The rope began to whiz through Narlette's small hands, burning her palms and bringing tears to her eyes. Roger stomped into the water, grasping for the back wheel. The rubber slipped from his grip. He stumbled, pushing the bike farther into the river. Narlette gave up and let go. Roger would have done the same. He could, after all, easily afford to buy Ed another motorcycle. Unfortunately, his leg had become tangled in the dangling ropes. He stood up and tried to brace himself, hoping he had the strength to hold the thing still.

He didn't.

The weight of the bike pulled him over as it continued its rush downriver. He could feel his wet clothes growing heavy. He thrashed at his jacket, fighting to rip it off.

"Narlette," Roger yelled, again losing his footing. "Narlette!"

The motorcycle caught in the fast-moving belly of the river. It whipped and turned, picking up its already speedy pace. Once again Roger was pulled under.

"Mr. Williams!" Narlette screamed. "Mr. Williams!"

Narlette took off running toward the boardinghouse. Her feet scraped loudly against the December ground. When she reached the others, it took almost a whole minute for her to catch her breath and get the words out.

Roger Williams was in trouble.

## 69

# Teach Ye Adequately

December 5th

Sunday morning I received a call from Brother Morose, the Clearview Ward Sunday School president. He solemnly explained that Sister Winters was under the weather. He then told me that I would be teaching gospel doctrine today. I felt like I needed to say thanks for being picked.

"Thanks."

"I'm hesitant to ask you," Brother Morose whispered. "What with all the talk of you and your bad decision this last Wednesday."

"Excuse me?"

"Noah Taylor is a respected visitor."

"Noah Taylor is a—"

"Respected visitor," he reiterated. "And you, Brother Williams, seem to have let your emotions get the best of you. But that's neither here nor there. Today is Sunday, and I'm giving you an opportunity to redeem yourself."

"Thanks," I said again.

"The lesson is on Alma, chapter 32."

"Okay."

"It's largely about faith. And seeds."

"I'm familiar with the chapter."

"A few lessons back the topic was repentance," he snipped. "Pity you couldn't have taught that one."

"Well, I—"

"Good-bye, Brother Williams."

Click.

The last couple of days had not been my finest. When I returned home from Leonard Vastly's on Thursday morning, I found my mother crying at the kitchen table. She was not expecting me and was very embarrassed to be caught knee-deep in actual emotion. When I asked her what she was upset about she refused to answer me. When I asked her if it was concern for my father that was making her cry, she just hollered at me and warned me about prying into other people's business.

Mom was worried about Dad.

It really was no great surprise. We were all pretty concerned about where Dad had gone and when he would come back. It had been well over a week since he had last called. Mom was beginning to fear abandonment. It was no secret that my parents' relationship had not been one of marital bliss these last five or six years. They had begun drifting apart when my father threw himself into building up his tiny empire. Consequently, many important parts of our family had grown soggy in the wake of his neglect. But for him to simply walk out on us seemed unbelievable. And the thought of him just walking out on his business and all he had created seemed absolutely unfathomable.

Grace and I had not had much of a chance to talk about what had happened between her and me. I had tried to get her to go out with me on Friday night, but she kindly brushed me off, claiming she had volunteered to help Sister Barns collect food donations for the auction. When I told her I would be happy to come along and help, Grace told me that Sister Barns had specifically requested that I not come.

So I asked Grace out for Saturday night. She said she would like to, but that the missionaries were coming over to Wendy's to teach her the third discussion. When I asked her if I could join her, Grace explained that the elders were frightened of me, and that it would probably be best if she did this alone.

We were losing big chunks of ground. Our once full relationship was thinning, making what we had feel bald and barren. Alopecia of the heart. I didn't know quite what to do. I had called Wendy and asked her if she could please let Grace know how sorry I was about hitting Noah, and asked if there was any way I could make it up to her. Wendy answered by listing all the things that Noah Taylor did better than I.

It was an embarrassingly long list.

"But I grew up with you, Wendy," I argued.

"Maybe we've grown too familiar."

"Wendy, what are you saying?"

"It's over, Trust."

"What's over?"

"I don't know," Wendy admitted. "I've just wanted to say that for a long time and I've never had the chance."

Doran was continuing to pursue Grace. He had gone to a recording studio downtown and made a tape of himself singing a song he had written for her. It was called "Amazing Grace." He parked his truck outside of Wendy's home and blasted it on his truck's beefed-up stereo system. His voice wasn't as bad as his songwriting abilities:

*Amazing Grace how fine your face,*
*How nice your body too.*
*I think it's time you changed your mind*

*Give that other guy the boot,*
*Give that other guy the booooooooot.*
*Dooodoodoo, ooohwaahhwahhhdiddy.*

Etc. etc.

Things were just getting more and more confusing. So Saturday afternoon, I bought Grace a card and made Abel deliver it to her. It was one of those cards that guys only buy when they know they're in trouble. There was an angel on the front with a poem underneath. On the inside, there was a broken heart with a big bandage on it. Like I said, under normal circumstances I would have gone with something a little more classy, a little less desperate.

With Abel reporting back that the card had been successfully delivered, I spent Saturday evening with my sister Margaret, shopping for sweaters at the Gap. I wasn't willing to admit defeat just yet.

Margaret and I returned home from the mall to find a note from Noah taped to the front door. He was basically apologizing for having done anything to offend me and pleading for my forgiveness. This guy was unbelievable. He didn't flinch. For days I had felt nothing but rage and disgust for the man; now I found myself actually wondering if I could have somehow misunderstood him. I replayed our conversation in my head, finding nothing open to any other interpretation but that he was a jerk in nice guy's clothing.

I wanted desperately to talk to someone about everything going on in my life, but my only real confidant at the moment was Leonard Vastly. And even though I was beginning to sort of like the guy, I wasn't about to start sharing secrets with him. Besides, the only way I had to talk to him was by visiting his garlic-scented doom dome. I considered calling President Heck in Thelma's Way. Chances were he was hanging around the boardinghouse and I'd be able to catch him. But President Heck was not only a friend, he was also the father of the girl that I was currently stewing about.

Saturday night I went to bed feeling more lonely than I had felt in a long while. I stared at the ceiling for hours, running all the things that were bothering me back and forth across my mind. I eventually fell asleep in uncertainty.

After I got off the phone Sunday morning with Brother Morose, I put on my new sweater and yelled down the hall for Margaret and Abel to hurry up. Church started in half an hour, and I didn't want to be walking down the aisle late. I was already feeling conspicuous enough in my new outfit. I didn't want to give anybody anything extra like arriving late to use against me. When I got downstairs, my mother informed me that she wouldn't be going to church.

"Are you feeling all right?" I asked her.

"I'm fine," she insisted, looking at me. "I just don't feel up to going. And your sweater doesn't match your tie."

I left that discussion right there.

Grace knocked on the back door and Margaret let her in.

She looked as beautiful as usual—her hair full and loose, her green eyes not letting on to the fact that she knew just how pleased I was to see her. I stared at her, taking in all the subtle changes she had undergone since being here. It wasn't that she was fading into someone else, or that she was shedding her old self to take on the new. Who she was and had always been was just getting more polished in Southdale. As if Southdale were toothpaste with whitening agents. She had moved up at least seven shades, currently residing at a brilliance two notches above blinding. The only real tainting she had sustained was her willingness to take Noah's side over mine. But with the things I had done, I couldn't completely blame her.

Grace took my hand.

"Thanks for the card," she said.

Who can resist a bandaged heart?

"You're welcome," I said humbly.

We got into my mother's car and drove over to the chapel. It was a wonderfully nice day for December. The sun was out, and on the ride over, I spotted at least three pedestrians brave enough to sport shorts on a warm winter morning. The sky was clear above Southdale, making the world seem that much wider and that much warmer. Suddenly, I felt self-conscious about my sweater.

I watched a small plane streak across the blue, two thin trails of smoke behind it. From down below, it gave the illusion of being the toggle on a smoky sky zipper.

The church parking lot was about two-thirds full when we arrived. Everyone was walking in past Bishop Leen, who was out front with a couple of deacons trying to extract a kite that had become tangled up in our steeple over the weekend. They were having very little luck.

Before we reached the building doors, Sister Cravitz stopped us and asked if she could talk to me alone. Grace went in with Abel and Margaret to save us seats.

"What can I help you with?" I asked as we stood outside.

"Your hair's getting better," she observed.

"Thanks. Did you need something?"

"Well, I'm aware of how things are going with you and Grace, and I'm afraid I took a little liberty," she said, as if she had just swiped a hotel towel or taken a salt shaker from some restaurant.

"Do you want me to help you put it back?" I asked, trying lamely for humor.

Sister Cravitz just scowled. I mean that as a statement of fact like "grass is green" or "the sky is blue." Sister Cravitz's face only had one gear. She never smiled, she just scowled.

"Trust," she said. "I'm doing you a favor."

Warning bells began to ring. The last time Sister Cravitz had done me a favor I had found myself signed up and committed to teaching orphans how to make piñatas at the Southdale orphanage.

"I have a niece," she continued.

"Sister—"

"Hear me out," she said, holding her wrinkly palms up at me and flashing the deep, long life-lines that she was always bragging about. "Cindy, that's her name, Cindy Finders. She's a relative on my side. Doesn't have the Cravitz name, but she has a nice share of the Cravitz's levelheadedness. She's also served a mission in Spain. Speaks pretty Spanish though I can't understand a word of it."

"Sister Cravitz, I'm honored, but—"

"Trust, you're a sharp-looking man. I've always thought that. I can't say that I'm giddy about all your choices, but I'm well aware of how handsome you've become."

I hadn't thought I could become any more uncomfortable.

"Grace and I—" I attempted to say.

"I know," she said soberly. "Things aren't the best for you and her. So that's where that liberty I took comes in. I e-mailed my sister back in Georgia, and she's going to see about getting me a picture of Cindy for you. I know, I know, it seems mighty shallow to swap pictures, but you can't be too careful these days. Did you see who Margaret Chad married?"

"Actually, I did, I—"

"Well, I suppose he's got really nice insides. Anyhow, I don't have a single picture of Cindy past the age of twelve, and honestly, Trust, she didn't bloom until at least three years after that. I could have sworn I had a picture of her in a sweater and poodle skirt, but my sister tells me I'm getting Cindy mixed up with pictures of myself when I was a girl."

"Oh." Dear merciful me.

"My sister says she'll get me a current picture of Cindy," Sister Cravitz went on. "Who knows, there might be one in the mail as we speak. In turn, however, Cindy needs a picture of you."

"Really, Sister Cravitz," I tried to inform, "Grace and I are doing great. I'd hate to get this Cindy involved when I'm already committed to someone else. Do you see what I mean?"

"So, do you have a picture?"

I don't know what I was more bothered by, the fact that Sister Cravitz wasn't listening to me, or the fact that she thought me to be the kind of person who carried around a picture of myself.

"I don't," I answered.

"No big deal," she scowled. "I brought my camera."

From her huge handbag, Sister Cravitz pulled out the oldest-looking camera I had ever seen. It had a giant lens and an accordion-like body that seemed to blend with the folds of her old hands. On top of it was a big row of square flash bulbs.

"Stand up against the building and I'll snap a couple of you."

"Sister—"

"Trust," she scolded. "Let's make things happen."

"But I need to get inside."

"It will only take a moment," she insisted. "We've got a good five minutes before church starts."

"Actually," I insisted, "I'm teaching gospel doctrine today and I wanted to set up the room before sacrament meeting."

"Set up your room? With what?" She called my bluff.

"Um, I was going to see if the library had a tablecloth or something."

Sister Cravitz eyed me suspiciously.

"They've got two of them," she said. "Donated them both myself. I must say it's sort of refreshing to see a man take the time to pretty up a room. Doctrine sits much easier when there's a homey feeling about."

"Isn't it the truth," I agreed, slipping away and into the building.

Sister Cravitz followed me in. I began heading straight for the chapel before she informed me that the library was the other way. I begrudgingly went to the library and checked out one of Sister Cravitz's tablecloths. I ran to my classroom and threw the tablecloth over the table. Then I hurried into the chapel. I took a seat by Grace just as the prelude music stopped.

"I missed you," Grace said kindly.

My sweater was working its magic.

Sacrament meeting was rather uneventful. Brother Jack talked about gospel hobbies, and how we Saints would be best to avoid them altogether. He then went into great detail about how he had mapped out the stars and made timelines of all prophecy dealing with the last days. His conclusion was that Noah Taylor's December seventeenth date was off by maybe two weeks, give or take a day.

I had noticed that Noah was not around this morning. I knew that he visited other wards, and had even been peddling his services to some of the other denominations in town. I figured he was simply off doing the fraud thing. My thoughts of him continued to mellow. Sure, he was a two-faced phony, and yes, this December seventeenth thing was made up, but at least he was getting our ward prepared. I'd have to hope that a few wrongs would make this all right.

After sacrament meeting everyone drifted off to their classes, flowing down the halls like leaves in a crowded gutter. Grace came with me and took a front row seat in the classroom where I would be teaching. I wrote a couple of things on the chalkboard as people continued to stream through the doors and fill up the room. By the time I turned around, we had a full class. I stood there in relative amazement. I had thought that most people would avoid my classroom when they saw that it was me teaching. Instead it was like a feeding frenzy. The smell of blood had drawn a nice-sized crowd. Even Doran was there; he had taken a seat right next to Grace. He and she exchanged a few words as Brother Morose looked at his watch and coughed, calling attention to the fact that I was running two minutes late.

"Good morning," I began. "When I got the call to teach this morning I was excited to find out that we would be covering Alma, chapter 32. So if you would all . . ."

Brother Morose raised his hand.

"Yes," I responded.

"Usually we begin class with a prayer, Trust," he said as if he were auditioning for the part of an undertaker.

"Of course," I apologized. "Sister Barns, would you mind?"

She obviously did, looking visibly upset about me picking her. Of course she really had no choice but to say yes. If she said no everyone would be forced to spend the entire class period wondering just what she had done to prevent her from praying. So rather than suffer the wondering imaginations of her fellow classmates, she stood and prayed.

"Amen," the class said in unison.

"Thank you, Sister Barns," I nodded. "Now if everyone would please open their scriptures to Alma, chapter 32."

People pulled out their scriptures and opened them as if they were presents they had received from a cheap aunt. I could tell this was going to be one enthusiastic class period.

"Before we begin," I started, "could I get those of you who have already read the lesson to please raise your hands?"

Three arms went up. I acted like I was okay with this, counting the three hands slowly to make it seem like they were more.

"All right, Brother O'Shawn," I asked. "Could I please get you to tell the class what the definition of faith is?"

"Well," he said, clearing his throat. "I think what Alma is trying to say in this chapter is that if you lose sight of the Savior, your vision, or your spiritual eyes as it may, becomes blinded. Making us less than our Father expects."

"Okay," I replied, suddenly remembering why Brother O'Shawn was never called on in class. "So the definition of faith is . . . ?"

"I'm not sure you can put a definition on it," Sister Treat replied for him, trying to sound intellectual.

"Actually, you . . ."

Sister Cravitz's hand went up.

"Yes," I motioned.

"Would it be possible for you to remove your sweater?" she asked.

"What?"

"Your sweater," she insisted. "I just don't think your skin will photograph well against it."

"Really, Sister Cravitz, I'm not sure this is the appropriate—"

"Faith is believing in something not seen," Brother Morose spoke out.

"Thank you," I sighed. "Believing in something unseen. Sister Luke, will you read verse 28 for us?"

"Can I say something first?"

"All right," I nervously agreed.

"I don't know if many of you remember Richard Dot. He was in this ward about ten years ago. Tall, sold trampolines, kept gum in his pockets for the Primary children."

A number of heads nodded.

"Well, he used to tell that story about that father in the manhole."

"I remember," a few members said.

"I'm not great at retelling other people's tales, but the story was about a father who was down in a manhole fixing or cleaning something. And I guess his little daughter came to visit him one day. She was delivering a message, or just stopping by. Well, either way, when she looked down the hole all she could see was pitch, dark, black darkness. Close your eyes," Sister Luke instructed us.

Everybody except Grace and me quickly closed their lids. We used the sudden privacy to make eyes at one another.

"Imagine a darkness ten times stronger," Sister Luke continued. "Now open your eyes."

Everyone opened and blinked like blind men receiving sight.

"Well," Sister Luke went on. "This girl's father told her to jump down into the manhole and he would catch her. Remember, she couldn't see him. Then this little girl . . ." Sister Luke paused to find a Kleenex in her purse. Unable to locate one, she settled for a crumpled grocery store receipt. She dabbed her moist eyes. "I'm sorry, but this part just kills me."

She was not alone.

"Anyhow," she continued. "This little girl just jumps down and her father catches her. Blind faith, Brother Williams, blind faith."

Brother Rothburn raised his hand and I pointed toward him.

"If you don't plant a mustard seed, you can crush it to make mustard."

I wasn't sure where that had come from. Luckily no one was really listening anyway.

"Thank you, Brother Rothburn, and thank you, Sister Luke. I think that's a great example of faith," I said with less than complete honesty.

"Wait a second, Brother Williams," Sister Leen said, coming to life. "Why would a caring father ask his young daughter to jump in a deep dark hole?"

"I think it's just an analogy."

"Well, it's a poor one," Sister Leen huffed. "Besides, what kind of work does a man do down in a manhole? The one in the alley behind us is filthy and infested with cockroaches."

"I hate to say it, but this warm winter's not going to help that," Brother Rothburn commented.

"I think the point is," Sister Luke defended her story, "often we have to take spiritual leaps into dark places."

"I thought God was a God of light," Brother Treat said.

"I have been reading this book by a Mark Lemon," Brother O'Shawn began talking. "In it he tells about how this life is all just a giant computer program and we all are a virus. I find that very interesting, and not entirely contrary to doctrine."

"Is Mark Lemon one of the General Authorities?" Sister Leen asked.

"No," Brother O'Shawn replied. "Actually, he's not a member at all. But if you remember, the thirteenth article of faith talks about us seeking after all good in all things."

"That doesn't sound good to me," she said.

"Well, in context it's—"

"Sister Luke," I interrupted. "Would you please read verses 30 through 33," I motioned, desperately trying to bring the lesson back on track.

Sister Luke begrudgingly read the verses. Then we all sat there in silence for a moment. I raised my finger as if to make a point and was temporarily blinded by the flash of Sister Cravitz's antique camera. A giant blue dot now hovered above everything I saw. Old Sister Timmons looked normal, but everyone else had suddenly aged.

"Sister Cravitz," I began to protest.

"I think it's an interesting use of the word 'the' in verse 28," Brother Morose interrupted, backtracking just a bit and speaking louder than I felt was necessary. "'The' can mean so many things, but Alma clearly meant it to say 'the word.' Not 'a word,' not 'thee word,' not just 'word,' but 'the word.'"

My word.

"Interesting observation," I commented. "I think that every word in the scriptures actually can—"

Sister Cravitz shot picture number two. I held my hand in front of my face, trying to will my sight back.

"Don't mind me," Sister Cravitz said.

It was too late for that.

"Let's read the next couple of verses," I said, discouraged about how poorly my lesson was going. "Who would like to read?"

Sister Cravitz raised her hand.

"Please," I acknowledged.

"Actually, I just wanted you to move over in front of the chalkboard more, those curtains behind you seem to wash you out."

"Please, no more pictures," I pleaded.

Sister Cravitz snapped one more.

"Okay," she then agreed.

I caught Grace smiling, and suddenly it wasn't all that bad.

"Grace, will you read verse 34?" I asked.

Grace did so.

"And 35?"

She did.

"And 36?"

"Brother Williams, I advise that you break up the reading," Brother Morose scolded. "People lose interest if they are not involved."

"Sister Laramie, would you please read verse 36?"

Janet Laramie read the verse and then told a short, unrelated story about a niece of hers that had recently had such a hard time finding a modest prom dress.

"Thanks," I sighed. "We're running out of time and I wanted to get the main point of this chapter across. And that is that Alma wasn't . . ."

Brother Rothburn raised his hand. I hung my head, realizing that now I would never be able to make my point.

"Yes," I said in defeat.

Brother Rothburn stood up, indicating that he had more to say than the circulation in his sitting legs would allow. "When the Saints assembled in the Kirtland Temple, most people thought that they had achieved Zion. But as we all know, Zion was far from established. I've got a cousin that moved to Missouri just so that he could be ready—"

"Brother Rothburn," I interrupted. "Since you're standing, would you mind giving us a closing prayer?"

"Not at all," he said, having been properly tricked.

Ten minutes later class was dismissed.

"So?" I asked Grace after the room had emptied.

"You did great," she replied affectionately.

"I used to think the branch in Thelma's Way was so weird," I remembered as I put my things into my bag. "Brother Rothburn's almost as bad as Jerry Scotch."

"I don't know," Grace debated. "I just think that time has faded your memory."

"I'm sorry about what I did to Noah," I apologized as we walked out together.

"I know," she replied. "You just don't know him."

"I know he's not telling the truth."

Grace was quiet. We parted ways in front of the foyer bulletin board. Grace went off to Relief Society, and I stood around to read what was posted. There was a fireside coming up on manners, taught by a Dr. Dave Knuckols. There would be a stake choir retreat in two weeks at the Dintmore Lodge. Members were encouraged to bring both their voices and spouses. And, of course, there was a large piece of orange poster board encouraging folks to get prepared before the seventeenth. In big letters on top of the poster it said, "Those prepared will be spared."

By the time I had finished reading all the posted information, priesthood had already begun. Not wanting to interrupt, or at least trying to make myself believe that was the reason, I stepped outside to enjoy the beautiful day. I walked down the side of the building and sat down next to a big tree that was growing by a row of bushes. The sun smashed through the leaves above, making me look cracked and broken. The large park across from the church was filled with people playing and acting as if Sunday were Saturday. A couple kites flew low in the thin December sky. I was just beginning to feel guilty about not going to priesthood when a pair of hands came up behind me and covered my eyes.

"Guess who?" the voice said, the inflection letting me know it was Leonard.

"Leonard."

"Not so loud," he whispered.

I turned around to see Leonard Vastly. He looked like I had last seen him, except now he had what appeared to be magnets strapped all over his body. He was crouched down behind the tree and leaning into the bushes. He had on a hat and dark clothing so as to be less obvious.

"What are you doing?" I asked.

"I came to talk to you," he said softly, wincing ever so subtly.

"What's with all the magnets?"

"This Bio-Doom isn't exactly a moneymaker," he said. "I'm looking into a few business opportunities."

"Magnets?"

"Multilevel magnets. They help balance out your electrolytes," he said as if rehearsed. "These on my ankles help firm up my skin. The ones on my forearms are actually rearranging the molecules in my hands to make me stronger. How about you, Trust, have you noticed a lack of energy in your life lately?"

"I'm not buying any of your magnets, Leonard."

"They're your electrolytes," he said, as if I were condemning myself to poor physical health by not taking him seriously. "I'll leave you with this," he offered. "These magnets have changed my life. I can't imagine . . ."

Leonard paused and then pulled a pamphlet from out of his shirt pocket. I could see him read a line to himself, trying to remember what to say. He pressed a hand to his head as if in pain.

"I can't imagine a pain-free day without them," he finally finished.

"Are you okay?" I asked, noticing that he was wincing quite a bit.

"I'll be all right," he said bravely. "It's just a little headache."

"Did you take some aspirin?"

"Phhheww," Leonard scoffed. "Aspirin is so passé. I've got a four-pound magnet in my hat. That'll cure it."

I tried not to smile.

"So, did you come to sell me magnets?" I asked.

"Nope, I did some checking on this Noah Taylor."

"And?" I questioned.

"Clean as a whistle," Leonard puckered. "Everybody that ever knew him loves him."

"I just don't get it," I mused.

"If it's any consolation, neither do I."

It wasn't.

"Well, I just want you to know that I'm on the job," Leonard said, patting my shoulder. "How's the women frontier?"

"Grace and I are doing okay."

"Good."

"How's the Bio-Doom?"

"It's not easy living in a fishbowl." Leonard tisked. "It can be awful restricting being cooped up 24 hours a day."

"You're not there now," I pointed out.

"I burned some dehydrated broccoli and had to get out for a while."

"Well, I'd better get back to priesthood. Do you want to come?" I asked.

"I'd love to," Leonard said. "But I'm a victim to commitment."

"We've all got our crosses to bear." I smiled.

Leonard was gone.

I stepped back inside, hoping to salvage some bit of Sunday. But as I was walking down the hall Doran stepped out from the nook that the nursery door created and stopped me.

"Can we talk?" he asked.

"Sure."

"Listen," he said kindly. "I really think we should work this Grace thing out. It's not doing either one of us any good to go on like this."

"I agree."

"So I've come up with a plan," he said quickly, as if hoping to get his idea in before I could stop him. "I'll date her on the T-days, that would be Thursday and Tuesday. Then I get to bring her to church every other Sunday. I get one Monday a month, or two, if it's a month with five Mondays. I'd like an occasional Saturday evening, but I've talked with the full-time missionaries and they have her scheduled for the next three."

"Doran," I began to protest.

"Hear me out," he begged. "She'll still technically be your girlfriend, I'm giving you that. I'll refer to her simply as a friend until such time as she is willing to upgrade me to steady, or even fiancée."

I like Doran Jorgensen, I always had. I loved the way he tackled everything in his life with such openmouthed, wide-eyed enthusiasm—like a dog with his head sticking out of a speeding car. It bothered me that he simply couldn't understand the fact that Grace and I were an exclusive item, but a tiny bit of me was flattered by how absolutely taken he was with her. How could I be mad at someone who saw as much great in Grace as I had?

"Listen, Trust," Doran continued. "I was about ready to give up on Grace altogether. Believe it or not, I get discouraged as much as the next guy. And I haven't exactly been getting positive signals from her. But last night I had a dream, or a vision . . . actually it was a dream. But in it I saw Grace in white. She was beautiful, Trust."

"I'm sure she was," I agreed.

"Not just worldly beautiful, but forever pretty," Doran insisted. "I can't just ignore that."

"I'll tell you what," I said. "Let's forget your T-day plan. But I'm fine with you seeing Grace as often as she will let you."

"You mean it?" he wagged.

"Sure. It's up to her."

"I knew talking would help," Doran grinned. "I just knew it. Thanks, Trust."

Doran and I both walked down the hall and entered priesthood late. I took a seat next to Brother Scott McLaughlin, the ward hermit. Brother McLaughlin was a fifty-year-old single man with a huge head.

He still came to elders quorum because he didn't like the slow-paced lessons in his high priest group. He was a loner who was best known for the fact that he used Wite-Out to highlight his scriptures. He found it much easier to simply cover up the verses that he didn't understand, or was offended by. I saw him eliminate two before the lesson ended.

I left my meetings that day uplifted.

# 70

# Smear

December 6th

Doran had really fouled things up for me by taking my job with Brother Barns away. I strongly disliked looking for work. I had thought about just not working until school started in a month, but I needed something to do. I had volunteered to help my mother out around the house, but she wasn't as enthused about that idea as I was. Brother Victor had come over the night before and informed me of all the possible positions that he was aware of. There weren't many glamorous options at the moment. Two of the better ones were taking part in a three week diabetes test, or cleaning out kennels at the Southdale econo-pound.

Brother Victor had left my house more depressed than I was.

Now it was Monday morning and I had an entire day of job hunting ahead of me. I put on an outfit that didn't look like I was trying too hard while still looking like I'd tried enough. My first stop was the large bookstore about a mile from my house. The store was called Ink Tonic.

There was a huge banner hanging outside that said "Four-Day Sale." I wondered which four days, seeing how it had been hanging for months. I walked inside trying to appear assertive. After asking a clerk named Timmy where to apply, I was directed to a woman named Opal. Opal, the manager, led me upstairs and asked me a few questions about myself while I sat on a couch that was so puffy I seemed to get lost in it. Opal sat behind a thin desk that had a fish tank on it.

"Have you worked in the last six months?" she asked without looking at me.

"I've done some work for my father," I answered, sounding a tad more pathetic than I would have preferred.

"And before that?"

"I was serving a mission for my church."

"Oh," she said unenthusiastically. "What are you, some sort of Christian?"

"I guess you could say that."

"Well, as long as you aren't a Mormon."

"Actually that's what I am," I said awkwardly.

"Well what is it? Christian or Mormon?"

"You can be both," I pointed out.

"Not me," she snubbed. "I couldn't stand being just another cookie-cutter sheep."

Opal had the same hairstyle as every other girl downstairs, was wearing exactly the same boots that Timmy the clerk had been wearing, and had so many name brand logos visible on her outfit that it would have taken me a full ten minutes to read them all. She was quite the picture of individualism.

"Express yourself," I joked, hoping she might lighten up just a bit.

"Ha-ha," she said coldly.

"I'm a pretty good worker," I tried.

"Well, we are short-staffed, and my sister said Mormons were reliable despite their restrictive beliefs. Plus, you aren't too hard on the eyes."

This was such a proud moment.

"I can only guarantee the job for the next month. And it will only be about three days a week," she sighed. "After the holidays, things will die down considerably."

"Sounds fair."

Opal looked me up and down.

"Can you be here tomorrow?"

I left Ink Tonic feeling pretty good about myself. I figured that I had to be doing something right to procure a job on the first try. I decided to get something to eat at the small bagel shop next door. While I was eating, Noah Taylor came in and ordered lunch. Once he noticed me, he smiled and asked if he could sit down. With my mouth full I couldn't properly decline.

"So, Trust," Noah said after he had been seated. "What are you up to?"

"I was wondering the same thing about you," I answered back.

"Sorry about nobody believing you." Noah smiled. "It must really hurt to have Grace take my side."

"What's your deal, anyway?" I asked.

"I'd tell you more, but our last conversation left me looking less than perfect."

"I can see that," I said, knowing full well that the effects of my fist were no longer visible.

Noah smirked.

"So are you getting the town all prepared?" I attempted to be civil.

"It's a daunting task," Noah said while smiling at one of the female employees.

"You know, I can't understand how Grace has not discovered what a phony you are. She's usually so perceptive."

"Love can be blinding."

"Don't flatter yourself," I said, taking a bite of my bagel sandwich.

"Why should I when I have Grace around to do it for me?"

"You're nuts," I shook my head.

"You're jealous."

"Am not."

"Are too."

The couple sitting one table over looked at us as if we were a couple of silly grade school kids.

"Oh, Trust," Noah said. "If I wanted to, I could make this so much harder for you than I have. You do know what I mean, don't you?"

"I know what you mean," I said defensively.

I didn't have the faintest idea what he was talking about.

"What do you mean?" I backpedaled.

"I'm certain Grace would jump at the chance to go off with me when all this is over. Maybe I'll just extend the invitation and see what happens."

"Like I said, you're nuts." I stood and picked up my trash.

"If believing that makes it easier," Noah said, "then you just keep on believing."

I was tempted to hit him again, but I restrained myself, walking out of the restaurant without further altercation.

I had gotten only a few steps out of the bagel shop when all of a sudden a ragged homeless person approached me. I thought it rather odd, seeing how this was the east suburbs, and I had never seen a vagrant or a wino in this area before. I had just begun to think of King Benjamin and his beggar speech when this particular bum addressed me by name.

"Trust," he whispered hoarsely.

"Leonard?"

"Not bad, huh?" he said, referring to his getup. Then he did a little spin so that I could take in the complete ensemble.

"What are you doing now?"

"I was tailing Noah. I wrote down the entire conversation you two had in there."

"You could hear us?"

"No, but I'm not half-bad at reading lips," he said proudly.

"My back was facing the window." I laughed.

"I had to just guess at your dialogue."

"So what were we talking about?" I asked, amused.

Leonard pulled out a pad of yellow legal paper and began to read back my and Noah's conversation.

"You said, 'Have you been to see Leonard Vastly's Bio-Doom?' And he said something about being jealous. You said, 'I can't believe how prepared that Leonard is.' And he said, 'Southdale sure had a long growing season.' I'm not sure why he said that, but I guess it's in reference to planting grain. How'd I do?" Leonard asked.

"Well," I began to say.

Leonard pulled out a glass bottle from his long wrinkled coat and took a big swig. It was obvious the drink was part of his undercover disguise. He wiped his mouth with the back of his sleeve and *ahhhed.*

"What are you drinking?" I questioned.

"I'm glad you asked," Leonard brightened. "This is Fiji prana juice. It's from Fiji."

"That would explain the name." I smiled. "Where'd you get it?"

"I'm selling it now. I ditched the magnet deal. Too many complications."

"Complications?"

"Well, yesterday after I talked to you, I was walking downtown through the swap meet and I unknowingly attracted a few pieces of jewelry to me. Long story short, did you know you can post bail with a credit card?"

"I had no idea."

"Technology is really changing things," Leonard reflected. "Anyhow, I've decided to try selling this juice. You need some of this,

Trust. It's from a rare fruit, and it stabilizes your entire body. Only fifty bucks a bottle."

"I can't afford it." I smiled.

"You can't not afford it." Leonard smiled back.

"I'm not buying any of your juice, Leonard."

"Just hear me out," he said, handing me his bottle to look at. "This is the only company that takes the juice in its freshest form, seals it up, and sells it to you. You might have seen Fiji prana pills, but those things are ineffective, processed until all the good is taken out of them. This juice goes straight from the tree to the bottle."

"But it says it's bottled in Provo." I pointed to the bottle.

"Listen, Trust, if you're not interested, just say so."

"I'm not interested."

"See, wasn't that easy? I don't believe in high-pressure sales. If the product is good, people will come to me."

"That's smart."

"Before I go, however, I just want you to take this tape."

"Leonard."

"Listen to it in your spare time. It tells all about the Fiji prana fruit. Fascinating really. If you have any questions just call the 800 number on the cover. If they ask who gave you the tape give them my membership number there on the back."

"753CON?"

"Those letters are assigned randomly," Leonard lamented. "I'm trying to get mine changed."

"Thanks," I said, slipping the tape into my pocket. "I'd better head home."

"You go ahead," he said, giving me permission. "I'll keep an eye on Noah."

"That's not really necessary, Leonard."

"Oh, Trust," he said, shaking his head as if I were a little child and there were still so many things that I didn't understand. "I'm doing this

. . . there he goes!" Leonard whispered fiercely, having just spotted Noah coming out of the bagel shop and heading the opposite way.

And with that Leonard was gone.

I went home and told my mother all about my new job. She said, "That's nice" at least twelve times.

It was time for my father to come home.

71

# LOVE VIGILANTE

Roger Williams was not in good shape. The motorcycle had pulled him down the Girth River until he got snagged on a rotting tree that was reaching into the water. He was lucky. A few hundred more feet and he would have been thrown over the falls. By the time he was rescued, however, he had been knocked around enough to do his body some harm. The town had carried him back and put him up at Sister Watson's house so that she could be on constant watch. Toby was called for. He brought his Ace bandage and wrapped the worst-looking bump on Roger's head. Then he prescribed lots of rest and maybe some fresh air when he was feeling better. The prescription fell on deaf ears. Roger was out cold. Toby gathered his things and quietly came out of the room.

"Can I see him now?" President Heck asked Toby as he emerged.

"Sure," Toby replied, wondering why he was asking him. "He's just in there."

President Heck walked into Sister Watson's spare bedroom and looked at Roger as he lay there. Sister Watson followed him.

"Does he look a little purple to you?" Ricky Heck asked her.

"That'll pass," she hushed.

"He could have died." President Heck tisked.

"He's lucky to be alive," Sister Watson agreed.

"Should we call someone or something? I mean he might have family that could worry over him." President Heck fretted with concern.

"No one knows who to call." Sister Watson sighed. "He had his bags all packed as if he were planning to leave, but there were no papers with his things. And I think his wallet must have washed downriver."

"You think it's okay if we just leave him here?"

"Sure," Sister Watson said. "The body's an amazing thing. He'll heal, and then he'll tell us what to do."

"I'm glad you're around to know that," President Heck said.

"Why Ricky Heck, did you just pay me a compliment?"

"Sorry," he said softly.

Sister Watson fussed with the blanket lying across Roger.

"You know what would be real nice?" she asked reflectively.

"A big dish of hot pie," President Heck answered without thinking.

"Wouldn't it be though," Sister Watson said distractedly. "But I was also thinking that Roger here might enjoy a nice haircut. Wad's always complaining about how people never sit still. I bet he'd sort of enjoy cutting on a knocked-out person. Plus, when Roger wakes up he'll look better."

"Mavis Watson, you are a genius."

"You're a married man, Ricky Heck." Sister Watson blushed. "Don't go flinging honey in places you can't reach."

Ricky Heck laughed, pretending that he knew what she was hinting at.

"You know, I think he's lost a little weight," Sister Watson observed.

"I think I found it," President Heck joked, patting his round belly.

"With his face a little thinner, he sort of resembles our Elder Williams," Sister Watson pointed out.

"You know, you're right."

"I tell you, the first thing this man is doing when he comes to is his genealogy," Sister Watson snipped. "Who knows, Elder Williams could be his long lost cousin or nephew."

"Or relative," President Heck said sincerely.

"You just never know, do you?" Sister Watson mused.

"Nope, I really don't."

72

# Dating Myself

December 9th

The idea behind this date auction was this: if a cake auction can bring in a couple hundred dollars, then a people auction should really clean up. It was skewed logic.

The auction was to begin at six. The actual auction being done by seven, everyone besides those who had bid would depart, leaving the participants and bidders to dine in the cultural hall for a very informal group date. It was sort of an exclusive ward activity that only those who contributed could attend.

"You'd better get me." Grace smiled as we got ready to head out. "I don't want to get stuck with anyone else."

"We'll see how the other girls look," I joked.

"I'm serious, Trust."

"You don't have to do this," I informed her.

"I need to support Noah."

I tried not to roll my eyes too loudly.

"What?" Grace smiled, perfectly aware of how I felt about her boss.

Grace and I had talked a couple days earlier about what Noah had told me at the bagel shop, and once again Grace had chosen not to believe. It wasn't that Grace thought I was making up lies to turn her against him, she just felt I was misunderstanding what Noah was actually trying to say. I had volunteered to wear a wire and get a conversation with him on tape, but Grace simply told me to be the bigger man. Actually, she begged.

"Noah's just using this town," I said, trying to not sound too heavy.

"Let's not talk about it," Grace said, fixing her hair.

"I didn't mean to spoil your big night," I joked.

Grace looked at me and smiled.

"It's only one date," I added. "And it's a fixed group date in the cultural hall at that. It won't be too bad."

"We'll see," she said. "How do I look?"

"Perfect," I answered, unable to think of a single English word that accurately described how beautiful she was.

"Your opinion's no good," she piffed. "You're in love with me."

"Uh, huh."

Grace leaned up and kissed me.

The last two days had been so nice. Grace and I had gotten along perfectly. We had both worked during the days and spent the evenings talking and being together. The more I found out about Grace, the more enamored I grew. And the more she discovered about me, the more . . . well, we really liked each other. The only unpleasantries we had encountered over the past couple of days were the constant phone calls that Doran was making to Grace, now that he had my permission to pursue her. He was going at it "full guns." I'm not really sure what that meant, but it had been the last line of the latest poem he had written her. The other concern in my life was the emotional deterioration that my family was going through. My father had still not called. Even his partners at work said they didn't know where he was. They added that if he didn't report to work in two weeks, they would have to take disciplinary action. It didn't look good. But Mom refused to call the police to report him missing. That would be going public, according to her, and she had more faith in Roger than that. Besides, she said, she felt strongly that he was okay. Whatever he was doing was important and we just needed to be patient. Abel, Margret, and I prayed for the best and tried not to fear the worst.

The sky was dark by the time Grace and I arrived at the church for the auction. The cultural hall was one happening place. It was trickier getting in than we had anticipated, due to Brother and Sister Phillips protesting the auction outside. The two of them were marching around carrying signs that said, "Going once, going twice, going down the drain," and, "The low bidder isn't the only loser." Apparently, I wasn't the only one bothered by Noah and his ideas. Either that or Brother Phillips didn't want to put out any money to bid on his wife.

Once inside, I hung up our unneeded coats and looked around at the large crowd. Everyone was there, looking and smelling their best. The Scouts stood inside the doorway to welcome people to this, hopefully, once-in-a-lifetime event. The walkway looked sturdy enough, and tables lined the walls filled with covered food and drink. There were hundreds of chairs scattered everywhere, and garlands were looped liberally through the basketball hoops on either end of the room. Grace wandered off to take her place behind the curtain. I took a seat near the middle of the room, right next to Sister Cummings.

I didn't really know Rachel Cummings all that well. She and her husband, Keith, had moved into the ward while I was serving my mission. She was an attractive woman with a mousy disposition. She was one of only a handful of women in the ward who didn't color her hair, letting a touch of gray show through the dark. Keith was in the military and had an amateur magic business on the side. They had five very little kids and lived in a nice house they had fixed up themselves. It was no secret that she was a nervous woman. She was always worried about finding the right thing to say.

She nodded politely at me.

I picked up a program lying on the chair beside me. I looked it over and set it back down.

Sister Cummings suddenly pointed across the room toward my brother. "Abel looks nice in his new Scout uniform."

I looked at Abel. He had come earlier to help set up the chairs. His neckerchief was hanging loosely around his neck, his hair was matted in a hat ring, and his shirt was untucked and wrinkled. Sister Cummings was obviously just being kind.

"Thanks," I replied.

Sister Cummings sighed, happy that her comment had gone over all right.

I think she was about to say more when Noah Taylor strutted out onto the walkway and stood there waiting for everyone's attention to be focused solely on him.

"Brothers and Sisters," he finally began. "I am honored and sobered by your participation tonight."

I started to get sick. Noah was wearing another sweater with khaki pants, and his hair was doing that hair thing. He held the microphone like an Englishman would hold a cup of tea, his pinkie sticking up and out.

"I would like to thank all of those who have helped put this together. Many hands have made light work. I'd list you all by name, but this old mind of mine isn't quite as sharp as it used to be," he said in an attempt at self-deprecating humor.

A few folks chuckled. I noticed, however, that people weren't quite as quick to find everything Noah Taylor said as amusing as I had thought.

"A brief reminder to us all," he continued. "The proceeds from this event will go to help those who cannot afford their own preparedness.

We will take this money and stock up all those who are less fortunate." Noah cleared his throat loudly. "Also, we have been busy getting the warehouse on Frost Road ready. I'm happy to say that all of you who have made the monetary commitment are now one hundred percent prepared. Take comfort in knowing that your food storage is up-to-date and stored in a climate-controlled place where you won't be tripping over it. It's sobering to think how close the seventeenth is, but come heck or high water, we're prepared."

A few people clapped.

"Back to the matter at hand," he chirped. "After the auction, all those who have been lucky enough to get a date will stay here and enjoy a great meal put on by Sister Barns and the Relief Society. Sister Barns, will you please stand so that all of us can recognize you?"

Sister Barns stood and bobbed out a couple of curtseys. She was wearing a bright yellow dress with puffy sleeves that made it hard for me to see her whole face. From the parts I could see, however, it appeared as if Sister Barns had chosen this night to experiment with new makeup. On a normal day, Sister Barns was above average in height, but tonight, with the heels she had chosen to wear, she towered over most people in the room. She smoothed and tucked her dress behind her rear and sat back down.

"Thank you, Sister Barns," Noah said. "Now, our auctioneer tonight will be Brother Clyde Knuckles. So after our opening song and a prayer from Brother McLaughlin, we will begin."

Noah Taylor stepped down from the walkway, and Sister Morris began playing "Count Your Many Blessings" while young Celion Morris directed poorly. After the song, Brother McLaughlin walked to the front and gave a long prayer begging the heavens that even with his limited income he might be able to afford one of the nicer-looking sisters being auctioned for dates tonight.

Brother Knuckles climbed up onto the walkway. Clyde Knuckles was an active Mormon—as long as "active" meant activity. He came out to all the ward plays, the barbecues, the socials, anything that meant food served up in the cultural hall. He just usually didn't make it to Sunday services. He worked for a big bank in the city. He was a tall, thick-haired guy with a smooth voice. Brother Knuckles was always chosen as MC. If the activity required a vocal tour guide, Clyde Knuckles was the one doing the talking.

"Good evening," Brother Knuckles said. "I hope you're all as excited about this as I am. I know that . . ."

Bishop Leen slipped him a note.

"This just in," Clyde said. "The bishop wants me to say that he hopes this evening will go over in the spirit in which it is intended."

"The spirit of slavery!" Sister Phillips shouted out from the back of the crowd. She had just slipped into the room to cause trouble. Two young Scouts quickly whisked her away.

"All right then," Clyde continued unscathed. "Without further fuss we'll begin. Volunteer number one is Sally Wheatfield."

Sally stepped brashly out from behind the curtains as Noah Taylor handed Clyde a small stack of cards. Sister Morris played soft music on the piano as Brother Knuckles described Sally's attributes.

"Sally is the seventh child from a family of eight. She has just recently received a degree in veterinarian studies and prelaw. Sally describes her age as moderate . . ."

Sally Wheatfield was an attractive young woman. She had big blue eyes and an innocence about her that made it hard for you to believe that she could be interested in prelaw. She was currently dating Michael Fits, a member of the Rockwedge Ward. As she walked down the runway, she smiled and waved to Michael. Michael got out his wallet.

"All right," Brother Knuckles said. "Who will be the first to bid?"

"Two hundred dollars!" Brother McLaughlin yelled, having been suddenly struck with auction anxiety and prematurely bidding everything he had the first chance he got.

"Two hundred dollars?" Clyde asked incredulously.

"Two hundred dollars," Brother McLaughlin tried to say with confidence.

Sally Wheatfield looked worried.

Brother McLaughlin was considerably older than Sally. And even though the winners weren't required to hold hands or do much more than simply eat next to each other, the idea still smacked of inappropriateness. I saw Michael Fits frantically count the bills in his wallet and realize he couldn't match the current bid.

Michael looked at Sally. Sally looked at Clyde. Clyde looked at Noah. Noah looked at his papers and shrugged. Sally buried her face in her hands and ran from the stage crying.

I had a feeling we would see a lot of that tonight. This wasn't such a good idea.

Brother McLaughlin walked up to Noah Taylor and handed him his two hundred dollars. Then he walked back and took his seat.

Noah nodded to Clyde, indicating that he should continue.

Brother Knuckles cleared his throat. "Our next contestant is Daisy Cravitz."

Everyone gasped. No one could believe that Sister Cravitz would willingly submit herself to be auctioned off. Even more than that, no one could imagine anybody bidding for her. Sister Cravitz walked out with confidence. She had on her biggest and shiniest brooch, and her hair was done up like one of those old movie stars that no one but she could possibly remember.

"Daisy Cravitz is the second child of a family of twelve," Clyde read. "She was raised up north in the wholesome environment of Idaho but has spent the last thirty years of her life out here. She is currently retired and addicted to latchhooks, whatever that means . . ." Brother Knuckles added. "She would like for her bidders to know that she is all woman, except for her artificial knees."

Everyone winced silently. I wondered who the marked man was that was supposed to bid on her. The idea behind the auction was that no one would participate unless there were a surefire bid. I didn't have to wait long to find out.

"Who will start the bidding?" Clyde asked.

"Twenty dollars," Brother Victor waved.

Everyone turned to stare. There was obviously something going on with these two older singles that the entire ward had been previously blind to. When no one else offered a bid, Brother Victor yelled out, "Fifty!" topping his own amount.

"Fifty, going once, going—" Clyde began to close.

"Seventy!" Brother Victor hollered.

Everyone looked at him, wondering if he was familiar with how auctions actually worked.

Brother Knuckles rolled his shoulders and continued. "Seventy, going once—"

"One hundred dollars!" Brother Victor yelled, acting as if he had just discovered gold.

Sister Cravitz blushed onstage, happy to be the subject of such attention.

"Is there anybody here besides Brother Victor who would like to bid on Sister Cravitz?" Clyde asked.

I had never seen the ward in such universal agreement.

"Sold to Brother Victor for one hundred dollars."

Clarence Victor gave Noah his money and then sat back down.

Brother Knuckles took a sip of water, licked his lips, and continued.

"Our next contestant is Grace Heck."

Grace walked out from behind the curtain, smiling with embarrassment. The entire room lit up. She was like a golden grain in a sea of common rye. Her red hair and white skin shone under the makeshift stage lights like stars in the night sky. She had on jeans, with a brown shirt tucked into them. Never had brown looked so fetching. Her green eyes flashed out at me, sending hurricane-like winds to every region of my soul.

"Grace Heck is a native of Thelma's Way, Tennessee," Clyde Knuckles described. "She is the oldest of three children and is currently working with Brother Noah Taylor. She lists her age as twenty-three. Grace would like for whoever bids on her to be about six-foot-two, with blue eyes, and have a name that starts and ends with 'T.'"

Everyone turned and looked at me as if I personally had written Grace's card for her.

"Who will start the bidding on the lovely Grace Heck?" Clyde hollered out.

Brother McLaughlin raised his hand. "Will you take jewelry, or does it have to be cash?"

"You already have a date," Clyde pointed out.

"I know," he huffed. "But I think I spent my money too soon."

"I'm sorry," Clyde said. "No refunds, no exchanges."

"But—"

"And no buts," Clyde joked. "So, who will start the bidding on our lovely Tennesseean?"

"Twenty dollars!" seventeen-year-old Leon Treat hollered, his voice cracking as he spoke.

"Thirty," I threw out.

"Thirty-two dollars and . . . sixty-eight cents," Leon bid, looking at some loose change in his hand.

"Fifty," I yelled, actually feeling a little bad about ousting Leon.

"Shoot," Leon complained and looked toward his father in despair.

"One hundred dollars," Noah Taylor jumped in.

"Two hundred," I hollered.

"Three," said Noah.

"Four," I offered, personally vowing that there was no way I would let Noah win.

The crowd inhaled at the bid of four hundred dollars.

"Five." Noah smiled.

"Seven hundred dollars," I said, knowing that I had just over that amount in my checking account.

The audience *ohhhhed.* Sister Laramie fanned herself as Brother Knuckles looked at Noah.

"Too rich for my blood," Noah said.

"Seven hundred dollars going once, going twice—"

"Nine thousand dollars!" a voice boomed from behind me.

The entire room gasped. Necks craned to see who it was. I turned around to see Doran Jorgensen holding the biggest wad of cash I had ever seen in my life. I had forgotten he was going to come out tonight. I was reminded in a big way.

"Nine thousand dollars?" Brother Knuckles asked in disbelief.

"Nine thousand dollars," Doran bragged as he strode to the front of the room waving the money.

Noah's eyes widened to the size of bike tires. Clyde Knuckles looked at Noah as if to say, "what should I do?" Noah was amazingly quick to hiss, "Close the bid."

"Nine thousand going once, going twice, sold to the young man with more money than sense."

Everyone cheered. Everyone except me.

Doran gave the money to Noah Taylor and climbed up on stage to claim his prize. Grace stood there looking wounded. I tried to explain to her with my eyes that I didn't have that kind of money, and that if I had, I still probably wouldn't have tried to outbid Doran, because all she would have to do is put up with one lousy group date and then she and I could go out and spend the nine thousand dollars that I didn't actually have on something far more exciting and worthwhile. Unfortunately, my eyes just weren't that expressive.

This was awful. I just kept thinking that I had let Grace down, and that Doran was an idiot not to have bid lower. Grace would have been his for the taking for a mere seven hundred and fifty. And where had he gotten nine thousand dollars? He must have come from a far wealthier family than I had imagined.

"That tall kid is nuts," a hooded woman sitting on the other side of me said. "More nuts than a squirrel."

"Yeah," I said, staring at her out of the corner of my eye. I turned away from her and then looked quickly back, realizing that there was something oddly familiar about her.

It was Leonard.

He was dressed in a huge muumuu and house slippers. He looked half-Arab, half-frumpy housewife.

"Is that you, Leonard?" I whispered. "What the heck are you doing?"

"Hiding," he whispered back.

"This is ridiculous," I whispered back. "Someone's going to notice that you're not a woman."

"I can't help it," Leonard said urgently. "I've always had big hands."

"It won't be your hands that give it away," I said, looking at the hairy ankles that his disguise didn't quite cover.

"I had to tell you about Noah," he insisted.

"What about Noah?" I asked, trying to not look like I was talking to him.

"The warehouse he's supposedly stocking is empty."

"What do you mean empty?"

"Empty, not full."

"But I thought—"

"Forget what you thought, you were right about him, Trust." Leonard congratulated me.

"Are you sure about this?" I asked.

"I couldn't be more sure."

"Like, halfway empty?" I tried to verify.

"Completely empty," Leonard said squarely. "I knew Noah would be busy with this auction tonight, so I snuck into the warehouse to see if I could find anything on him. I found something all right. Nothing."

"I can't believe this," I mumbled.

"It's true," Leonard insisted. "And now he's got that skinny kid's nine thousand dollars. You have to do something about this, Trust."

"What can I do?" I said, turning to find Leonard gone. I thought maybe he had quickly jumped up so as to get out before he was noticed. Then I spotted him over by one of the serving tables picking at food that was covered and set there to feed the winning bidders later tonight.

I looked up at Noah Taylor on the walkway. He was blabbing about how Doran's nine thousand dollars was going to help a lot of folks get prepared. He was also going on and on about how surprised everyone was going to be when they saw how well he had organized their food storage for them.

I couldn't just sit there. I stood up and tried to say what I had to in the most tactful and unsensational way possible: "Noah Taylor is a big fat liar, and I can prove it!"

Everyone turned to stare at me in disbelief.

"The warehouse is empty," I said, hoping that someone would believe me.

"Brother Williams," Noah said, looking hurt. "I know that you and I have had our differences, but is this really necessary?"

"The warehouse is empty," was all that I said.

"Is this true?" Bishop Leen asked Noah.

"Of course not," Noah scoffed. "I'm afraid Brother Williams here is just a little sore about losing his date tonight."

A couple of people laughed, but most folks were more willing to hear me out than I had anticipated. Grace looked at me with angry green eyes. She seemed to say, I can't believe that you would bring this up now and in front of all these people since there is no possible way that you could actually know what you are saying because you've never even been inside of Noah's warehouse, so I'm figuring that this is just some last-ditch effort to make Noah look bad.

Her eyes were far more expressive than mine.

"Listen," Bishop Leen said. "I'm not sure that this is the time or place to be making such accusations."

"If I've been paying Noah for nothing," Brother Treat yelled, "then this is the perfect place to make those accusations."

"Someone's been in the warehouse and seen if it's full, haven't they?" Brother O'Shawn asked in a panic.

Nobody responded.

"Grace?" the bishop inquired. "You work there. You've seen all the food and supplies."

"Actually," Grace said, uncomfortable about being put in such a spot. "I work in the front office. I've not been into the warehouse. Noah keeps it locked. But I have seen trucks coming and going."

Everyone began to holler and stamp their feet. Noah Taylor held up his hands.

"Listen, everybody," he yelled. "Your food is all there."

"Prove it!" someone screamed.

"Right now?" Noah asked. "What about the auction?" he whined.

"Right now!" Sally Wheatfield hollered, sensing a chance to get out of sitting next to Brother McLaughlin the rest of the night.

The whole body of Saints began filing out of the building, running swiftly to their cars. I found Grace and pulled her to the side.

"Trust, this is ridiculous," she said above the rush of excited members. "Noah's not a crook."

"We'll see," I replied, happy that everyone had taken me seriously. "Let's go and check if it's empty."

"I thought you knew already?" Grace questioned.

"Not firsthand."

As we were shoving our way out of the cultural hall and into the parking lot, Doran grabbed my arm.

"Trust," he said with great animation. "Could I get a ride with you?"

"Where's your truck?" I asked, slowing just a bit.

"I sold it."

"You—"

"Sold it," he said curtly.

"What for?" I asked, the answer coming to me as I spoke. "For nine thousand dollars!"

Grace was shocked. "You sold your truck to have dinner with me?" she said, sounding more flattered than I felt was necessary.

"Grace, I had this dream, and—" Doran began to say, but before he could get it all out Sister Cravitz knocked him down making a beeline for her car.

"Let's just go," I insisted.

Grace and I got into my car and Doran followed. We followed the stream of vehicles up Frost Road and over to the warehouse. Everyone got out and surrounded the building's entrance. One after another people tried the front door to see if it would open, working themselves into an angry mob.

"Where's Noah?" someone hollered.

"There he is," someone else screamed.

Noah was pulled and pushed through the crowd until he was finally standing in front of the door. He fumbled with his keys, trying to tell everyone to calm down.

It was too late for that.

The moment the door swung open, people crunched and shoved to get inside. The front offices were packed in no time. Once again Noah groped desperately for the right key that would open the door to the warehouse.

"Hurry up!" Brother Lewis demanded.

"Listen," Noah tried. "This is all one big mistake."

"Open the door," everyone yelled.

Noah found the key and unlocked the door. The crowd moved though the small door and into the huge warehouse with one big surge. Someone flipped on a light. We all just stood there staring, slack-jawed, wide-eyed.

I was in big trouble.

The walls were lined with food and supplies. Mountains of cans rolled throughout the warehouse like sand dunes of self-reliance. Boxes of wheat and grain and noodles and vitamins and so on flooded the floor, leaving us neck deep in emergency preparedness. There were little signs labeling what was whose and how much each had purchased. Labels and canisters sparkled under the long fluorescent lights which were blinking as if the glow had just awakened them.

I was dumbfounded—and found to be dumb.

Every eye turned to me. When I said nothing, Noah spoke for me.

"I've kept this room locked off because I wanted this all to be a surprise. I didn't think anyone would challenge my honesty."

I guess I was anyone.

"Trust," Bishop Leen said in his gruffest voice. "What is the meaning of this?"

"I . . ." I looked around at all the angry faces. "Leonard Vastly did it," I said, folding like a spineless jellyfish with a weak threshold for pain. "He said the place was empty."

"Leonard Vastly's locked up in his own house, everybody knows that." The bishop hung his head out of shame for me. "I hope you're happy, Trust."

I wasn't.

"Listen, let's not let this ruin our whole evening," Noah said graciously. "If we hurry back to the church, we may still be able to salvage some of tonight's festivities. People paid, after all. And the food's still there."

Everyone began to walk out past me. If I had any doubts about how people felt, they were quickly dispelled by the comments thrown as they walked by: "What has Noah ever done to you?" "I can't believe you would do this." "Your mother will be ashamed . . ."

I offered weak apologies to each of them, but it did no good. Grace looked at me as if I were someone with an embarrassing tattoo on his forehead.

"Grace, you have to believe me," I tried. "Leonard said it was empty."

Doran stuck out his arm for Grace to take hold. She looked at me. She looked at Doran. She looked over at Noah. She took Doran's arm and the two of them walked off together. Grace looked back and sighed. I guess they were going to find a different ride back.

I was now all alone except for Noah. He glanced around to make sure no one was within listening distance and then said, "Trust, you really are a piece of work."

I held my tongue.

"It's been fun messing with your head, but this time you saved me the trouble." Noah smiled meanly. "I'll almost miss you when I'm gone."

I walked out toward the parking lot, making an effort to ignore him. Most people were already pulling away, heading back over to the church. Noah locked up the building with his keys, got into his shiny little car, and waved sarcastically as he drove off. I got into my car and started it up. I looked in the rearview mirror to back up, and there was Leonard's face, staring back at me.

"Leonard!" I scolded, "you've got to stop sneaking up on me this way!"

"Sorry," he said. "But how'd it go?"

"How'd it go?" I asked incredulously. "How'd it go? The place is loaded with food."

"I was afraid it might be," Leonard said abashedly.

"I thought you said it was empty!"

"I thought Noah's warehouse was the one over on Pine Street. When everyone pulled up here, I realized my mistake."

I banged my head against the steering wheel and moaned.

"What?" he asked innocently.

I looked at him full on in my rearview mirror. He still had on the pink hood and the exaggerated makeup. He looked so stupid in his getup that I suddenly felt pity for him. I decided not to take the discussion any further.

"Do you need a ride home?" I asked dejectedly.

"Sure." Leonard smiled. "But drop me off at that park near my place. I wouldn't want anyone to see me coming and going from the Bio-Doom."

Leonard Vastly was one curious individual.

We passed the church on our way home. I could see shadows in the cultural hall windows mingling about. The steeple was lit and cars were in the parking lot. I felt confident that had I rolled down my window I would be able to hear the sound of laughter coming from the building, but I left my window shut. I was also pretty certain about what they would be laughing over and I didn't want to hear.

"So, do you think the auction's going all right?" Leonard asked, taking off his hood and primping his hair with both hands.

I had enough to think about.

## 73

# Fries Like Us

My night was ruined. After dropping Leonard off I drove back over to the church in hopes that it had caught fire and the group date had been forced to be cut short. I had the worst luck.

The chapel was just fine. In fact, it seemed to be inappropriately dark.

I drove home slowly, thinking about Grace, steaming over Noah, stewing about Doran, and wishing Leonard had not decided to make perfume an integral part of his most recent disguise. I rolled down the car window and stuck out my head in the hope of getting some fresh air. The wind whipped around me, cooling my still-uneven haircut. As I pulled up to my house, I noticed a red car parked at the curb. There was a blonde head decorating the front porch. I retracted my noggin and turned off the engine. I stepped out and faced the music.

It was Lucy Fall.

She stood there in a black sweater and faded jeans. Her blonde hair under the porch lights made her look angelic. She was smiling at me. She was laughing. I thought perhaps that she was just really happy to see me. It turns out, however, that she was just reacting to my windblown hair. I smoothed it down and caught myself trying to act cooler than I actually was. Despite all that life had led me through in the last few years, Lucy's effect on me was still just as strong.

"What are you doing here?" I asked as we stood on the porch.

"I just got here," she said, brushing a still-standing piece of my hair down. "I've been trying to call you for a while now, but you're never home."

"Really?" I asked with far too much enthusiasm.

"I was wondering if . . ." Lucy paused as a car drove past. "Do you think we could go somewhere to talk?"

"Margaret's inside," I nodded toward the front door of my house.

"Are you hungry?" Lucy asked.

"A little, why?"

"We could get something to eat," Lucy said seductively.

Okay, it wasn't at all seductive. In fact, she probably used the exact same inflection and flare when asking the price of dish soap at the supermarket. But for some reason the air between Lucy's lips and my ears had always been against me. It was as if her words were warped and manipulated to make my mind go crazy.

"Eat?" I asked, unable to tackle more than one word at a time.

"Just a quick bite."

There she goes again.

"Well . . ." I hesitated.

"I need to ask you something, Trust," she seemed to plead, a sense of nervousness appearing for the first time in our conversation.

Normally, I wouldn't have even entertained the idea. Grace was so much more than Lucy could ever hope to be. Sure Lucy had this effect thing going, but it was all just smoke and mirrors. Grace's hold on my heart was no illusion. But truth be known, I was more than a little sore about Grace not believing me, and then skipping off to spend the evening with someone who threw cash around like it was lawn fertilizer.

I mean, if she was on a sort of date, then what harm would it do for me to do the same?

"Okay," I agreed. "Where should we go?"

Lucy took my arm and led me to her car. We drove over to a small diner called Nick's Pit. We sat down at what felt like far too cozy a booth and pretended we were adult enough that this situation didn't faze us. Lucy was far more convincing than I.

I was just beginning to enjoy myself when a beautiful redhead came into the diner, hooked onto the arm of a tall thin-haired guy.

Apparently the intimate ambiance of a packed cultural hall was not good enough for Doran and Grace. I waited for the rest of the ward to come in after them.

They never did. The two of them were alone!

I would have been completely disgusted if it had not been for the fact that I was sort of in the same spot. Regardless, Grace and Doran had shifted from a group date in an open place to a cozy meal in the most secluded corner of Nick's Pit. And I couldn't decide if I should stamp over to them in self-righteous indignation, or try and sneak out the back door.

Lucy noticed the storm in my eyes.

"What is it?" she asked, unable to see who had come in from where she was sitting.

"Nothing," I said abruptly.

The waiter brought our food. I found myself peering through the bush partitions between tables, over at Grace. I swirled my fork through my meal and tried to fake interest in the things Lucy was saying. I must have been somewhat convincing, judging at least from the fact that Lucy kept on talking.

Images pushed and scattered through my mind like a theater crowd at the cry of fire. Now that I thought about it, Grace had never said straight out that she didn't have feelings for Doran. I mean, it's possible she had just been stringing us both along. Maybe this last little while had simply been a time of sifting for Grace. Sure, Doran wasn't exactly what I would call "dishy," but I suppose in a sort of "I just got done plowing the north fields and I'm looking for a soap strong enough to clean me up" type of way, he was okay. Maybe Grace preferred that. She did hail from a rather small town. That was it. All those years of living in Thelma's Way had made her go for tall gangly guys who chewed on toothpicks and were intimately acquainted with gun racks. She was probably just sort of teetering on the line between choosing Doran or choosing me and the nine thousand dollars had tipped her over.

"Trust, are you all right?" Lucy asked again, pulling me back to my meal. I gazed across the diner at Grace. She was sitting closer to Doran than she absolutely had to. In fact, a real gentleman would have asked the waiter to put a chair on the end of the booth so as to eliminate the possibility of accidental footsies.

Lucy's shoe brushed my ankle as she shifted.

"Sorry," she said, blushing.

Need I say more?

I took a bite of my meal and *uh-huhhed* at Lucy's latest remark.

Grace was laughing. Things were worse than I thought. Doran had a speck of sauce on his cheek and Grace brushed it off with her fingers. I couldn't believe it. I remembered Grace comparing Doran to Leo Tip from Thelma's Way. She had said they seemed so similar. But wasn't it Leo that the entire town had thought, although wrongly, Grace was sweet on? Maybe subconsciously she had felt sorry for letting everyone down with Leo, and liking Doran was a way to put things right.

That was it. It all seemed so clear.

Lucy asked if she could have one of my fries.

"Go ahead," I answered, as if nothing now mattered.

I watched Doran slyly spill his water, causing Grace to have to dab his table setting and shirt with her napkin. It was obvious that I had played Doran for a far bigger fool than he actually was. The old spill and dab was a brilliantly devious trick.

Our male waiter came to our table and asked if everything was all right.

"Yes," I lied.

Then he took a long look at Lucy and left.

Lucy kept talking for a minute and then stopped.

"Trust, you haven't been listening to a word I've said, have you?" she asked.

"If that's what you want," I replied, looking past her at Doran who tenderly split a breadstick with Grace and then scooted at least an eighth of an inch closer to her. The nerve of that guy.

"Would you rather just leave?" Lucy asked.

"Isn't it the truth?" I fidgeted.

Suddenly Lucy sounded hurt. "Trust, I thought you would help," she cried. "Here I am pouring my heart out to you and all you can do is keep staring at that bush?!" She reached up and brushed her tears away indignantly.

She was making a scene. People all over the restaurant were starting to notice.

I panicked, not wanting Grace to see me here with Lucy.

I quickly slipped to the other side of the bench and put my arm around her, hoping to quiet her down. But it only seemed to make things worse. She sobbed without holding back. "There, there," I said. "Shhhh . . ."

Out of the corner of my eye, I could see Grace with Doran. It didn't look like they had noticed all the hubbub. Doran was saying something with great animation. He was pulling his wallet out and fishing through it for money. He threw some of it onto the table and the two of them stood up to go.

Lucy pressed her palms against her eyes and continued to unravel. I leaned my head in close and tried to calm her. At the same time, I tracked Grace with the corner of my eye like a laser beam as she and Doran reached the exit. Doran pulled open the door for her. Somehow, they had not yet noticed me and Lucy. It seemed like the whole rest of the restaurant was staring in our direction. But as Grace started to step out into the night, Lucy wailed. Like a spigot with a busted nozzle, she bubbled forth with force and volume.

Grace paused.

She turned slowly, her green eyes locking onto my blue. She saw me sitting there with my arm around Lucy and my head on her shoulder, looking as if I had just been caught with both my hands deep in some grand cookie jar that the heavens themselves had forbidden me to snack from.

Grace's eyes darkened as if in mourning. I tried to tell her that this wasn't what she thought, but the words didn't come. Doran noticed us too. He shook his head and pulled Grace from the building as if he were a cop removing her from some gruesome crime scene.

The doors swung shut. Grace was gone.

I thought about running after them, but I was worried about leaving my heart on the floor where it was now lying. Plus, Lucy was really in distress. I couldn't just leave her there alone. I weakly smiled at her, trying hard to appear put together.

"I'm sorry," I said. "I know you're going through a lot. I'm sorry I wasn't listening."

She waved it away, embarrassed over everything she had been through.

"I'll be all right," she said bravely. "It's not your fault my life's a wreck."

I asked our waiter for a to-go box, and helped Lucy out to her car. It took some effort, seeing how I wasn't exactly in any wonderful emotional state myself. When we reached my house, Lucy insisted she would be all right, so I got out.

She drove off slowly.

I watched out my window until 1:30 in the morning, but Grace never came home. It was obvious to me that catching me with Lucy had persuaded her to give even more serious consideration to Doran. It seemed like a good time to take up swearing. But since there was no one around to swear to, I resisted the temptation and fell into a restless sleep instead.

## 74

# Assume

December 10th

I woke up early the next morning. I wanted to make sure that there was no way I could miss Grace coming out of Wendy's house. Giving little thought to personal appearance, I ran downstairs in my shorts and T-shirt. I went out front and sat on the porch, watching and willing Grace to emerge. My powers were weak. Actually, pathetic was a far better description. Instead of Grace emerging, I conjured up Doran walking down the street. He cut across our December lawn and stepped boldly up to me, claiming that he had something important to ask me. I would have responded with a few questions of my own, but as if it had been previously orchestrated, Grace stepped out of Wendy's front door and walked across the yard to join us. She looked radiant in the morning light, but her eyes were still dark. I wanted to feel for her, but my own insides were rapidly bruising.

"Grace, I . . ." I started to explain.

"Trust," she interrupted, "I need to tell you something before I go to work." Whatever it was, it was obvious that she wouldn't be comfortable saying it.

"Doran," Grace greeted him.

"Grace," he replied sweetly, "I'm glad you're here, seeing how what I came to say involves you and all."

This was it, and what a way to go. They had both come to break my heart in stereo. Grace took a deep breath as if she were about to dive into a deep pool when Lucy's bright red car distracted us all by pulling into my driveway.

"Is that Lucy?" Grace asked.

"I think so," I replied, as if it could possibly be someone else.

Lucy stepped out of her car and walked up to the three of us.

"Hello, Grace," she offered.

"Lucy," Grace replied back.

"Hello," Doran said, offering his hand to Lucy. "I'm Doran."

"Nice to meet you." She smiled.

"So, now everybody knows each other," I tried to joke. They all just stared at me like I was out of place. It could have been my outfit, seeing how they all were dressed nicely and I looked like someone who had just rolled out of a dirty clothes hamper.

"So what are we all doing here?" I asked.

"Don't you remember?" Lucy sighed. "We sort of had a date."

"A date?" Grace asked.

"Well, not a . . ." Lucy began to explain.

"Actually, Trust," Doran interrupted, "I feel I should speak my piece and get it over with."

I shrugged, not sure if I really wanted to hear what he had to say.

"You see, last night—"

"Maybe I should speak first," Grace interrupted, touching Doran's arm.

Doran consented.

"I can come back later if you want me to," Lucy said, sensing that she might not be welcome.

"That's all right," Grace said with a tinge of jealously. "I don't want to ruin your early-morning date."

"Really, it's not a date, it's—"

"So, you two are seriously dating?" Doran asked Lucy, finally catching on.

"No." Lucy hesitated. "We . . ."

"That makes no difference." Doran stood tall. "I have a couple things to say, and I'd best say them quickly."

"Maybe Lucy should speak first," Grace considered.

"I'm all right," Lucy insisted.

"I'd agree with you there," Doran complimented her.

"Thanks." Lucy blushed as if she meant it.

"I really do need to get to work," Grace pointed out, hoping to speed things along and acting more bothered than I had ever seen her.

"What I aim to say," Doran spoke, "is that Grace and I . . . well . . . as you both know, we spent a little time together last night. And I wanted to let you know—"

"Listen," I said, holding up my hands, not wanting to hear what was coming. "I think that Grace and I should talk first. Alone."

"Really?" Grace's eyes grew brighter. "What about?"

"Trust," Lucy interjected uncomfortably. "We can meet up later," she said, taking a step back.

"I didn't know you were dating other people," Grace said, ignoring Lucy and focusing in on me.

"I'm not, I . . . what about you and Doran?" I helplessly flared. "I saw you two sitting there last night, laughing—*sharing breadsticks.*"

"The electricity went out at the chapel," Grace explained. "Sister Barns snipped the main wire while trying to find a way to dim the lights."

"Still," I defended. "Splitting breadsticks?"

"It was the last one," Doran explained.

"Besides," Grace simmered, "what were you two doing there?"

"Oh, no," I said. "You can't turn this around on me. Lucy lured me there. I can't help it if she wants us to get back together."

"Get back together?" Lucy fumed.

"There's no need pretending," I insisted.

"Who's pretending?" Lucy snipped. "I just wanted a blessing."

"What?" I asked. "What did you say?" Her words sounded so out of context that I almost didn't understand them.

"You told me you would give me a blessing this morning before I went looking for a job," she said in disbelief.

"I did?"

"I knew you weren't listening," Lucy complained, her emotions surfacing again.

Everyone glared at me.

"Well, what about this big marriage news that Doran has?" I tried desperately to change the subject. "Or the fact that you never came home last night, huh? What about that?"

"Me?" Grace asked.

"Yes, you. When I fell asleep at 1:30, you still weren't there."

"I must have gotten back before you did," Grace said in disbelief. "I went to bed early."

"Well," I tried, "that sure is convenient."

"Trust," Grace said kindly, her eyes now open to the reality of what a big misunderstanding this was. She smiled and once again said, "Trust."

"So what's Doran's big news then?" I said, making a last-ditch effort to take the focus off of me.

"I just wanted to apologize," Doran said. "I don't want to marry Grace any longer. We set things straight last night, and I now know that she and I can never be. I was hoping you'd forgive me for everything I've done."

"Uh . . . sure." I tried to be gracious.

It was too little too late.

"I'll be leaving town in a few days," Doran added. "I hope I haven't ruined everything for you guys."

Doran nodded and turned. He had said all he was going to. He walked across our brown lawn and off down the street. I watched him for a moment and couldn't help noticing that without his truck he looked like a fish out of water.

"Maybe I'll talk to you later, Trust," Lucy said, placing great emphasis on the word "maybe." She didn't wait around for me to apologize or say anything else. She got into her car and drove away, leaving Grace and me alone on the porch.

"So I guess I sort of blew it," I sighed.

"Yeah, you could say that."

"You think you'll ever be able to forgive me?"

"I'll work on it," she said. Then she added, "Marry Doran?" trying not to laugh.

"Well," I defended, "you thought I was capable of dating Lucy."

"You used to date her all the time," Grace pointed out.

"Well, Doran looks a little like Leo back in Thelma's Way. And everyone used to think that you liked Leo and all. And I just . . ." I stopped speaking before I said anything else stupid.

Grace smiled, more with her mouth than her eyes. "Trust, we've been through a lot together. How could you even think that there could be someone else for me?"

"I don't know," I said lamely. "You've surprised me before."

"When?" Grace insisted.

"Taking Noah's side."

"Just because I think you don't understand him doesn't mean I care for him any more than as an employer."

"Really?"

"Really."

"Sorry," I offered. "About everything," I added.

"I should be really, really mad at you," Grace pointed out.

"So are you?"

"Only if it means we get to make up in a spectacular way."

"What you see is what you get," I said, holding my arms out.

"Let me get back to you on that." Grace smiled again, more with her eyes than with her mouth.

Was it any wonder I loved her?

75

# One Wish

Sister Watson's home was packed. Everyone crammed to get in and get in place. It had been only an hour or so ago that Sister Watson had noticed Roger stirring. News of his possible coming to whipped though the meadow at breakneck speed. Everyone came bearing gifts and bulk food. President Heck occupied the best seat in the house—a folding chair pulled right up to the bed. Everyone else was forced to stand and huddle over. Ricky Heck took Roger's hand in his and stroked it.

"Are you there?" he asked quietly.

Once again Roger stirred, and it looked as if he were making an attempt to open his eyes. It took every ounce of self-mastery that the town was capable of mustering to simply not cheer.

"Roger, it's Ricky," President Heck said. "You're here in Thelma's Way. Do you remember us, Roger?"

A shallow and barely audible "Yes" escaped from his lips like a ghost of good things present.

The entire house emotionally and collectively *hurrahed.* The very foundation that everyone was standing on expanded and contracted in one giant and joyous sigh. No one cared about being on the front of a book at the moment. All anybody felt was happiness over their friend having held on to life.

President Heck held Roger's hand to his face and cried.

It was a great day.

76

# I Think We're Falling

December 13th

Monday morning I sent Grace flowers and begged her to forgive me for doubting her. I even asked her forgiveness concerning Noah Taylor—for falsely accusing him. She was willing to accept the flowers with the condition that I would not bother him again.

I sort of promised that I wouldn't.

Monday night after work, Grace and I went to hear the tri-ward choir concert being held at the Southdale community amphitheater. All three wards had practiced separately and were now coming together in what would be a beautiful "pre-Christmas, bring your nonmember friends, missionary and goodwill, family home evening program" (at least that's how the flyers had described it).

Unfortunately, before the first note was sung, problems had surfaced. The three wards began squabbling over who would get the center section and who would be stuck singing from the less-prestigious wings. They ended up drawing straws to solve that one. Our ward drew the long straw and won themselves the center spot. Then they all became concerned about who would direct whom. The solution to this was to have one director facing each individual ward choir. Three directors, one voice. Brother Stablin, our ward chorister, took his place in front of the group.

Brother Stablin had been directing our choir since before I could remember. He was a thick man with flowing white hair growing from both his head and his ears. He had flaming blue eyes and a belly that his belt had a hard time confining. Often he would pull his trousers up over his belly, only to have them work their way down until his stomach sprang in release. He taught physics at the university here in Southdale and took the position of choir director very seriously.

Grace and I spread out a blanket on the ground in front of the open-air theater. It wasn't cold enough to warrant jackets, so I just had on a heavy shirt and Grace was wearing a hooded sweatshirt. She looked like a casual Eskimo with her hood pulled up around her face—her hair spilling out like red grass from an Easter basket. We had brought Margaret and Abel with us, but they ran off to be with friends as soon as we arrived. My mother was supposed to be singing with the choir, but she was not in the mood to do anything festive. I worried about leaving her home alone anymore because her depression was getting worse. We had not heard anything from my dad in weeks. I was worried, but for some reason I felt certain he was all right, and would be coming back soon. I hoped it wasn't just that I had seen too many Christmas specials on TV.

Grace scooted up next to me as we watched the three ward choirs bunch up together in preparation for the show to begin. All those singing tonight had been instructed on what to wear. The men were to wear dark green sweaters, and the women were in red. Two notes into the first song, however, I noticed that nobody had given any thought to where certain people would be standing. Thanks to the way everyone had ended up on the risers, the women's red sweaters spelled out a big red minor swear word—a word that could have been used to describe their performances so far. The moment after I noticed the sweater message, Grace did also.

"Do you see what I see?" she asked festively.

"I do," I replied, trying to appear disgusted by it.

The expletive looked huge, and perfectly arranged. It could not have been clearer if they had tried.

"Should we say something to someone?" Grace asked, giggling.

"And ruin the performance?" I scoffed.

Margaret came up to Grace and me with a couple of her friends.

"Trust, can we borrow some money?" she asked. "We want to get something to drink at the concession stand."

"I'm broke," I told her, stretching my legs out on the blanket.

"I've got a few dollars," Grace volunteered. "Mind if I come along?"

Margaret gave the fifteen-year-old "yes" nod. Grace stood up, leaving me alone. I listened to the music for a few minutes, closing my eyes to get a stronger effect, and to block out the hidden message of their wardrobes.

"Nice night, isn't it?" a voice said from above me.

I looked up to see Leonard's big head eclipsing the moon.

"Should I be concerned that you always know where I am?" I asked.

"I think 'comforted' is a better word."

I thought so too, but unfortunately that's not how I felt. Leonard had on a long-sleeved shirt and ball cap. And for some reason both his hands were tucked into a muff that was strapped around his neck and hanging at waist level. He saw me look crookedly at his muff.

"If you're going to make fun of the muff, I'm leaving," Leonard said as if he had already experienced his fill of muff jokes tonight.

"I didn't know they still made them" was all I said.

"They don't." Leonard sat. "I made this myself out of big and tall socks and a bungee cord."

"Impressive."

"Keeps the hands warm," he explained. "Plus, it's a lot cooler than those goofy-looking fanny packs."

That was an issue for debate.

"So, what are you doing here anyway?" I asked.

"I came to see the show."

"Can you read the message they wrote out for you with their sweaters?"

Leonard squinted. "Crab?" he said. "I bet the final number has something to do with the ocean," he reasoned.

"That's a *p*," I pointed out.

"Oh," Leonard realized, "it seems mighty unChristmaslike." Then he sat down and lay back on our blanket.

"You know, Grace will be here in a moment. She'll see you're not in your dome."

"All right," Leonard whined, sitting up. "I'm leaving. Before I go, however, I was wondering if you drove here tonight?"

"I did," I answered. "Do you need a ride?"

"Actually," he smiled, pulling a small bottle of something out of his muff. "I had a product I wanted to show you."

"Leonard."

"It cleans your car without any water," he said excitedly. "You just smear some of this all over your vehicle and then brush it off."

"I appreciate it, Leonard, but I'm going to pass."

"It's your future."

"I'm glad you see it that way."

"I'll tell you what, though," Leonard tried again. "I'm walking in on the ground floor of this one. Do you want to know how much money I deposited yesterday just from selling this product?"

"I don't suppose I can stop you from telling me."

Leonard ignored me, pulling a pen and a piece of paper out of his muff.

"I'm going to write down a figure here," he said, biting his tongue as he did so. He then handed me the paper.

"Fifteen hundred dollars?" I read.

Leonard just smiled.

"You made fifteen hundred dollars on this stuff?"

"Well, not actually, but if I sign you and four other people up before January, I'll be eligible to win a two-day cruise to Alaska."

"So you didn't make fifteen hundred."

"That's just an example, Trust."

"An example of what?"

"I didn't come here to be made fun of," Leonard said, adjusting his muff.

"Sorry, Leonard," I said, laughing.

"So I guess things are going all right with you and Grace?"

"I think so."

"I hear your father's still gone," Leonard said casually.

"He is."

"I know I'm not exactly the first person people turn to for help," he said, blushing shyly, "but if I can do anything for you . . ."

"Thanks," I replied, surprised by the offer.

"You guys got enough food?"

"We're fine."

"Well, let me know."

Before I could say "thanks" again Leonard was gone and Grace was approaching. She sat down in front of me so that I could wrap my arms around her. I pulled her hood down around her neck so as to let loose her red hair. I kissed her on the ear and whispered something about liking her.

I could hear her smile.

The choir began singing some somber, reverent song that I didn't recognize. A few bars into it, however, the three directors fell out of sync. By the time the song was really going it was as if they were singing it in a round. It was like a sacred "Row, Row, Row Your Boat." The pianist was desperately trying to keep up with one of the directors, but eventually the task became impossible and she stopped playing altogether. The choir continued to sing three rounds of what was supposed to be a very somber and peaceful piece.

I noticed Sister Johnson from the ward sitting six blankets in front of us. She seemed to be enjoying the music until her bad eyes focused in on the word that the choir's sweaters spelled out. She frantically tried to cover her kids' peepers. Then I watched as she instructed her husband to do something about it. He argued with her a little and then got up and wandered down to the stage. I saw him whisper something to a woman standing on the side with a clipboard. The woman stepped back a few steps and read for herself. She gasped and then in a frenzy tried to sneak on stage to rearrange the sweaters. The choir members were already confused by the round they were singing, and now this woman was tugging madly on selected members and making them move to different spots.

The lady with the clipboard quickly finished shifting them. They now spelled "crud." Brother Johnson returned to his wife. She nodded over a job well done, taking her hands off of her children's eyes.

Grace bent her head back and kissed me on the underside of my chin—the only spot she could get to from her position.

"What was that for?" I asked.

"I was just making sure you were still there."

"Wouldn't dream of leaving," I said, sounding sappy. I pulled Grace closer as the choir began to sing "Jingle Bells."

"You know, Christmas is only thirteen days away."

"I thought there'd be no Christmas," I joked. "Seeing how the world will end on the seventeenth."

"Noah's not saying it will end, just be disrupted."

"And do you believe him?" I asked.

"No." Grace smiled.

I pushed Grace's hair to the side and kissed her on the nape of the neck. I could feel her respond warmly. I lifted my head to see her amazing profile. Her eyes were softly closed, as if she were soaking in everything that was transpiring around her. I kissed her ear and whispered something about it being such a nice night.

"Mmmmhuumm" was her only response.

The choir finished "Jingle Bells" and tore into "Here We Come A-Caroling." Halfway through the song, however, it became obvious that the choir was now facing a new dilemma. With the reshuffling of members to correct the sweaters, somehow all of the heavier singers had ended up on the back row of the risers. Now whenever those in the front row would lean back, the entire set of bleachers would tilt, lifting a couple of inches off the ground. The singers didn't quite understand what was going on, thinking that it was simply their beautiful voices making the earth move. Unfortunately, the next song was a fast-paced, get-into-it number. The singers all smiled and swayed. Then in one fluid motion, the whole group leaned back. The risers rose. The entire choir flew backwards, men and women falling on top of and over each other.

The congregation went wild.

Well, as wild as a choir congregation could. The concert was temporarily postponed while cuts and bruises were attended to. The singers also took this time to remove their sweaters, seeing how it wasn't cold enough for them anyway.

By the time they began singing again, Grace and I were long gone.

77

# Grainy Days and Tuesdays Always Get Me Down

December 14th

Tuesday evening Grace went with my mother and Wendy to enrichment meeting at the chapel. I made myself some dinner and waited impatiently out on the porch swing for them to return. It was a nice night. High above me the sky was clear, and the pinpoint bodies of a million stars were pulsating in the hard black.

But by 9:00 Grace still had not returned home. I found myself counting headlights as they passed, teasing me with their flashy beams. At 9:30 I went in and lay on my bed. The mattress was soft and warm, and I wondered why I hadn't been waiting there all along.

I let my mind wander over the things in my life. Not the least of which was that I was contemplating asking Grace to marry me. We both knew it was coming, and I couldn't think of a single reason to make it later instead of sooner. I felt very sure of who, and how wonderful, she was. Part of me wanted to wait until she had some schooling. But another part of me thought getting hitched before the semester began was a better idea. My mind buzzed as I considered the possibilities. But I grew sleepy and dozed off before Grace had returned.

Sometime a little while later I felt hands brush against my face.

"Mmmmm," I said, imagining that it was her.

My imagination could not have been more off.

"Save it for Grace, Trust," Leonard said, slapping a piece of duct tape over my mouth just as I opened my eyes. I tried pulling away, but my wrists and legs were taped together. "Sorry about this," Leonard apologized. "But believe me, it's for your own good."

Leonard tried to lift me out of my bed, but I was too big for him. He pulled a piece of rope from his bag and tied it around my ankles. Then he yanked me off the bed and dragged me out of my room and down the hallway. For a man that was so much smaller than I was, he was amazingly strong. I struggled to break loose.

"Maaaaaaahhhhhhh!" I tried hollering.

"Shhhhh," Leonard whispered. "You'll wake your family."

I couldn't help thinking that was the idea, but it didn't work.

Leonard kept dragging. He approached the steps leading down and didn't slow his pace one bit. With big strides, he hurried me down the steps, the back of my head whacking against each corner. By the time we reached the wood floor at the bottom, I was seeing stars. Leonard noticed Abel's skateboard. He rolled me up onto it and pulled me out the front door and over to his car, my head dragging against the side-walk. With a huge heave he shoved me into the backseat of his car and slammed the door. He got in and we drove away. I struggled like mad, willing him to stop and remove the tape from my mouth. I had a few words I wanted to say to him. Eventually he pulled over and turned around to face me. He reached back and yanked the tape off my mouth.

I wouldn't need to shave again for a year.

"What's going on?" I demanded.

"I needed to talk to you," he said importantly.

"You could have just called, or rang the doorbell, or thrown pebbles against my window," I said out of frustration. "I think those stairs gave me another concussion."

"I did throw a rock at your window," Leonard insisted. "But I guess I was tossing it at the wrong room."

"What room?"

"A room in the wrong house," he added.

"Leonard," I said, shaking my head.

"I didn't know glass could shatter into so many pieces," he contemplated, pulling a pocketknife out of his glove box and cutting the tape around my wrists.

"So, what's so important?" I asked, wondering if he had yanked me out of bed simply to pitch another product to me.

"I got something on Noah."

"Oh, no," I waved him back. "I'm done messing with Noah. I've learned my lesson. I'm not making another fool of myself."

"This is different," Leonard insisted. "You remember Sam the cop who was married to my sister Tina?"

"Yes," I replied.

"Well, I had him run a background check on Noah Taylor. And guess what he found?"

"I have no idea."

"Well, he didn't find anything exactly, but he discovered a Noah Talmage that had prepared a town in Maine for a coming hurricane he had predicted."

"Noah Talmage?"

"No, do you?"

"Leonard."

"What?"

"Anyhow," I prompted.

"Anyhow, this Noah got everyone prepared and then the warehouse burned down. It appeared to be an accident, but after Noah collected the insurance money, he disappeared. The case is still open in Maine."

"And you think that Noah is our Noah?"

"Could be."

"What did Sam say?" I asked.

"He told me I was watching far too many mystery shows, and to please not bother him at work. So what are we going to do?" Leonard asked.

"Nothing," I said adamantly, unwrapping the duct tape from my ankles.

"Nothing?"

"There is no way that anyone would listen to a word I said," I reminded him. "My credibility is pretty pathetic at the moment."

"I'd listen to you, Trust," Leonard said seriously, reaching over the back seat and putting his hand on my shoulder.

"Thanks," I joked. "But the only way I'm going to believe any of this is if I wake up one morning and the warehouse on Frost is burned to the ground."

"I just feel real bad about Brother McLaughlin," Leonard said.

"All right, Leonard," I bit. "What are you talking about?"

"Well," he said with new excitement, "at this warehouse fire in Maine, the security guard got hurt real bad."

"How?"

"Seems the electricity was off, and the guard lit one of those hundred-hour candles to find the fuse box and *kabamo.* All the gas that was stored in there with the food and supplies went up in flames. The guard was wounded, and blamed for it all."

"That's awful," I said.

"Yeah," Leonard replied coolly. "But I guess there's nothing we can do."

"What do you have in mind?" I asked in defeat, beginning to wonder if there really might be some connection between our Noah and this fire in Maine.

"I say we arm ourselves with weapons and hold the warehouse hostage until Noah clears out of town."

"Any real suggestions?"

"We could knock out a couple of the city's power grids," Leonard schemed. "Then, in the dead of night, steal everyone's car keys so that no one will be able to drive. Once that is accomplished. . . ."

I shook my head.

"Too complicated?" Leonard asked.

"Just a little."

"I'm tapped out as far as ideas," Leonard said, as if I'd be disappointed in him.

"I thought you had already run a check on Noah?" I asked, remembering my conversation with Leonard. "You said he was clean."

"I had spelled Noah wrong when doing my search on the Internet," Leonard said, embarrassed. "Turns out I was getting personal information on some other guy."

I sighed in defeat.

"I'll tell you what," I offered. "Let's just drive over to Noah's place and tell him what we know. If it's true, he's sure to get spooked and leave town. If it's not, well then, he'll throw us out, and we can go home and get some sleep. Does that sound okay?"

"You realize it's 12:30?" Leonard pointed out.

"So *he* loses a little sleep for a change," I said callously. "If what you say is true, we need to know now."

We drove over to the edge of town and back into the Dintmore Hills. I knew Noah was renting a farmhouse in the hills, but I had no idea where it was. Luckily, Leonard had a small hand-drawn map that he had sketched out a few days ago after secretly following Noah home. When we were close enough, we flipped off our headlights and crept over the small crest in front of Noah's temporary house in the dark. At about two hundred feet away, Leonard stopped the car and shut it off. In the clear night I could easily see the outline of the house and barn next to it. It was a nice-sized home, with a huge square barn sitting no more that fifty feet away. Next to the barn were what looked to be a couple of old grain silos. They stood next to each other, one significantly taller than the other, looking like giant batteries with their weathered tops eroding and gone. A tiny porch light was on at the house. It was a small light, little more than a decoration, but in the moonlight, I could see Noah's tiny white car parked out front. He was home. With any luck he would still be up.

I hesitated, both mentally and physically.

I knew that Noah was capable of lying and deception. But insurance fraud and arson really didn't suit his sweater-wearing charms. The last thing I wanted to do was walk in there and accuse him again, only to have him blab to Grace about what a complete idiot she had for a boyfriend, or ex-boyfriend if he chose to put it that way.

"Go on," Leonard prompted.

"I don't know," I stalled. "Besides, aren't you coming with me?"

"And blow my whole dome thing?" Leonard asked incredulously. "Besides, from what you've told me, Noah seems to talk a whole lot different when it's just you and him."

"I need a witness, though."

Leonard looked hard at the house in front of us.

"I'll tell you what," he whispered, forgetting that there wasn't another hearing ear within two hundred feet of us. "I'll slip into that barn and hide. You see if you can talk Noah into having your conversation in there."

"How am I going to do that?"

"That's up to you," Leonard said. "But if you can get him to talk in there, I can witness everything that's said. Plus if he goes ballistic on you, I can let the cops know what happened afterward."

"Thanks for the comfort," I said.

Leonard quietly got out of the car and crept across the field and up to the barn. The barn was old enough that getting in presented no problem. After a few moments, I said a quick prayer and drove the rest of the way up to the doorstep. I got out and looked down at my wrinkled clothes. I was thankful that I had fallen asleep dressed.

I walked to the front door, the dry ground shifting under my feet like sheets of paper. I could hear a TV or radio on inside. I readied myself and knocked.

Thirty seconds later I was staring into the uncertain face of Noah.

"Trust," he said uneasily. "What are you doing here this late?"

"I wanted to talk to you," I said.

"Well, I do have a phone," he snipped. "Why don't you just run on home and call me in the morning?"

"Actually, it's about Maine," I threw out, wondering if he would bite.

He flinched ever so slightly. My heart began beating faster.

"What about Maine?" Noah feigned disinterest, looking over my shoulder to see if anyone else was around.

"We're alone," I said.

"You came out here by yourself?"

"Do I have reason to be afraid?" I asked him.

"No, of course not."

"Well then, could we just talk a moment?"

"Maybe we should," Noah conceded. "Why don't you come inside."

"Actually, I was hoping we could talk out here."

"And why is that?"

"Well . . ." I had no idea what to say. My mind whipped wildly as my thoughts fought to align themselves. The best I could come up with was, "My grandmother died in a farmhouse like this one."

"Really?"

"Yeah," I said, knowing I had no choice but to complete the lie. "It was awful," I mournfully explained. "Somehow one of the old walls collapsed, and, well . . . well, she and I were really close."

"What's going on here, Trust?" Noah asked, obviously not buying my story.

"Nothing," I insisted. "I'd just rather talk out here."

"It's so windy," Noah said, informing me of something I already knew quite well and falling right into the conversational trap that I had so brilliantly been weaving.

I looked around and acted as if I was just noticing the barn for the first time. "We could go in there," I suggested.

"You're okay with barns?" he questioned.

"Sure," I shrugged. "My grandmother loved barns."

"I don't exactly know what you're trying to pull, Trust, but I'll play along for fun," Noah said snidely. "Just let me grab a sweater."

"Of course." I smiled.

A few moments later Noah stepped outside. We walked over to the barn, both of us keeping our distance from each other. We went in the same door I had seen Leonard go through moments before. Once inside, the sound of wind died down and the night seemed to become even emptier around us. My forehead hit against a small hanging object. I pulled on it and light flooded the room. I hoped Leonard was well-hidden.

"So is this all right now?" Noah asked.

"This is fine."

"Well then, speak your piece and get on with it," he demanded.

"Listen," I said, trying to start the discussion on a good note. "I know you and I have not exactly gotten along, but I didn't come here to make any more trouble than I have to."

"I'm not afraid of you, Trust," he snipped. "Say what's on your mind."

"All right," I sighed. "Have you ever done one of these emergency preparation operations in Maine?"

"And what if I have?" He grimaced.

"Well, does the name Noah Talmage sound familiar?"

I had asked the question in a nice enough way. But I guess Noah felt differently. He pulled a gun out from under his sweater and motioned with it for me to put my hands up.

"What are you doing?" I asked in alarm.

"You're a real thorn, Trust," he said. "I took you for smarter than this. And let's just say, I knew you were no genius."

"So that *was* you in Maine?" I said, amazed.

"I'm not going to answer a single one of your stupid questions."

"Listen, Noah, I don't care what you did in Maine, really. Just don't do it here."

"You act as if you have some control over the situation."

"This can be worked out," I reasoned.

"Actually, I'm doubting it can," Noah sneered. "You know, I've never shot anyone before. Then again, I suppose you've never been shot before. Huh . . . I guess there's a first time for everything."

I was just about to make a break for it when I noticed Leonard up on one of the haylofts behind Noah's back. He crept into position as if to jump down on top of him.

I tried to stall. "Really, Noah? I'd guess a guy like you had killed dozens of people."

"You think you've got me all figured out, don't you?" Noah asked. "Well, you're wrong. You've been wrong from the start. And anyway, it doesn't matter now. You know, Trust? Maybe after you turn up missing, I'll go over and comfort Grace. She really is a nice girl. You were right about that." The words were like grease dripping from his lips. "I know I was shooting my mouth off about the babes in Tahiti, but there's just something about that Grace."

Noah licked his lips and smiled.

"I'll have to make sure and spend a little time with her before I leave town."

"Don't make me sick," I spat.

"I'll make you more than sick," Noah laughed. "I'll make you dead . . ."

From the top of my eye I saw Leonard leap off from his perch. He seemed to hover in the air for a moment before plummeting down. I guess he was planning to land on Noah, but unfortunately he missed completely. He smacked against the dirt floor two feet away. But the commotion was enough to distract Noah, and in that split second, I threw myself into him, pushing up his arm. The gun fired into the barn ceiling as the two of us fell backwards into a mound of moldy hay.

Leonard grabbed a loose board lying on the ground and swung it wildly toward Noah's head. It would have been helpful had he hit Noah instead of me. The already bruised and swollen back of my head throbbed with pain. I rolled off of Noah and into Leonard's legs. My momentum threw Leonard off balance, flipping him forward into Noah. I blinked my eyes, trying to remain conscious. When my double vision finally became one again, I saw Leonard struggling with Noah on the ground, the gun lying in the dirt about three feet beyond them both. I started crawling for the gun. Noah kicked Leonard free, sending him flying into a large wood beam that was supporting the upper loft. Leonard's eyes almost burst from the impact of it. He slid to the ground in a lifeless lump.

"Leonard," I yelled, taking my eyes off the gun.

Noah began scrambling for it, pulling my focus back. Both of us got to the gun at the same time. I reached out and Noah bit my arm. Then he tried to scratch my eyes. I was not at all surprised he fought like a little girl. I fell onto him again and we rolled about, trying to gain possession of the gun. Finally I got a good enough hold on it to be able to toss it up into the air and away from the two of us. It flew into the hayloft.

Noah dug his knee into my chest and pushed my face down as he fought to get up. I let him, only to grab his ankle as he jumped onto the ladder leading up to the loft. He kicked like a mule on fire, the back of his shoe clipping me in the face. I stumbled backwards as he made it the rest of the way up the ladder. I felt the blood on my face. With new resolve, I jumped to the middle of the ladder and pulled myself onto the loft. I stood up and realized that we were higher up than I had expected. Noah was digging through the hay like a madman. But it was no use—the gun was gone. I walked up behind him.

"You'll never find it," I said, wiping my bloody mouth with the back of my hand.

Then he did what I considered to be a rather thoughtful thing. He turned toward me just enough so that I was able to connect a strong punch to his jaw. He stumbled back, trying to catch himself. As he got his bearings, he looked around in a panic for some sort of exit. There was none. The ladder leading down was behind me, and I was blocking him from the edge of the loft. He glanced over at what looked to be a grain chute on the wall behind him.

"Give it up, Noah," I said, exhausted.

"I never should have spoken to you," he said hatefully. "This is my fault. I knew you were a moron, so I thought I'd have a little fun with you."

"You mean this isn't fun?" I joked.

"You really are a piece of work," Noah said. "Grace talks about you like you're something great. She's just as dumb as you are."

"Excuse me?"

"She's as stupid and deluded as you are, Trust," he said childishly.

Silly me, I had thought I was through hitting Noah—I ran to him and slammed him against the wall. He rolled out of my grasp. The entire barn seemed to moan and wobble. He grabbed the edge of the grain chute and pulled himself down into it. I could hear him banging around as he slid his way down. I should have just let him be, but I didn't want to risk him getting away. I took a big breath as if I were diving underwater and jumped in after him.

The grain chute was about ten feet long and connected to one of the silos I had seen earlier. It was rusted and weathered, but I still fell through it at a pretty good speed. I flew out the end of it and down into the empty silo. My hands hit first as I rolled into the ground and up against the inside wall. I felt around for anything broken. I seemed to still be latched together. I quickly glanced around the silo floor for any sign of Noah. The moon outside was just bright enough that I could see. Noah wasn't there. I pulled myself up and tried to open the door leading out. It was sealed shut. I thought for a moment that Noah had made it out and locked me in. I felt panic flush through me until I looked up and saw his dark form hanging upside down from a rope near the opening of the chute. It appeared his leg had gotten caught in it as he flew out. He was wiggling around trying to disengage himself. I followed the rope with my eyes up from Noah's leg to where it was hooked to a little door high up on the silo wall. I could see through the eroded roof that the little door fronted a chute from the other, taller silo next door.

"Help me down," Noah pleaded.

"How?" I asked. "I can't reach you."

Noah flipped and turned as he dangled up above me. The rope slipped a notch, becoming completely taut and tugging hard against the little trapdoor.

"Maybe you shouldn't be moving around so much," I hollered. "There could be something behind that little door."

"So what?" Noah yelled. "Get me down!"

I tried the latch on the lower door again, knowing it was no use. Noah swung his upper body up to grab hold of his ankle. It was that move that did us in. The rope jerked, pulling the door above us open. Grain doused us like a weighty waterfall, the pressure of it knocking Noah out of the rope and pushing him down to the floor by me. I fought desperately to keep the stuff off of me. It was no use. In a matter of moments we were waist-deep in wheat.

I frantically began to bail, scooping grain away from me with my hands as more rained down. It was a lesson in futility. There was no place else for the grain to go. The flow of wheat surged, suddenly burying us up to our shoulders. I thought about trying to get my arms up before it was too late.

It was too late.

The wheat packed around us, binding my arms to my side so tightly I could scarcely wiggle my fingers. We were strapped in for the long haul. I tried to move my legs but the weight of the wheat was crushing. I prepared myself for suffocation, certain we were going to die. Wheat flew around my head like bursting fireworks. It was in my hair, in my ears, and rising over my shoulders and up my neck. I kept my mouth shut, desperate not to breathe in the dirty grain. The wheat was inching up right below my nose when suddenly the flow from above miraculously stopped. I wiggled my head and tried to pull my arms out. I couldn't do it. Wind dipped down into the open-topped silo and seemed to suck the dust from the old grain up into the night. I opened my eyes expecting to see long-dead relatives waiting to greet me. There was no one there except for the top half of Noah's head. I assumed I was still alive, though just barely.

Noah was a couple inches shorter than I but I must have been standing lower in the silo because the level of our heads above the grain was just about equal. He spat out wheat and tried blowing it away from his mouth. I did the same, experiencing similarly weak results.

"Can you breathe?" I finally coughed, wishing away the dark.

"A little," he answered.

"Can you move?"

"I don't think so."

"Save your strength," I huffed. "Leonard will find us."

I don't think either one of us felt comforted. The wind kept reaching down into the open-capped silo and whipping around in our hair. I pushed my head back as far as I could and opened my mouth wide to breathe. I noticed a few stars through the rotted roof. I cast my eyes over at Noah and almost started to laugh. The sight of his half-head sticking above the wheat seemed so absurd and brought me a small amount of joy. I said a prayer begging God to please not let me die this way. Then I willed Leonard to find us.

A number of hours later, I felt pretty confident that neither God nor Leonard had been listening. It was almost impossible to stay awake any longer. Noah had knocked off a while earlier. I panicked for a bit, not knowing what the consequences of falling asleep like this might be. I remembered learning that if you dozed off in the freezing cold, you would never wake up. I just couldn't recall ever having discussed what to do when you were buried in wheat. So I kept myself awake by reciting anything I had ever memorized. Songs, poems, ads, the Boy Scout Oath, anything. I drifted in and out, dozing off a couple of times, but the pressure of the grain pushing up against my lungs made it impossible to breathe at moments and helped to keep me awake. The sun eventually rose on the two of us planted there like tulips. And sometime near its zenith, Noah began to stir and started sobbing.

"We're going to die in here," he moaned. The small bit of his head that was visible looked like a hairy anthill.

"Well, it's not my fault," I huffed.

"Where's Leonard?" he cried. "You said Leonard would find us."

"He hit that pole pretty hard," I reminded him. "He's probably in worse shape than we are."

"I don't think that's possible," Noah complained.

"Just hang on," I encouraged. "Someone will find us and dig us out."

"Who knew you were coming here?" Noah asked. "Anyone?"

"Just Leonard."

"We're going to die."

"Can you get your arms above the wheat?" I asked him.

"I can't even move my hands," he snapped.

I tried again myself, but with no luck. The grain had a suction-like hold on my whole body.

"This is it," Noah lamented. "Killed by food storage. How befitting."

I couldn't help chuckling. He was right.

"This could have been avoided," I sputtered, spitting wheat all the while.

"Thanks for pointing that out," Noah yapped.

"I only—"

"Just shut up," Noah said sharply. "We're going to die."

I was just about to agree with him when I heard something outside the silo. A couple of seconds later, I could distinctly feel the grain being pulled down and away from my body.

Someone had opened the lower silo door.

The wheat continued to slide out until we could see our waists again. As it lowered I saw two teenage boys standing there in the doorway. One of them had a pack of cigarettes, and they both were looking surprised. I think they were hoping to find a little solitude, not a few tons of wheat with a couple of dirty-looking bodies in it. The moment they realized we were still alive, they backed away and took off running.

"Stop!" I tried to holler. But being teenagers like they were, they didn't listen to a word I said.

I put my hands under my right knee and pulled my foot out of the grain. It came up shoeless. My body was so exhausted I could hardly stand. Noah was leaning on his hands, slowly extracting his legs as well. There was dirt and wheat clinging to almost every part of his body. I thought about tackling him so he wouldn't get away, but I was too spent. Instead, I crawled through the waist-high wheat and fell out the door onto the ground. I looked across the field and noticed that Leonard's car was gone. I just lay there for a moment, thinking how curious that was, when I drifted off into sleep.

## 78

# Tall Drink of Water

Lucy couldn't believe how nervous she was as she answered the door. Even though her father and mother would be back from their long European vacation in a little more than two weeks, Lucy had decided to call the full-time missionaries and finally get the blessing she had so desperately sought. She figured they were the perfect people to ask. They wouldn't judge her. And even if they did, they would be transferred out of Southdale before long. At this point, she didn't really care what anyone thought anyway. She only wanted some comfort for the pain and confusion she was still wading through.

Lucy opened the door and Elder Nicks and Elder Minert entered, followed by Doran Jorgensen in a denim shirt and tie.

"Three of you?" Lucy observed out loud.

"Brother Jorgensen is driving us around in his new truck," Elder Minert explained. "We were just over at the Williams' house giving Sister Williams a blessing. I guess she's not feeling too well."

"Was Trust there?" Lucy asked without thinking, still bothered by how he had reacted a few days back.

"No," Elder Nicks said, fielding the question. "Actually, they don't know where Trust is."

"I hope that you don't mind me coming along?" Doran said shyly. "I thought, since we'd already met and all . . ."

Such sincerity.

"Not a problem," Lucy replied, looking Doran up and down and recognizing something comforting and strong in the way he held himself. "I'm just thankful that you came," she replied.

"Me too," Doran said softly.

"Who would you like to give the blessing?" Elder Minert asked.

"It doesn't really matter," Lucy said, while sort of hoping it would be Doran.

The choice was made.

The blessing was given.

Lucy was comforted.

## 79

# Confined

Roger Williams yawned, causing the checkerboard that was lying across his lap to jiggle. He had been confined to his bed for some time now. And even though it was not what he would choose to be doing, the locals had done a rather nice job of keeping him entertained. Narlette put on a puppet show with some of Digby's old socks. Pete Kennedy gave him a personal gun safety course, and Leo Tip read to him from some of his favorite comic books. And now here was President Heck taking time out of his not-necessarily-busy schedule to play a game of checkers.

"I can see that," Ricky Heck joked as the board jiggled again.

"See what?"

"The old tilt and cheat," he said. "You think Roswell's never tried that on me before?"

"Have you played a lot of checkers with Roswell in bed?" Roger laughed, the color rising in his face as he did so.

"Well, not lately." Ricky scratched his head. Then he jumped Roger's playing pieces until he was victorious. He smiled wide.

"Happy?" Roger asked.

"I suppose I am," he answered. He glanced at the clock on the wall. "I better get along. Wad needed me to help him paint his shack. Can I get you anything before I go?"

"You've already done too much," Roger said.

"You sure now?"

Roger paused as if remembering something. "You know, I would like to make a phone call. Do you think you could help me over to the boardinghouse to make one sometime?"

"I'd be honored to." Ricky sort of bowed. "But the phone doesn't work. Lupert accidentally chopped down one of the phone poles thinking it would make good firewood. The phone company hasn't been able to make it out here to fix it."

"I don't suppose anyone here has a cellular phone I could use?" Roger asked.

"Is that the fancy kind without the round dial?"

"No, actually it's the one that you can carry with you and use from anywhere," Roger smiled.

"Nope, none of those. Although I bet the stake president in Virgil's Find has one. He's real progressive," Ricky stated. "I can try and get it for you if you'd like."

"I'd really appreciate it," Roger said.

"Consider it almost done." President Heck stood. "Anything else?"

"Actually, there is," Roger remembered. "You know, it won't be too much longer until I can go home. And, well, I was hoping to do a little fishing on the Girth before I leave."

"You get your legs back, and you're on." President Heck clapped. Then he left Roger alone in the spare bedroom of Sister Watson's home.

Roger sat himself up and sighed. His strength was coming back slowly. He looked over at the small nightstand and saw the blue paperback Book of Mormon that Toby had given him. He picked it up and thumbed through it. Toby had mentioned that he had highlighted a few of his favorite passages. Roger could find only two markings in the whole book. The first one was First Nephi, chapter 13, verse 22.

*And I said unto him: I know not.*

Roger wondered for a couple of minutes about what had possessed Toby to mark that certain scripture. He finally concluded that it must be some sort of personal motto. The second and only other marked verse was Helaman, chapter 4, verse 15.

*And it came to pass that they did repent, and inasmuch as they did repent they did begin to prosper.*

Roger touched the word prosper upon the page. He smiled, thinking about how wise Toby Carver really was.

## 80

# A Normal Blood Flow

December 15th

By the time I woke up, the sky was turning dusky and my body was stiff. I pulled myself up and looked around for Noah. I couldn't see him right off, and his car appeared to be gone. I walked to the farmhouse and tried the door—it was locked. I picked up a huge rock lying near the mat and heaved it through the front window. The sound of falling glass almost made me feel as if I were having fun. I knocked out the remaining shards and stepped through.

No Noah.

I looked around for his phone, but couldn't find it. His whole house appeared in disarray. Drawers were pulled open and papers were thrown about as if Noah had been in a hurry to leave. I figured he must have packed up and gotten out while he still could. Most likely he had taken his phone as well. I decided that instead of just waiting around and taking the chance that someone would come find me, I should start hiking home. I noticed a crumpled piece of clothing that had been crammed back behind the couch and left behind. I picked it up and shook it out.

It was a sweater.

I slipped it on and found a towel to tape around my shoeless foot. Once improperly prepared, I set off. By the time I walked out of the Dintmore Hills, it was pitch dark. I thought back to when Grace and I had done this same thing just a couple weeks back. I longed to have her with me. I was just not the high-caliber company that she was. I called my home from the same gas station that Grace and I had used before. My mother answered and sounded so relieved to hear my voice that I was suddenly glad to have been lost for a while. She promised to get Grace and hurry over to pick me up.

When they arrived, both of them fawned and fussed over me like I was a two-thousand-dollar hairdo after an afternoon in the wind. My mother had discovered me missing shortly after Leonard had dragged me out of my house. She called the police, but it wasn't their policy to get involved until more time had elapsed. So, my mother and Grace had done nothing but sit around and worry for the last twenty hours. Mom had even become so overwhelmed by everything that she had asked Doran and the elders to give her a blessing.

I filled them in on everything that had happened as we drove home. Both of them were absolutely blown away by how wrong they had been about Noah. Grace apologized repeatedly. She couldn't believe that her instincts had failed her. I watched her eyes gloss over as she realized how wrong she had been. It was a moving moment. She kissed me on the hand, promising there would be more once I cleaned up.

It was nice to be alive.

81

# Setting Things Right

December 16th

The day before the end of the world was a day like any other. The sky hovered, clear and open, the ground was dry, and the sun shone like a mother's face at a child's first recital.

At around noon I called Scott McLaughlin and warned him about lighting any candles over at the warehouse. He asked me why, so I told him the entire story. He was speechless. I made him promise to stay away from the warehouse until the police could have a look at it. He thanked me, still a little unsure of what to think. Then I called the police and recited the story again. I thought that they would congratulate me for making it out, for stopping Noah and revealing him to be what he really was. Instead, they insisted I come down to the station immediately so that they could question me in person.

When I got there, they asked me every possible question about Noah. I looked at pictures, filled out forms, and gave descriptions.

"About yay high and wearing a sweater," I said.

On the way home, I decided to drive over to Leonard's to make sure he was still okay and find out what had happened to him.

I pulled up to the front of the Bio-Doom and parked. He had his bay window curtain open and was inside doing exercises. I got out of my car and stepped up to the window. The second he recognized me, he became extremely animated, waving me to the side of the single-wide as if I were a winning horse coming down the final stretch. I slipped around back and crawled under the skirting and up into his kitchen. Leonard was waiting.

"Where have you been?" he said with excitement.

"That's what I was wondering about you," I responded. "The last time I saw you, you were knocked out against a pole."

"That's right," Leonard gleamed, acting as if we had both just recalled a thrilling memory. "Boy, what a night, huh?"

"So, where did you go?" I asked, frustrated.

"Well, when I came to, you weren't there. So I went down to the mall to finish up my Christmas shopping."

"You went shopping?" I asked in disbelief. "You're serious?"

"They're having some great sales." Leonard clapped his hands. "Look at this," he said, pulling a pair of snowshoes out from behind a pile of canned olives. "Got these babies at forty percent off. And how about this," he beamed, walking up to the wall and pointing to a small framed plaque. It was one of those common biblical parchments with your name and its meaning written out in calligraphy. It had the name "Leonard" written in big letters and the definition below it read: "Reorder."

"I think knowing what your name means really builds the old self-esteem, you know? Mine's not bad, is it?" He elbowed me. "Reorder. I'm sure it has something to do with the reordering of the Melchizedek Priesthood."

I didn't have the heart to tell him.

"So you didn't even wonder what had happened to Noah and me?" I asked, bringing him back to the conversation at hand.

"I figured you would work things out."

"The last you saw he was pointing a gun at me," I huffed.

"So, is he all right?" Leonard asked.

"The gun was pointing at *me.*"

"Trust, you're repeating yourself," Leonard said, acting like a second grade teacher.

"We both almost died," I argued.

"I guess we've got a lot to be thankful for."

"You could have at least called the police and sent them out to find us."

"And jeopardize my dome life?"

"This is amazing."

"So where's Noah?" he asked.

"Who knows?" I blurted out. "He took off when I slipped into a state of exhaustion. The police are looking for him now."

Leonard looked at me with renewed interest. "I should have signed him up for pre-billed legal while I had the chance. Could have saved him a bundle in law fees."

"You're selling law consultations?" I asked. "What happened to the waterless car soap?"

"Turns out people enjoy using water," Leonard said sadly. "But that's in the past. Now I'm part of a huge team of important lawyers."

I didn't want to know any more. I went back down through the hole in the linoleum and outside, leaving Leonard to sell to himself.

Late that afternoon, Grace and I snuck off together and headed down toward Southdale River. We climbed up under one of the covered bridges and spread out a blanket on the steep slope beneath it. We pulled out the few items we had brought along to eat.

"You know, this could be our last day on earth," I said coyly.

"Well, I guess that makes it no different than any other day," she replied.

I lay down on the blanket and listened to the river rushing below. Water flopped down its course like a clumsy adolescent snake. I looked up at the bridge above us as a car rolled across.

"So, I guess I was right about Noah," I said, not confident that I had yet milked it for all it was worth.

"Let's not talk about him," Grace replied, her green eyes deep and dark in the light of the afternoon.

"All right," I agreed. "Let's talk about tomorrow."

"What about it?" Grace asked.

"Well, it's the seventeenth," I reminded her.

"Did you bring me here to this secluded spot to talk about unimportant things like the end of the world?" Grace smiled. "Or was there something more pressing on your mind?"

"Well, now that you mention it."

"I didn't realize I had mentioned anything." Grace shifted in her cross-legged position, bringing her knees up next to the side of my chest. She leaned over so that her long hair dangled above my face. I could smell the ends of it teasing me. Her lovely mouth smiled in delight over the feelings she knew she was inducing.

"Do you still love me?" she asked.

"More than ever," I whispered.

Grace bent over farther and softly touched her pink lips to mine. My toes exploded like a string of firecrackers, each one setting off the next. And my fingers all detached and rolled helplessly down the river bank. I was in awe of what was happening. Visions of my childhood and every day I had lived since seemed to be rushing toward me like some great wind.

It was a hard feeling to describe, but similar to when I was seven years old and our family owned a huge Labrador retriever. I used to go out into the backyard and call for her, not knowing exactly where she was. The moment I hollered her name, she would appear, running as fast as she could and hurling her weight toward me. It used to scare me, and yet thrill me too, to see her heading straight toward me. Each time I had to steel myself against the urge to run, standing my ground and waiting for the inevitable. The fear would build until the moment when she would bowl me over, covering me with her paws and licking my face.

That was the feeling I had now. Every part of my life was speeding toward me at breakneck speed. I looked myself straight in the eye as it approached, falling on me like hail, stinging me all over, and reminding me I was alive.

I opened my eyes to see Grace looking down at me. She pulled back her hair with her left hand while touching my face with her right.

"Will you marry me?" I asked.

"Of course," she replied.

I moved up onto my elbows and kissed her. I could feel her warm breath and cool skin as she kissed me back. Her hair surrounded me like light. She pushed me nearer to the ground and then stopped to smile a knowing smile at me.

"I thought you'd never ask."

82

# Oh Buoy

December 17th

By the time I got out of bed in the morning, it had already been raining for four straight hours. I looked through the kitchen window at the now-flooded streets and sidewalks. I wondered if I shouldn't start shoveling sand bags. The rain was thick and heavy, drops slapping against the window like overripe plums.

"Can you believe it?" Margaret asked me as she came down for breakfast.

"Amazing," I smiled.

"Noah Taylor should have built us an ark," Abel joked.

"Noah Taylor should never have come," Margaret added.

"So, Trust," Abel asked with a mouth full of cereal. "When are you and Grace going to get hitched?"

I had come home the day before and told my family the good news. Everyone was excited. Even my mother seemed mildly pleased. Mom was doing better. The blessing the elders had given her a few days back had seemed to lift her spirits. She still worried night and day about my dad and touched base with the police regularly, but we all seemed to sense that whatever happened would be for the best.

"We're thinking of this spring," I answered Abel.

"I think spring is the best time to get married," Margaret said, pulling out a cereal bowl from the cabinet and taking a seat at the table.

My mother came into the kitchen looking like she had just seen a naked ghost. Her hair was a mess, and she appeared emotionally disoriented. It looked like she had had another bad night. She walked over to the table and sat down.

"Are you all right, Mom?" Abel asked.

"Your father," she said. "He called."

"Daddy called?" Margaret asked with excitement. "What did he say? When is he coming home?" My sister gushed, barely able to contain herself.

"He sounded so different," was all my mother said.

"Good different, or bad different?" I asked nervously.

"He couldn't talk long." She shook her head and started to cry. "He said he'd be home soon . . . and that he loved me."

Margaret burst out bawling, tears dropping into the bowl of cereal she had just poured—her shredded wheat getting soggy before any milk even touched it. Abel wiped his mouth with his sleeve. From my seat it looked like he had just rubbed on the world's biggest smile.

I called Grace and told her the news. She ran over as fast as she could. When she came into the kitchen, my mother hugged her even though she was now wet.

My father was coming home.

My mother was hugging Grace!

We all ate breakfast talking like we had just received free tickets to the celestial kingdom in the mail. My mom went over and over the few words my father had said to her. He said he had been hurt, and that he was fine. He told her he couldn't talk long because it wasn't his phone, but that he would be coming home as soon as he possibly could. And then he told her that he loved her more than anything in the whole world.

I had never seen my mother so happy. It made me more proud of my father than I had ever been.

I think we would have all stayed indoors, basking in our state of bliss, if it had not been for the fact that shortly after eleven o'clock, water began building up against our house and leaking through the door. Mom called over to Wendy's to see if she was doing okay with all the rain. As soon as my mother got the question out, the phones went dead. Two minutes later, Wendy was knocking on our door, begging to come in. Abel opened the door and water rushed in like loose mercury, sloshing across the floor and into every corner of the front room. I expected it to be cold on my feet, but the high temperatures had kept the rain warm. It took both Abel and me to get the door closed after Wendy came in.

"What should we do?" Wendy asked, wearing a white silk pajama top and fishing waders. "Should we make some of those sandbag things or something?"

I would have answered her, but the electricity suddenly went out, distracting us all from her question. I could see the flood level rising against our large front window as rain continued to dump down. It was too late for sandbags. Everyone ran around the house collecting things and moving them up to higher ground where they'd be safer. We all made some lame jokes about how it looked like Noah Taylor was right about the end of the world after all. But by twelve o'clock no one was laughing. Our front window gave out first, shattering inward, allowing a huge deluge of water to push into our home. Luckily, Mom had had the foresight to gather us together far from the windows before it got to that point. We climbed up on the kitchen table and chairs.

By 12:30 Margaret was genuinely scared, and Abel was asking my mom things like, "If someone stole a baseball mitt from a friend, and he didn't get a chance to return it before he died, would he go to heaven?"

Mom would have answered with a stern lecture, except I think she was too busy worrying about what to do next. She was a determined woman—determined to still be around when my father came home. He had said that he loved her.

We all moved up into the second story as the water climbed the steps at an amazing rate. Grace and I sat on the top step watching it rise toward our feet as everyone else huddled in the master bedroom looking out the window for some sign of relief.

"Can you believe this?" I said, more in awe than in anger. "I keep thinking that we should do something besides just sit here."

"I've never seen so much water," Grace replied. "What happens if it doesn't stop?"

"I suppose we get really wet," I answered, trying to keep things light.

"Your house is ruined," Grace said sorrowfully.

"I'm sure my parents have flood insurance." I *wheewed,* thinking about how nice it sounded to say "my parents" with such confidence for a change.

The water was six steps away from us.

"Should we move up?" Grace asked.

I would have replied, but it was suddenly silent. I was a little spooked by the quiet until I realized it meant the pounding rain had stopped, at least for now.

"There's some blue sky rolling in," my mother hollered, fit to burst.

Instantly the fear fled, and hope eased its way back into the room. I could hear Abel begging my mother to let him swim around the living room, and Margaret asking if we still had the air mattresses up in the attic. Suddenly everyone was all right. Our poor house was ruined, but we were thankful to be alive.

An hour later the skies were clear, and the water was at about half the level it once had been, allowing us to walk around the bottom floor of the house. I stepped outside and surveyed our street. It was like a mighty river slowly draining away. As I turned to go inside I heard someone holler from off in the distance. I looked to see Bishop Leen and his wife paddling toward us in a rowboat. They paddled up to me and he jumped out of the boat, fastening it to a tree nearby. Bishop Leen was wearing a long yellow coat and had a shortwave radio strapped to his belt.

"Are you all okay?" he asked.

"Just fine," I answered. "Can you believe this?"

"God can do some mighty works," the bishop declared. "There'll be some lush lawns this summer."

The Lewis family across the street came out of their house and waded over to us. I could also see the Phillips children two houses down beginning to swim over as well. Grace and Margaret came out, followed by Wendy and my mother. A couple of seconds later, I spotted Abel paddling up to us on an air mattress. I could tell this was a day he would never forget. It wasn't long before we were surrounded by a nice-sized portion of our ward and neighbors.

"I've never seen anything like this," I said, baffled. I put my arm around Grace. "It came on so fast. Those drops were huge."

"The ground was pretty dry," Bishop Leen suggested. "Water stacks up quick when it can't be absorbed."

"I'll say," Sister Lewis chirped. "We've got a watermark as high as our second floor."

Everybody nodded, anxious to let each other know that they too had high marks.

"So was Noah right?" Brother Lewis asked the bishop. "Is this the end of the world?"

"We're still here, aren't we?" a wet Sister Phillips pointed out. "This has nothing to do with Noah."

"Not only that," Bishop Leen spoke up. "But I just got a radio call a few minutes ago from an employee of mine who lives near the warehouse. I guess Noah hadn't made sure that old warehouse was secure after all. All this water pushed down the walls. My employee wasn't sure, but she figures that almost everything that was in there is ruined."

"You're kidding?" I asked in astonishment.

"I'm not," he said.

"He's not," Sister Leen confirmed.

I wanted to laugh out loud at how dumb we all had been.

"We trusted in the wrong person," the bishop said sadly.

I felt "I told you so's" were in order, but I held my tongue. Grace squeezed my hand, indicating that she was well aware of my restraint.

"Trust was right?" Sister Lewis asked skeptically.

"Dead on," Bishop Leen replied.

People began slapping my back, and apologizing profusely.

"What do we do now?" Wendy asked.

"Luckily this water should be gone soon, and at least it's not too cold," the bishop continued. "We'll have a muddy mess, but we should be able to operate somewhat close to normal. I guess God's going to give us a chance to do it right."

Some final clouds passed and sunlight lit down across the receding waters, lighting the surface like an electric globe. I was just about to comment on the astonishing beauty of it, when I noticed a number of small objects floating toward us all. As they got closer, I realized that they were Ziploc bags full of red licorice.

"These are Leonard Vastly's." I laughed, looking up to see hundreds of other bags drifting down the street. I couldn't imagine what might have happened to have caused Leonard's life supply of food storage to now be flooding our street. Fortunately I didn't have to wonder long.

As the entire neighborhood began harvesting the bobbing manna, a noisy engine sounded in the distance. It grew louder and louder until it was on our street heading toward us. The source of the sound was a small truck with huge wheels racing through the knee-deep water, creating waves that were at least ten feet tall. The truck slowed as it drove by those people collecting food in their front yards. Eventually, it stopped in front of our house. A number of people from the ward piled out of the back of it. Sister Cravitz, Brother Victor, the Morrises and Brother Clyde Knuckles, who obviously viewed this as enough of an activity to attend. Doran stuck his head out of the driver's side window.

"Everyone okay here?" he asked.

"We're fine," the bishop answered.

"So what do you think?" Doran asked me.

"About the rain?"

"No, about the truck."

"Very nice."

"I know my father warned me about getting into debt," Doran said. "But I figure he never set his eyes on this beauty."

Leonard Vastly climbed down out of the passenger side. The moment people realized it was Leonard and that this was his food floating about, everybody stood silently wondering what he was going to do. The truth was, a lot of the people in this neighborhood needed this food. Most kitchens had been soaked, ruining any immediate supplies anyone had had on hand. Plus, it would take a while for the stores to clean out and get running again after this water. Leonard looked at everyone.

He held up his hands, silencing an already silent crowd.

"Just so you know," he spoke loudly, "all the food you see has already been prayed over. But I don't suppose God would complain if you thanked Him again before you ate it."

Everyone cheered! Then they continued to grab anything floating their way. Cans of food and sealed bags of dried fruit were everywhere, dotting the surface like oil spots on the surface of cold soup. I reached down and pulled up a bag of beef jerky.

Leonard was about to feed our entire neighborhood.

Everybody gathered what they could and began trading for what they wanted. Eventually we all figured it would just be easier to all eat together. So as the water lowered to a manageable level we sat anywhere we could find, feasting on not half-bad food.

Bishop Leen labeled it our "doomsday buffet," compliments of Leonard Vastly.

Leonard explained what had happened as we ate. His mobile home had been washed over by the flood, splitting an entire wall and sending all his hard-earned supplies everywhere. He said that he had fought to remain in his dome, but that nature had finally washed him out. He also claimed that because of the flood's course, Varney Street, one block over, had received all his best food and above-ground pool.

The water continued to recede and people began to help one another clean up. Men lifted wet couches through doors and out of houses while children scraped mud from out of living rooms with shovels and buckets. Leonard used his newfound popularity to try and sell tea tree oil to anyone who would listen. It didn't take long for him to realienate himself from everybody. My mother let those who would be interested know about my father's phone call and even bragged a bit about my engagement to Grace.

After helping Sister Lewis drag a huge muddy area rug from her family room I stood outside surveying all that was before me. The end of the world had knocked, but then it just walked away. Some major damage had been done, but I felt like more had been repaired.

It would be a cold wet night.

No one seemed to be complaining.

83

# One Last Fling

Roger Williams cast his line and watched it wiggle through the cold air and snap just above the moving water. He reeled it back in, glancing over at President Heck who was trying to extract yet another fishing fly from his right hand.

"You got it?" Roger asked.

President Heck tugged one last time on the bait. It came loose with a minimal amount of blood. "Not a bad day," he observed, ignoring his small wound.

"Not at all," Roger replied. "A little cold, but who's complaining?"

Roger stepped across the snow and close to the river. He was packed and ready to leave Thelma's Way. He was simply taking a couple of hours to fish with a friend. He had recovered nicely from his entanglement with the motorcycle and river. The entire town had helped nurse him back to health. And not since the day he had woken back up had a single person besides Roswell even mentioned the book that he had lied about planning to write.

People just helped him because they cared.

Roger had forgotten that that was an option in life.

"I'll sure miss this place," he said.

"We'll miss you," President Heck replied, tightening the homemade scarf around his neck. "That's the nice thing about Thelma's Way, though. We'll always be right here. You can go away, change, get married, lose a loved one, but we'll still be sitting here. All you got to do is wander back for a spell. Wad will still be cutting hair, and Toby will still be mending breaks."

"You're a lucky man," Roger said, amazed that those words were coming out of his mouth.

"We're all lucky," President Heck said. "God fills our lungs with air, then lets us wander around till we're stupid enough to step in front of a bus or eat something that will kill us."

"Well, God seems to keep a pretty good eye on you here," Roger sighed, flinging his line back out across the Girth. "I wouldn't be at all surprised to see Him step out from behind the boardinghouse, or rise from the snow in the meadow."

"Wheeew," President Heck whistled. "That would scare the tack out of me. Not that I would mind it, but I just don't think I would know what to do with such an experience."

"Think of how strong your faith would be afterward," Roger reeled.

"I s'pose. But you know an angel could come skippin' down the Girth tossing out gold coins and I wouldn't be any more impressed or sure about God," Ricky stated soberly. "People are always looking for stuff to touch, or see. Like Toby after he heard Pete could do that unsettling thing with his ears. I told him, Mavis told him, and Frank told him. But he didn't believe us until he saw it for himself. Now he won't stop whining 'bout how he can't get the image out of his head."

"I guess you're right," Roger said.

"I am?" Ricky said, surprised.

"My life is one giant bag of signs and markers illustrating clearly that I'm being watched over. I had to come here to remember that."

"The world loves to help you forget," President Heck said. "That's for sure."

Roger Williams thought about what was just said. It was almost unbelievable, the amount he had changed within the last month. He couldn't wait to get home so that he could begin mending everything he had once forgotten about.

"Had enough?" President Heck asked.

Roger smiled, patting his friend on the shoulder. "For now," he replied.

Six hours later he was at the airport in Knoxville waiting for his flight home.

84

# Ding

December 22nd

We had all just sat down to dinner in our water-worn dining room when the doorbell rang. Thanks to the flood our ringer no longer ding-donged, it just went "Diinggggrrr-rrrrrr-rrrrrr-rrrrrrr," until someone pounded the box on the wall by the stairs. Abel got up from the table and ran to do the pounding. A couple seconds later we could all think straight again.

We had been expecting Wendy to come over, so there was little thought given to who might be at the door. Grace passed me the pepper and Margaret began to pick the tomatoes out of her salad. After a bite of food I began to wonder what was taking Abel so long to let Wendy in.

"I think Abel must have gotten lost," Margaret said, apparently thinking the same thing.

I took another bite and stood up to quench my curiosity. I walked into the living room and spotted the back of Abel as my father held on to him as if he were life itself.

"Dad's home," I hollered.

I was practically bowled over by my mother and Margaret as they came bolting out of the dining room. Dad hugged us all as Grace looked on. This was a different man than the one who had left us so many weeks ago. His face was hollow and bearded, and his hair was short and light. He was dressed in casual clothes that reminded me of someone. I just couldn't place who.

As we were smothering him, my father noticed Grace standing off a ways. He stood tall and walked over to her. Without saying a word or explaining why, he wrapped his arms around her. She responded in-kind.

The four of us stared at the two of them. I looked at my mother as she cried, my sister as she beamed, and my brother as he sighed.

Dad was back.

85

# When All Is Over-Done

December 24th

Abel tugged on the plush purple bath towel that he had pinned around his head. He crouched down in front of Grace and me as we hovered over an elongated punch bowl with a small, blanket-wrapped fire extinguisher lying in it. I watched Grace as she knelt beside me. She had a faded quilt draped over her head, looking every bit like Mary of old. Me? I was Joseph.

My father read from Luke as Abel, the head shepherd, waved his cronies in closer. Mom and Wendy approached the manger.

"And the angel said . . ."

Margaret raised her arm as if she were an angel addressing the world. She had on a large white garbage bag with arm- and neck-holes torn out of it. The whole scene was rather authentic looking.

We had not reenacted the nativity on Christmas Eve for years. It was a family tradition that had been dropped a long time ago. Well, things were changing around the Williams house.

After my family's production, Grace and I slipped out into the backyard to be alone for a few minutes. We walked over to the long flat bench that sat behind the big leafless elm tree. Grace sat pretzel-style as I straddled the seat facing her, our knees touching. The wood bench was cold as we sat down, but it soon warmed under the presence of Grace and me. The motion sensor light that we had triggered by stepping out the back door flicked off, no longer able to detect our movement. The clear sky burned black, the lights from the city giving it a glowing base and tinting the canvas of God.

"I love you, Grace Heck."

"I love you back," she smiled.

"We're engaged," I pointed out.

"I'm aware of that," she replied.

"That means marriage, and . . ."

I would have finished my rambling statement if it had not been for the presence of Grace upon my lips.

Once again my life flashed before my eyes, the past speeding up to run headlong into the present. As the ever-alluring now grew nearer, my mind slowed, replaying the events of the last week.

I had spent days shoveling mud out of all the houses on our street. In all of Southdale only the lower areas and the warehouse district near the river had suffered much damage. Our entire neighborhood had become one in purpose—putting things back together as much as possible before Christmas. Well, tomorrow was Christmas, and even though there were still watermarks and warped walls to contend with, everyone had a home to celebrate in. For the first time in my memory the Clearview Ward had banded together and grown. We had collectively discovered that we could not only be wrong, but we could be watered. The flood had been a soggy wakeup call to bring us all to our spiritual senses.

I had needed to take time off from work to help set things right, but Opal at Ink Tonic refused to make allowance for my cleanup schedule. So I had been forced to quit. Actually, it wasn't as if I left Opal hanging, seeing how I offered her Leonard to take my place. Amazingly, she agreed. Leonard was loving having steady employment again, and Opal saw him as some sort of odd nonconformist that gave her store character.

Luckily Leonard's ruined mobile home had flood insurance. Just yesterday I had gone down to "The Real American" mobile home and RV center and helped him order a brand-new double-wide trailer. We had matched carpets with appliances and paint colors with moldings. I felt so domestic. His new home wouldn't be here for about six weeks. He had already made arrangements to stay at Scott McLaughlin's apartment until it arrived. I could only imagine the conversations those two would have.

The ward had come together to mourn the loss of their food storage. The water disaster had completely destroyed the entire warehouse. Unfortunately, Noah had not taken out any flood insurance. Plenty of fire, but no flood.

The good news was that Noah had not gotten away. He had been apprehended by the law. He was caught making a phone call at a rest area just over the state line. He had on a fake beard and sunglasses. He would probably have been overlooked, but the arresting officer said the sweater gave him away.

Justice was sweet.

It was nice to know that he was behind bars. The state of Maine was already making motions to get him back and try him. I felt confident that he wouldn't bother my city again.

One nice thing had come out of all this. Thanks to the auction Noah had put together, Brother Victor and Sister Cravitz were seeing one another in the open. Tiny Brother Victor had been taken with the assertive and opinionated Sister Cravitz for quite some time. It had been the auction that had finally given them courage enough to be openly adoring. I would have said that they made a cute couple, but a few days ago I had seen her pick him up and carry him over a big puddle, and, well, that sort of ruined it for me.

Grace still talked about how foolish she felt about believing in Noah. I would always brush it off, insisting she needn't worry, and then ask her to tell me more, after which she would go on and on about how cute she just remembered he was. It didn't bother me—Noah was one competitor I need not worry about. I suppose I could also say the same for Doran. Doran Jorgensen and Lucy Fall appeared to be an item. The blessing he had given her seemed to have made a long-lasting impression.

I was amazed to the point of disbelief.

Unbeknownst to any of us Doran had gone back the day after he gave her the blessing to confess his love to Lucy. He claimed that the only reason the heavens had told him to pursue Grace was so that he would be around to find Lucy. He had seen her every day since. I just couldn't believe how much Lucy had changed. The girl I had dated all those years ago would have been too busy listing Doran's faults to ever take him seriously—not to mention the remarks she would have made about his truck. But now she seemed to hang onto him, amazed by his devotion to her, and she was so relaxed about life that her entire being seemed almost unrecognizable. Mixed with my amazement was a huge pile of honest happiness for the two of them. It was also nice not to have him hanging around Grace anymore.

Young Leon Treat probably would still have had his mind set on Grace if it hadn't been for the accident that had occurred during the flood. I guess Leon had gotten his natural disasters mixed up, mistaking a flood for a fire. When his mother started panicking over the heavy rain he ran up to the attic and jumped out of the window, landing on top of his father's old van. He had broken one leg and one wrist. While recovering in the hospital he developed a crush on a candy striper named Nicole. She was ten years his senior, but the way she dispensed magazines and pillows made age seem so trivial.

The elders had finished their lessons with Grace, and in doing so had really hooked Wendy. Wendy had sat in on most of them, and had begun to see some things that just might fit in her lifestyle. She had already asked them if they would teach her again, promising that this time she wouldn't keep saying things like, "What kind of fool could swallow that?" The elders agreed, seeing how they both had just received word that they were going to be transferred out of Southdale next week. They would leave Wendy to whomever replaced them.

So with everyone out of the picture only I was left to fumble over Grace. Unless of course you were to count my father's newfound fatherly interest in her. He still had not told us where he had been, claiming the experience was too personal to talk about just yet. He promised, however, that in time he would fill us all in. Whatever the story was, it had caused him to see Grace in a completely different light than he once had. He asked her constantly about her hometown, and about each and every person there. He was most interested in her father and all he had been through in his life. I was rather impressed with how fast my dad memorized everyone's names, and how respectfully he spoke of them. He had even suggested that we take a trip back there someday.

I was all for that.

I missed Thelma's Way horribly. I was glad that Grace had come here, but deep down I hoped that she would beg me to take her home soon. I missed the meadow, the mountains, the people, and the problems. I thought of the two Christmases I had spent there, and how I had ached to be back in Southdale. I can't believe I could have ever been so naïve.

My mind moved to the present.

"What are you thinking about?" Grace whispered, her lips next to my ear.

"Home," I replied, kissing her on the eyelid and then the cheek and then the mouth.

I put my hands on her back and pulled Grace toward me. I could hear her breathe and felt her eyes close. My fingers became tangled in her long red hair as she moved to get even closer.

I was just about to confess my love again when I noticed Leonard crouched down about six inches away. He was staring right at us. We both jumped.

"Looks like things are good for you two," he commented, raising his bushy eyebrows.

"Leonard," I protested.

"Don't let me bother you," he insisted. "I just had a little something I wanted to drop off for the both of you."

"Leonard, you didn't have to," Grace said kindly.

"I know," he replied. "That's why I gave it to Opal. I hope you don't mind."

Grace smiled before I could. My father pushed open the back porch door and called us in for cake and cider.

"Want to join us, Leonard?" I asked.

"Well I did need to . . . sure," he said with excitement.

We walked inside, passing the Christmas tree in the living room on the way to where my family was gathered. Leonard broke away, leaving Grace and me alone again. We looked down and noticed that there wasn't a single present under the tree.

I could think of nothing that bothered me less.

My family broke out in song in the other room, their voices mixing with the smell of the Christmas tree. I felt Grace shudder under the weight of how perfect this was. It didn't matter that our carpets were still damp, or that no presents had been purchased. God had stocked us up with more than we could ever possibly rotate. Once again He had moved me around until I stood where I was supposed to. I lifted my face to the ceiling, almost expecting Him to be there.

"What are you thinking about?" Grace whispered.

There were no words to properly describe it. I thought back to when I had reached into my mailbox over two years ago and pulled out my call to serve. I remember the disappointment I had felt about Tennessee and the fear I had experienced worrying about being stung by bugs.

I looked at Grace.

Who knew I would be bitten so hard? I could feel the venom flowing through my veins, warming me up and making me feel invincible.

"What are you thinking about?" Grace insisted kindly.

"Bugs," I whispered.

"Oh," she said frowning. "I was hoping for a completion of that kiss."

I smiled, more than happy to accommodate her wish.